Cover art by: Muhhamad Waquas

Edited by: VEXFC

A fair warning:

This novel was written by a rebellious, sarcastic, partly insane teenager. As such it contains vividly disturbing descriptions, some heavy concepts, and a lot of swearing. Also, other than name concepts and language translation, absolutely NO Machine learning (AI) algorithms were used to create this novel. It was written entirely by me, the guy you know as VEXFC.

Enjoy :)

CHRONOLEFT: TIME PARADOX

"We have no need for this place anymore," the screens above blared loudly. She fought to stay alive, turning pages frantically as the flames melted her face, exposing bare bone the color of the rusted walls around her. Her heart stung with pain, and her eyes were gone, blood pouring out their sockets into the fire, turning it red, as if the two had conjoined. Now, her senses were gone, burned away, but she didn't need them. **She** was dead. But she remained fully conscious. "Live or die, it won't matter. Soon they'll all forget. Soon it will ALL be forgotten. It will all be left behind to die in the flames. ALL OF IT!" The voice continued to blare impossibly loud above. She bit down her teeth hard, with the little strength she had left, half her face a flesh-baren skull. "And if you ever see the creator.. say hi for me." She smiled with her mischievous grin, and her neck twitched a bit, then her fingers went limp, and the papers fell to the ground, engulfed in flames.

The e-

·*ERROR: plot misplacement in: 3.*

·*attempting to correct paradox.*

·*failed.*

·*restarting to avoid further corruption.*

·*begin-CL*

·*cycle: begin*

·*correcting anomalies*

·*beginning.. again…*

Neverland Colorado, 2000.

Chapter 1

A girl sat alone in the woods. Dim sunlight shone through the

trees, and into the miles of grass surrounding her. A dog could be heard barking faintly in the distance, as the sound of the wind in trees embraced her. She sat on a wooden bench, staring down. Ocean blue eyes stared back, through the ripples, and messy brunette hair blew in the wind. She rested her hand into the water, playfully, and retrieved a handful of mud. It was cold, and covered in water plants. A grasshopper jumped behind her, and she startled, letting the mud slip out of her hand. The sun beamed down into the pond, illuminating dark green plants, and small fish. "Avery!" A voice called from behind, and Avery sat up. "Whatcha up to?" Her father appeared in thick brush, secluding her. He brushed his long brown hair out of his face, his handlebar mustache bouncing with him slightly in the wind. A goofy look only he could pull off. "Oh you know," Avery said sheepishly, smiling awkwardly. "Pretty far away from home," her father asked, curiously. "What's out here that isn't at home?" She turned her head so he couldn't see and rolled her eyes. *not you.* "Well, uh dinners ready," he announced, happily, unsure of her mood.

Avery stared mindlessly at the pond, as the sun set behind the trees. Her reflection was no longer visible, and the bright light illuminating the pond was gone without a trace. In its place was a dark shadow. Something jerked out of the water and snapped at her feet. She yelped, staggering backwards off the makeshift bench she'd made. "You okay?" Her father asked, worried. Avery stood up quickly, brushing the mud off her knees. "Uh, yeah totally fine," She replied with a smile that was *not totally fine.* "Their offspring are large this year," her father said, pointing to the snapping turtle. "Hey, let's get you home," he urged gently, taking her hand.

Avery wasn't paying attention. She stared at his face, something familiar glaring back. *They can't, no they won't, they can't take-..* "No!" She yelled, and her father staggered backwards, both of them surprised. "I mean uh, yeah, no.. I just wanna watch the uh sunset, yep," she said, recovering quickly, holding her hands behind her back and smiling as if nothing had happened. The sun was already set, and the woods were growing dark.

"Av, are you okay?" Her father asked, a look of concern on his face. The question stuck in her head like a knife in a tree. *"Av,"* the name echoed. Only two people ever called her that: Her father, and her old friend Sean.

They'd met out by a lake when they were in preschool, and talked to each other, playing with sticks and trees, and the water. Avery leaned her head on her shoulder, enjoying the nostalgic feeling of the environment around her. When they were a little older, they'd created a fort out of loose pine branches. They'd spend nights together in that fort: camping and watching the stars. He was like a brother to her. When she was scared, he'd be there. When she had an idea he knew what it was at the first word, always finishing her sentences. They grew up together, venting and going through life, trusting one another with their personal issues. *Even if he pushed me into the lake too many times to count.*

She smiled to herself, memory's flooding back. They did this every day as time went by, depending on each other. He was her safe space, and she was his best friend.

The world was now dark. *Too dark to see.* A Coyote howled in the distance, and she snapped out of her dreamy state. Her pupils focused on a tree in the distance, adjusting to the light. After a moment, she could see a little better, but didn't need to. She'd grown up in these woods, she knew the path back by heart. Reluctantly, she stood up, and turned around. A part of her didn't want to leave her tiny pocket of peace. "Dad?" She called out.

Her father was no longer there, no footprints, no indication of any human life behind her, as if he hadn't been there to begin with. *Thanks.. for the space...?* She smiled, and walked forward, stepping on a twig. The environment blew around her, and the air grew cold. She squinted as the trees around her blurred in her vision, becoming that of inky blobs on a paper. *Too cold...* Somehow, in a way she couldn't articulate, something felt off. A stick snapped to her right, and her heart skipped a beat. Panic set in, her ears began ringing. The brush grew gray in her vision, as the moon went behind a cloud. Something moved behind her, and a tree fell to the ground... ***run...***

Light reflected off the glass from the window, and shadows of a book's open page reigned through the room brilliantly. A boy sat on his bed, his hands placed at his sides, as if patiently waiting. His eyes focused on the shelf in front of him, hastily nailed to the side of the wall of a closet, its door barely ajar.

The light leaked in through the door, illuminating the shelf with a bright beam. He stared intensely at a teddy bear, a mini bobble head like-stuffed animal. Its eyes were pitch black, facing downwards in a sad aura. Yet its teeth said otherwise, glinting below its big nose softly in the light. They were square, not unlike human teeth.

It hardly had fur, a solid plastic structure with little tuffs of green cotton. The image didn't sit right with the boy. He'd been told it would "help him sleep" when he was very young. Yet he only slept less. Metal and plastic parts stuck out, from where he'd "accidentally dropped it" many times.

The white had rubbed off its teeth over the many years and all that was left were shiny silver squares, which made it smile, and shine even in the dark.

A voice called his name, but he didn't budge. He continued to stare, and it stared back. His eyes were deep gray, and he wore a black shirt and jeans. He thought back to the time his sister had locked him in that closet. He'd stepped in her room, and exposed secrets to her friends. He did everything he could to be as annoying as possible, and she had enough of it, thrusting him in the closet, and slamming it shut, locking it. *"God just get out of my life and crawl back to the hole you came from!!" His sister screamed.*

He remembered the shadows closing in on him, as the metal jaws that made up the structure of the door enveloped him. "Hey, Hey! Come back! You jerk!" He'd yelled out loud, and then smiled softly to himself, having a new *excuse* to look closer at the bear.

Suddenly, a bird flew outside, slamming full force into the window. But he did not even remotely take his eyes off his target. He simply continued staring into the things eyes, unfazed by the blood splatting in the corner of his eye. *Blood? No. Just bird poop.* But it had indeed been blood, covering the shell and the screen. The voice came again "Come down! Dinners ready!"

Without warning, swiftly and cleanly, he kicked his legs out, holding onto his bed, slamming the closet door shut, with a bang. He furrowed his brow, and gazed out the window, spotting the blood splatter from the bird. *I'll clean it up later*. He felt no guilt, and paid no mind to the stains that most would've usually lost their mind over.

He was a witty, quiet and clever boy. He'd always been smarter than his sister, outsmarting her in games they played, and making her look bad in front of her friends. He didn't try in school, he didn't care to try. If he'd did he'd ace his classes easily. But he preferred struggling. He liked having to work hard for what he wanted, and doubted himself when he got it. The voice called again more angrily this time. "Come down!!" He jilted his eyes about the room, not moving his head from its direction of the closet. The clock ticked softly behind him, ringing in his ears, nearly the only sound in the room. The big hand reached near eight, and something satisfied him. Then he walked out the door, closing it swiftly behind him.

He emerged from the stairwell, and into the dining room. The door to the basement loomed behind him, a cavernous staircase rounding the corner, and disappearing into the darkness. "Hey son," his father smiled brightly, and he smiled back, hugging him. The boy stopped shortly, realizing there was something he needed to do. "Hey, where's mom?" He asked curiously. "Oh, guess you haven't heard. Your sister's out in the woods again, moms looking for her. She doesn't want to hear it from me, so I figured your mother could talk some sense into her."

The boy nodded, not really caring about what his sister was doing. "I'm gonna go use the bathroom," he stated, in an odd tone, and ran down the basement stairs before his father could respond. His father rolled his eyes, and smiled proudly, turning around, and walking to the window, eagerly awaiting to lecture his daughter.

Avery set off, rushing through the woods, whipping through the wind. Her heart skipped a beat, her adrenaline response to match as she hit a root, and tripped. She felt her ankle crack, and pain rang through her leg, sending her tumbling down a hill and crashing into a tree. Her head spun, and she turned around, keeping her eyes behind her. Her ankle seared with pain, as she tried to get up, but despite her best efforts: she couldn't.

The leaves rustled, and the thing moved closer. The sound of metal being drug behind, scraping against rocks with an awful sound. She clenched back, and squared up her chest, bracing herself. It was silent for a moment, the only sound being the sound of the wind in the trees. Then it stopped. The world grew completely mute, as if someone had pressed a pause button. she made no sound, she couldn't even hear her own body.

"HELLO DARLING!" A man's voice rang out, and Avery staggered back. "Sorry, didn't mean teh' startle yeh." His face appeared, an old buck tooth grin, and a gray beard. He wore a camouflage hat, blowing in the wind.

Avery sighed in relief. *Great, yeah, hi Ronny. Thanks for not being an ax murderer.* Though he *did* donn one: a large fire axe, which he'd been dragging behind him. Avery managed to speak up, still in pain. "So uh, what are you doing out here?" She asked, trying to make conversation. "We-hell' I could certainly ask you the same question young lady," he said accusingly. *Okay he actually has a point.* But she said nothing, staring at him confused. "Gathering wood for the winter, that's all," he said finally, gesturing to his axe.

"Well, uh good seeing you," Avery mumbled, and tried to get up. Pain rang through her leg, and she was pulled back down. "Woah there, you okay?" she bit her tongue. *Yeah, you know, just..broke my fucking leg because I thought you were gonna kill me.* "Uh yep, just fine," she replied, very clearly lying. "Let me help get you home," Ronny said, echoing her father. He extended his boney old hand to her, a little too close to her face. She hesitated for a moment, staring down at her apparently nonfunctional ankle, then back at his hand. She took it. *Not like I have a choice.*

They walked together slowly, as she staggered with him. "Phewy, yeh' sure don't weigh the same as you did when yeh' were three no-more. *Wow thanks genius.* She let out a small fake chuckle in respect. *He's helping you, be grateful.* "So what are yeh' doin' out here?" He prodded. "I ought to tell Gary," he added sheepishly. "He must be worried sick, ya goof!" Avery held back a laugh."Oh uh, dad knows I'm out here,"she said, not wanting to continue the conversation. "Really? Well to each their own I suppose." *Ugh how much further?* "I tell ya' Avery, the last time I saw you was.."

He paused as if something had interrupted him. "Was when you were three, he finished. *Three...* The number floated in her head. She stared at the luminescence of her house ahead. The basement lights were visibly on through the storm shelter exits. She could make out the vague boxes and trunks. A boy's silhouette could be seen grabbing something that looked like a book. He turned to the side, hearing something and slammed the trunk he'd taken it from, latching it quickly and bolting out of sight. *Oh boy, What's he up to this time?*

They were closer, and the basement was more visible now. A single shelf stood deep in the hallway. *Shelves...* She stopped suddenly, falling to the ground, "woah there," Ronny called, but she didn't hear him.

Her ears rang, and her knees bent uncontrollably. ***Three…***

Memories flooded back, gone in seconds before she could even process them. The wind was no longer silent, it screamed as if in pain. A thousand thoughts rushed through her head, her blood draining to her stomach. *Three…* "-rey?!" Ronny's voice shot into existence, as he knelt beside her, his joking personality gone, a grim worried look burned on his face. "Um yeah, thanks for helping me back," she said, as she stared up at what was apparently her front door. *When did we get to the house?*

Ronny eyed her carefully, then knocked on the door. Her fathers face appeared in the crack of light instantly. He spotted Avery like a sentry guarding a prison, and his appearance relaxed. Then immediately turned back, eyeing her with suspicion and angry eyes. *Time for the 10 year lecture.*

"Dad I-" Avery began. But was interrupted by Ronny. "She tripped and fell, and passed out. I was out serachin' for firewood, and I found her and helped her back."

Her fathers face dropped, and the anger in his eyes turned to worry. "Thank you so much," He said. Ronnie grinned with a bucktooth-grandpa-smile. "Of course. Y'all have a good night now." Her father walked back into the kitchen, and Avery turned to follow but Ronny stopped her.

"Avery.." He dropped his voice, almost whispering. His tone was serious again, and his accent was nearly gone. "Stay safe, okay?" She nodded, smiling. "Avery I mean it." His tone grew darker, and his persona slipped ever-more away. "If something comes up, anything at all.." He began, "I'm just across the woods. "Okay?" he asked, almost panicked. "Okay," she echoed, though it was more of a question."- "Goodnight now," he said, loudly, his old southern accent returning. She stepped forward and her eye's grew with confusion. **Her ankle was now fully working to its best ability.**

They all sat down, and their father sighed a heavy sigh. "Well, sorry dinner is late everyone," their mother commented stressfully. She glanced at Avery, worried. Avery stared forward, not willing to even breathe. The boy picked up his fork and began eating. It was a nice basic meal: meatloaf and potatoes. Their father followed suit and began messily devouring his plate.

The boy took a sip of milk, and wiped it on the inside of his shirt. *Why waste resources when I can just use it and wash it later?* "Oh **Grey**," Their mother remarked, disappointed. Grey's gray eyes darted between the three of the family, each waiting awkwardly for someone to say something. Grey, unsurprisingly, had indeed been named Grey, not just in his name, but as if the creator of his rights to life in general had given him that title. He rarely ever showed signs of true happiness, he wore bland colors, and acted boring around his friends, though he had few. He rarely put effort into interacting. Even at his young age, he found dating to be a waste of time. He never truly tried at anything, it just came naturally. He had brown hair like his fathers, but it had a small hint of gray. Grey was gray, in every way.

Finally Avery jumped in, preventing a silent war of awkwardness. Grey stared into space. what *was there to talk about, what was new, ever?* He rolled his eyes but no one noticed. "Well I broke my ankle, so that's new," Avery said as if reading Grey's mind, though she knew she was sort-of lying.

Grey looked down at the open flesh wound at his right knee, hidden behind the table cloth. *Oh boo hoo suck it up.* He gritted his teeth speaking through them disingenuity. "Sorry to hear that." Their father glanced at him confused, but worried. "I'm fine,' he said, and he wasn't lying. Though the *stone object* had sliced into knee when he tripped on it, he hardly felt any pain. It had always been this way for wounds. *Thank you, high pain tolerance.* He looked at the flesh wound, bloody and fresh in his knee.

Their mother stood up, and Avery watched as she looked down at Grey curiously. She had noticed the flesh wound but paid no mind, and rubbed her eyes, as if ridding of a bad vision. "Anyone want crushed pepper?" She asked cheerfully. "Count me in!" Avery answered happily. "Me too!" Her father echoed.

In a happy, normal family Grey would've answered "Me three!" Or "I'll have to pass", enjoying the dinner with his loving family. Instead, he just stared at his mom, the gray in his eyes piercing into her's. He smiled, but he was far from happy. She bore no resemblance to him at all, he didn't look much like Avery either, but very much like his father. He'd taken after him, studying old myths. He moved his eyes between the two of them, and centered on their dad. He smiled, secretly happy their mom was gone, feeling a moment of peace.

"So," their father began. "How's school?" - "Fine," they both said in unison. Avery took another bite of the meatloaf. *Too dry.* Though for some reason she craved salt. Grey shared this craving, and they both reached for it at the same time. "Older first," she teased. "Newest the best," he responded. *Newest generation who does he think he is?* She rolled her eyes, "What are you like four? I honestly forgot." Grey furrowed his brow. "eleven," he said, moving his head and eyes, jeering at her. "Funny, I thought middle schoolers out grew comics"? Avery countered, smirking, her mischievous eyes glinting in the orange light above. "**The artifacts aren't comics, and I'm not-**" He stopped himself, breathing out heavily. *Damnit she's good.*

"I *AM* in middle school," He admitted, exhaling angrily. "BU-" He was interrupted by their mom in the other room "Stop bickering!" She appeared holding fresh crushed red pepper in a container. "And Gray, stop harassing your sister, can't you see she's injured!?" Grey bit his lip, his anger growing. "ME? WHAT DO YOU MEAN HARASSING, AND YEAH I AM-" He stopped himself, looking down carefully at his knee. He looked up, and smiled. His mom shot him a look, with a slight grin, knowing she'd won. *She knows...* He gritted his teeth silently. Panic arising. "Fine," he said at last.

Avery raised an eyebrow, slightly a bit worried. She loved teasing him and their sibling wars, but she *did* genuinely care about him. Grey didn't know this, he cared for her deeply, more than she did for him. But he never expected the same back. Avery was naive, never recognizing her situation, or if she was being tricked. Grey was smart, and protected her in the shadows. When she was twelve, she had a friend who used her, manipulated her. Avery was small, and could fit through vents. Her friends used her to steal things, and she never noticed anything bad. They were her friends, trustworthy and good people. Because they were "nice" to her. She didn't know better, but Grey did. Even at age seven he was good at manipulation. He never used it for school or people, simply because it came naturally. It wasn't hard for him. He tore apart her friend group, bringing her back together with new friends. He was her *shadow*. Bleak and unknown. But he looked out for her, even if he was far younger. Grey secretly enjoyed the sibling war too, it was the way they interacted, a normal language. To outsiders it would seem aggressive and unhealthy, but to them they had a silent understanding, it was just another language, even if it involved yelling.

Grey glanced at his knee again, smiling briefly at her gaze. He picked up his fork and swirled his hand, making it "lose its balance" and fall out of his grasp underneath the table. *Ah shoot darn who could've seen that coming?* He glanced around. They were all staring at him. He smiled "Don't worry, I'll get it"

He reached down to pick up the fork, stopping for a moment under the table. He eye'd the wound in his knee, and squinted his eyes, making a plan. "Oh cmon, damnit, where is it?"

I could tie a napkin over it? No they'd be suspicious. Milk, how would that help? Burn, no. Bathroom, pointless. Admit it, no. No, there's a way. Time, pm. The night, masks. Yes! The month, Halloween. Halloween... "Ah there it is." He emerged from under the table, holding the fork, and smiling triumphantly. "Avery rolled her eyes, and smiled, confused." *Uh okay then buddy.* "You Alright?" Their father asked. "Yeah, yeah, no problem, it just fell into the crevice. I should probably go get a new one though." Avery squinted, suspicious. *Why are you talking like that?* Grey stood up, and his wound was immediately visible. "My, Grey, what happened!?",his mother asked, the slightest hint of a smile in her eyes. "Oh right!" He looked down, pretending to be surprised. "It's a costume! I'm going all out this year, I made it in school!" He said confidently. "Uh, cool?" Avery remarked, not fully convinced. "Yes," their mother said, her lips falling to a frown. "Very cool." His father nearly leaped through the ceiling in excitement. "Agreed, you should go for costume of the year! It looks... so..

realistic," he said, completely convinced. Grey smiled, and nodded. Pretending to be a "humble, good artist." then turned around, and brushed past his mother, side eyeing her, standing tall as he walked out the room.

The stairs were dark, and the ceilings were low. Cobwebs blocked the path forward, through the tiny crawl space like door at the bottom of the stairs. Grey darted his eyes around, searching for his goal. The light was dim, and the walls were old and dusty. An unplugged refrigerator stood just outside of the crawl space entrance, leaving a tiny gap between it and the ceiling. Inside that gap was a watch, which read: 8:03.

Grey peaked around the corner, staring at the watch, making sure his eyes didn't deceive him. *Exactly as planned.* He leaped forwards, jumping over the boxes and shelves fallen over on the ground. His head came just inches away from the ceiling, and he came skidding to a stop at his destination, sliding against the dusty concrete. He was at his goal, and bit his lip with satisfaction.

Bingo. The trunk clicked open, revealing a dark leather interior. *Okay.. didn't plan this part.* He dug through the random clay artifacts and scrolls that filled the trunk, at last grabbing something. He'd felt the texture, and didn't need to read it. He smiled, satisfied. "Grey?" Came his moms voice, echoing through the crawl space with a metallic ringing. Something caught his eye. He paid no mind to his mother outside, and simply stared into a paper on the floor. He didn't bother picking it up, for some reason, he didn't understand why. *Just don't.* His eyes darted back and forth as he began to read it on the ground, crouching down next to it.

September 15th. Something isn't right. I've seen lights in the sky more than usual, and the air is colder than normal. Yesterday I found something I'd never seen before on the ground, strange metal with a spring, it was damaged, thrown there as if it had fallen from the sky. I don't know what it is, and now I'm finding more. A child's toy, peculiar metallic parts that resemble a wagon. They're massive. No one knows what they are. We've quarantined them to study them in hopes of learning from them. Some hope to rid of them, others hope to use them. I don't know.

but it's getting violent quickly. Whatever these things are..

*They're not meant for us. And if they are real, The C–***..*

certainly don't want us finding out what they are.

Grey shook his head as he stared at the blotched out ink on the

paper, kicking it underneath the shelfs cautiously. He nodded, not

quite disturbed by the message, more-so intrigued.

Ink doesn't just.. splot like that randomly. Someone did it with

purpose. They're covering something up...

Just then he perked up, hearing a twig snap in the distance. He

stared up through the small grimey window above him. In the far

distance, a man held a girl's hand, and she collapsed on the ground.

Avery? He began to panic more. *Snap out of it! There's no time!*

He didn't wait for his plan to be ruined, and ran behind the corner,

disappearing into the shadows.

Objects rubbed against his legs as he ran through the long halls in the dark. The basement wasn't normal, it protruded further than the surface of the house even was. The halls ran wide, becoming cave like. three doors passed him, as he ran into the darkness. He stopped, reaching an end, and rounding a corner. Suddenly the air grew cold, and he could feel spiders crawling around his body. The room hadn't been used in a very long time, if even.

Okay, you don't bite me, I won't bite you. He stared at nothing, and it stared right back. *Right, left, left, left, right. So we take the far corner back, and then right. Wait, no. Left.. no it's...* he paused. He realized, in the dark long halls he ran through, and random corners he took. "Where am I?" He asked aloud, knowing no-one could hear him, being far away from the actual house.

Despite his vast knowledge of the basement's layout, he knew for a fact that he hadn't been here before. The air was different, stale and old. He stepped forward, and his foot dropped a few inches, landing on stairs that led slightly down, evening out the slope of the hall, though the design felt as though *they were meant to go further down.*

Grey stopped, reaching the new ground. His nose was inches away from an old Russian doll, a set of them on a shelf, covered in spider webs. He continued down the halls, a weird surreal feeling in his mind. The floor was unstable, and cracked violently with each step. Suddenly, he stopped dead in his tracks. The door in front of him slammed shut. "Grey…" A woman's voice called out, deep and hard to hear, echoing into oblivion.

He took off running, bashing through the slammed door, rounding corners he could only guess existed. He ran through halls he didn't recognize, old posters and shelves everywhere. The air was unnatural, and the walls almost felt like they were manipulating around him as he blind guessed turns, guiding him forward through the pitch darkness. As if the house itself wanted him safe.

Something fell in front of him, and he caught his foot in its mouth, sending him falling face first to the ground, ripping open his jeans, slicing his knee. He winced in pain, though he didn't feel any. His face lay smashed against the concrete floor, and he watched curiously as his blood dripped thick into the gargoyle statues mouth, leaking out the fountain hole where water should've been.

He kept his death grip on the paper, holding it close to his chest. His vision blurred, as he got up and his ears rang, but as soon as it began, it was gone. *Get a move on, you're gonna get caught!!* He got up, limping into the light, as he emerged on the other side of the basement. "Grey!" His mothers voice yelled again from above. He peered through the crawl space into the world above, his exit was blocked, his mother stood directly at the foot of the stairs. *Time to improvise.* He spotted the vent in the corner that he'd once used to play hide and seek with Avery countless times. *Like a mother like a daughter, if it works on her, then it'll work on her mom.*

He darted to the vent, and climbed in, moving into the metal, as the darkness swallowed him. There was a ladder inside, and paths diverged in all different directions. But he *wasn't* in a maze, and simply kept climbing up, still holding the paper over his hand. He reached a cover in the living room. "Dunno, I haven't seen him," his sister said in the next room behind him. "Okay then," his fathers voice admitted, deep, and sad. "Grey?" His mothers voice called, annoyed in the distance upstairs. Grey took the moment, and began to climb out of the vent. *Wait!* he paused. *The paper!* He folded it up in a rush, tucking it into his back pocket, then covered the vent back up, and emerged from the wall, ripping around the seat just in front of it, and sitting down at the dining table. He glanced at the clock above the kitchen cabinet. It now read: 8:15. *That could've been bad.* He relaxed. "Son? Where have you been?, His father asked profusely. "Sorry forgot to tell you guys I came down," he replied, smiling.

His mothers face appeared heading down the staircase. She said nothing, and simply glared at him, worry on her face, *but not worry for her son.* She, too, glanced at the clock, frowning. Grey rubbed his eyes, exhausted from what lay just under his feet. *Plan perfectly executed.* His sister appeared, "limping" around the corner. *You too, huh?* - "Well, shall we?" Their father asked, gesturing to the table. "We shall," Avery replied, grinning.

"Welp," their father began, exhaling loudly. "That sure hit the spot." Grey nodded, though he didn't even touch his food. "You can say that again," He agreed.

Just then, the phone rang in the next room. "I'll get it," their mother said, as if she'd been expecting it. She stood up without a word, and disappeared around the corner. Avery leaned into the wall, peaking over the small pillar that separated the kitchen and the dining room. "Mhm. Yeah. Oh, really?" Her voice was muffled through the walls. The three of them exchanged glances, and their mother appeared around the corner again. She gestured her head at Avery. "Yeah, I'll put her on for you." Avery cocked her head, but Grey already knew who was on the other end, rolling his eyes and smirking. Only one person would call her at this random time of night. Avery picked up the phone.

"Uh, hello?"... A voice jumped into action on the other line, deep and slightly excited. "Hey Av," a boy said. She paused for a moment, covering her mouth, at a loss of words. After a few moments she finally responded. "Oh uh, hey," she said, walking into the other room away from her family. She hadn't seen Sean in nearly two years, or any of her old friends, for that matter, after the argument between them.

"Long time no see," He said, trying to cover up his excited voice. Avery raised an eyebrow, "See?" .. "Uh, yeah, you know, radio waves, you can see them, right?" She chuckled, happy to see he still had his sense of humor. "No? Just me? Right, I should've told you about that spider I got bit by." She laughed again, loudly, and Grey heard from the other room shaking his head, he'd predicted everything the second the phone rang. *Yep, what a surprise.* "Hey, uh I know it's been a while but.. would you want to-" - "Yes!" She covered her mouth, immediately longing to take back the word. "Oh uh, but you didn't even hear what I was gonna say" He laughed. She missed that laugh, and the genuine safe aura that surrounded it. "Well, I guess I already got your answer, but we're all going camping for Thanksgiving-break, up in the woods. The group." He paused, worried he'd say the wrong thing. "Look, I know it's been a while since we were all together, but I mean, hey we've all grown, right? I'm sure we'll all have some apologizing to do, but like, I just.." He paused again. "I just miss the old days, and I think we'd all still get along well. Plus, you never know, it could be a really good opportunity to *find yourself.* I know it's a lot to ask of you, but if you're willing to, I-" He cleared his throat. "We..Would really, *really* like to see you again."

Avery stopped for a moment, considering what may come of the decision she'd make. *Too late now, great self control Av.* "Av." She found herself calling her that name all of a sudden. "Well, too late to say no now, right", Sean sighed in relief, then inhaled quickly, trying to hide it. "Sweet. Then that's all of us. Well I mean except Jane. But she doesn't really live around here anymore. *Jane. Jeez it's been a while.* "Yeah," She went to say more, but stopped herself. They sat in silence for a moment, then Sean spoke. "Well, Cam's family has an awesome trailer we can take, um, at least he says so, but you know him. Anyway, it's not exactly the most liveable, so we'll have to sleep in tents. That alright?" He asked nervously.

Avery squinted and shook her head, confused why he thought she wouldn't have been okay with it. *Dude we literally grew up together sleeping in tents.* "Pft, it's not camping without tents," she replied, grinning ear-to-ear. "Couldn't agree more." - "So, uh, how's life lately?" He asked, seeming genuinely interested. The question bounced around her head, a million different answers generating. Only to be deleted moments later. *How is life? Good question.* She searched her head, but found nothing. It refused to work. "Oh, you know, just school." Was all she could come up with. "Right? Good lord, learning about different forms of rocks is SO interesting." - "All I think of when I wake up," she responded. They both laughed, happy to hear each other again. To be interacting *at-all* again. "Jeez, it's.. honestly really good to hear your voice," he remarked, not bothering to hide it. "Yeah.. you too." She echoed him, and she meant it. They stayed silent for a moment, both smiling to themselves. "Well how-" "Oh dammit," Sean said in distress. Avery moved the phone closer to her ear. "You alright?" The sound of coins being inserted came through the phone. "Gah, Yeah sorry Av I'm using a phone booth." Avery looked up, surprised. "Why's that?" She asked, confused. His response was static, and scratchy through the weak signal. "Well, I'm helping my family set up for the winter. Ah crap, okay Avery, I'll call you back. I'm really sorry, the signals about to die. "Oh, uh okay, well-" She stopped talking, at a loss of what to say. "I'll call you back tomorrow afternoon, Sunflower still gets out at two?" - "Uh, yeah," she responded. "Okay cool, I'm sorry, I have to go. Talk to you tomorrow, it was.." He stopped, and it wasn't because the signal was dying. "It was really great to talk to you A-" The line hung up. She wished he would have finished what he was saying. She wanted to hear the name… "Av," the boy finished, but the line hung up. He was standing in an old red phone booth, shaking hard in the cold wind. He sighed, and hung the phone up, pushing hard against the door as it blew back against him, trying to shut him in. His brown hair blew behind him in the night as he walked into the darkness

"Sean! Come help me move it!" A man's voice called, and he vanished into the shadows. The phone booth door blew in the wind for a moment, *resisting the force of nature.* It curved all the way back against its hinges then lurched forward violently, slamming shut.

Chapter 2

The shadow of the boat moved ominously through the sand, scaring fish and ocean creatures away. "Mark twenty-three, depth at nine-hundred meters." Two figures fell into the darkness of the cave, ropes attached to their backs. "Copy that." The light shone down through the water from above, but didn't reach the bottom of the cave, dying in the dark inky water. Massive rocks stood, light waving through their bumpy textures in the water. "What is it this time?" One of the figures pushed a button on his wrist, and a purple light sprung to life. "Dunno, but he said it's close to being found. Plus it's a high pay retrieval. I ain't complaining." The other figure shook his head in his black visor. "You think I am?" The first one cracked his knuckle through the thick suit, and it echoed strangely through the water. "Nah, but let's make this quick. I've got bad claustrophobia." The other one put his hand to his face, still falling fast through the dark water. "And you still took this job?" The first one shrugged, pushing against the pressure of the water. "A man's gotta eat." Their boots crashed into the ground simultaneously, sending sand and rock bits flying around them. "C-45, on record, we've reached the bottom."

Ahead of them was a massive crater, with a metal and stone capsule. The material emitted brilliant blue light. "Alright," The figure said, gesturing to the other. "C-Ninety-seven, on record, we're extracting the object now." The man spun his wrist and a blinding red laser shot out of his arm. The light grew around the capsule, overtaking the blue light. Then stopped. The light emitted was now red, and the capsule echoed sounds of pulsing energy. Suddenly, the material folded in on itself, each panel retracting onto the previous one. There was another layer that looked like stone. It stayed dark for a moment, and then cracked apart, spiraling out into the water. The inside gleamed with the red luminescence, and an object came into vision. A sword lay vertically, glowing. Marks of an ancient language burned on it. Attached to it, drifting in the water was a piece of parchment, long sense destroyed. It began to shake violently, and its Ink floated off of it into the water, growing massive and covering the crater, shining in the red light. The figures starred up, in awe as letters began to form. ***To M.L…***

Avery rushed down the road, frantically trying to do her hair, not paying any mind to the speed limit. The trees rushed behind the car, as she sped through the wind. "Cmon, stay green." The light turned yellow, and she floored it, barely making it as the light switched to red. She pulled into the school lot, brushing past long trees, and skidding to a stop, at last parking. She looked around frantically checking her watch. 7:44. *Two minutes.. we can make it.* Her hair rocketed out behind her in the wind as she rushed to the doors, preparing to be yelled at. *I'm late.* She told herself, knocking frantically on the door. *Mr Johnsons gonna kill me!* She waited a moment, anticipating her fate. The glass was foggy, and nearly impossible to see anyone. *Okay.. he's late. So we use that against him!* She thought, smirking, continuing to wait. But the doors didn't open.

Perplexed, she looked around and realized she'd been running on full auto. The brick building stood looking over her in the fog, the roof barely visible. The fog blended it to where it seemed to echo off into the heavens. No one was around her. The school was abandoned. A chill ran down her spine, and the air grew stale. She looked down at her watch again. *November 16th.* She heaved a heavy sigh and smacked her face hard. The pavement was hard, and hurt with each step as she walked back to the car. She stopped, surprised, and took a step back. A cop was parked behind her car, trapping her in between the median. He stared at her curiously, his handlebar mustache blowing in the wind. He wore a stern, strict frown, gesturing his head to her car. Avery reluctantly opened the door. No sooner had she closed the door, then the cop wrenched his own door open. He got out, and walked over, somehow seeming excited. "Hmm," he hummed, barely audible through the freshly opened window as he walked. He extended his hand out to knock on the glass, but was taken aback, realizing it was already open. His sunglasses bounced with him, as his red hair and mustache blew softly in the wind. "Do you have ANY idea how fast you were goin'?!'" He demanded, in the most stereotypical *cop way.*

Avery held back a grin, biting her lip. *No way, they're REAL!*

The cop adjusted his sunglasses, his hair blowing into his face. *I*

believe I was going the speed limit. A phrase her mother had

burned into her. But she knew that was a lie, and would probably

get her in more trouble. The man waited patiently, shaking his

head, ridding the hair in his face. "I'm sorry, I just needed to get to

school." *I'm not lying.* The cop raised his eyebrow. Avery looked

up, his appearance was completely different. Her panic had created

an image that wasn't even real in her head. He had no long hair,

He was built like a stubby kid, clearly a newbie. His mustache was

only slightly established, really just peach fuzz. "Isn't it

Thanksgiving break for you kids," he asked, his voice wasn't

nearly as deep as she'd just recalled. *Wasn't it just spring break for*

middle school? She fought back a grin. The man was short,

probably her height. "Yeah I… I forgot," she admitted, honestly,

sulking her head.

The cop sighed. "Well.." He looked around, contemplating his

decision. "I suppose it wouldn't be fair for your one break to be in a court." Avery glanced up, surprised. "Look, I'll let you off with a warning for now, but be careful and drive safely next time alright?" Avery smiled genuinely. "Right, yes I will officer."

The cop took a deep breath, something in his demeanor changing. His childish voice was gone, as if he, in an instant, became someone else. "Look, I'm new here, but I can see you're an honest kid." His eyes were barely visible through the sun glasses, and he blinked them rapidly, making a confused face. They looked different for a moment, vividly someone else's. But it disappeared as soon as it came. Then went back to normal "I remember my days of rushing late to school like it was yesterday."- Though judging by his appearance it was quite literally "yesterday". Avery eyed him, curious. "Just know, if you ever need anything, or you're in trouble, let me know." Avery nodded, smiling. "Oh uh, right, I forgot abou…" He turned his head, and his mustache bent inwards, his teeth showing through as he bit his lip. "Just, have a good day Ma'am," he said haphazardly, and ran back to his car, pulling out of the lot in a hurry. Avery squinted, as he sped off into the fog, faster than *she* had been going. Her face was left confused, she never pulled her wallet, her insurance, nothing. *Well that worked out.*

A tumbleweed blew across the driveway as she pulled in, the fog was mostly gone now, and the sun shone down, lighting up the trees beautifully. Her mother stood worried at the front door. Avery got out of the car. Her mothers eyes lit up at the sight of her. "Avery! Are you okay? I was so worried! Where were you?" Avery squinted, overwhelmed. *One question at a time, maybe? Would be great.* "I uh- I just forgot it was break. I'm fine." Her mother stared at her with suspicion. *Well I got pulled over and almost killed someone too but ya know.* "I'm fine mom," she assured. Grey leaned back against the far wall, shadowed in the dark corner, exhaling sarcastically, but he secretly admired his sister's power to bullshit. Her mother appeared in her face as she zoned out, startling her. "Well, at least come have some breakfast, I don't want you not eating, sweetheart." She walked back inside, and Avery grabbed the wall for a second. Her mother had good intentions, she knew that. *But still, I'm not dead, mom, chill out for once,* she thought to herself. Grey walked over from the corner, emerging from the shadows. Yet he looked no lighter, as if his own persona wasn't capable of being any brighter than just "Gray". He brushed past Avery, who was wiping her mouth in her sleeve as she went by. They exchanged glances for a moment, then she walked to her room. She felt the air clear as she closed the door, and took a deep breath, collapsing back onto the bed. The ceiling was all she could see, and exhaust overtook her. The world went dark, and she fell into a dream.

"Get her in, we don't have much time." A man sliced open a vine, clenching a knife in his mouth. "What about you?" A woman asked, a tear in her eye. "Doesn't matter. You deal with her, keep yourself safe." The man breathed heavily, and they moved forward into the fog, trees all around them. "What if I get caught, what abo-" The man spun around, grabbing a piece of metal. "you're not gonna get caught! Just... just..." He shook his head. "There's no time." Yelling sounded in the distance, and the vision blurred into a thousand memories. **"Av.. we need. Quiet. One day.. don't. It's not y.."**

Avery jilted awake with a sharp breath. The world around her was blurred, colors black and white, the universe glitching in and out of existence. She forced herself to blink through it, and meaning returned from the nonsense. She looked around frantically. Her pillow lay on the floor from where it had fallen, and her alarm clock was embedded slightly into the carpet. It looked as though it had been thrown there hours ago. The clock was still plugged in, and Avery looked at the time. 2:43Pm. A burst of adrenaline ran down her spine. *Shit, Sean!*

The stairs made a horrible sound as she raced down to the kitchen, flying past her mother, who was watering flowers. She looked at Avery for a moment, surprised and offended, then went back to watering, rolling her eyes and smiling. *Oh kids.* Avery ran down the hallway, the phone ahead of her. She felt something catch on her sock, and the string ripped from the seam, sending her leg to the ground. She paid no mind, and got up quickly. Her mother stared at her confused, wanting to rush to her aid, but Avery waved her off, and continued running. She reached the phone at last, skidding to a stop, the seam of her sock flapping violently behind her. She stopped, and checked her watch. 2:45pm. *Any second now…* she waited, tapping her foot nervously. The phone didn't ring. Seconds passed, her mother began to approach her, her phasique looking sad. *No it's gotta.* But the phone didn't ring. She checked her watch. *2:47pm.* Avery's eyes dropped, and her mother extended her hand to her for comfort. "I'm sor-" She didn't finish. The phone exploded into ringing, louder than normal. Avery could've sworn it was deeper, more diluted then usual, but picked it up excited nonetheless. Her mother backed up, raising an eyebrow, then nodded and went back to her flowers. "Oh, there you are, I was beginning to worry you wouldn't pick up, I've been calling since forty-four," he chuckled. "Haha" Avery managed to spout, awkwardly. *44?* "Must've just been problems with the phone," she said, smiling with approval as if he could see her. "Ah, yeah gotta love the fall storms." She looked outside. He was right. It was foggy, and stormy, gray clouds and faint thunder. "So, uh.. how are you?" Avery asked sheepishly. "Doing great Av, how about you?" She smiled at the name. "Never better," she replied, and she felt it in the moment. "So, game plan," he began, happily. "Game plan," she repeated. "Alright, so Cam's dad has a truck we'll take, things a monster. BUT!" He stopped himself. "Cam insists on taking his raggedy, shitty old Scooby doo van." Avery chuckled. "Fine by me." Sean echoed her. "Alright, well we'll stay for about four days. No need to bring a tent, We've got tents for everyone, uh you'll have to share with Sasha though." Avery nodded. *Sasha.* She missed her. Brown hair, stylish, smart, always caring for everyone. "That all sound good?" Sean asked confidently. Avery snapped back to reality, her daydream fading. "Uh, um…" She glanced back at her mother, who was now staring in the kitchen mirror, seeming sad. it reflected Avery and they made eye contact. She looked away pretending to have not noticed her. "Yeah!" She said finally, clearly lying. "You sure you don't want me to go over it again, I have a while, ha." She thought hard, but her brain wouldn't let her concentrate. "Nope," she said, in the same tone as before. "Alrighty then, we'll see you tomorrow, nine-am sharp. Not a second late, Or else…" he joked, laughing. Avery's eyes skyrocketed open. *Wait what?* "So.. how's life today?" Sean asked. Avery struggled to find a response, her mind was going a thousand miles an hour. "Got pulled over," she said, and her mother turned around, staring her down with worry, and anger. "Uh oh," Sean replied. "What did ya do?" He asked, mockingly. "Hahaha," Avery laughed sheepishly, "just joking." Her mother raised an eyebrow, then walked to the living room, disappearing around the corner. "Oh, ha," Sean coughed out, trying to be nice. "What are you up to?" Avery asked, accepting she now knew absolutely nothing of what she was supposed to do. "Just been around, you know, chopping limbs, adding to my kill count." Avery laughed, and he echoed her. "I don't know, I've just been trying to not get eaten by school, and hanging out with friends here and there." Avery nodded. "Yeah, pretty much the same here." She waited a moment, and neither of them spoke. Then finally Sean coughed, breaking the silence. "Alright well, I'd better go Av." Avery looked down, surprised. "Oh, uh yeah. Have a good day." - "Pft, don't be so sad I'll see you in less than twenty-four hours." - "Oh, right," she said, smiling awkwardly. "Av, you sure you're okay?" He asked, sounding genuinely concerned. "Yep," she said, clearly not okay. "Well alright then. See you tomorrow morning!" - "Yep," she repeated. "See you then." She hung up the phone slowly, disappointed. *Great job, me, now we have no clue what we're doing. Sweet, great, just great!*

She ran past her mother back up the stairs, crashing through her door. She wrenched open her dresser and threw open her closet. *Camping, camping. What the hell does one do when camping?* Her mind was racing, and wouldn't let her think. *You got that? You got that.. uh. Cams dad, four. four yes, four days.* She tried to focus on the number. *Okay four days of clothes. How hard can that be?* She opened the drawer to a mountain of *nothing. Oh, laundry. Crap.* Her closet was full of a pile of clothes, and various random metal bicycle parts. A bag lay on its side softly deep in the closet, in the darkness. It was a camouflage, old leather utility bag. To the right was a pocket where a pocket knife stood out haphazardly. To the left was a zip strap that had been duct taped back together countless times. She grabbed a flashlight off her dresser and shoved her hand into the closet, grabbing the bag. It made a loud zipping noise as she pulled it out, and threw it to the ground, holding the zipper, and violently opening it. *Okay, knife, blanket.* She exhaled and shook her head, her mind still racing. *Just take the whole thing idiot.* Suddenly, a knock came from her door, echoing through the metal frames of the closet. She sighed. "Yeah?" A face appeared through the crack in the door, and she turned her head around to face them. *Grey. What a great surprise, why are you bothering me?* "Hey buddy, sport, little man," she greeted sarcastically, mocking his existence. But Grey looked at her differently, something of concern and fear in his eyes. Avery raised her eyebrow. "You been reading too many spooky comics?" She asked, confused. Grey simply stared back, his eyes blank. His arm dropped for a moment, and his eyes lost their gray, there was nothing in them. *Grey...?* It disappeared as fast as it came. "I found something, I want you to see it," he said, his voice serious. Avery looked at him like he was an alien. "Uh okay?" Grey reached into his pocket, and retrieved a hastily folded paper. He shoved it in Avery's face and she looked at him blankly. She ripped it out of his hand reluctantly, and Grey startled back, looking offended. It uncrumpled in the most unnatural way possible as she unfolded it violently. Avery's eyes became active. It was a letter, with something of a diagram below, labeled in symbols that looked like gibberish. She darted her eyes across the parchment, a spark of curiosity forming in the massive blue ocean within them.

To the other two, at M.L,

it brings me no pleasure, having grown with you to

deliver this letter. While I'm not sure what I can possibly

do next, having seen the most one can possibly see in this

time frame, I assure you no information will be retrieved,

nor given. I wish to start a family, and live peacefully for

what I can. The illustrator will give no information, I will

ensure this. You have my word. I'm aware my departure

from the operation will disrupt elements of the plans, I

must do this for myself, and my morality. I understand the

feeling of power and knowledge, I know you find yourself

in your position well. But I advise that you do the same as

me. What we've been "graciously" gifted is knowledge no

man should have. We're assisting in things we can't even

begin to understand. I don't trust THEM. What they have

us doing cannot be for good, it's nature in itself makes

that clear. I wish nothing but the best for both of you,

however I hope in my departure, you take your thoughts

and actions seriously. Think about the consequences that could arise from them. I believe if you look further than what's here, in this time, you'll find it's a lot more than just yourselves. The war is over. It's BEEN over. Come home. I miss the old shack, I miss the hunting every day. I miss you both. There's nothing left for us. Please at least consider joining me in leaving all this shit behind. Farewell, to both of you. May our friendship remain ever true, though we all know we're not just "friends."

-The third.

Avery's eyes widened, and she felt a chill down her spine. Grey looked at her curiously. "What do you make of it?" Avery stared slowly up at him, then looked back down at the letter. "You find this in the comic book, ha." She laughed, but inside she knew she was dismissing something. Greys eyes turned serious. "No," he said grimly. "It was in the basement." Avery stared at him, her face going blank. *The basement.* She thought back to the figure in the light. *So that was you.* "I don't.." She shivered, but couldn't finish her sentence. *I don't go down there.* Grey waited patiently, frustrated at both their lack of knowledge. Avery skimmed over the words in her hand again. *The third. No info?.. What info?* Grey spoke, breaking the silence. "The most one could ever see in this time? What can that even mean?" Avery looked up at him. "I think it's something that shouldn't be messed with, it's clearly not for us," she said, with a slight hint of fear in her voice. Grey curled his eyelids, and made a face of offense, and confusion. *Ain't that ironic?* "Not for us?" - "Not for us??" He repeated, his tone of voice matching his face. "Avery, it was in the basement. *OUR* BASEMENT. In *OUR* HOME." Avery turned away to look out the window, but the blinds were closed. *He's right.* "I don't know," she said, turning back around to face him. "Grey, I'm about to go camping for a week. I don't need thi-" - "four days is not a week," he said, rolling his eyes. Avery raised an eyebrow. "What? How did you.." Grey returned the raised eyebrow with a mirrored look, his left eyebrow slightly above the other one, vertical to Avery. "Unimportant,' he spoke, ominously. She narrowed her eyes in curiosity, but didn't have time to prod. "Okayyy, well uh, see you later," she called calmly, waving him off. Grey's jaw almost fell off his face. "See ya.. later see- HOW CAN YOU NOT CARE ABOUT THIS!?" Avery stared at him blankly. "Dad loves fictional stories, I don't know, maybe it's a Halloween decoration." Grey fought hard not to tear his eyes from their sockets. "A Halloween decoration. Uh- huh, yeah, a Halloween decoration, that's definitely the answer." Avery simply stared back at him. "Look, I don't know dude. It could be from a book or something." Grey heaved heavily, anger rising in his face. *Why do you have to be SO DUMB?* "Yes," he said patiently, but passive aggressively. "Yes, perhaps it is a book. It doesn't change the fact I found it in *OUR* basement, and had to LITERALLY run-" He stopped, suddenly turning to her closet. He stared as he had before, at the bear's eyes. A pink, less disturbing version as the one in *his* closet. He eyed her alarm clock, still on the floor. *3:30 on the dot.* He stared back at the bear, its pink tuffs hanging from its ears. "Haha, good one sis," he said, and walked out of the room. Avery stared in confusion at the door. *Uh, yeah. Okay, good talk?*

Grey ran out the front door before his mother could stop him, into the woods outback. A place he could think. His mind raced as he darted around trees. *The third.. the other two. There were three, had to be. Who had put it down there? Why was it hidden, locked away?* He ran through a soft puddle, leaving muddy footprints in the ground behind him. *How.. why? Mom and dad are the most stereotypical parents, why would they have that in the basement. And who was that woman.. that voice?* He reached a gap in an irrigation river and leaped over it, grabbing onto an overhead branch and launching himself to the other side, sending the branch rubber banding, violently. *No info.. What info?* He thought back to the books he had read. *M.L.. I've heard that name. In the woods.* He felt a chill down his spine, and it wasn't the rushing wind. *I've heard that name…*

The house was miles away now, as he continued running into the woods. The light beamed down faintly, making the shadows of the massive trees above look like dark rooms. Grey felt his foot hit a root, and he tripped, sending him spiraling to the ground. He made a roll maneuver, and carried the momentum forward. A common mistake, that only made him faster. He ran forward, jumping over holes in the ground, and massive roots that used to be covered in water. He reached a fence, and stared into it. old dry rusty barbed wire, glared menacingly back. The wire seemed to threaten him from remotely getting near. As if it was more than just an object. He reached down, and made his way through the hole in the fence, as he had a hundred times before. At last he reached the end of the irrigation river he'd been trailing. The muddy ground faded into the destroyed sharp concrete, dipping down into the river, at a steep incline. There was a massive open storm drain pipe at the bottom, covered by a thick dark green brush. Grey crawled his way down the slippery sharp concrete, and into the mouth of the storm drain. He pushed hard on the vines, heavy in mass from their extended time growing there. The storm drain was revealed. A little Further ahead was a massive sharp rusty gate, with a tear just big enough for a little boy to fit through. He crawled over it like a laser maze, as he had many times before. He continued descending further, diagonally down. The tunnel was wide, easy to stand on. It was pitch black, any normal person would trip over everything, terrified of what lay in the darkness, needing a bright hefty flashlight. But Grey didn't need one. He knew the tunnel by heart, having been there many times. He reached a rusty gear, blocking the path in the middle. Mechanisms that controlled the Irrigation. He reached out for it, and took hold of a cog, and pulled down hard. A gate squealed loudly open in the distance. He went through the newly opened tunnel, and headed left, then right, further into the darkness. The path grew even more damp, stenches getting worse as he continued downwards. At last, he reached a hole in the tunnel, open ominously on the floor, leading straight vertically down. All around him he could hear the sounds of dripping water, old pipes struggling to support their weight. It was damp, and there was no light to be seen anywhere. He positioned himself above the hole and grabbed hold of the makeshift ladder he had made. A series of old branches, tied together, and hanging from twine from the old dripping pipe in the ceiling. Carefully, he made his way down. Two meters, five meters, ten meters. He was far underground now, into the world below. His world. His personal thinking spot. He dropped a few feet and landed softly in a mucky puddle below. Ahead of him was a ramp, which he slid down with grace, and landed softly on a catwalk. with a metallic bang. The air was stale and old, different from the outside world. Smells and sounds trapped below, where they couldn't escape, where they would never be found. Beneath him was an old sewage ditch, long since drained of its water, overgrown by thick vines. To his sides were entrances where the catwalks connected. The archways were barely visible, and caved in by bricks and debris. The ditch had no water, and was instead flooded with something else. Grey smiled, he was at peace. This was his little world, his spot to think. To be present. *Never gets old.* He thought, staring at the old pipes and machinery below. *God, I love it. I'll never tell anyone about this place. I'll take it to my grave.* He smiled, staring like a child seeing a rainbow. But the sight below was far from it. Birds. Hundreds of them, thrown down here, made to be part of the room. Their decomposing skin melted together, and into the structure of the ditch, seeming to have become a natural part of the wall. Grey didn't know how they ended up here, they just did. It was peaceful really. A topic to think about, death. A thing most people were afraid of discussing, to them a bad word, a bad thing. To Grey it was simply the cycle of life, another reason to enjoy being alive while he was. He sat down on an old rusty oil barrel, just inches away from the balcony that dropped into the darkness. He sighed.

He was at home. His seat, his relaxing thinking spot, his little

world.

Grey stared out into the darkness. *Okay.* He took a deep breath.

Here we go. He wrenched his hand into the pocket of his jeans, and

retrieved the crumpled paper. *No use in leaving it at home.* His

eyes darted across the paper for the hundredth time. *The third.. ML.*

What does it all mean? The ink glowed ominously with a red hue

from the small light above. *Avery was a giant old help, really*

helpful insite. He rolled his eyes in annoyance and disgust. *She*

didn't even look at the diagram. Grey's attention was suddenly

pulled to it, having thought of the word. It was a clock. An old

fashioned analog clock. It appeared to be resting on a man in a

business suit's head. A classy old top hat on top of the clock, as if

the head of the man itself was the clock. The image had no labels,

nor any signs of writing. But it had indeed been a diagram, drawn

in a blue print fashion. The ink had been smudged at parts of it,

dripping down off the page. The clock man appeared to have his

hands on a blank table, and his fingers crossed. A modern day hand sign of a business deal. Grey stared at it, confusion overtaking him. *I've seen him in the books, I swear I have.* He read the letter again, and again, but to no avail. *The consequences of your actions. I wish to start a new life..?* This "third" is clearly writing to another *two.* He shifted his vision to one of the collapsed entrances. "I advise you to do the same as me?" He said aloud. The light above flickered ever so slightly, as if in response. *THEM? Okay, so an all powerful being, what did THEY give you?* He shook the paper in his hand, and scratched his eye. "Find yourself well." He said again, out loud. The light flickered again, a little more this time. He paid no mind. *M.L.. Mr Lego?* He thought back to his childhood. *Nope, definitely not. Okay then wha-..*

Suddenly he felt a chill go down his spine. *M.L, the name of the company in the books. They aren't just legends. This illustrator person exists.* His eyes widened as the world came to make sense. His hobby, his imagination. *It was real..* The light burst out in the sound of a gunshot as he finished the thought. It was pitch black. Quieter than anything ever. Yet the air was full. Gone were the empty blank trapped sounds and smells. Something new was there.

Someone else was down there with him. Grey fought with his eyes, blinking rapidly, to get them to adjust to the darkness. He tried several times but to no avail. Something moved in the bushes in the ditch. Grey waited, still sitting at the edge of the catwalk, its rail broken and sharp. Nothing came. It was silent. *Damnit. I'll have to come back with a light.* He began to stand up, but something moved in the corner of the ditch below. *Stupid rats. No..* he stopped himself. *I've never once seen a rat down here.* Panic began to creep in, and the walls around him felt like they were closing. He stood up, but was pulled back down. Something grabbed his leg, and drug him back to the oil barrel. He kicked at it, fighting like his life depended on it. It released its grip finally, but he could hear it just underneath the catwalk. *We're not out of the woods yet. Haha, good one, me.* Panic began to overtake him. *HAHAH THANKS ME.* He couldn't see the exit. The air was hard to breathe, thick and full of decay of dead animals. "Gr- E-E-Y" the thing groaned with a thousand voices below, its voice echoing in a metallic sound through the openings in the railings. He felt arms shoot up through the holes in the catwalk. *Okay yep, definitely don't stick around, thanks thinking spot, bye bye!* He ran for the exit, knowing it was there. But couldn't reach it. He felt his ankles be grasped suddenly by a crusty, mucky hand. Then two. Then 3. Grey stared out helplessly. The exit was in the room, without a doubt. Yet the air felt trapped, never to be released again. There was no exit, not now. He could hear as the thing squeezed through the holes in the floor, ripping and tearing of muscles, flesh and bone crunching. It was up to his waist now, hands, little and big crawling up him like spiders. Grey fought for freedom but couldn't escape. Hands grasped around his arms and chest, pulling him further into the ditch. He felt his head smash against the wall, and his vision went blurry. He tried to hold onto the wall, but the thing kept pulling, and his fingernails bent inwards, ripping the skin off his fingers. He could feel his blood drip, as his fingers were dragged down the sharp concrete, like a carrot in sand paper. The stench of the birds grew closer as he was dragged further down into the ditch. ***But the birds weren't there.*** He grabbed onto the sharp destroyed metal railing, holding on with all the strength he had. But the thing didn't let go. He was pulled further down, his arms stretching, nerves snapping and popping in his wrist. The thing pulled hard, but his grasp stayed on the railing. It bent inward with him, as the thing dragged him further down in. It tugged hard again, and his hand was torn from the railing, thrashing against bits of torn metal, leaving a gash through his hand. He felt the hands crawl up his body as he was pulled even further down into hell, the surface disappearing. His neck twitched with sensitivity as the hands crawled further up, digging into his ears, and nostrils. He tried to breathe but couldn't. The last thing he saw was a hand, grasping over his face, and shutting out the world to his eyes, the gaps in between the fingers closed. He screamed but nothing came out, the hand covered his mouth. He felt his lips being wrenched open, and something crawling into his mouth. The hand covered his eyes, as he tried to scream, And then the world went black.

Chapter 4

The room was joyful, happily lit by the rising sun beams, casting

through the faint transparent curtains. The vent echoed softly through the room, a peaceful white noise, fit in its context. Avery lay peacefully on the dark wooden bed. She was silent, asleep in what one would assume to be a nice comforting dream. A telling of the future. Good things coming, seeing the things and the people she loved. She moved violently in her slumber, her neck twitching disgustingly. ***It was the opposite.***

The man ran to the side of the building, spinning a red valve. The woman scrambled anxiously with the child she held hands with. "Sh. Shh it's okay Av." Avery sat staring, unable to move. Isolated in a three year old's body. She let out a cry, but couldn't speak. "Shh. Shh, it's okay, everything's okay," The woman whispered, holding her close. She walked forward involuntarily, into the mouth of the massive trees, blocking out the sunlight above. "We need you to be really-" The woman's voice cut out, and she stared dead outwards. Her eyes widened, and her face went purple, struck with fear. a bright light blasted from around the corner, and the man rushed to the two, reaching into his back pocket. In an instant people were rushing in, yelling. Screaming. Avery stood, her eyes a blank slate. Only one word ran through her head, corsing thickly through her veins in pain. ***Run...***

The air rang with a loud obnoxious sound, as her alarm clock blared with red light. *BEEP BEEP BEEP! WAKE UP! WAKE UP! WAKE THE HELL UP!!!* Avery sat up fast, her eyes wide, breathing loudly, her body tense. She looked around. *Room. A room it was a room, the-* she trailed off in her thought, as she regained her sense of reality. *My room… Mine. So then it's safe..* She dropped her shoulders, and relaxed her body. The alarm was still blaring. *BEEP BEEP.* She shook her head, and smacked it, and it fell right back to where it was the previous day, shutting off with an angry *BEEP!!* Avery smiled. *My arch nemesis defeated.* She laughed to herself, and checked her watch, for she wouldn't give the alarm clock anymore attention than pain, the thing it deserved. *8:58.* She relaxed, and sat back. *Break. Nice relaxing break. Nothing to do-*

She stopped, and her eyes skyrocketed. Her brain forced her back to a memory. *"See you at nine, on the dot, don't be late, ha."* The blankets nearly grew wings as they were thrust into the air, and she leaped out onto the floor, reaching down and grabbing the bag she'd placed for herself the previous day. The dresser almost broke as she frantically threw on crappy old shorts, and a sweatshirt.

She shook the railing as she ran down the stairs. *Okay.. nine on the dot, say bye to mom, then gun it out the door.* She raced through the kitchen, skidding to a stop where her mother was. Her mother stared at her, confused. "I uh, yeah," Avery said. "Sweetheart, are you okay?" She asked, looking *into* her with worry. "Ah, yeah. I have to go, I'll see you in a week, love you." Her mother raised an eyebrow, a hint of anger showing through her face. "A week..?" She eyed her with suspicion. "Uh yeah, four days right, sorry." *Thanks Grey.*

She thought back to what she'd told her mother yesterday. "I'm leaving for four days with friends." Not: Can I go? She simply stated that she was going, and her mother allowed it, making sure to pack her things extensively. Very, extensively.

Avery spoke nervously. "So uh, bye mom." She went in for a hug, and her mother dropped her suspicion, gladly returning it. Averys arm fell, unstable in her mothers arms. The bag on her back weighed her shoulder with all the things her mother had packed her. "Mom, do I really need cooking spray? Do I really need a hard hat? They already have a tent mom." But she insisted Avery take these things. Avery wanted to argue, but her mothers look told her she wasn't going unless she agreed to the *EXTENSIVE* pack of "necessities".

"Okay, but just be careful, and have fun. I love you too sweety." Her mother smiled, and Avery didn't wait another second. She ran upstairs, and Swung from the door frame into her fathers study. He was sitting with his legs crossed, and glasses perched on his nose, staring at a newspaper. "Oh hey Av!" He said, noticing her presence in the doorway. "Did you hear about this new internet thing?" He asked, showing her the newspaper. Avery smiled awkwardly. "Uh, yeah.. that's.. that's cool," she replied, and her father smiled, blind to her insincerity. "Dad I gotta-" Her father interrupted, yawning loudly, and stretching, sending his glasses falling to the floor. He picked them up, and dusted them off. "Ah, what a lovely day out," he remarked, staring at the closed shaded blinds. Avery squinted, but the widow was irrefutably closed. *Uh, you good dad?* "Uh, yes well, dad, I'm-" Her father sneezed loudly, shaking the seat he sat on. "Phew. It's certainly allergy season," he said, repositioning his glasses. He aligned them with his eyes, but they immediately fell back to his nose. "Dad!" Avery snapped, finally.

Her father looked at her, and sat up. "Oh right, the camping trip!" Avery bit her lip. "Yeah," she muttered. "Stay safe Av, love you," he said, smiling with his big goofy smile. "You sure you don't want some camping lessons before you go?" He phrased the offer like it was a trophy, though inside he didn't even slightly have one. "I'm good, love you too," she said, extending her arms. Her father raised his eyebrow, and it took a moment to figure out what she wanted. "Oh," he said out loud, and returned the reach, pulling her into a hug. "Love you Av. Stay safe, alright." Avery smiled. "Alright." Then she turned around and left the room, racing back down the stairs.

She reached the door, and grabbed the handle, but her mother appeared suddenly, out of nowhere, and stopped her. "Avery.." She scalded. *Oh my god what now?* "Say bye to your brother." Avery held her breath, and bit her lip. *Just smile and nod.* She did so, expecting it to work. "Uh yeah haha, tell him bye for me!" She said, grabbing the door knob. But her mother stopped her. "Nuh uh," she snapped, with textbook motherly disapproval. "Go tell him goodbye."

Avery gridded her teeth, and nodded, smiling with her mouth open, teeth blaring. The stairs creaked loudly as she bolted back up them. "Hey bud, sport, friend, little man," she called in her famous Grey greeting, a ritualistic tradition at this point. But there was no Grey to greet. The blinds were closed, and his bed was still made perfectly. It was dark, a quiet ringing sound echoing through the room. *Grey?* She shook her head, clearing her mind, staring down at her watch. *9:00. That's my cue!* She turned around, but stopped. Her mother was waiting patiently below, listening. Begrudgingly, she popped back into his room. "Alright man, hope you have a good break, see you in a week- uh, four days," she corrected. She turned around, and nearly jumped down the flight of the stairs, her bag trailing behind her, bouncing and hitting her back. She glared at her mother and smiled. *Do I have permission to use thine door now, dear mother?* Her mother stared at her blankly. She knew well that she was lying, but saw it as a lost cause. "Alright sweetheart, stay safe, I love you," she concluded, stepping out of the way of the door. "Love you too," Avery mumbled, as she ran out, and jumped down the steps.

A van sat outside in the fog, facing the house where Avery walked. It's headlights blinded her path. The sound of a door being jammed open echoed into the woods, then two figures' faces appeared in faint light. Without warning, they ran forward and jumped at Avery. She flinched, and braced herself, ducking. One figure landed on her, and wrapped its arms around her. "Avery!!!" Sasha cried, with glee. "Long time no see!" She said, helping her back up. "Haha yeah," Avery responded, in pain, but happy to see her old friend. Sasha looked at her, guilt and worry shooting into her eyes. "Oh, sorry! I couldn't contain myself." She laughed awkwardly. Avery looked up. Her Indian slim, and slightly sly eyes looked no different. Gleaming, as if beckoning literally anyone to fall into her sarcastic traps, of which she had many. She wore a brownish red sweater, and simple brown pants. She smiled, and pushed her long black hair back. The second figure walked into the light. "I thought I told you nine on the dot. Tsk tsk." He smiled, and Avery met his gaze. "Ran into some.. complications," she replied, walking up to him. She smiled back. His brown hair blew in the soft wind, his eyes matching it. He too looked no different than she remembered, stoic, and standing confident, dawning a Gray camouflage jacket and jeans. She smiled, it was somewhat nostalgic. "Welp," his deep midwestern voice echoed out into the fog around them. "Shall we be off?" Avery smiled, the weight of the bag still holding her down. "Lead the way." The van door opened loudly, and the three hopped in.

"Ah, about time," the driver said, smiling. He cranked his neck around, glaring at them like a weird owl. "Have you grown at all?" He joked, his blonde parted hair blowing into his slightly squashed in looking face, like a human-pug. Avery smirked. "Just as much as your maturity," she replied, eyeing a certain shape drawn crudely on his arm next to his simple white T Shirt, visible as he stared back. The boy laughed. "Nate's fault." - "Can confirm," Nate said proudly, popping his back against the old, bright orange leather seats. Avery smiled with her signature mischievous grin. *Never change, never change.* "Uh, Cam?" Sasha nudged. Cam crossed his eyes for a second, as if trying to restart his brain. "Right," He said, turning around to face the wheel. "Alright," he began, putting the van in drive. "Ladies and gentlemen, please keep your hands inside the van at all times. Flash photography is not.." he stopped, seeing them sit down. "Ah, fuck it" He smirked evilly, cranking the radio up and flouring it.

The van lurched forward, sending Nate flying out of seat slightly. "Hey!" He yelled, Cam simply kept his evil smirk. As he landed, another object flew over the back seat and collided with his head. "Alright that's i- oh." His vocal attitude changed like a car being put in reverse. He reached up and grabbed the small Gym bag perfectly balanced on his head. "Finally!" He complained. "Been trying to get this damn thing for like..sixty minutes!" Sasha furrowed her brow. "Sixty minute- just say an hour!" She palmed her face. Avery held back a laugh and continued watching *the friendship comedy club*. Nate smiled with a big dumb grin, and patted the gym bag on its "back" like a pet, only for it to fly out of his hand, further into the back seconds later as Cam took a sharp right. He clenched his fists at the sky, and fell limp on the back seat. "Caammm!" He yelled, but his face was buried in the leather. "Oh stop your drama Nate, we'll be there soon, you can get it out when we get there," Sasha scolded him, rolling her eyes. Nate pulled his head from the leather, and took a deep breath. "Yeah… Yeah you're right," he said, calming down. He turned around, but only made it halfway, tugging hard. "God, just- go- the damn-" He struggled against his seat belt. It unbuckled, and he looked up. Avery sat, smiling at him. "Locked?" She asked, just slightly teasing him. "Hah, yeah," he replied, feeling stupid. "Well hi, Avery," he said, his face going from anger to happiness in an instant. Avery nodded. "Hi Nate." And laid back in her seat. She felt at home, next to Sean. "So uh, should've asked this before but where exactly are we headed?" Sasha asked, a little shy.

The mirror reflected Cam widely, who was rolling his eyes hearing her question. "Didn't Sean tell you?" Sean frowned. "Oh sorry

Cam, I should've realized it's *MY* job to plan *YOUR* camping trip." Cam ignored him, and kept his eyes on the road. Avery watched, feeling slightly more safe. *At least someone had common safety sense here.* "Hey don't you ignore me!" Sean said, jeering at Cam. Sasha looked at them confused and concerned. Cam looked back smugly through the rear view mirror. "Gotta keep the peepers on the road, numbskull."

Sasha's eyes widened, and she reached into the air as if calling timeout. "Boys, stop it! It's only been an hour together, and you're ALREADY arguing." Cam and Sean both began to laugh. Cam's face moved in the rear view mirror. "Pft, nah we're chill now, best of bros." Sean smiled genuinely. "Got that right, I missed this little man." Cams face went from satisfaction to offense in an instant. "Hey, who you calling little!?" Sean smiled, happy his jabs were working. "You." Cam furrowed his brow. "Yeah my bad, forgot I'm the shortest one here," he joked, eyeing Avery and Sasha. Sean seemed slightly disappointed, finding Cam had learned to ignore ridiculous insults. "That's the spirit," he said, patting an invisible Cam on the back in front of him.

The van shook as it trudged down the gravel path. Sasha cleared her throat. "Anyway, where are we going?" Cam smiled through the mirror. "You know, just an abandoned building. An industrial factory with absolutely no wild-life." Sasha frowned. "Okay smartass, could you at least tell us if there will be woods and trees?" She brushed her thin pants, which were clearly not made for camping. Cam smirked. "Gee, I don't know Sasha, are we going camping in Colorado?" Sasha rolled her eyes. "Can you for once just give a normal response?" Cam frowned. "You're no fun." Sasha nodded, crossing her arms, expectantly. "Alright alright, sorry I had to mess with you guys." Sasha nodded again, in the same tone. "It's called Butterfly sanctuary. Locals just call it **"Monarch"** . Avery froze for a moment, unsure why. Something about the name was familiar, the air felt colder than normal, and motion felt like it had stopped. "Av?" Sean asked, and her mind immediately snapped out of it, the smell of the old van and sounds returning. Sasha dropped her death stare, nodding with engagement this time. Avery and Sean followed, and Nate was zoning out, staring out the window. Cam continued. "But considering no one in their right mind would go camping for thanksgiving break of all times, we should have the place to ourselves. No one to get in our way, a whole thirty mile mountain all for us, where no one else can get to," he finished with excitement.

Sasha raised an eyebrow. "And you're sure that's a good thing?" Cam laughed smugly. "Please, I know how to camp." Avery and Sean exchanged glances. *We'll see about that one.* "So, obviously the elephant in the room," Sasha began. "Van," Cam corrected, fighting back tears of self congratulatory laughter. They rolled their eyes consecutively, and glanced at each other nervously. "I know how we all left each other last time was.. not ideal." Avery nodded politely. Sean bent his neck, and closed his eyes, affirming her statement. "But, that was a while ago. And we've changed." Cam smirked through the mirror. "Yeaaahh," he muttered. Sasha shot him a death glance, and he instantly started whistling gleefully. *Nothing to see here.* "So, I think we should all tell our side of the story, and apologize to each other." Sasha glanced around hopefully. Avery nodded again, hearing her out. *Though inside she didn't want to.* Sean stared forward and smiled, letting his vision unfocus. "Yep. Yep. Great idea Sasha." He tried to stay genuine, glancing at Avery and smiling. She smiled back. She thought back for a moment to what he'd said. *"It's really good to hear your voice."* Sean seemed to share the same energy, Almost as if he could read her mind. The van hit a bump in the road, sending Avery and Sean into the air for a moment. They landed back down, with a loud clunk.

Cam laughed a bit in the driver's seat. "Haha, oh shoot darn, whoops, sorry." Avery scowled at him, and he darted his eyes back to the gravel road. Sean sat up, recovering from the landing. He gestured towards the seatbelt, which was nearly non-existent. Avery realized what he was trying to say, and passed him the buckle, pulling the strap behind him. They were sitting in a two person seat, and the buckle covered them both, snapping securely. Sasha shook her head, and redirected everyone. "So, who wants to go first?" Nate rolled his eyes, and turned his head towards Cam. "Cam, we good homie?" Cam smirked back, nodding. "We good." Cam gestured to Sean and Avery. "You two?" He asked, as if labeling them as a pair. Avery raised an eyebrow. *What are you implying?*

Though in the double seat, they quite literally were. Sean nodded, smiling awkwardly. "Yeah, no worries guys, we're all cool here." He glanced at Avery hopefully. She nodded. "Yep, all cool," she echoed. Sean smiled to himself for a second. He seemed to enjoy representing both of them, together.

Sasha sat, her mouth slightly ajar. "I-" She frowned, and dropped her hand, slapping it in her lap. "Okay then, yep nevermind. we're cool, so cool," she muttered begrudgingly, though she did mean it. "So, there's five hours of ideas and planning wasted." Sean shrugged. "Well then, how's everyone been?" The van reached a stop sign, buried in pine trees. Cam turned around, checking for cars. He sighed, having seen none. "I've been alright, just fishing. That's about it, fishing and archery." Though something in his demeanor read that he was lying. Sasha nodded, and gestured at Nate. He startled a bit, having no answer. "I.." He took a moment to think. "Ah, I've been fine. Just school and rock climbing, working out. Finally benched three-hundred the other day," he smirked, but no one seemed to care. "Uh, I got my squat to three-hundred too," he said, starved for attention. Avery stared up at him. *Could you flex more please?* Sasha nodded politely, trying to care, and Sean gave a confident, prideful nod. "Well, I'm proud buddy," Cam assured, his voice bouncing off the metal walls of the van. Nate starred up, hopefully. Sasha moved her gaze to Avery and Sean. "Uh, you go first Sasha, how have you been?" Sean led, nervously. Sasha raised an eyebrow, but smiled, knowing they cared. "Been learning biology and…" Her voice trailed off.

Avery stared past her through the window, bending Sasha out of focus. Alone lay a building. Covered in vines and plants. A voice stabbed into her head. ***"Av, it's gonna be okay. I have to go, stay with your-"*** *the words blurred into a thousand memory's, as if something blocked her from hearing them.* ***"You'll be safe with her. I promise. I'll see you again. One day…*** *day…* DAY. The words rang from her head into her perception. Echoes of a thousand memories. They blended together, seeming to collide into the real, waking world. Everything was a blur, the van blinking in and out of her reality. *She was in a room. Sean was there. It.. was*

Sean? And the others? Her mind raced, as words echoed through. *A.. a... V... v...* "AVERY?" Sean's voice called, fresh in the real world. They were all looking at her confused, even Cam glared back, his face with genuine concern. A stark contrast to his almost universal attitude. Avery's vision blurred back into the van. "Avery! Are you okay!?" Sasha asked, loudly. Avery smiled frozen, as the world came back. *The van. The oth-.. friends. Safety.... Safety.* -"Ha.. ah, uh. Yeah I'm fine guys, just dozed off, sorry." Their eyes pierced straight through her lies. "Yeah, that wasn't just a Power Nap, I've seen power naps. That ain't one," Nate said, shooting a glance at Cam. He nodded strongly. Sean said nothing, staring down at her with concern. Yet something in his eyes said he understood what she was feeling perfectly. "Uh, yeah I'm fine guys don't worry," Avery repeated. Sasha eyed her suspiciously.

Just then a car pulled up behind them, honking. "Oh haha, look at that, better get going," Avery said, smiling awkwardly. Cam shook his head, and took a deep breath. "Yep," he said simply, turning around, and pressing his foot to the gas pedal.

The walls were dark, and the ground was wet. The red light poured in from Above, pulsing against the dark brick walls. It reflected in the water below, barely reaching the bottom. A brick loosened from the ceiling, and fell with defeat into the depths of the pit. It landed with a loud bang, echoing through the chamber. A boy awoke, covered in muck, and blood. He tried to open his eyes fully, but couldn't. The mud sealed them. *Sewer… fell… hands…* he felt the brick next to him, it had landed just mure inches from his face. He picked it up. It was heavy, and filthy with mud. With no other choice, he reached to his eye, and began scraping the mud. The brick hadn't fully been covered, in the murk, and still had a few sharp corners left. Slowly, he raked it across his face. It hurt. But he didn't care. He didn't feel the pain.. He felt his eyelash bend as the mud was scraped off his face and eyes. It cut slightly into his forehead, leaving tiny marks and bruises. *Hands… water… tunnel.* His mind was spinning, nothing clear. The brick had done its job, he dropped it into the water with a plop, and slowly began to wrench his eyes open. He gritted his teeth as the mud pulled and stretched against his eyelids. *Arms.. crunching… thinking.* He opened his eyes, but saw nothing. *Paper… writing…* His eyes widened, breaking free of their restraints of reality… *dad?* His mind settled on the thought, as if recalibrating, and the letters echoed through his head. *M.L…* He began to stand up, fighting against the concrete-like mud that held him down. After much effort he got up, standing in the mucky water. There was no space around him, simply walls of endless black, piling up into the darkness above. Grey struggled to separate what was real from what was fake, tearing at his mud covered hair. The walls changed their appearance for moments at a time: *Rats, brick. Vines.* His vision blurred, and his head went light. The wall spun and twisted, sending tiny ripples through the air, changing shape. They danced for a moment, in a beautiful evolution of terror and confusion. Humans eyes stared back. *Ten. fifty. a-hundred…* The vision blurred again, and was gone as fast as it came. Then it stopped. The world went silent, and his head stopped spinning, shutting down, and focusing on the situation at hand.

Grey looked around. He stood alone in a pile of rotting dead birds, underwater, all around him. His eyes widened, and fear began to creep in. *How many are there?* Though this was a question of curiosity, and genuinity, rather than concern and fear. He didn't need to know how they got here, they simply did. That explanation was good enough for him. He looked down. There were more. Underwater, piling up. They stood, mangled and twisted around him, closing him into a sort of nature's grave. *Though it was not natural.* He blinked a few times, as his head began to settle. *Time to leave. He* told himself. The walls of birds around him were massive, and tall. Grey scanned them hastily. *fourteen meters, forty-five feet.* He predicted, feeling satisfied he was *mostly* correct, a quality good enough for him. Slowly, he began to climb at the birds, grasping a wing. There were scarcely any heads, or real bird shapes. They were one massive amalgamation, conjoined with the room. He grasped it. The wing was grimey, and he could feel the dry, decomposing structure of the Skeleton inside it. He lifted himself up. *Glad I'm not fat.* He mumbled aloud, trying to make light of the situation. It didn't help. Slowly, carefully, he made his way up the wall. It was steep, and fragile, held together only by mold and mud. *And blood.* He thought, feeling a dry sticky liquid at each new appendage. He reached up, he was around half way up the wall now. The light was more vibrant now, reflecting on the birds. He could see the red light beaming down in rays, softly illuminating his way out of hell. He clenched his neck, as he reached up. *Almost there.* Just then the birds began to crumple, and move in the pile that made up the wall. Grey bit his lip. *Please stay-...* The birds fell to the ground, bouncing off the other corpses, along with Grey, who landed again in the water. He watched in horror as the mud began to absorb him again, like quicksand. He fought for control, but it wouldn't let him go. The pile collapsed down into the water, in an avalanche of dead birds, burying him with it.

"Ladies and gentlemen!" Cam began loudly, as the van roughly trudged down the road. Avery had fallen asleep on Sean's shoulder, and he had done the same with the arm of the seat. *Avery twitched a bit. Grave... Fan...M.L.. visions and words echoed through her head, becoming one. As if the concept of them being separated had disappeared. To most normal people, dreams have elements, visions, words, people, plots. To her, there were no words and phrases, there was simply the content of reality, a jumbled mess that only WAS.*

She jilted awake at the sound of Cam's voice. Sasha yawned. "We there?" Cam looked back at them, as he drove up the mountain. Nate was now sitting next to him. He echoed Sasha's yawn, stretching and bouncing along with the van. Cam frowned. "No." Sasha gave him her death stare. "BUT…" Cam continued. Nate rolled his eyes, and flipped around in the passenger's seat. "We still have at least an hour." Sasha nodded, and scowled at them. Sean was still asleep against the arm. "So why wake us up?" Avery asked, sheepishly, having been sleepily watching. Sean began to rise, yawning just like the others had. He spoke in a muffled morning voice. "We there-" - "No," Sasha stopped him. Cam shrugged, and reached into the glove box. He fished around in it for a moment, then pulled out a crumpled up piece of paper, handing it to Nate, who was now riding shotgun.

He stared at it confused. "What's this supposed to be?" Cam made a jeering expression. "It's a map, and you can use these crazy things called eyeballs if you want to know where we are so bad,"

he said, ripping it from Nate's hand and tossing it behind his back.

Sean caught it, and began to unravel it. Sasha curled her nose at the

sorry sight. It was old, and covered in coffee stains. "Ugh, Cam."

Cam rolled his eyes and frowned. "It's from like the wild-west,

what did you expect?" Sasha nodded, still disgusted by its potent

smell.

Sean stared at it, analyzing their position. "Okay, so west on..-"

"i-seventy?" Avery nodded, and completed his sentence. "Then we

should be around.. Here." She pointed, touching the old nasty map,

Wiping her finger on her shorts, making a face of disgust. "Huh."

Sean exclaimed. **Mr. Monarch's magnificent survival camp**"

Avery squinted her eyes. "Wonder what that is." Sean stared out

the windshield. "Looks like the universe heard you."

In front of them was an old ugly chain link fence, with a small

rusty metal sign. ***Mr. Monarch's magnificent survival camp***. The

title would suggest a happy kids theme, made for children to go

have fun and learn to camp. This was the opposite. It stood on an

old wooden pole next to the fence, which appeared to be grown over by trees. Threatening barbed wire poked out behind branches, grown over and nearly fused with the tree branches. The sign itself looked to be done by a toddler, with hastily made etchings and engravings in the metal. Sean eyed the gate, and the map, alternating his view. "What.. that doesn't..?" Avery glanced over his shoulder. "Those.. THIRTY MILES.." He glanced at Cam sarcastically. "Are unmarked, private territory," he finished. Avery stared ahead. He was right. The road they drove down had a fence on each side, each one looking more threatening than the other, as if trying to compete to scare people away. Cam stopped the van for a moment. "Oh.." He said, his confidence being swept away. Ahead of them was a dark, overgrown road, winding and twisting up the mountain. Beams of light shone briefly through the pine-trees, illuminating the path only slightly. The fences continued with the road, turning and expanding as the path went up.

"Well.." Cam began, staring at what lay ahead nervously. "Guess my hour estimation was wrong," he said, scratching his head. He thought for a moment, while the others waited, unsure of what to do just as much as him. Nate looked curious, but didn't seem to mind the ominous sight. Sasha shrugged. "We're already here." Sean looked at the map. "Where exactly is **here**?" Avery looked around, as if the universe would offer an explanation. "Cam, you sure you took the right path?" Cam nodded grimly. They all looked at him, expectantly. "Well then," he began, slamming the stick into drive again. "Axe-murderer-land, here we come!"

The air was freezing cold, and reeked with death. All light was gone, and the room sounded like it was collapsing, horrific sounds of metal and rocks crunching above, falling and fading into the bird ravaged water. Grey's eyes shot open. He had been knocked out for a few minutes, his face barely sticking out of the water, saving his life. He looked around. He was surrounded in a tiny air pocket of the bird amalgamation. His nose was but a few centimeters from the roof of his tomb, his hair bent back in the mud, stuck, and jammed against the dead birds around him. *Okay...* The walls felt like they were closing around him, swallowing him in the darkness. *Okay... okay.. so we fell.* He rationalized the situation, but felt no fear or panic. He squinted his eyes, trying to see in the dark, but to no avail. *Well that's a problem.* His brain suddenly clicked on, then came the smell. It was randsent, invading every bit of his sinuses in an instant. It stunk of rotting flesh, and his eyes and nose began to sting. Slowly, he pushed his way up. *There's a pocket. Left, up. And... Got it.* He found a crack in the amalgamation, and gave in a firm shove. It didn't budge. The smell began to worsen, and the walls felt closer. His motivation suddenly became VERY clear. *OKAY... we should get out of here, NOW.* Without any caution whatsoever, he bruit forced his foot from the water, and kicked upwards. In return, his foot bent in a way that couldn't be less natural, snapping and crunching. Yet he felt no pain. *good enough for me.*

His leg was now bent at his chest, and he pressed hard up, kicking at the birds. They crumbled, and hard dry flesh clashed against his face, splitting on impact. He was covered in them, struggling to breathe. *Four.. five. Twenty five...* He thought, feeling the weight above. The roof had fallen, but he was free now. Slowly, he lifted his legs, and braced his hands against the mucky, fleshy floor. He kicked hard up, in a perfect motion, blasting the birds apart, and opening the roof. He stared outside, but saw nothing. Just another roof of flesh. He exhaled hard, and the smell worsened. Threatening to singe his nostril hairs off. He stared up, a massive open beak, sharp and deadly gleaned softly, barely visible in the darkness. The head of the bird was broken, vandalized. As if someone had deliberately cut it up, in a fit of rage. Grey was not startled, he knew it was dead. He kicked up as hard as he could, and the roof broke, sending bird parts tumbling down the hole. The beak fell straight down to *god knows where*, and he dodged his head out of the way just in time, as it landed *somewhere* below. He kept fighting and kicking, and it got easier each time. He slowly made his way up through the layers. *One meter… Four meters… Eleven meters…* He emerged from the pile of flesh, gasping for breath. The air was open again, he was free. The light was visible again, and it glinted off the flesh bird pile. It had, *apparently* collapsed on top of itself, no longer a hole with walls, but a loose, sketchy pile. Something crossed Grey's mind. *It was a pile before I fell down there.. did it… change shape?* Somehow this thought made the whole situation ten times worse. He was closer to the surface now, maybe five meters from the ledge. He scanned the makeshift room. *Okay, so maybe off that wall, and onto the ledge?*

He nodded, confidently, and ran at the wall, then thrusted his hands

out, and extended his legs, bouncing off the wall, and flying fast to

the other side. He saw it, the surface. His hands grasped the metal

rail, still sharp and bent. They dug softly into the metal, adding

new cuts, deep in the ones he already had. Yet still, this didn't

mind him, his pain tolerance kept him from feeling anything at all.

He pulled himself up hard, and onto the ledge. He was back, safe.

Cautiously, cold calculated, *gray.*

He scanned the soft red light, but the letter was nowhere to be

found. He stared down for a moment, looking at his almost

permanent tomb. He shivered at the thought, but more out of

curiosity than fear. He would suffocate down there, drowning in

the horrid amalgamation of flesh. His body would join the birds,

blending into them, becoming just another one of them. Just

another forgotten, tortured victim, never to be found till the end of

time. He nodded, thanking the universe that wasn't the case, then

glanced at his watch. It was covered in mud, and he brushed it off.

7:13Pm. Time for dinner.. he smiled, Then walked back up the

slope that made the entrance, and out of his tiny little world.

•**Chapter 4:** A figure ran through the trees at impossible speeds, leaving soft bruises in the ground as its heavy feet impacted each time. It reached a barn, old and red. It didn't slow down, still running at an unreachable speed. Then, without warning, It impacted with the barn, and smashed through the wall, leaving wood bits falling around it. The figure continued running, reaching a fence, thick and electric, but it paid no mind to its threatening existence as *it was the greater threat, tearing through* it, and continued speeding on.

 A deer suddenly jumped in the way, and the figure skidded to a stop, digging its long nails into the thick ground. Curiously, It watched it for a moment, then lurched forward, grabbing it with terrifying speed an instant. The deer squealed in pure agony as It dug into the poor animal's bloody flesh with sharp needle-like claws. "Hello darling," It spoke, in a deep, metallic, scratchy voice. It plunged its hand into the deer, and grasped hard on its heart, ripping it out with a god awful sound. "Bye bye… Darling," It coughed, breaking into a run again. It glanced to the side, and suddenly stopped running, freezing in surprise, as the lights of a certain rusty old van bounced up the road in the distance..

"Alright," Cam began nervously. "Ten minutes." Avery glanced out the side window, and Sean followed her gaze. The fence seemed to have no end. It continued up the mountain, shrouded in trees. She shot a glance at Sean, and he nodded. "Well, at least the trees are pretty," Sasha commented. No one nodded, or even acknowledged her statement. Avery's eyes widened. Something was caught within them. Deep, camouflaged in the tree was a shadowy, large figure. *Just a tree. No.. wait. No, just a tree.* She dismissed it, not giving the universe more attention. Though she knew deep down what she'd seen.

Nate smiled. "Hey, I mean at least we've got a good… view…" He stopped. As they entered the fog. The "view" became clear. The fence curved around cruelly like a hunters trap. Avery continued investigating, following its reign as they went by. The endless stretch itself appeared to warp all the way the trees surrounding the mountain, in the shape of a sharp hook. Sean glanced at her again, and she nodded with her eyes. In the dead center, A sign was haphazardly nailed into the metal. "Butterfly peak lookout." Sean squinted. "Must've been a lookout spot, maybe a pullover?" Sasha nodded. "Then who would fence it off? Who even has the authority to do that?" Cautiously, she glanced down, just out of the dusty old window, her eyes suddenly fixating on something. "Hm," she frowned. "There's a hole in that one section." Sean grinned, catching on, immediately defaulting to every tenagers mindset: "Maybe someone could squeeze through?" All eyes turned to Cam, who, as per usual, waved them off. "Please, look at Avery, she's the shortest."

Avery glared at him, offended, and gestured to her self proclaimed: "crappy old shorts." Cam rolled his eyes. "It ain't my fault you wore shorts. Who even does that for camping??" Avery kept her eyes on him in response, glaring smugly. *Someone who's an idiot… that person being me,* she thought proudly. "Well, those two may be short, but you're skinny," Sean added, shrugging. The others followed Avery, looking at Cam, and nodding. "You've been elected by the group," Sean concluded, standing up and walking to Cam. He patted him on the back and gestured out the door. Cam scowled. "Why don't you do it?" To this, Sean echoed Avery, making the exact same gesture, comparing their body sizes. "I triple-hotdog-dare ya," he muttered, a tradition they'd had since the sixth grade. Cam rolled his eyes, standing up. "Fine, besides, no-one's gonna care if *I'm* dead," he jeered. Everyone laughed, though Sasha squinted her eyes confused. "You wusses are too scared to do it anyway," Cam continued, yanking open the door, and jumping down the steps.

The group sat silent for a moment, but Sasha interrupted. "Finally, someone put him in his place." She rolled her eyes though in some way she was perfectly mirroring him. The door burst open, and Cam's face popped in. "Hey, let's not forget who's driving you!" He snapped, in anger. Sasha rolled her eyes again. "Back so soon?" Cam nodded. "Yes, to tell you idiot- ahem. Friends," he corrected. "To move the van if someone's behind us. Or call me so we can get the hell out of here." Avery nodded, sensing his fear. *Can't blame you bud.* Cam tripped on the steps a bit, and corrected himself, coughing. His head bobbed up and down where it peaked in through the door. "Now I know you guys have never driven anything bigger than a Prius before, but if worst comes to worst, get me, and we'll get the van out of here." - "And us," Sean added. They all nodded in agreement, slowly realizing how safe this "extraordinary idea" actually was. "Alright, be back in a jiffy!" he concluded, disappearing out of the van.

It ran through the trees, flying through the wind, destroying sticks and logs. It smashed through the fence as a tree fell behind it, distinct in the dry, cold fog. The ground shook as it crushed through old soil, destroying plants that had worked so hard to grow there. It reached an old Ferris wheel, on the ground, murky and overgrown, then lurched down, and picked up the rusty, heavy metal with zero effort, and threw it across into the trees. Then it took off again, darting up the mountain. Something glinted in the distance, and It turned its head. It was a boy, blonde hair, thick jeans, an orange coat. They stared at each other for a moment, then the boy turned around and took off running. It ran too, staring at the boy for a moment, echoing his movements, then it leaped forward across a chasm and further into the desolate, inky trees, vanishing in the fog.

The fog grew stronger as Cam approached the fence, making the van barely visible. He thought back to what Sean said. *Cam, you're the smallest, why don't you do it? Yeah, and you have the smallest balls. That's why you WON'T do it.* He rolled his eyes to himself, and reached the hole in the ground. It was slim, barely big enough for him to squeeze through, but he knew he could do it. Bits of metal poked out underneath, and the dirt below was covered in sharp rocks, a spikey death crawl on all sides. "Great," he said aloud, and bent down, leaning into an army crawl. Slowly, He made his way into the hole, and was immediately struck with a rock. It stabbed quickly into his skin, but not enough to penetrate. "Ow, god d-" He hit his back on the metal bits above, as he recoiled in pain. "FUCK!" He yelled, pressing himself against the ground hard, trying his best not to hit more rocks. Eventually he got his head through, and forced his arms out, grabbing at the ground. His hand caught a pipe, and he pulled on it hard, dragging his torso and legs down the sharp rocky path. They stabbed fully into him this time, creating cuts and slits.

Determined, he bit down the pain, and yanked himself through, standing up fast then he bit his finger hard, wanting to feel a different pain, something to distract him from the cuts all across his leg. "Well. Thanks guys," he winced, limping forward. He looked up. What he saw surprised him. A massive carnival-like tent, with a ticket booth. Paths sprawled out in all directions, and attractions stood in the trees, overgrown and long-since disabled. One particular statue stood out from the rest, desolate and decimated. Cam stared at it, with curiosity and a slight hint of fear. It was an old wiry, spider-like stick figure, with a butterfly for a head. Yet it was nothing like a butterfly. The antennas had been torn off in stone, and human-like eyes stood in the wings, wide and disturbed. As if the statue itself had just been awoken. A smile curved, crossing the middle of both of the wings. It had human-like teeth just like the eyes, which glinted in the fog. Its four arms held a sign up, old and decrepit. ***Mr. Monarch's magnificent survival camp.*** The last words still didn't fit, leaving a disturbing tone in his head. "Okay…" He called out to no one… *it responded*; Something booming in the distance.

Suddenly the air grew cold, and *the hair on the back of his everything* stood up. He felt a chill down his spine as he turned back around, swallowing. The sign no longer read the happy go lucky camp feeling, nor the words themselves. Now, in their place were four, bearbone, etched in words. ***There's something behind you…*** He turned around slowly. A tree fell in the distance, loudly. They were moving now, their leaves falling. Cam was frozen, unsure of what to do. *There's something behind you..* Those four words were all the motivation and clarity he needed. Everything made sense in the world now. Chills began creeping up his spine like a long, desolate spider, and an awful sound of bending metal echoed horrifically in the background, accompanied by a loud clash through the trees. He stared out, and ***IT*** stared back. It was impossible to describe, as he'd only seen it for a mere second. It was like an object, completely still and meaningless, yet infinitely alive and even more infinitely threatening. Cam didn't wait another moment. For, what there was to do was quite simple: ***Run…***

The trees blew softly in the wind, and the curtains inside the house flapped about, making a loud annoying sound, and covering the light that illuminated the dark backyard. Grey's face appeared in the bush, dark and hard to spot. He glanced down, checking his watch like a spy movie character. He looked both ways. Something his mother had burned into his brain. *Clear,* he told himself as he left the bush. He crept up slowly, keeping low to the ground. The grass was wet, and itched at his skin. *Alright..* He could hear his parents through the window, muffled and distant. They sounded concerned, and their talking didn't stop. "Ye.. I.. ju.. like… sis… I ont.. th.. k… **Grey**," his father said loudly, finally a word Grey could hear. *Right, time to move.* In one fluid motion, he dove forward, and rolled tactically, then jumped through the window, and dropped to the floor. He slammed it behind him, and steadied the curtains, then ran forward, kicking the bathroom-door with a satisfying *click.* "Grey?" His mothers voice came. "Yeah?" He responded, as if nothing had even happened. "Where have you been?!" Grey bit his teeth together. "Was out with Tommy late, sorry!" He opened the shower curtain, and began to step in. "How did you even get in? The front door is locked!" His mother scolded, with high suspicion in her voice. Grey smirked to himself. "No it's not!" He knew it wasn't, having studied it before entering.

"He's right!" Came his fathers voice down the hall. "Grey, I'm coming in sweetheart" His mother said, her voice suddenly shifting, subtly changing as if she started to *care*. Grey, like he'd done to every other furnishing that even remotely had an opening and closing feature, slammed the curtains shut, as the bathroom door opened wide. His mothers shadow appeared through the curtain, and she immediately noticed his smell. "Ugh, Grey!" Grey said nothing."What did you go rolling in?" She asked, as if he was a mut. "Haha, sorry. Just mud," he replied, pretending to be embarrassed. He stared down at his mucky, feathery, blood covered body. *I'm not exactly wrong.* He shrugged to himself. "Grey, sweety, is that blood?" She asked, concern growing. *Crap! Didn't think of that..* "Grey, that's a lot of blood, showering won't help that." Grey squinted, looking offended. *Yes mom, it actually will.* He had studied medicine and gotten a minor bloodborne certificate, part of the "required nerd quota." He was smart, and knew most things better than his mother. "Sweety, let's clean that up with some hydrogen peroxide, I'm gonna open the curtain," she said, reaching for the fabric. Grey flattened himself against the shower wall, cringing in fear. But the curtain didn't open. "**Martha**, let's leave him alone. He can handle himself, he'll be okay," came the voice of his father. "Oh please, I raised you, it doesn't bother me at all. I'm your mother," she said, though not with certainty. "I've given you baths hundreds of times." Grey suddenly felt a chill. "I'm your mother." The words echoed through his head. *"I'm your mother Grey."* He fell backwards slightly, against the wall, and his eyes went blank for a moment. *My child. My (...)* The words were blocked from his memory as if his brain had a missing file.

"Martha, Please. Let's just leave him be," his father's voice echoed back into reality, now in the bathroom, his silhouette curling its nose. His mother nodded, begrudging, and they left the room, closing the door behind them with a soft creak. Grey sighed, and dropped his shoulders, turning on the shower. Cold water blasted out, hitting his skin. But he didn't mind it. He glanced at his body, covered in *death. How is all this even going to drain?* He thought as he scrubbed at his arms. Eventually, he got his skin to state that was remotely seeable. He looked down. His arms and legs were covered in cuts and scratches, and the skin on the bottom of his fingers had been mostly torn off, his index and middle finger stuck together with blood. Despite looking like a soldier in an all-out war, he felt only a little bit of the pain, like nothing but a small taxing of his appearance. *Alright well, we're home at least.* He thought to himself, continuing to scrub at his arms.

Sasha looked out the windshield. "Where is he? It's a lookout, there can't be that much to see?" Avery shrugged. "Maybe he's enjoying the view?" - "Yeah, quite a view," Sean laughed, gesturing at the tall ominous fence before them. Avery furrowed her brow. "Well not from here, obviously. But I don't know, it's a lookout, there's gotta be SOMETHING behind it." Sean nodded. "I'm sure there is, but it's too foggy. There'd be nothing to see." Avery's eyes narrowed. "He's right," Nate affirmed, reading her mind. Sasha nodded, seeming to be more interested in the massive blockade itself. Avery shrugged. "Well, he hasn't given us *THE SIGNAL* yet," she said, making air quotes. Just then a terrible sound of creaking metal echoed in the distance. Sean stood up. "Uh oh. Think that might be *THE SIGNAL*." They all nodded, and Sean walked down the van, grabbing the key, which sat buried slightly in the front seat. "Alright Cam, your call…" He waited for a response from the universe. But nothing came, just silent cold air.

"Alrighty then!" Sean said, a little more panicked. "Careful what you wish for!" He yelled, starting up the van.

Just then something fell from a tree, landing with a squeak. They all stared, though not in fear. "Cam?" Sasha gasped, surprised, running out the van. "Yea," he winced in pain, the breath clearly knocked out of him. "You okay?" Avery asked, now outside next to the others. "Yea," he repeated, in the same struggling tone. "What happened!?" Sean demanded, admittedly a little mad. Cam thought for a moment as he stood up. *Well I saw a shadow demon that tried to fuckin' kill me.* He stopped, and sat back down. *No* they wouldn't believe that.. *and they wouldn't think of me as tough. Uh- because I am!* He considered his options, then got to his feet, quickly this time. "Just wanted to get back quick, and it's easier to go up than down," he said, gesturing at the cuts on his legs. Avery's face went from worry, to fear, to confusion. "Then what was back there?" Cam leaned against the tree he'd just dropped from. "Nothing really, just more trees, maybe a view but it's too hard to see," he lied, breathing out. "But… it wasn't all for nothing," he relayed, retrieving something from his pocket.

"Ladies and gentlemen, introducing the *CAM-era*!" He boasted proudly. It was an old, barely working disposable camera, a glorified tourist tool that looked like it hadn't been used in decades. Avery looked at Sean, and he looked back. *Oh boy.*

They all stared, unimpressed, saying nothing. "Yoo! Awesome!" Nate interrupted, genuinely intrigued by the tiny device. Cam smiled, and looked at the others braggingly. "At least someone around here has taste," he snapped, performing a secret "bro handshake" with Nate. Sasha glanced at Avery, something in her eyes different. Not the smiley, sarcastic, voice of common sense, but something darker, more fearful. Something was wrong. Avery's breaths shortened. The fence began to feel like it was closing in, entrapping her in the fog. She looked at Sasha. She nodded, responding through what looked to be confused pain. Avery stared her dead in the eyes, locked with one similarity, as if all other qualities had been ripped away. Confusion, and pain. *So it's not just me.. "uy?" "Uys?"* -"Hello, earth to the women?" Cam asked, jeeringly.. Nate waved his hand in front of Avery, and her eyes darted open. *Fence... Friends... safety...*

She awoke fast from her daydream, still staring at Sasha. She seemed to have been awake. "You okay Avery?" She asked, in her sweet voice. "What.. I?" *No, no you were there too. It wasn't just me, you were there, I know it.* "Uh guys?" Came Sean's voice. He was standing maybe twenty feet away, staring into the trees. Cam took off into a jog, with Nate following him, and Sasha gestured for Avery to walk forward. "Wanna go see what that is?" She asked, in the same genuine sweet tone. Avery looked at her, confusion and hopelessness fighting for control over her face. "I.." *Why are you talking like that? I.. I know that voice. That's.. I don't..* Her neck twitched slightly, maybe in the present, maybe in her head. But Sasha did not react. *Why are you acting like-* Avery fell to the ground, grabbing at her head. It screamed with vibrating pain, pulsing through her veins. She was trapped in an inescapable prison. She could feel it in her physical body, an electric shocking pain, irradiating through her existence. There was nothing left but pain, she *WAS* pain. She fought, her blood vessels becoming visible on her face. *YOU SOUND LIKE... LIKE-..* But she couldn't find the name. "Avery?!" Her eyes shot open, and the pain was instantly gone. "I don't want to remember that name," she muttered aloud, in a monotone voice. *The pain. I can't. I won't. Never. Again..* She cleared her mind, taking a deep breath. "What did you find?" She asked in her "normal, happy voice" Sean stood in front of her, kelt down. Avery dropped her shoulders, relaxing. "Oh." Immediately, Sean shot up to the ground. "Av.. Are you okay?" He asked, his face looked as if he was ready to burst into tears. "You were.. I… Av, I think you had a seizure," he said, reaching to comfort her. "Nah, I'm fine, don't worry," she replied, in an obviously lying voice. "I.. okay. But seriously, We don't have to do this, okay?" She nodded, and Sean waved to the others, who were scarcely visible in the fog. Sean looked outwards. "Well, turns out there is a campsite. We were just blind to it. Avery cocked her head, confused. They walked forward, reaching the group. "Oh," she spoke aloud once again. A small, wooden frame was cut out, lining the fence. It was empty. "What? It's just more fence?" Avery asked, confused. "There isn't one," Sean responded. She stared out intensely. The space inside the wood was empty, and the ground behind it had been painted. "The perfect angle and everything," Sasha exclaimed, marveling at its architecture. Avery narrowed her eyes. "That's.. Huh.." Sean was right, there was no fence in between the wood, just a painting of one designed perfectly to look like part of the fence, a 3D illusion. "That's not all," Nate added, gesturing towards a sign down the road. ***Butterfly sanctuary: next right.*** Sasha smiled. "Well, now that we've seen a creepy ass government black base, I thin-" She turned around, but no one was there. "You coming?" Cam's voice called from the distance. She blinked a few times, and glared out at the fog in disbelief. "You can't be serious," she muttered, jogging to catch up to them.

The ground shone bright with orange light, from a flashlight, illuminating the trees above. "Go hunting in the fog he said, It would be fun HE SAID," a man jeered, shaking his head at his partner. "Yeah well, who knows, all kinds a' creatures come out in the dark." The other man stared at him like he just said the dumbest thing he possibly could've. "That's what all those idiots in horror movies say. You tryna' get us killed John?" John rolled his eyes, reloading his bolt action rifle. "Yeah well, news flash there BRAD! This *IS* real life, not a horror movie." He sighed, taking aim. "Dunno what you kids are into these days." Brad Gritted his teeth. "YOU KIDS!?" He demanded, in his heavy southern accent.

"I'M THE SAME DAMN AGE AS YOU!" He yelled, crossing his arms and turning away. Just then, a noise sounded in the darkness, echoing closer and closer. "It's a bear!" John yelled, getting Brad's attention. A screech of bending metal echoed out through the fog, and a single ominous figure began to appear. Tall, and bulky. "BEAR!" John yelled at the top of his lungs, the number one thing you're *NOT* supposed to do when hunting. Seeing a *"golden opportunity"*, he fired the bolt action, startling Brad. It hit the "bear" dead in the chest, but did absolutely nothing. The thing kept approaching, its inky black skin melting with the heavy fog. John fired another shot, and Brad grabbed the rifle. "You idiot!" He snapped quietly, a far smarter approach than John. But it was too late. The second shot had hit the figure again, perfectly in the eye, yet it still did nothing. It just kept on waking forward, completely unbothered. "Uh oh," John remarked. "UHUH," Brad whispered sharply, and they frantically ducked behind the hill. The air grew cold, and the trees began to shed pine needles, landing in their hunting setup. John stared out. "Now. Now just a minute!" He demmanded, standing up gleefully. "Oh you damn prankster!

You're not a bear at all!" He exclaimed, anger growing on his bushy red face. "STOP!" Brad tried to call, but it was once again too late. "Now listen here son, your first mistake: dressing up as a bear! You can get arrested for that you kn-.. *IT* lurched forward, grabbing John by the neck, effortlessly. A bullet impacted into Its leg, burrowing inside of it. But it did nothing, falling out from its skin in pieces a second later. "Your first mistake…" Its metallic, disturbing echoing voice rang out. It reached for John's arm and to his head, digging into him, and drawing blood. "Having limbs," It said grimly, as it tore him apart..

"Annd' we're here!" Cam announced proudly as the van pulled up to the campsite. Avery stared out the window, her lips fogging it up slightly. *Beautiful woods, a great big view of the mountains. I can't wait to se-* Her smile faded. It was foggy, and drizzle poured down heavily, now battling the very thin metal top of the old van, drips leaking down threateningly to where they sat. "Well?" Cam asked, putting the van in park. "Is it everything you hoped and dreamed of?" Avery exchanged a glance with Sean. He matched her concern. A tire swing blew in the wind from an old lanky tree to the right, barely visible in the fog. Cam signed. "Well I tried, okay?" Avery shook her head. "No.. it's fine it's just.." Cam shrugged. "We got the whole mountain range to ourselves!" He said, pointing at the simple, ugly fog. "Yeah," Sasha coughed, trying to be uplifting. "Welp," Nate muttered, directing a not-so-subtle hint to get out of the van, grabbing the sports bag he'd been battling with earlier. Cam nodded. "Let's get to work, boys," he smirked, annoyingly, staring at Sasha and Avery. "Honorary boys," he corrected, ameliorating absolutely nothing. Sasha rolled her eyes, "You're right, you're boys, we're women." Avery nodded sternly, but kept a hint of a smile, enjoying the gag nonetheless.

Sean exhaled with relief as he finished pounding in the last stake. It was dark now, nearly night time. "Oh good, you finished it," Cam remarked, sitting back in a hammock, for some reason still wearing aviators. "Yeah, thanks for your help," Sean responded, sarcastically. Cam nodded braggingly. "Anytime bud." Avery pulled the knot on the hammock her mom packed for her, tying it tightly. "So… fire?" She asked, gesturing at the inky fog that surrounded them. "Yeah," Nate responded, grabbing a bottle of rubbing alcohol. With a total of zero thought, He dumped a good amount of it into the fire pit, and Sasha ran forward to stop him. "What are you doing you idiot?" She covered her mouth, instantly wanting to take it back. Nate wasn't offended, he just nodded. "What, how else are we supposed to start one?" Sasha smacked her head hard. "Well you're not supposed to USE *THAT MUCH*!" Nate shrugged. "Eh, Fire is fire," he spat, picking up a lighter. To absolutely no one's surprise it lit ablaze when he flicked the lighter, and his old jeans immediately caught flame. "AHH!" He yelled, dancing around. Sean jumped to action, and smacked him in the butt with his shoe, putting it out swiftly. Nate exhaled, falling down flat on his face. "So.. let's not-" He began, his voice muffled in the moist ground. Sasha palmed her face, not even having to say I told you so. His vision cleared as he rolled around, face up, Sean's hand hung above him, inviting him out of embarrassment. He took it, and Sean pulled him up with mild struggle, nodding and dusting off his shoulders. "You good?" He nodded, and gestured at the newly born fire. "And we now have a source of heat!" He exclaimed, flexing proudly.

Time passed bleakly as they sat around the fire. It was night now, and the rain had stopped, but the fog had not depleted, if anything it had only gotten worse. "Y'all wanna tell a ghost story?" Cam asked, looking around the group. The shadows of the trees loomed over them like gods. Avery snorted at his request. "What are you, twelve?" Cam rolled his eyes. "No, I'm just not a girl." Sean stared at him disappointed, matching Avery. "Yeah so twelve," she repeated, and Sean faintly nodded, joined by the others. "Well I do," Sasha joked, posing for her spooky ghost story-mode. They all nodded in variation, and She smiled. "There was once a boy named… Oh I don't know… hmmm.." She *thought hard,* "Nate," she concluded proudly. Nate squinted, obviously taking the bait. "Now Nate messed with elements NO human boy should have.." She continued, building the *suspense.* Nate rolled his eyes, and Sean and Avery chuckled slightly under their breaths, joined by Cam. "Fire!" Sasha yelled, *"jumpscaring"* the group. She dropped her pose and the universe almost *cut the scene,* the light feeling reset. "Pffttt," Cam laughed aloud. "I'm just joking Nate we love you".. *yeah man... you'r-*

Their voices trailed off into the distance of the space around her. Avery's vision began to blur once again as she stared at the aspins in the distance. They had always looked like eyes to her, their irises only existing because of the reflection from the fire.

"**Avery**?" "Avery..?" *"Avery.."* A woman's voice pierced into her mind, echoing as it injected itself into her consciousness. It was her mother, undoubtedly. Though her face felt blurred, the universe was static like an old radio, particles floating around, trees melting in and out of the ground. She was a young little girl, but she could not tell her age. She looked down desperately in her head, but her body was not young. She maintained her teenage look and size, yet her hands looked like that of toddlers. "Don't get too close to the fire sweetheart," her mother warned in her sweet soothing voice. The trees were there, still like eyes in her memory. But they felt different. Hard to see in her mind, melting into nonsense, as if the information had been scrambled and scattered across her brain. "Martha!" A man called in the distance, his voice deep and scratchy. Avery fell forward even closer to the fire. *Dad..?…* *"Av?"* The man responded. *"Av?"* He called again, his voice sounding different. "Avery?!" Sean snapped, his voice bleeding back into the *mortal* realm. She was awkwardly leaning toward the fire, and the others were looking at her like she just killed someone, for all she knew she may have done just that. They were silent, all staring at her, as if the world had just paused. It felt uncomfortable, radio silent. -"Very?" Sean asked again, his voice split off. They were close to her now. "I think we should all get to bed," Cam offered, rather seriously, and Sean nodded, attempting to rest his hand on her shoulder. Avery shook her head, and Sean understood, taking it off respectfully. "You guys go ahead. We'll catch up later." Cam gave a thumbs up. "You wake me up and you're both dead." Sean laughed, and echoed his thumbs up.

"You okay?" He asked gently. Avery shook her head. "I.. I don't know. I just keep having these weird thoughts and visions." Sean smiled, as they stared at the fire. "Yeah, I know what you mean." Avery shook her head. "You don't," she responded coldly. "Sorry," Sean said lightly, looking in the opposite direction of her. "No.. I'm sorry," she replied, remorse in her voice. "For what?" Sean asked. "I don't know man, I feel like I'm a burden." Sean frowned with sadness, and shook his head. "Av, you're my bes-" He stopped himself, glancing down briefly. "You're our best friend to all of us," he reached out to wrap an arm around her, but changed his mind, backing it out awkwardly. "You're not a burden at all." He smiled, and his face turned slightly red in the light of the fire. "I.." He stopped himself. "You're a part of the group," he concluded, cringing at that statement. "You'll alwa-" Avery lost foccus. Something moved out of the corner of her eye. *"Come home! We miss you.. you.."* She sat up fast, and Sean's eyes widened, but nothing came. *Just a shadow.* Sean cocked his head, noticing the fear in her expression. "Avery?" Avery stared back at him to the side, expressionless. She wasn't ready to admit she was wrong. *I saw it.. I fucking heard it I know I did!* "Yeah, just tired." She smiled forcefully. "Okay then," he assured, trying his best to smile. They were silent for a few minutes, not vocal but both enjoying eachothers company. "I'll give you some space," Sean spoke, respectfully, and sat up, making his way to the tent. She sighed in relief, and stared into the fire, something she'd always loved doing. The wood was dying, turning ashy white as it breathed its last breaths. For a moment it shone bright in the reflection of her eyes, her face cast vividly in the shadows, an aura of life almost having new meaning. Then the wood fell with the loud crack, crumbling to pieces.

 It was almost morning, and she'd barely slept, a common thing for her. Something she was used to. *Just another day.* She stretched and opened the tent to go outside. The world slowly came into view as her eyes adjusted, she had thought about the vision she'd seen the previous night, eyes lit by flame. She stared at nothing, and it stared back. Her blood was running to her stomach, and she felt queasy, grasping the pole of the tent for support. The world around her blurred out of vision, except for a single pine tree in the distance. She focused on it, trying to anchor her reality, the rest of the world an insignificant void.

She was a little girl in the woods. "Are you sure it's safe?" A woman was standing in the shadows of a tree. "Martha there's no other way," responded a man, frantically packing items she couldn't make out into a trunk. Avery stood, unable to speak. She was staring at an old brick building swallowed in foliage, with a *rusty metal garage door at its center, scarcely visible in the dim sunlight, peering through the thick trees. The man began turning a valve at the corner of the building, and the garage door started to open with a painfully loud squeal. "Avery honey, we need you to be really quiet, okay?" The inside of the building came into view, but there was nothing.. Complete and total nothing. The light shone into the building, but all she could see was a void. No color, no shade, simply nothing. As if the concept of anything itself refused the room. She began walking forward, unwillingly, still speechless. Out of the corner of her eye, an object appeared, looming in her direction behind a tree. She squinted for what felt like hours, time having no meaning, nonexistent. After a long time, the image began to spin and distort like ink in freshwater. It was a bright flashlight pointed directly at her, threateningly. The woman screamed bloody murder as her being was illuminated in the light, scattering like a bunch of bats.. "**Run.**"*

Suddenly, a knife landed softly just inches away from her foot, stabbing into the ground. "Sorry!" came a voice. Avery snapped back to existence, shaking her head to rid of the memory. She looked up. Cam stood awkwardly next to a tree, his hand still in the air from when he'd haphazardly thrown the knife. "You're up early," Avery managed to cough up. "Yeah well someone's gotta keep the camp safe." He smiled awkwardly, clearly having no actual come-back. She glanced at his hand in the air, then back to the knife in the ground, confused. "In the dark?" She gestured towards his hand. "Uh, flash-lights are bright these days." *Flashlights.* The memory came flooding back, and she froze. The sound of rushing blood in her ears, yells, screams. Running. Trees passing by as sounds blared behind. That feeling.. *Run.* "Uh hello, earth to Avery?" Cam stood next to her concerned, the knife now in the his hand. The tent rustled behind them, and a figure appeared. Sean arose, rubbing his eyes. "Mornin." He bit his lip in curiosity, noticing the peculiar nature of how they were standing. "Campfire stories keep you up?" - "Haha, you wish," Cam teased. Avery wasn't listening, *who were those people, why were we there? -*"Yeah right, I swear the tent was gonna blow away, right Av?… Avery?" - "Uh, um yeah, good one," she coughed up bluntly. Cam raised his eyebrow, and fiddled with his knife, heading back to the tree. "You okay?" Avery looked up. Sean was staring at her, concerned. "Uh, ah yeah. Just didn't sleep much."

"You and me both," he laughed. "Av, what's up?" She didn't

answer, staring into his eyes unsure of how to respond. "I just…"

She hesitated for a moment, this was something very private, but

she trusted him, as she had nearly her whole life. "I just keep

having this memory," she mumbled, so Cam wouldn't hear. Sean

waited for her to continue, his eyes patient like a hunter. "There's a

building in the woods, a- and a man and a woman." Avery began to

twitch just slightly, shedding a tear. Sean reached to comfort her,

but she lurched back. "They tell me I need to go with them, and

then…" Her face switched back and forth from confusion and

anger, searching desperately for answers in her mind. "And then

I… The woods, there's woods, but I just- I don't-" She lost herself,

becoming increasingly more incoherent. "I don't know!" She

yelled finally, and Cam glanced over his shoulder in the distance, a

look of rare genuine worry on his face.

"Av I-" -"I don't know," she repeated in a sadder tone. She glanced

into the trees searching, but found nothing. Defeated by her own

mind, She dropped her shoulders and sulked towards the ground, giving up. "Avery I believe you, it's okay." She glanced at him thoughtfully, surprised at what he had said. "Hey uh, do you wanna take a walk?" His face turned pink, smiling awkwardly. Avery liked the idea of a walk, getting away from her friends for a bit. *Get away from life for a bit, but Isn't that what we came here to do?* She stood up. "Sure." Sean glanced around, checking that everyone was still asleep. Satisfied, He turned back to Avery, who was no longer there, but far out towards the exit of the campsite. He rolled his eyes, grinning nostalgically, and sprinted to catch up with her.

"Took you long enough," She teased. "Lady's first," he replied, smugly, and Avery scoffed, cutting through the thin bushes in front of him. They left the campsite together, walking behind Cam and out of view. "Yeah okay, sure, real great friend-group communication guys," Cam muttered, spinning around, thrusting the knife into a random tree with zero concern for safety.

The wet autumn leaves fell amongst the ominous fog, as they walked along a barely established trail.. "So, how's Grey?" Sean asked. "Oh he's fine. Really into comics." - "Huh, Grey? Never would've guessed. He doesn't strike me as a Nerdy type." Her natural teenage sarcasm screamed at her. *Have you even met him?* She just shrugged. "Well to each their own I guess." - "Yeah." They were quiet for a moment, walking faster not looking at each other. "So uh, do you want to talk about the thing?" Sean asked. After a few moments. Avery took a deep breath. "The memory's?" Sean smiled, unsure where he stood. "Yeah."

She glanced at him, side-eyeing him up and down. "To be honest, I just didn't want the others to hear." They stopped in their tracks, and she faced towards him. He smiled genuinely, and she returned it. *I trust him,* she reminded herself. She echoed his smile with a slight "Avery branded" smirk, happy she came to this conclusion. He reached to comfort her on her shoulder, and this time she let him. They stayed for a moment smiling, everything else around them paused. Nothing else mattered. Then Sean retracted back, his face bright red. He looked the other way and acted like nothing happened. Avery gave a school-girl chuckle, and covered her mouth trying to hide it, a very rare event to occur for her as a person. "So.. memory's," Sean said ending the awkward tension.

"Right," she replied, a slight hint of disappointment in her voice. They resumed walking. "It's just.. woods. Pine trees and bushes. There's a brick building that looks like uh, just super old." She glanced at him, and he was staring ahead, but clearly listening intently. "I remember a tall man, and a woman. But I can't see their faces.. it's like".. She paused, choosing her words carefully. "It's like someone used white out on a crime scene report. I can see their body's, their.. figures. But not their faces." Sean's face grew with concern, still looking ahead of them. "They tell me I need to go into the building, but there's nothing inside. I just.. can't see anything in there. It's like somethings **jamming the signal**, and blocking it out of my memory." She consulted the trees, unsure of what to say. "I remember a flashlight, someone with a flashlight. There was commotion, something bad. The woman, uh I, the woman was screaming. And the trees." Something snapped into place in her mind. She felt a shiver shoot down her spine, spreading through her body. The air was different all of a sudden, and her eyes turned bloodshot, her breathing becoming unstable. She kept walking, but the world around her became nothing. *It was there.. the Door, the grave, the room...* She tried desperately to hold onto it, but it left as soon as it came. The world came back, spinning, particles of her minds eye rippling through the air. "I don't.. I can't." *Cmon think damnit!* "I- uh- um" She stared into the trees begging for something to appear, but nothing did. The memory was gone.

 "Hey it's okay." Sean turned to face her, a look of hope and longing in his eyes. "I don't get it!" She yelled angrily, kicking a pinecone into the abyss. "Every time I'm right there, someone.. something blocks me out!" *THINK!* "It's okay Av," he replied, kindly. They stopped again for a moment. "It.. It means a lot that you were willing to share this with me at all to begin with," he muttered shyly, as though he'd been waiting for a long time. Avery met his gaze, and he reached out his hand. She hesitated. *I believe you. I can trust him. It's okay.* She took it, and he smiled, giddy with happiness. She smiled back, and they walked into the woods, together. Suddenly the trail stopped, as if something had deliberately cut it off. "Oh it's dead en-" Avery stared up, and Sean echoed her. In front of them was a massive open tunnel that looked to have been burrowed deep, and hastily into the terrain. It was dark, with parts of grass and dirt pouring down, hanging over the freshly dug hole. "What..how?" Her eyes were wide, but she wasn't staring at the tunnel. Below it lay a small, crumpled old paper. Sean noticed it, and reached to pick it up. He unraveled it, and furrowed his brow in confusion. "Uh.. weird," he muttered, eyeing it up and down profusely. "What is it?" Avery asked, though deep down she knew very well what it was. Sean glanced at her with a grave expression, the faint sun glinting in his eyes. "Have you ever heard of something called M.L?"

Chapter 5

"Come now, One. We've been through hell and back, it wasn't me." Two men sat at a table, glaring threateningly at each other. The light shone down from massive screens above, illuminating their faces like a faint night sky. "Your promise wasn't kept, Three," One said, crunching his knuckles. "You argue we've known each other forever.." He stopped, drawing a pen from his pocket. "Then why.." He began, pricking the ink barren pen into his thumb, he drew blood. "Then why was info received, Garrison?"

The sun shone brightly, casting beautiful beams through the massive trees. "You gonna throw that thing all day?" Sasha jeered. "All morning," Cam responded, rolling his eyes. Nate patted him on the shoulder as he was about to throw the knife, and Cam recoiled a bit, shaking his head, annoyed. "Yeah!" Nate said, curling his nose at Sasha. "You got an extra?" He asked, looking hopefully at Cam. "You bet your sweet ass. Back corner of the trunk." Nate nodded, and took off running. Sasha rolled her eyes. "Ugh, why I am I stuck here with YOU TWO while Mr and Mrs. Love bird go for a private walk." Cam shrugged. "You could go take a walk." Sasha frowned. "Yeah! Maybe I will!" A knife went flying out the trunk as Nate dug through it. Cam raised his arms, offended by Nate's recklessness of his PERFECTLY PACKED van. "Okay, do that then," Nate replied to her in the distance. She opened her mouth to respond, but stopped, staring up at *Caveman 1 and caveman 2, idiots. It's a lost cause.* Nate arrived at the tree, and held a smaller, more fragile knife proudly in his hand. Cam smirked "Ayyyy!" Nate joined in with his energy. "Knife club! Yeaaah!" Sasha rolled her eyes, and began to walk away. Cam and Nate performed their secret bro shake, knives still in hand, completely unaware of any concept of safety. "Hey Nate, imagine NOT being a part of the knife club. HAHAHA," Cam cackled loudly. Nate smirked nodding. "Yeah, guess it's KNIFE BROS!" Sasha curled her lips, muttering mockery of the two, as she walked off. "Hey bro!" Nate began, in his college frat bro voice. "Yeah bro?" Cam replied, tipping his sunglasses, only to realize he had none. "Wanna do a ULTIMATE DOUBLE KNIFE CHUCK?" Nate asked, in a deep- announcer voice.

Sasha stared at the ground in disbelief, now in the distance. *Are you two filming something, what are you, the jackass cast?* "Hell yeah dude!" Cam replied, preparing his knife. "Alright ready.. 3… 2… 1- what the!?" A paper blew into the tree, right as the knives collided, stabbing it into the tree. "BRO!" Nate exclaimed. "BONUS POINTS!" He added, holding his hand up for the "bro handshake." But it didn't come. Cam had dropped the bit, genuinely curious as to what the paper was. He was a smart kid, he just loved feeling tough. "Uh, Sasha?" He asked, in a normal voice. *Oh now they want me great.* She rolled her eyes, and turned her gaze to the mountains. She was sitting on a sharp, mangled stump, barely visible through the thick trees. "Sasha.. I'm not kidding anymore, we really think you should see this." His tone was more grave, and his voice was slightly louder. *Fine.* She thought, as she walked back begrudgingly. "What?" She said, impatiently. Cam handed her the paper, a grave expression that matched the voice on his face. Sasha's eyes widened as they darted across the page.

Had to rush this One, because the last one took so long. I'm coming for you, One. See the other note if you want, or don't, I'll be out before you know it. -Two.

"What… was this intended for us?" Cam shook his head. "It doesn't seem like it." Sasha raised her eyebrow. "Then what are the numbers?" Nate shrugged. "We thought you'd know better than us." Sasha nodded, smiling to herself. *You sure did.* Just then two figures appeared in the corner. "Guys!" Sean called, out of breath. "Oh great, Santa's back." Cam jeered, leaning against the tree. Sean didn't laugh, and simply stood, staring. His expression was far from comical, his eyes slightly bloodshot from running, and his face full of fear. "I-" "We found something." Avery interrupted, her face matching Sean's. She held up the paper, as it blew in the soft, somehow ominous wind. Nate and Sasha cocked their heads. "Well, wouldn't ya know. We found one of those too," Cam said, holding up the paper from the tree. Avery recoiled back, and looked at Sean. "Anyway, you guys wan-" She ripped the paper out of Cam's hand and began to read it intensely. She handed him the other paper, and he began reading, echoing her same intensity.

Hello, One. It's my understanding you've grown... jealous of my work. We always knew I was better. I still am. But listen old friend, your attempts to take me down were for nothing, and thanks to you I have a very happy little workforce of soldiers now. It didn't take much to convince them, just a few syringes of, well that's not important.

Can't have you stealing my business right, haha. Speaking of stealing, I'm actually on my way to the old lab right now. I need more material, and you, my friend, have it. I'll be out before you know it, don't worry. But don't cross me. C1 already ordered you to stand down. I'm untouchable. So enjoy watching from the sidelines as I rip everything you've ever loved away. Byebye.

-Two.

"Pft, seems like a real professional guy," Cam spat, cracking his neck, and stretching, still tired from his lack of sleep. "Yeah, well, it's not just the paper we found." Avery added, glancing at Sean. He nodded slightly, and she grabbed the note out of Cams hand, putting the two together. "Okay.. look." Sasha cocked her head, and Cam and Nate glanced at each other, confused. "My little brother, Grey. You remember him right?" They all nodded, and Cam laughed a bit, remembering good times. *Miss that kid.* He'd always gotten along with Grey, sharing his crazed theories. "Yeah, well he found a note.." Avery stuttered, glancing around for answers. The trees stood tall all around, as if blocking sight of clarity. "He found a note just like the ones we found, right in our own basement *in our own home*." Nate opened his mouth to talk, but Avery waved him off. "I've been having dreams. I can't describe them.. it's just. I know.." She stopped, not wanting to share quite as much with them as she had with Sean. "I know this is connected somehow. I know I used to say I have a confusing past." She laughed nervously. "I know I sound like some stupid character in a movie right now, but something isn't right. I can just.." "Feel it?" Cam asked, in a cold voice. "Yeah," She responded, dropping her hands in defeat. "Yeah, not gonna lie Avery, your parents have always been weird, and you mentioned your basement, I mean we were never allowed to go down there when we all used to hang out." She nodded. Sasha squinted, trying to sort her thoughts. "Avery.. What are you asking from us?" Sean stepped forward to her back, as if to literally "have her back." Avery nodded, and let him. "That note wasn't all we found," She began, ominously. "At the end of that trail, there's a dead end. And.." She paused, considering something. "And a dug out tunnel." Nate raised an eyebrow. They remained silent for what felt like an eternity, awkwardly waiting for the other to say something.

"Uh, so what exactly is this tunnel?" Avery bit her lip. "I think the person leaving those notes dug it. But.." Cam shivered just slightly, suddenly remembering what he saw earlier. *"There's something behind you."* Cam shrugged, "It *would* be impossible, but then how would.. Or, why would whatever this is write notes?" "Yeah, and why would *we* find them?" Sasha added. Avery brushed the hair out of her face, as it blew in the cold wind."Look, call it hunch but there's no way all this isn't connected." The group exchanged nods. "It's like a book, but someone tore the pages out. I can just.. I can feel it. But.. that thing. I mean, whatever, whoever dug that hole.." She paused, glancing briefly into the desolate trees. Still, they offered no answers. "I don't think they're going to want us to follow."

Cam shivered. *Nothing human.... The shadow thing.* He flashed back in his mind. *Darkness. The cold.. The trees moved. "Not human." She's right.* "Alright so all in favor?" They all turned towards him. "Cam?" Sasha asked, her face a mix of annoyance, and concern. "Yep. Couldn't agree more guys, let's do.. that." *What the hell, I was only dozing for like five seconds?* Sasha raised an eyebrow, and Nate stood, looking confused at him. "Alright, the council has decided!" Sean concluded satirically. "Ten-pm tonight, we head out." Cam' shook his head like a wet dog, suddenly processing the words he'd just heard. "Okay wai-" "So we decree!" Nate interrupted, Drawing a flashlight from his bag. "Uh… yep." Cam managed to reply, accepting his fate.

"I let you leave, Three. That was your chance. And you.." The man stopped, beginning to write with his blood on paper. "You betrayed that," He finished, coldly. "Negotiating is devoid, Three. I respect you as an inventor. You know that. But now your family does too… that's a problem, Garrison. Go say goodbye while you can." The **third** *man lurched forward angrily. "You say you respect me?" The first man nodded begrudgingly "Then you'll at least use that respect to let me choose where she dies." Angered,* He shook his head, slamming his fist on the metal table with a loud **gong**. "What happened to you? Both of you…?" The first man said nothing, staring ahead soullessly. "I tried telling you already." He gritted his teeth, regretfully. "THE WAR IS OVER!" The first man rolled his

eyes, shaking his head. "And why exactly do you think that is?" "You only think in this narrow minded wa -" "It's over." - "Have you forgotten why it stopped in the first place?" The third man shook his head. "He's using you. You really think they need one SINGLE human on earth, much less in this timeframe to manage their wasteful artifacts?".. "What about everyone in **THE ZERO**? What about retiring for once in your goddamn life! You ever thi-" The first man strung his arm straight out, at an impossible length like a spider, and nailed the third man in the head. *The first man nodded, diligently. "You want to pick where she dies, sure. But you aren't ever seeing her alive… ever again."* He stopped, looking at the other man with deepest hatred, a long history. *"You're choosing to create collateral. You betray us again, Three.."* He began, *raising the pen. "Then you can say goodbye to the mere concept of existence." He finished, stabbing the pen into the paper, with a bloody mess.* The other man shook his head as he sat up. "I don't know what you are…" He grabbed the wall, blood on his fingers, staring at the man like he was a complete stranger.".. "You're not my fucking brother."… "Goodbye, **One**." He finished, slamming the door, his long brown hair barely covering a bright blue eye as he left.

"Alright, yep that's dark." Sasha's voice echoed into the depths of the dark woods., stepping out of the tent. Sean stood in the faint rain, a thick brown coat sheltering him. The fog still had not let up, looking even worse illuminated by Sasha's flashlight. Sean took a deep breath and gave a confident nod. "Everyone ready?" Avery gave a thumbs-up, a red flannel fastened tightly around her upper body, and her childhood switchblade secured tightly in her back pocket, ready to be drawn at any second. Nate wore a hood, barely visible in the darkness, and Cam donned.. Nothing. He wore the same yellow jacket from the previous day, and the exact same dark blue jeans.."Alright then, follow us," Avery called, joining Sean, and leading the group. The flashlight bobbed up and down as they walked, illuminating the trees and bushes. Cam mentioned something about night being less creepy than the day, and they argued passionately for the entire fifteen minute walk. Avery shook the water out of her flannel, the rain was coming down harder now. Sean shot her a glance, reading her mind. *Shit, this might be difficult.* The weather only worsened as they reached the dead-end in the mountain."There," Avery commanded, pointing at the wall. "Oh." Sasha exclaimed, as she shone the light onto the tunnel. It was dark, and inky, as if the dirt had grown it's own, original new dirt. Dirt that demanded credit for its originality, in the sheer amount of its presence, a black sea of mushy, gross- god knows what. Cam curled his nose, and made a worried face. "Uh.. you sure about this?" Avery and Sean simultaneously. nodded, confidently, The tunnel itself was small, barely big enough for them to fit through, and it leaked the black mud in massive amounts, making whatever was in there darker than the pitch darkness around them. It was high up, hard to reach, dangerous: Sharp rocks and thorns just under it, each being pummeled by the downpour. They waited for a moment, and Sean took the lead, leaping into the air with a grunt, and barely grabbing the base of the tunnel, which crumpled a bit at his touch. He slammed his knee down hard into the rock, cleaving his foot into the dirt, and lifting himself up. He knelt, nearly crawling in the mud, and reached his hand out for the others. Avery jumped forward, and grabbed his hand. His arm was pulled from her weight, and he struggled to pull her up, wrenching backwards violently, and dragging her slowly up the rocks. "Ow," Avery winced, mildly slicing her forearm on the sharp rocks. "You good?" Sean's voice echoed through the tunnel, a weird, squishy calling back, as if the mud itself was mirroring him in some sick twisted way. "Yep, just a paper cut," She whispered back. Though it wasn't, it bled heavily, and the blood dripped down the rocks with a loud dripping sound, combining with the awful mud, never to be seen again.She bit down on it hard with her lips,the only safe way to apply pressure, a sort-of vacuum seal.The bleeding stopped, and she sighed in relief. *Okay, well we're alive, thanks, survival tea-* She was pulled into a crawl, and Sean turned her forward, securing her place in the tunnel. "Alright next,." He called, navigating around Avery, but Nate was already right behind. He had scaled the wall easily, a simple task for a rock climber. Cam looked at Sasha and shrugged. "Well." He scoffed, breaking into a run, and leaping to the tunnel. His hands met the wall, and he hung from the base of it, slipping a bit in the mud. The plants flailed around him, as he started to climb. "OW!" He snapped, a new weight on his back. Sasha chuckled sadistically slightly, as she climbed up his hanging body. "you lit-" She kicked him a bit in the back, and he coughed, nearly letting go. Then she leaped up, and scurried inside. "Well, great, that sure works." Cam muttered angrily, clenching his teeth. He looked up. Sasha was crouched, her hand out, smiling evilly. "Cmon idiot." Cam took her hand begrudgingly, and she pulled him up surprisingly easily. Cam rolled his eyes. "Yeah yeah, thanks.. I guess." Sasha smirked in response, patting him on the back slightly, a little more intimate than usual.

"Okay.. so we're alive.,"Sean announced to the dark pit of nothingness ahead of them. Avery scowled behind his back. *I would've said that if you let me finish my tho-* "Let's go," Sean led, observing the shrinking ceiling of mud above them. "Before this thing caves-in," He added, turning the flashlight forward, and passing it back to Sasha, who was demanding it with gestures.

The mud was thick, and enveloped their feet. "Ew," Sasha whispered, disgusted. The walls were shallow, and thick with the black mud. "Uh oh." Nate called, glancing at Sean. He understood. *"We're too big to fit through."* The walls stopped, and narrowed curving, and opening in a tiny hole which looked impossible to fit through. They all looked at Cam but he shook his head violently, glaring at Avery. "Oh absolutely *nope*, now it's your turn." Avery sighed, and nodded. *No way of getting out of this one.* Sean raised his eyebrow at Cam, who was smiling watching Avery lower herself to the ground. She dipped down, but began to sink in the mud. "Umm," she began calling, uneasily, beginning to panic. She reached up, grabbing the ground but it was no use. "Avery!" Sean yelled, reaching to grab her, but their hands didn't meet. She was halfway into the hole now, too far into the small, brittle walls to reach. "Uhhh!" She yelled, fully panicked now. "Avery!" Sasha yelled. "Grab this!" She threw her backpack out into the hole, and Avery reached up desperately to grab it. But it was too late. Her arms were submerged. She fought with the thick, black oozy mud, pushing against its weight. But it didn't let her move an inch. She looked around desperately, but nothing was of help. "AVERY!" "HOLD ON WE'RE GONNA-" She breathed in heavily, and began to hold her breath. *"AVERY?!"* The voices became more and more drowned out as her ears began to fill with the mud. *"Avery Don-"* But it was too late. "She's.. gone." Nate muttered, in disbelief, staring out at the thick black mud in horror. Sean, without hesitation: took off his shirt and cracked head first after her. "WHAT ARE YO-" Cam's voice was cut off as he submerged.

"Avery...?" A voice called, echoing. "Avery.." It called again, whispering this time. Its words, its summoning rang through her body in sharp white hot pain. A figure began to appear. A smirk on its face, mischievous intentions it was born with. "Don't." It said coldly, its blood red lips moving subtle in the darkness. The figure pointed outwards, and Avery grabbed at her face in agony. She forced herself to look at what the figure was pointing to. Darkness. Nothing but- They were in the woods now. An old building, shrouded in overgrowth. The trees cast massively over them, covering them in a lack of light. A man was there, but only him. He was staring, frozen in time. His face was full of sorrow, yet something about him seemed insincere. The figure remained dark and shadowy, though the world should've been bright enough to see it. It pointed again, angling its finger, its arm gesturing at the ground in front of the building. "What..?" Avery said aloud. she was surprised she could speak. "It's just the ground?" She

remarked, not understanding what the figure wanted. It pointed again, shaking its arm, gesturing more aggressively this time. "I don't understand.. it's just the gr-" *PAIN rang through her head, and the world collapsed for a few seconds, only to reform. The ground shook, and the spot the figure was pointing at began to blur in her mind, as if it was glitching in and out of existence. The pain stopped, and the image changed. The ground was open, drug out. The figure smiled, only the bottom of its face revealing. It nodded, and Avery stared down into the hole…* "It's.. it's the-" **"grave."** The figure said, in an all too familiar voice. it was her own. *She stared into the open grave, another figure laying at the bottom. It was.. she fought hard, but the image continued to blur, as if something was blocking her from seeing it. Her mind spun, and the image changed. The figure stayed for a few seconds, but blurred out. She fought hard to remember, but the thing in the grave remained dark.* "Remember." *The figure said, still in her voice. She fought, and squinted in her mind, but nothing came. A blurry, blinking ground. The fragments were there, but they were scattered. Suddenly her head began to hurt, and the figure blurred out of existence, becoming someone else.* "No." *The woman said,* *as if talking to a dog. Her head rang in pain, as the world blurred out into darkness. "No more…" the woman yelled, her voice echoing into oblivion. The darkness hurt, stung like a needle. There was nothing left to remember now, she was no-one, and no-one was her. All she knew in that moment was pain. She was the very manifestation of forgetting. She closed her eyes, and everything went bright, the opposite of the darkness she found herself in.*

"No there has to be something we can do!" Sean yelled, frantically scratching his head, and tearing at his eyes. They all glanced at him, their faces just as shocked as his. "WELL?!" He yelled in Sasha's face. "I.. I don't know." Sean turned around and kicked the wall gridding his teeth tightly. "So that's just it? THAT'S JUST IT HUH?! NOT EVEN GONNA TRY!?" Cam looked at him with grief. "Sean." Sean turned around and stepped to Cam, towering over him, his eyes wide with rage. *If you make one of your SNARKY LITTLE JOKES I SWEAR.* "Don't you even-" He said coldly. He looked around the room in panic, and lunged out into the dirt wall, slamming his fist against it. "She's dead." Cam's voice echoed, blending with the ringing in his ears.He turned around, breathing rapidly, his heart racing, staring desperately at the mud.*You won't survive it. Don't.* His subconscious told himself. *No. No she's alive. No I won't let you take this from me, NO!* "I'm going in." He said, taking his shirt off. "Sean, no." Sasha grabbed his arm, and he yanked her to the ground. "Don't GET IN MY WAY!" He yelled, bending down to the hole. 'She's dead." Sasha repeated, in the same tone that Cam had."Wait.. "Sean.." Nate called, though not in his usual inflexion, his nose sounding far more nasally. Suddenly Nate's hand appeared, grabbing at Sean's arm, and ripping him from his goal. "She's dead.." Nate repeated, in the exact same tone as both of the others. "She's dead.." They said in unison, starting as a whisper. "SHE'S DEAD!" They screamed, piercing his ears, and manipulating his mind. "GIVE UP YOU WASTEFULL DEADBEAT, SHE'S FUCKING DEAD!" They all yelled horrifically. Sean fought desperately, pushing on the walls, begging the tunnel to change shape. "IT'S YOUR FAULT." They all said, dragging him back from the mud,his bare chest raking against the ground, ripping open. He could feel his naked rig cage snapping as they yanked him back out of the tunnel, desperately watching as they left a trail of his own organs in front of him. He felt the pain of each one being torn out, literally being destroyed from the inside-out. "SHE'S DEAD!" They repeated, a thousand other voices joining them. "SAY IT!" They demanded, dropping Sean's torn apart body on the thick muddy ground. "SA-AY -I-IT!" They yelled, morphing into one massive meat amalgamation. "SHE'S FUCKING DEAD AND IT'S YOUR FAULT!" Sean tried to scream, but couldn't, his vocal cords had been ripped apart, and strung into the depths of the blood conjoined mud.

The figure began approaching him, the entire concept of light fading, and losing its meaning. **IT** suddenly sprouted ten new horribly placed appendages, sprinting a distance Sean couldn't possibly tell. The thing came into light, and he could finally make-out what horrible monstrosity stood before him. "YOUR FAULT!" It screamed impossibly loud, Nate as it's main head, sasha's mangled body forming it's right arm, and Cam's head at its crotch. "EACH TIME!" It screamed, but Sean couldn't make out the rest. It was tearing the pieces from his brain that he needed to do-so. "SAY IT!" It screamed again, each head yelling in the most horrific pitch ever imaginable. Sean tried to scream again, to no avail as its horrible, spider-like fingers dug out the contents of his brain. He could feel it, his intelligence, his own personality, his awareness of his existence all being torn away. Unimaginable agony, with no-way to show it. "SAY.. IT," It demanded, as his optic nerve was sliced out his skull, blinding him completely. He yelled and pleaded in his head, one last phrase, permitted in his throat, one final dying breath..

"She's dead," He repeated, at last.

"Cam?" Sasha called. She was a child, no older than 6 standing next to the others. They were in a dark, rustic building. It smelled of smoke and dust. "Nate, have you seen Cam?" Nate was small, but had the same base muscle mass. "Nope, alright, who wants to be seeker?" Sean raised his hand in the air happily. "Me!" "Okay," Sasha smiled, and Sean began counting. "Hey, no cheating! Turn around," Sasha commanded, offended. "Okayy," Sean whined. Sasha nodded, then ran further into the building. Shelves and barrels fell around her, as she whipped around a

corner, and ran up old wooden stairs. At last she found a small cupboard and wedged herself inside it, rattling various bottles.

*"Ready or not, here I come!" Sean yelled from downstairs. Sasha watched from her tiny vessel as Nate ran by her. He spotted her, and ran towards her. "Can I?" Sasha stuck her tongue out, and spat a bit. "No, go find your own!" Nate nodded, closing **her** cabinet, and ran further into the building. Sasha listened as Sean ran past. "Hehe," She laughed silently. Sean bolted down the corridor, throwing open random vessels recklessly. "I know you're in there!" He yelled to a random barrel. He lifted the lid with minimal effort, but no one was in it. "Or not," He added, sulking a bit. At last he reached a door, pushing hard on it. It opened with ease. His little eyes widened. Before him stood an altar, massive and powerful, complete with a coffin sarcophagus at its center. Light shone down into the room, meeting the coffin perfectly. Yet something about the light seemed unnatural. Sean ran up. "You've gotta be in there!" He yelled, standing barely over the sarcophagus. "Darn it," Cam's little voice came, muffled, as he lay perfectly still. "Haha. Got you!" Sean bagged, and Cam nodded, reaching up and sliding out the lid, then standing up. Something*

changed in Sean's eyes, as he watched him attempt to escape. A "brilliant" idea crossed his mind. **He pushed Cam over.** *"Hey, what gives?!" Cam demanded, after crashing back into the stone bottom, which somehow seemed to have grown in depth. "Sean, let me out!" He called. Sean smirked with an evil little boy smile. "What if I don't?" Cam looked at him with genuine fear, and Sean continued to smile cruelly, enjoying this new power. Cam got to his knees again with an annoyed huff, but Sean pushed him back down. "Dude.. wha-" Sean began to heave heavily, sliding the cover back on top of him. "This isn't funny anymore Sean, let me out!" Cam demanded, a hint of crying in his voice. Sean laughed audibly, pushing the seal even further across the coffin. "Wait! Sean please!" Cam begged in horror, coughing as a massive stone slab with no air-holes began to swallow him. "Please," He gasped, Sean only continued laughing, and at last shoved the stone slab into place, where it clicked into a groove perfectly. Cam began to cough, as his world turned into a vacuum chamber. "SEAN!" He yelled in genuine agony. Sean continued laughing, seeing nothing wrong. Just then Sasha and Nate ran up behind him, having heard the commotion. "Haha found you!" Sean* *remarked. But they pushed him out of the way, trying to open the coffin. Cam coughed with wretched sounds, and slammed on the lid loudly, the bangs echoing through the building horribly.*

"HELP!" Cam managed to yell. Suddenly, the coffin moved downward, down a hole like an elevator, making Sasha and Nate jump back as the small, coffin sized platform descended a good twenty feet. Sean went to jump down, guilt flooding his entire body, but Nate stopped him. They all watched the coffin as the little boy struggled to breathe, his cries of desperation barely audible from the depth. A figure with a gas mask stared up at them, scarcely visible around the large rectangular cutout in the ground. It began to lift the lid, then waved ominously, and wheeled the coffin out of their sight.

"Cam?" Sean yelled, followed by the others, all three of the others, their voices approaching him. "Guys!" Cam called back, crawling towards the direction of their voices. He felt his body collide with Sean's, who, *apparently:* had also just emerged from the mud. Nate rushed to their sides, as they both reached solid ground, hoisting them back onto solid ground. Sasha clicked on her flashlight.

"Where's Avery?" Sean demanded, nearly crying.

Sasha shrugged in concern. "AVERY??" She called. To everyone's relief, she responded."Well, it's a bit of a swim, but that mud dips down into water, uh kinda," Avery's voice echoed from above, and slightly through the hole, creating strange reverberations.
"Are you okay?" Cam yelled back, his 'cool act" completely gone. "What, yeah?" Avery replied, as if nothing had happened. Sean raised an eyebrow, his tears fading into his face, still breathing heavily. "So.. how do we fit through?" Sasha called, studying the wall, the beam of her flashlight bouncing up and down. "Your backpack had a mini shovel, right?" Avery called back. Sasha retrieved her backpack, still wet and dripping mud next to the hole. "Yeah, I think it's still in there!" It was silent for a moment, as if everyone had been frozen in time. "Uhh, throw it over!" Avery yelled back. Sean Cam and Nate all exchanged glances. *WHAT DO YOU MEAN OVER??"* Sasha shined her flashlight up. There, far above was a slight break in the tunnel that led to the other side.

Sean smacked his face, and Cam fell into the wall in cringe. "Oh," Sasha remarked, trying to keep her cool.

She reached down to grab her bag, but something hit her, and she realized, looking around how dark it was. "Avery?" She yelled over the wall. "Yeah?" Avery called back. "How can you see in there? It's gotta be pitch black." It was silent for a moment, then she responded. "Oh haha, it's easier to see in *here*, brighter ya know."
Sasha glanced at the three boys, and they all nodded, the same suspicion in their eyes.

"Can you reach it?" Avery asked, her voice slightly different than it was before. "Yeah.." Sasha replied, barely actually speaking. "**Great**," Avery responded, having heard her perfectly. "Wha?" Sasha muttered, nearly whispering. "**What**?" Avery replied, her voice seeming to come more from the mud. "Haha nothing, Avery. Just grabbing the bag," Sasha said, glancing at the three boys again. Cam shrugged, and Nate echoed him.. Sean stepped forward. "Hey, Avery, it's Sean!" He yelled over. "Oh, Hi Sean!"

She called back. He shook his head. "Avery, do you remember that one time we climbed the tree, and went fishing?" The room fell silent, then her voice echoed back. "Oh, of course!" She replied, giggling with her very rare giggle. "Do you remember what I said to you that evening?" Sean yelled over. Everything went quiet. No one spoke. Suddenly the wall crumpled, and fell in their direction. "Run!" Cam yelled, and they all took off down the opposite way, as the wall collapsed into the tunnel. They waited for a moment, then made their way back. Sean shook his head. "This isn't right." Sasha nodded aggressively.

"Well, no shit Sherlock!" They reached the area where the wall had been, and the mud was completely gone, as if it was never there to begin with. "Avery?!" Sean called out.

She lay in the corner, twisted and fallen, unconscious. Sean tapped her shoulder, and she began to wake slowly. She turned to face them. "Sean? Sasha?" Her voice was dreary. Sasha eyed her with suspicion. "Avery, did you just ask us to throw you a shovel?" Avery squinted, still waking up. "What?" She mumbled, her voice was hers. Sean looked at Sasha and nodded, she nodded back. "Are you okay? What happened in there?" Sasha demanded. Avery lifted her arm, slowly beginning to get up. "I don't know. I went into that mud and… well, apparently, woke up here." Sasha nodded. "Are we all okay?" Sean asked, resisting the urge to hug Avery.. Sasha eyed Cam, who eyed Nate, who eyed Sean, a hint of rage in their faces. Sean nodded just slightly, *so we all saw..* He stopped himself in his mind. *-remembered it?*

"We ready?" Avery asked, standing, prepared. "I.." Sean began to respond. "I need a minute," he managed to cough out.
The others nodded. "So the mud causes you to trip balls," Cam stated. They all nodded. "apparently." Sean closed his eyes for a moment, reflecting on the pure horror he'd "*Apparently*" seen. He shook his head. *Just a bad dream…nothing more.*

After a few moments, they regrouped. "Allright, now we ready?" Avery asked, like a toddler. They all nodded in agreement, and Nate, Cam, and Avery continued forward into the cave. Sean went to follow but Sasha stopped him, tapping him on the shoulder. He narrowed his eyes, awaiting a lecture he'd been avoiding for a literal decade. Sasha's face grew intense, and she opened her mouth to speak, but stopped, for some reason deciding otherwise. "I don't get why THAT'S what we remembered." She bit her lip a bit. Sean echoed her, feeling the other side of an ancient coin. "I don't.. Either.. I want to know. I want to know why, Okay?" She shook her head, in disappointment, and opened her mouth to speak, but he interrupted. "Look, there's too much going on right now. We can do this when we're safe." Sasha frowned, holding back a thousand arguments, nodding nonetheless. "You slowpokes coming?" Cam's voice echoed out. Sasha gestured her head dryly at the direction of his voice. "Then unless your **victim** has something to say about it, we'll leave it at that." Sean rose his eyelids in confirmation, with a hint of coldness, remembering what had split them up to begin with. Sasha reciprocated, and lightened her expression, running to catch up with the others, who were incessantly insulting them about their speed.

They emerged from the tunnel after what felt like Days, a light peered out far ahead. Avery's heart started to lift with hope. *There's something at the end.* They were mostly silent along the way, except for Cam, who was cracking pointless, unfunny jokes all the while.

At last, They made it to a small corridor, where the tunnel protruded from a solid cave-wall. Avery scratched her chin. *Clearly it's new, but who.. Dug it?* The walls were Covered in red pipes, cold and rocky, and the air smelled of dust and rusty metal. Old Vines hung from the metal beams above, illuminated only by Sasha's flashlight, where an old rusty door stood. Engravings covered it, and inscribed in them looked to be some sort of ancient language. "What the," Sean exclaimed, his voice echoing miles back down the tunnel. "Maybe we shouldn't?" Nate offered. Avery shook her head.

 "There's gotta be a way through there." She pushed and prodded at the walls, but nothing came of it. "Okay," Sasha remarked, flinging her flashlight beam about the walls. "Maybe.." She searched the room for an answer, but nothing came to mind. "You could try kicking it," Cam suggested. Sean shook his head.

"Clearly whoever.." He cocked his head, choosing his words cautiously. "..Resides here doesn't want company. They might not take loud noises too kindly." Cam rolled his eyes. "Sorry, didn't realize we're dealing with a booby trapped temple." Sean exhaled, annoyed. "Have you really never seen any of the classic exploration movies? It's always the one guy that makes noise who gets crushed by the boulder." Cam frowned. "I have," He replied, in a much graver tone. "And you know what else is in those movies, Sean?" Sean opened his mouth to respond, but Cam stopped him. 'That's right, *coffins*." His eyes went cold, his pupils shrinking for a moment. He didn't look himself. Sean gave a quick nod, frowning, remorse in his eyes, before turning around and searching the other side of the room.

 "Oh!" Nate called from ahead, unexpectedly. In an instant, the door retracted backwards, mechanical snapping echoing through the room, startling them. Then, without warning it jerked into action, and shot down into the ground like a reverse rocket, leaving an open dark cavern in its place. Sean squinted. "How did you do that?" Nate shrugged nonchalantly. "Just gave it the good ol' Officer Dans breaking down my door for the money I owe him- kick." Sasha cocked her head. "Wha-" - "tallyho!" Nate commanded. Avery eyed Sasha, they shared the same exact thought: *What even the fuck?* "Kick, huh?" Cam muttered, smirking at Sean. He rolled his eyes, and smiled in surrenderance. "Okay," Nate sighed, as they walked into the room.

In front of them stood an elevator-like door with a large metal entrance and tubes full of wires hanging from the ceiling to the floor. To the right, a massive industrial fan was embedded deep in the rock, its shadow hiding parts of the room at different times as it spun.

To the left was a rusty old gate that appeared to lead further into the cave, which had no visible end, continuing down and out of sight. "No good," Avery remarked, *like every protagonist ever when faced with a locked door.* She glanced through the bars and noticed some wires attached to the side. "Looks like it's electronically locked." "Well, really, wow I thought it was locked with fairy magic," Cam joked sarcastically. "Glad to see your *being an asshole* to your friends, attitude is back," Sean scolded, glaring at Cam. Cam scowled in return, his face angled down, eyes forward, staring at him deadpan. "Don't talk to me," he replied coldly, turning his back. Avery raised an eyebrow. *What? What happened?* They all took turns examining the room. Etches and random photos of artifacts lined the walls, but they had seemingly no useful information. They all stood, confusion in their eyes. Sean curled his nostrils. "Somethings wrong.," He began. The others nodded. "It's like the room feels separate from the cave," He remarked. He was right. The hallway looked like it wasn't even a part of the cave, compared to the other rocky tunnel behind it. The smell displayed the same signs, no longer rusty and moldy, but sterile and air tight. Avery stared at the fan, its smooth air stream echoing slightly. "It's so… different." - "*Something isn't right,*".. The words repeated in her head. The stark contrast between the two environments gave an eerie vibe. Something about the air wasn't normal, and the atmosphere of the room almost eluded panic on its own recognizance.

Suddenly a red light blasted across the cave, and a loud industrial beep rang from the elevator door. Avery looked at Sean, his eyes matched hers: *something's coming..* She searched around desperately, having no idea how fast the elevator was approaching.

Sean ran out of the tunnel, grabbing Avery's hand. But the door slammed shut, and they retracted their hands just as the jaws collided with each other, breaking them apart. She was beginning to panic, as a sharp mechanical scratching sound rang through the room, and the elevator door lurched.

She darted her eyes around the room desperately, catching a glimpse of the door in the process. Something *was*, indeed coming, and it was moving rapidly closer, *faster*. She gritted her teeth, unsure of what to do. The sound was getting closer. **Snap, Snap.. SNAP.** A red light began to spill into the room as the doors opened, and Avery's instincts kicked in. At the last second, just before the outside was visible to the elevator, she gunned it for the fan on the wall, and dove straight into it.

Chapter 6

All eyes stared at Avery, faces of curiosity angled in her direction. She glanced quickly around the room and tried her best to see back out into the cave. She nodded, ever so slightly. Cam had wedged himself into a crevice in the wall, Nate took the ceiling after climbing the cave walls, laying straight down in a ridge like a spider, his hands pressing against the old damp rock. The red light still glowed ominously, casting shadows of things she hadn't even seen before. A door slammed to the left of her, and she readjusted her focus. She could barely see through the fan duct, her nose just inches from the razor sharp spinning blades. The air was freezing cold, and she could feel it brushing against her hair threatening to reveal her position at any moment. The world was upside down, and blood ran to her head. She could feel her legs hanging above her body, hooked on a tiny slippery opening in the vent above. "Worker 303," a rash, seemingly annoyed voice echoed out. "We regret to inform you that you have failed your mission, and we must let you go." A figure, scarcely visible in the dim red light, stood leaning on the far wall. It appeared to be the person the man was addressing. "Exit through here, you'll be taken to the pocket-complex where your three day debriefing will be conducted." The figure raised its hand to talk, but was interrupted by the man. "Please give your emergency handgun, rifle, and boots." Avery squinted, she could see the side of the speaking man's face. He was wearing old librarian glasses, and had a crooked nose. His eyes were swollen and tired, his ribs were visible through the thin plaid suit he wore, his cheekbones dropping down to his mouth. He looked impatient and unimpressed. The figure seemed to recognize this and didn't bother to argue anymore. The man's eyes grew more impatient, and a tapping started echoing through the room. *His foot.* The figure stared for a second, and the man's eyebrows angled down in an expecting angry look.

Avery's head began to hurt, hanging upside down. *Why would they need an emergency handgun?* She thought about what the man had said, "worker number". *Why dehumanize employees?* She snapped out of her day dream, realizing she spaced out. The man was now holding a pair of boots, a pistol and a rifle strapped to his back which he could somehow carry even in his physical state.The figure handed the man an object, and the man nodded. "Well?" The man demanded impatiently. The figure stepped into the dim light, barely revealing its face. It had curly black hair, and… green eyes… maybe? Avery squinted to see more, but to no avail. It was impossible to fully discern the figure in the shadows.. "Thanks for the opportunity," the figure said bluntly at last. Its voice was strangely metallic, and unordinary deep. Avery brushed it off - probably *just the room.* A moment of silence passed as the figure stood poised staring directly at the man. Finally, the man pulled out a book with a pen haphazardly attached to an old page, seemingly out of nowhere. He opened the pen with a loud click throughout the room, then scratched something off the page. "Go," He said plainly to the figure. It didn't wait. The figure walked further into the shadows, obeying the man. Avery's head spun with confusion. *Mission!? What mission?* The man walked back, entering the elevator and leaving with a loud buzz. Avery dropped her shoulders and took a breath. Then suddenly Avery realized the group had been following a dark tunnel in a direction they didn't even register. *How far down did we go...* She started to grab the ground, preparing to somersault back to a normal position below, when suddenly a skid sounded from the shadows ahead. She stopped dead in her tracks, holding her breath once again. The figure emerged into the light, passing by the pillars where Sean was still hiding. It stopped for a moment, turning around and glancing directly at him. Avery's blood ran cold as she watched in horror. But the figure made no move, and simply continued walking. *You saw him, there's no way you didn't! So why..* The figure turned its eyes directly at Avery. She shivered, swallowing all the remaining air she had to breathe. **It** stared into her soul, not blinking for what felt like an eternity. She tried to avoid it, but looked up and locked eyes with it. *You're crazy, it can't.* She lied to herself. The figure took a step further towards her, its eyes still trained on hers. *It can see me*, she admitted to herself. As if in response, the figure held up something that looked like a clock. It was moldy and covered in rust, yet it still ticked loudly and ominously. The figure smiled, glaring directly into her eyes.

"Figured he'd want you to have this," a small mechanical-like voice whispered out. It smiled - its buttery yellow teeth glinting in

the red light of the elevator. Avery shivered and tried desperately to avoid making eye contact, but couldn't manage to do-so.

She breathed in, accepting the fact that the figure knew she was there. But, her breath was cut short as the sudden sound of a metal ping echoed through the vent. The figure nodded, just ever so slightly. She looked down, and saw the clock-like-object, despite the fact that she hadn't seen the figure drop it, or even move its hand. "Who.. are you?" She asked, a faint, tiny begging whisper of curiosity. The figure's smile faded, then it turned around and sprinted into the tunnel, disappearing in the shadows.

The air was silent, and everyone was still for several minutes. She held the little clock in her palm. It was engraved with text, though she couldn't make out what it said in the darkness. The smiling face still stung in her eyes. She closed them, but it was still there, burned and embedded into her brain. For some strange awful reason, it felt *Nostalgic. But why? Why would some weird cultists looking dude's creepy ass smile feel nostalgic?*

Something stirred in the corner, and a face emerged out of the darkness. "Everyone alright?" Sasha called out. Nate fell from the ceiling and tumbled back through the now open cave entrance door, slamming into the wall and landing with a loud yelp. "Yep," he managed to say, winded. Sean strolled through the door stoically, his eyes wide. Cam emerged looking scared and hesitant. "Okay," Sasha seighed, and relaxed. She looked at Avery, who had her eyes sealed shut and was clenching her chest. *Why me? How did they see me, but not the others?* "Av?… You okay?" She felt a hand on her shoulder but didn't open her eyes. *I've seen that clock thing before. Grey... in The basement...* **They knew me.** "Av?" "Avery, are you okay!?" **"They saw me."** Sean startled back, letting go of her shoulder. "They saw me and they gave me something they were holding." They all circled around her, looking confused and concerned. Sasha raised an eyebrow and reached out to comfort her. "Who?" Avery didn't respond. "Avery who saw you?" *Was it even real? It had to have been!* "Av-" - **The figure,"** she said finally, jilting her eyes open. "The man that got uh, fired, or whatever?" Cam asked. *Man?* "The man?" Sean echoed as if reading her mind. "That was a woman." Avery cocked her head, still breathing heavily, confused. *You saw them?* "Uhh no, it was definitely a man, didn't you see his blonde mustache and blue eyes?" *Blonde.. blue? What, No, they had black hair and green eyes!?* "What?"- "Yeah it was definitely man, no question," Nate stated, confused. "Okay look, it doesn't matter," Sasha jumped in, preventing a group war. They stopped talking for a moment and all went to speak at once. Avery was overwhelmed and didn't know how to respond. *How could he.. or she? Have different hair and eyes?* Sean took the opportunity. "So you said this person saw you?" Avery nodded, barely listening. "Okay and what did they give you?" she reached into her back pocket, where she'd just put the device. *Kay, where in pocket-land are you?* She kept fishing but found nothing. *What?! Where is it??* "Where the hell is it?!" She began yelling out loud, frantically digging through every pocket she had. "WHAT THE HELL?!" She screamed, dropping her arms to her sides in defeat. Sean raised his hands to comfort her, but she pushed him away. 'I JUST had it!" "I LITERALLY JUS-" She felt a hand collide with her back. "Avery, it's okay we believe you," Sasha's soothing voice wafted through the room. "Most of us," another, rather annoying boy's voice joined in. Sasha shot him a death look, and he turned around immediately. Avery nodded, frowning with genuine rage. "Do you think they'll come back?" Sean asked, gently. She stared at him for a moment, her ears ringing, and adrenaline pumping. "No," she concluded, at last. "Alright well that's sure a relief." Sasha exhaled, calming down. Nate stepped in. "Yeaah we clearly stepped where we shouldn't be." "Let's get you to safety, Sasha said to Avery." She wasn't listening. *Black hair, green eyes. Black hair, green eyes, I've seen that face before, that ugly ass, needs to floss- smile.* "Get you to safety." She finally registered. "No!" Avery replied, annoyed, Sean stood next to her, and the rest stood next to the door. She shook her head and looked around, surprised at what had just come from her mouth. "No, I'm fine," she tried to fake, in a nice voice, a voice of someone that would *actually* be "fine", but it sounded the same. Sasha's jaw nearly fell off her face. "What? Avery are you crazy?! This is clearly a place we shouldn't be." *Whoever they were, there were three, I'm connected, but... why?* "No, let's keep going," she interrupted, finding herself with a new motivation. *I have to know.* Sean *cautiously* took her hand. "Av, are you really sure?" She didn't hesitate. *I **have** to know.* "Yes," she answered, immediately.

Sean sighed and looked at Sasha, they exchanged words through their eyes, both clearly understanding she wasn't taking no for an answer. "Okay," they all said at once, some reluctantly. "Okay," she echoed. Cam nodded his head, and brushed off his coat. "Then here we go," he said, pressing the elevator call button. The red light blasted once again through the room, illuminating their faces in ominous light. Avery stood ready to take on the world. *Here we go, indeed.*

The elevator was cramped, and smelled of old rust and mildew. They glanced at each other and waited in silence for a moment. The walls rattled, as if they could split apart at any moment. Avery looked around. She could see through the holes in the wall, as rock and metal beams flew by too quickly to look at. Tense, she shot a glance at Sean. *How far are we going?* She could feel gravity taking them downwards at an alarming speed, and her ears began popping just slightly. They were going underground, and deep. The opposite of what they thought would happen. Light bled through the elevator, illuminating their faces every few seconds. Sasha shivered, as the body of the room shook violently. They waited a few more seconds, then all of the sudden: *DING.* The elevator squealed, to a loud stop. The door-lock slid open with an echoey snap, resembling a muffled gunshot. Then the doors began to be wrenched open by a mess of mechanical arms and gears, visible within the side of the wall.

Slowly, loudly, the doors retracted into the elevator. Avery looked out, expecting illuminating light to guide their path. Instead, she found a massive black box, a void. Pure pitch darkness. The doors finished opening with the sound of an old wheel, then the light clicked off. They were left in the void, unsure if they were alone- in an old dark basement. Avery stared at the darkness, their new world. *Welcome to hell.* She shivered, and looked at the others expectantly, though she could see no one. "Ladies first," came Nate's voice, sacred and timid. Avery rolled her eyes in the darkness. *Then you go, miss precious.* Sean stepped forward, and his voice fell to a whisper. "There's a really big gap here, be careful." Sasha made a face of disgust and confusion. "You're *not* going in?" Sean's voice was forward, hard to hear. "We.. way.. nothing.." - "what?!" Sasha snapped. His voice angled back to the others. "I said we came all this way, c'mon, think about what could be down here." Sasha laughed like he was crazy, though in the moment he definitely could've been. "Yeah, that's *EXACTLY* what I'm worried about, what's down here," she spat, fear and adrenaline consuming her. Avery felt something brush past her skin, and let out a muffled scream. The room went silent. "Av it's me, sorry," Sean comforted. Her face dropped with immeasurable relief. "Okay, let's go," Sean led, his voice echoing further as he descended into the darkness. Avery walked to what she remembered as the exit, it was too dark to know. There was indeed a massive gap, big enough to swallow an adult whole. It echoed, sounds of rattling. Old beams supporting structures long since abandoned. *What if I fell down there?* She shivered at the thought. The echos alone told how massive the pit could be. She bit her lip at that thought. *Could be.* The others followed her reluctantly through the darkness. "Okay," Sean's voice said ahead. "This.. is weird." He didn't bother concealing his voice anymore. Sasha reached into her bag in the darkness, and pulled out a flashlight. She clicked it but it didn't turn on. She shook it a few times, and the rattles echoed through the darkness. "It's a rattlesnake!" Cam yelled softly. Sasha rolled her eyes "no idiot, it's a flashlight. You're welcome, by the way," she snapped, clicking it on, and illuminating the room. A long vertical hallway appeared. Shelves lined the walls, hundreds, stacked up, seeming to reach infinity- Rusty and black, matching the darkness that surrounded them.

Hundreds of thousands of books and boxes piled on them. "What.. in the?" Nate began. "Yeah," Avery affirmed, the same curiosity in her voice. The room felt small in the darkness as she stared up. The shelves seemed to never end. *How far down...* "woah!" came Cam's voice. Sasha shined the flashlight to him, sending the others back to the darkness. He appeared to be kneeling next to a shelf, grabbing onto its exterior. A box stood below his foot, and the shelf had apparently fallen over on him from when he'd tried to climb it. Sasha rolled her eyes, "We leave you alone for two seconds.." Cam shrugged. "What, can't a boy be curious?" Sasha rolled her eyes, eying at a specific part of herself, then began to walk away. "Uh, yeah but seriously though, could use a little help." She turned around, and walked across the room to reach out her hand. "C'mon, idiot." She smirked a bit, liking the feeling of superiority. Cam jumped down with her hand in his. "Thanks." He smiled embarrassed. "Yeah yeah, let's go find the others," Sasha said, and they walked back into the darkness, still holding hands for a second- which Sasha promptly cut-off immediately.

"Echo"..Echo..*echo,*" Sean called into the darkness. The darkness did not respond back. "Woah, Sick!" Nate called from the corner. The others rushed to him, to find him holding a massive sythe. It pulsed with a strange green light, making Nate seem like an ant in comparison. "What.. is that?" Avery asked, reaching out cautiously to touch the blade. Nate jerked back, and looked at her sternly. "Woah there. Careful." Slowly, he touched the sythe to the side of the metal shelf behind him. It began to melt away the second it touched it, its thick heavy layers dripping down to the ground, leaving slight tiny craters. "Nate," Sasha began,"You should put that thing down, it looks VERY dangerous." -"But sickk!" Cam cut in. Sasha smacked her face, and Sean and Avery stood watching them, like disapproving parents. "Well. Clearly we're in some sort of warehouse. "So, Avery," Sean offered. "What exactly do you think we're looking for?" Avery looked down at the ground, surprised at the question. *Um. Yeah, uh you know. Of course you* *know, right? "Nope,"* Her consciousness responded. "Uhh, I don't know." She looked around the room, catching Cam's eye as he played with their new *death toy.* "Maybe…" *The letter,* She thought. "The first letter I read had this weird guy with a clock for a head in it. That's really all I can think of." Sean smiled, having finally gotten an answer. "Well then.." he began. "Clock face it is." Out of no-where, a chill shot down her spine. *Clockface.. Clock? .. ticking.. Like that clock thing?*

The flashlight bounced, and swayed through the shelf's and artifacts as they walked through the warehouse. Avery threw the light beam, but immediately brought it back, something catching her eye. Alone on the wall lay an old, smashed poster. She squinted hard, holding the flashlight like a weapon. *M.L- 1977, artifact storage crew.* It depicted a number of men and women who she couldn't make out, all in a group photo. "They're uh.." She looked again. The poster looked like it had survived at least five floods. "They're storing.. artifacts." A chill went down her spine at the word. *Grey's into artifacts.* "What kind?" Cam's voice echoed through the shelving. Avery glanced behind the shelves. "Uh, I'm not sure," she responded, her voice echoing back. She studied the looming shadows ahead. The shelves resembled rooms with open roofs, spilling out into the infinite pit of darkness above. "So.. where do we look?" Nate enquired, still holding the scythe like a new baby. "Around," Avery replied, gesturing out into the void of infinity. Just then their flashlight flickered. Cam's voice grew frightened in the new darkness."Uh.."

In the distance, a single noise echoed through the maze of shelves, now the only noise in the pitch black void. A soft, quiet whistle of a chickadee bird. It was a comforting sound, a sound you'd hear when spring starts. A sound you would hear to signify nature, and safety. Perfect for the sunny, happy trees. But in the context of the pitch black warehouse, it *froze* the blood of any poor soul that happened to hear it. "*Whistle,*" It echoed through the shelves creating a metallic groan, two pitches, two whistles out of tune, out of place. "Guys.." Sasha began, as her flashlight clicked on again. Yet it was dimmer, as if the light waves themselves were being quieter, afraid.

Moments passed in the darkness, every atom in the universe silent. Then it came again. Louder this time, closer. One whistle, then another one, ominously out of tune. As if it was waiting for a response from another bird. Shasha and Sean cast the flashlights around the group, and everyone collectively locked eyes. *We need to leave.. NOW.* Sean took a step forward, and the whistle echoed again, this time directly in front of them, faster and more aggressive. Two whistles, two notes. He took another step, and the other followed, the whistle came again, this time with a footstep, perfectly matching the groups at the exact same time. They all backed up together slowly, and the footsteps once again matched theirs. *It* whistled again, on its own free will. They stood, perfectly still. Then, collectively, they all broke into a run. *It* immediately lurched forward after them, running seemingly at all of them. Matching their pace perfectly, just out of their reach. Yet there was one problem. In the chaos, they had all run in different directions. In the pitch darkness, with no way to see. The background erupted into a cacophony of whistle calls, and loud echoing footsteps. Avery brushed against the narrow metal shelves as she ran down the hallways, no way of knowing where she was. Suddenly, her foot caught on a crack in the concrete, and she tripped, flying into a nearby shelf. A loud clash exploded through the void as she landed, and in the distance a whistle call echoed in her direction, as if to say *"I heard that.."* Quickly, She fished around the shelf for any sort of weapon, but could find nothing in the darkness. She did; however, find something that felt like cardboard, and after feeling around a bit, she nodded. *Open box.* Just then, faster than she could even process, the sound of all of her nightmares combined erupted, and her blood ran cold, her eye's growing wider.

The whistle call was directly behind her now, echoing into the tiny space She found herself in. The aura in the room read one word: *Run.* She didn't waste another second, and began to crawl as fast as She could through the boxes on the shelf, like a rat in a crawl space. Her environment quickly turned back into an alarmingly tight, pitch black tunnel of boxes and things she couldn't see through the shelves. Crawling echoed behind her at the same pace as she forced her way through god knew what. She stopped. She could feel from her hair that there was a ceiling of shelving a mure inch above her head. *Okay, so it's a tunnel jammed in between shelf tiers, huh.* She glanced behind her, and her bones cracked a bit, echoing through the tunnel of boxes. She heard the same thing behind her, and a chill went down her spine. *Okay.. so it only moves when I do. At least god I hope.* She waited for what felt like hours, the threat behind her purely silent, yet evermore there, physically behind her. As time passed she braced herself, moving her arm slightly, and daring to stretch her arms. As expected, She heard the exact same sound behind her. She took a fast, deep breath. *Okay.. here we go.* The shelf's rattled as she lunged forward into a speed crawl, whistling and crawling now directly behind her, echoing and mimicking her every movement. She glanced back to try to see, and it did the same. Yet they both saw nothing- pitch darkness. But they were both aware of each other. More time passed, and still no light came. No sounds were heard. It was simply a void, impossible to tell time was even passing. She braced herself again, and began to crawl forward once-more. As expected, *it* followed behind her, perfectly in sync with her movement. She searched around desperately for answers, but only darkness called back. *How fucking long is this stupid thing?* She barged on the boxes, trying to break out of the seemingly infinite tunnel. But it didn't budge. The boxes surrounding her creaked loudly as she reached forward, preparing to crawl again. A faint reflected creaking could be heard behind her. *What the hell are you?* She found herself asking, terrified, yet curious. She felt around. *Boxes, darkness.. Sharp, flat..* **grip.** Suddenly it all made sense in her head, and a map formed in her mind in the blink of an eye. Confident, She reached down, and stood herself up with her hands, into a cruel, cramped hand stand. Then She shoved upwards with her feet against the top of the shelf section, grabbing the checkerboard hash texture of the "makeshift shelf-floor" with her bare fingernails. She winced in pain as they tore a bit, but she held on, struggling with the grip. *It* tried to do the same behind her, but she could tell it had failed. It was too tall, too big to mimic her perfectly. *Hah, Simon didn't say, bitch.* She flinched as a cacophony of whistles erupted violently behind her, demanding a call back, no longer asking nicely. Then, without warning, it lunged forward. On its own free will, its own choice to move. ***It had learned.*** *Okay.. NOW!* All at once, Avery thrust her hip to the left, upside down, still grabbing and pushing hard on the shelf. Her body went limp, as the momentum of the falling shelf took her. She smashed into the wall, left and right, then went flying out the side. The box had split in half, She was free. The footsteps had stopped, and she was once again left in perfect dark silence.

Nate looked around. He could feel Cam breathing next to him. They were hiding, deep within several layers of shelves, sitting in a massive basket, filled with various mechanical parts. "Okay.. so that just happened," Cam exclaimed, still a bit shocked. Nate's peach fuzz was illuminated as he smirked in the soft light of the flashlight. "We should make a horror movie about this." Cam nodded. "If we survive that is." Nate shrugged. "So.. this isn't a dream right?" panic slowly grew in his voice.

Just then, a series of angry whistles echoed from the distance, accompanied by a loud metal clash. "That sound like a dream to you?" Cam asked, slowly turning around, but he could see only darkness pass the dim beam of the flashlight. Nate shrugged. "Well, if this is some kind of stupid horror movie Truman's show thing, let's actually be sm-" The shelf burst apart, as *it* smashed through the basket. Nate yelled, and they both landed hard on the concrete ground. Cam stood up fast, thinking quickly. *Not enough time to lay here. Swiftly,* He grabbed Nate, and Nate yelled a little more. "Ah!! whistle man!" Cam slapped him a little. "Dude shut it, it's me," he whispered sharply, grabbing Nate's hand, and yanking him up. "There's no time, man cmon!" Nate stood up, reluctantly, but fell back down a bit. "Quit playing around, let's go!" Desperately, he tried again, to stand, but he couldn't. "I.. think I broke a leg!" He winced. Cam gridded his teeth, and reached down to pick him up. *"Whistle, whistle, WHISTLE!"* **It** screamed, like a toddler, desperately searching for its *dead* mother. Nate grabbed his shoulder, and Cam pulled hard on him, lifting him to the ground. Another whistle echoed again from the background, every trace of good gone. Now, it was a loud demanding yell, like the yell of an abusive parent, demanding a call back from their child. They began to move, but staggered with each step. Cam was tiny, barely able to carry Nate, a two hundred pound man-child. He gritted his teeth under the weight. "Dude you're not paralyzed, help me here!" Nate nodded, and planted his left foot on the ground. They moved forward faster, gaining speed by some miracle.

The whistles had stopped as they reached another corner of shelves, and everything seemed to be safe again. Cam slowed down a little, but somehow to no success. Suddenly, they were speeding up. Faster, then faster! They were running uncontrollably. Cam looked at the ground. *Fuck, we're going down hill.* They were indeed, moving fast down a sharp concrete hill exponentially quick, and uncontrollably. They both looked around frantically. *This can't be it.. there's gotta be a-* their body's smashed into the pitch dark ground face first, together rolling across the solid rocky floor. The world blurred in and out of view for both of them, as Cam's flashlight tumbled away, shattering, and sparking before dying in its final concrete grave. Nate stirred a little. "Gah, ow." Cam nodded, still on the ground, breathing heavily. "Concussion?" Nate asked, a little jokingly. "Yep," Cam groaned. "Probably." The world focused again. It was dark, and the flashlight was long gone. One old, chained light loomed, above them, swaying, back and forth, making them illuminated in increments. Cam sat up and his tailbone poked against the concrete ground. His elbows were anchored to the floor, and his face had a massive bruise. *Sure as hell a headache, I'll tell you that much.* Nate began to stand, only to fall back down. "Oh, right," he winced, as he remembered the state of his leg. They sat, in darkness, only in light every few thirty seconds. Cam looked up, studying the light curiously, following it from corner to corner, looking up and down at the results it created on the ground. "Who would even bother motorizing a light?" Nate asked, stupidly. Cam covered his head, and looked at him, his pupils glowing from the light, now in the upper right corner. "I don't think-" he stopped, suddenly looking up the ramp they had come from. "What?" Nate demanded, shrugging in confusion. The ground began to shake, and hundreds of whistles echoed, in metallic, disturbing order. Cam braced himself, backing to Nate, ready to fight. But they stopped. "Probably way out there. I think we're safe for now..?" Nate half asked. Cam shrugged, holding in the contents of his stomach, which had been encouraged to his throat during the fall. "Oka-" he coughed, anger spilling into his voice. "Okay, but what the hell is that thing?" Nate couldn't help but shrug uselessly. *Think man, how can you be safe?* Just then, the light swayed over them, illuminating an object in front of them. Nate raised an eyebrow. "That wasn't.." - "Yeah," Cam affirmed. In front of them now stood a massive tree that appeared to grow into the ceiling and out of the room. Nate smirked. "Well, still got those knives?" Cam shook his head, his mouth slightly open. *It really bothers me how fast you're accepting this situation.* "I.. don't think it's a good idea right now, man." He kept looking around, following the light. "Hey, I mean no time like the present right?" Nate laughed, a little too loudly, as he went to draw from Cam's backpack. He spun around fast, and frowned, visible in the temporary light already fading above them. "Dude, now is not the time. We need to find a way out of here, cmon," he snapped. Cam was smart, he knew when he'd stepped too far. He was a clever, cunning kid, he just loved being sarcastic and rude. Nate on the other hand, was more legitimately what Cam pretended to be, foolish and unsure, unconfident. He just followed whatever Cam did, like a puppy. Cam was his leader, and he was a follower. Wherever Cam went, he came with.

They waited, looking around again in the darkness. The light was now to the far left. Showing the corner. Yet something was off. There was a shadow in the spot in the light, of a tall, lanky man. Cam looked at Nate, and almost as if it heard them, a whistle echoed through the room. Once again, soft, and polite. Two notes, a chickadee communicating. It waited for a response, as if playing a game of Marco, pollo. Cam's eyes shot open, the light began to creak louder, and swing and sway faster. He nodded tactically. *You're above us, aren't you?* then to the right. **Then another whistle.** There it was again, the shadow standing tall. In the light on the right side. "Uh?" Nate asked to the void out loud. "Shh!" Cam snapped, glaring at the shadows. The light moved again, **left, middle, right.** Each time, the shadow getting closer. *It* whistled again, ever present in the room, yet no-one could see it. It stopped for a moment. "I thi-" *boom!* The light exploded into a spinning mess, violently shaking and swinging back and forth, and creaking loudly. The shadow was impossibly in each light, moving faster and faster, closer and closer. Angry whistles echoed through the darkness, matching the violent tone of the swinging light. Bangs and booms now exploded, each time the shadow appeared. Then, as if time had frozen, it all ceased. "Wha?" Nate asked, and Cam slapped his hand over his mouth. He looked around, ready for something to jump out. But yet again, nothing came. The creaking of the light began again, above their heads, at a normal pace once again. A new object was now there, as the light swung back into their view. It was a massive, mechanical elevator shaft. Cam smiled. *Oh good, Mr whistling fairy-magic fuckface gave us way out… or does it just want us to think that?* Nate paid no mind, and began to limp over to the door. "Wait!" Cam yelled, loudly. But nothing came of it. He was at the door now, limping fast. Cam caught up, breathing heavily, but it was too late. Nate reached out. "What does this but-" The mechanical door shot open with a screech of pain, revealing an empty elevator shaft. It was lit with faint red lights, shining off the metal shells that covered the walls. Cam shrugged. "Okay.. I guess this *IS* the way out." Nate nodded, and limped in. There was an emergency ladder in the corner, and a pull chain next to it. "Well, if we want to lock ourselves in.." Cam said to no one, studying the chain. They waited for a moment, unsure of what to do. The light still was moving outside, in the distance. It was now in the middle. Cam squinted, and his heart skipped a beat. *There's something there, .. yeah, no shit, sherlock.*

The shadow was now directly in the middle of the light, and then, without warning, the light went off. ***It*** whistled once again, in a happy tone. Two victory notes, as if to say *"found you.. "* Footsteps **EXPLODED** into an echo, approaching the door at what should've been an impossible pace. Cam ran forward, and pulled hard on the chain desperately, and the door slammed shut.

Pine needles fell as Grey ran down the path, swinging across "just stable enough" branches, back home. His gray shirt was soaked from the rain above, covered in mud from his *daily mischievous mission*. He donned several "war injuries" around his arms from said adventure, but he didn't mind. As long as he got answers, nothing that happened to him mattered. The house lights turned on, as he hopped over the gate, and he headed straight to the front door, ringing the doorbell. A shadow began moving through the faint window, and a *happy whistle* came closer to the door. *Lying mode: activated.* The door opened. He put on a great big grin, matching his fathers, at the sight of him. Though most of him was genuinely happy to see him. "Hey sport!" His father called looking down at Grey. "Hey pops!" Grey smiled. "Boy, what happened to you? You're soaked!" His father frowned slightly, somehow not even noticing his injuries, which were fairly visible. "Haha!" Grey laughed, overdramatically, putting on the perfect *puppet show.* He stared behind his father at the door in the corner. *Alright, get there and we're home free.* "Well, why don't you come inside?" His father asked, his trademark grin on his face, with the handlebar mustache. "Sure, I gotta use the bathroom anyway." Grey smiled, matching him. His father gave a nod, and moved aside. Immediately, he ran to the basement door, directly opposite the bathroom door, his perfect way in and out. He then opened the bathroom door, and the basement door at the same time, then waited for his father to look away. He smirked, and turned the bathroom light on, then immediately slammed both doors shut. *Plan perfect once again.* He maintained his smirk as He darted around the corner. *That's .. weird?* He found himself looking up as he made his way through the crawl space. For whatever reason, it was overly wet, and not just "rain-wet." he brushed it off, crawling through the tight tunnel into the basement at an impressive speed.

He was a pro at it by now, and could do it in a mere five seconds.

Void of any caution, he hopped out the other end, and ran to the

shelfs in the corner. The light swayed a little, and a whistling

echoed from the distance, through the vents. Grey smiled. *Perfect,*

he's distracted. Then he drew a paper out of his pocket, and

grabbed another one hidden behind a box on the shelf. *Alright..*

answers.

Long before gravity, space and all known physics existed,

*Sancthrus was at war with **igneous,*** and his two brothers. After

killing all humans, to improve and start again on new ones,

Sancthrus saw it as wrong, and left. Igneous, the natural leader of

the tree, being the oldest: did not take kindly to this and punished

Sancthrus by draining him of his blood. All of humanity was meant

to be controlled by demons, forged in hell, never to leave. But

sancthrus's blood changed this. It tricked down into the mortal

world, creating hope, and all things good. Eventually, Sancthrus

came to grow new blood, and felt his old soul on the new world

he'd made for the mortals. One ***time****,* he snuck out of *their* world, and into the mortal one. He brought with him the katana Igneous used to drain him of his blood. The brothers fought hard to get him back, to get revenge, but they could not. Sancthrus remained in the mortal world, sworn in as man's new protector. His protection… **has failed**. Which is why you now find this sword, once used for good. Now a weapon. That's why it's here. *Good things never end up here..*

His eyes widened as he finished reading. He didn't know what to make of it. *Okay, so you're depicting ancient stories in modern century language… why?* He frowned, and searched the old, moldy hall for a sliver of an answer, but yet again found nothing. Frustrated, he looked back down at the paper, his gray eyes darting back and forth for meaning. something caught his attention. A new word now stood boldly in strangely scribbled ink, as if demanding his attention. He furrowed his brow, as the dim light flickered just slightly behind him. *That wasn't there before? Ghosts? Who cares, it's answers.* Below, crudely written in old ink lay one word: **replica.** He looked around at all the shelf's, and the papers he held in his hand. There was a box that appeared to contain a gear cog, an old clock, and a strange metal katana, each reading the same word in hastily written ink: ***replica.*** He shivered, and leaned against the wall. *Then where are the real ones?*

Chapter 7

"Sancthrus, huh?" Sean asked, reading a certain old piece of paper, laughing a bit. "Guess the aliens have Greek gods." Sasha frowned, her flashlight pointing directly at him.. He raised his hand to block it. "Aliens?" She asked. Sean nodded. "What else would *this* be?" He asked, holding up an object. It was a silver, shiny katana, with a slight blue glow emanating from it. "I guess.." Sasha seighed, then immediately rose up again. "We have to go find them, you know, don't you care about Avery?" Sean scowled. "Of course I do, but right now it's not safe. Plus she's smart, she'll be okay." They were sitting on the edge of a giant shelf, their legs hanging off like a ski lift. "Hints the reason I'm searching around for.." Sean bent to the right, and dug through a box. Sasha raised an eyebrow. "Weapons." Sean finished, holding the sword into the air, its blue glow illuminating the many shelves in front of them. "Maxine's door hinge?" Sasha turned around, and raised her arms. "Wha-" "Ooh, Norsiah's kitchen spatula." She frowned, and he interrupted her again. "Neverou?" Sasha's eyes raised. Sean set the paper down, along with the objects. "Pft, what are these, constellations?" - "It's the tenth planet." Sean stared at her blankly. "You know.. the gaint anti earth that's supposed to kill us all." Sean frowned. "In legend, yeah." Sasha shrugged, and began tapping her foot on the bottom of the shelf, swinging her leg under, and letting her foot collide with the bottom. "Yeah.. well.. CLEARLY **legends** are real." Sean shrugged a bit, then nodded. "Yeah, fair enough."

He paused, searching the air for the right words. "You know, I'm surprised I'm not freaking out. Ghosts, cryptids, myths, they all are real, apparently, but I'm so.. calm." Sasha side eyed him. "Ghosts?" Somewhere far off, a whistle went off in the distance, requesting a call back. "Yep," he whispered. "Ghosts." Sahha made a face of disgust, and began to tear at her hair. Then she let helf slip off the shelf a bit more, and spun her hips to face Sean, whispering sharply. "Can't we just "find weapons"- She elaborated with air quotes.- "faster?" Sean shrugged, looking everywhere except at her. "Can we just hurry out of here, so you can go rescue your all important girlfriend?" Sean crushed his face, offended, finally shifting his eye contract to Her. "I.. don't know what you're talking about." Sasha rolled her eyes. "Dude, I don't care but just know it's PAINFULLY obvious." He blushed slightly, and turned his face away, though it was virtually invisible in the faint glow of Her flashlight. "Well.." He began, suddenly turning around. "Any advice?" Sasha nearly burst out laughing, slapping her hand over her mouth to cover the noise, and checking her environment like a grazing deer. "You serious?" He nodded, attentively. "Well, Avery's not exactly an open book, and uh. No offense but look at where we are now." To this, he frowned. "That's not her fault." Sasha stared at him blankly, pointing the flashlight at Him to match. In an instant, his face went from defense to realization, then back to defense. "Right, Well.." - "Adventurous," she offered. He smiled, stifling a laugh. "Not wrong about that, I can tell you that much." Sasha extended her arm, as if presenting a chalkboard. "Yeah, exactly." Sean raised an eyebrow. "What?" She covered her face and shook her head. "Dude, you literally know her better than me, you two grew up together. Trust me, you know her a *LOT* better than me." Sean shrugged. "Yeah well, I'm also not a girl." Sasha seighed. "You really want advice? just be yourself." He nodded. "But.." She began. "Don't kill your friends trying to get her." Sean looked down, starting to sulk. "Yeah," he muttered, a little louder than Her whispers. "Like you know, don't go locking your best friends in coffins.." His face went blank immediately, but quickly turned into not just defensiveness, but angry defensiveness. "Look, we were six.. *SIX*, Sasha!" She raised her hand in panic, holding a finger to her lip. "I know, I'm sorry, I just want-" She stopped herself, holding back a small tear. "I need to know what it was, all three of us do." Sean scowled, not a frown, but a scowl, an angry scowl. "And did it ever occur to you.," he began, keeping his voice down, somehow feeling even more passive aggressive. "Did it ever occur to you that maybe I want to know the shit that happened down there too?" … She shook her head, and placed her fingers around her chin. "Yes, yes it did, Sean." She bit back Her tears of trauma. "But I think the answer might be near. Why else would w-' **Whistle…** whistle... *whistle.* **It** echoed in the distance.

She bit down her jaw, rapidly looking around, cold calculating strategies, her biggest passion. "Whatever that is, it's clearly not good. I say we steak camp here, and *QUIETLY* try to find things of use." He gave a simple, communicative, cold nod, and they faced away from each other.

For the next few minutes, they continued silently sitting, refusing to accept each other's company. Then without warning, Sean *leaped* down to the ground, causing a loud echo. *Shh!* Sasha gestured, once again holding her finger to her lips aggressively. "Sorry," Sean whispered, a sense of kindness restoring within him. He fumbled with the deadly katana, which he'd discovered was a viable source of light, as he made his way around the shelf. He began to walk through the aisle of shelves, each footstep echoing loudly, and Sasha jumped down and followed behind, landing with a soft quiet scrunch. The boxes moved slightly, as they crawled through them, breaking the tiny safe house they had built, her flashlight suddenly being swallowed by the darkness around them. "Maybe give me a heads up next time you wanna just up and le-" He waved her off. "Just, shh." He stared down, and gestured for her to echo, shining the light. Two, signature, ominous words glared back: *To M.L..* Sean breathed heavily, shivering and nodded. *So we're in the right place.* They emerged to the other side of the safehouse shelf, and immediately the air was cold. It felt like they'd left home base in capture the flag. Out now, venerable, unprotected. Sean shined the light of the katana to Sasha and gestured to the right, where the space appeared to be empty. She shrugged aggressively back. *It's infinite. Just pick a direction!* He repeated her shrug back, then proceeded with his original plan, veering right and further into the void. The concrete shook as they both walked through. Sasha frowned, distressed. "Keep the footsteps down!" She whispered sharply. "I am LITERALLY being as quiet as humanly possible!" Sean responded, the same aggressive whisper echoing all around them. "Well, be more quiet than a human!" Sasha whispered back, shaking her head as she followed behind him. They reached a shelf section again, and Sean began to climb through it. "What am I supposed to do, just stop being a human?" He demanded, ducking under a shelving beam. "At this point.." Sasha began, struggling to keep up with him. "I wouldn't be surprised if that's what happens." Finally, they stopped, and Sean jumped onto a shelf in the corner, covering the only entrance with a box before doing so. "That's.. weird," he exclaimed, observing the walls. "I mean, sure the other one we made a little fort but.." Sasha shivered. The shelves were filled in each section with boxes, and metal sheets, scrap and paper, and plastic wrapping. The floor was covered in cans, and boxes of frozen foods. It looked like an abandoned home, built crudely in an unforgiving maze. Sasha knelt down, and picked up one of the cans. "Yeah. Someone's definitely been here before." Sean seighed. "Well, now what?" She shrugged. "Now what, what?" They were talking now at normal volume, feeling safer with the walls that surrounded them. "How do we get out of here, and find our friends?" He asked sarcastically, crossing his eyes. Sasha looked up at the boxes. "I mean, your plan has been to run around in random ass directions the whole time, so I have no idea. Cardinal directions, maybe..?" Sean frowned. "Well first of all thanks a lot, and second of all how?" Sasha glanced up at the many boxes surrounding them, bouncing the flashlight beam on every available surface. Her eyes focused on something, and she grinned, then leaped up to a shelf, and began digging in a random box. Sean shook his head. "What are you doing?" He asked, treating her like an idiot. "How about one of these?" She asked, proudly holding a large golden compass, and a map of the warehouse in her hand. "Yep," Sean affirmed, slightly in pain from swallowing his ego. "Yep, that would help." She nodded, sassily, and he opened his mouth. "I-" - "Thank me later, let's go find the others."

"Then what, we just stop ridding their minds, and kill them in total!?" *The* three men sat in an interrogation room, dark and damp, a yellow light shining barely down on them, the only natural light, though it was the opposite of *natural.* "three, the universe runs on survival." The second man paused, gridding his sharp, nasty teeth slightly. "on natural selection," he finished, his sharp, frizzy hair poking into the light. "***They*** ordered it." The first man muttered, frowning in the dim light. "No.. no.. ***they*** didn't, One." The first man's frown turned into an aggressive scowl, and he began to crunch his fist. To this, the third man matched his expression. "You don't scare me, **Ignelious.** The first man angled his eyes into a warning stare but the third man continued before he could talk. "I'm a founder.. not your soldier.. not your hire." The second man nodded slowly, observing, and the first one echoed him, reluctantly. "Then you should know well.." He began, leaning back into the shadows. "Business.. is business.."

Okay.. okay. Grey, could REALLY use your insane luck of navigating right now! She leaped over a gap in the ground, rolling to break her fall. *Thanks Grey,* she thought, recalling back to when he'd taught her the maneuver. The floor shook as She ran as fast as she could forward, not stopping for a single second. *Uh, Yeah problem alert.* She found herself looking to the side, where, alone lay a poster, taped crudely on the wall. ***"They are always watching."*** She shivered, not fully sure why. She stared at the poster, and it stared back. For whatever reason, she felt entranced by it, still sitting there alone. *Someone deliberately put it there.. why?* She stopped, **but she didn't.** She looked down. And suddenly she was running at an alarming pace, and the poster had long since passed, nearly half a mile back.

Panicked, she looked forward, having no control of her spinning legs, going faster, and faster. Her eyes fluttered around as her mind kicked into gear, realizing the problem her brain had been trying to warn her about. About twenty feet in front of her was a solid metal wall, complete with a thousand bends and burns. Effectively a molten hot knife. *YEAH, PROBLEM. ALERT!* She yelled in her head. For a brief moment in time, she accepted her fate, and then closed her eyes, letting her instincts take over. Her skin burnt slightly as she veered straight to the right, barely missing the wall by a few centimeters, and diving into a pile of boxes. The world spun as she got up. *Okay, so we're alive. So that's good. Uh.. headache? Check. Complete lack of any sight? Check.* She moved forward, and her eyes widened. *Massive.. pit.. of.. ..flesh?.. Check.*

Indeed, that's what it was, with a colossal square of millions of pounds of flesh, accompanied by molten lava fusing the flesh together. She peered into the distance. *It's.. a factory?* The walls were massive with looming flood lights casting up into the sky, their beams still not reaching the pit itself, providing no effective light. Cat walks and factory equipment stretched on for miles in the distance, all to manage this one massive pit of death. She scoped the whole area, but could see no end. *What the fuck?* She took a deep breath. *Could this get ANY weirder, any creepier?* A single sound answered her. This time it was louder, but not just slightly. The whistle boomed throughout the void, hurting her ears. Then silence. Nothing. Just an empty black shadow of the real world, a hell of uncanny clarity. Then suddenly, randomly, a million different whistles echoed out at once, all in different pitches, all in different tones. Avery grasped her head, covering her ears as she struggled to breathe, the sheer number of sounds disturbing literally her heart beat. Then there was silence again. Not a whistle in the universe. She got up slowly, and looked down again. The pit no longer seemed so static. It was lit with bright fluorescent light now, and tiny whines echoed from every corner. She shivered, her face horrified. *They're all alive.* As if in response, a light clicked on, bright and blue. Below, etched and marked and painted in a military fashion was one word: ***Prototypes***. The letters were covered in blood, and had been scraped away over many years. Then, all at once: colossal mechanical arms began falling down, each with a panel that looked like a rocket thruster. They all formed together like dominos, creating a new mile-wide roof. It was silent for a moment, and Avery sighed. Then without warning, the new roof ERUPTED into flames, and shot down at a horrifying speed into the pit. Avery stumbled backward. She could feel the heat on her face from a distance. It stung, and burnt painfully, and she crawled backwards, watching in horror as the massive mechanical arms dug and smashed into the collective pile of living things. Bones being cracked, and flesh and blood being ripped echoed through the void around her. She winced in genuine mental and physical pain. They were all whistling now, yet their whistles were not calls for attention, they were desperate calls for help. No longer communicating, but screaming in pain. Because it was all they could do. It was all they existed for. They had no other purpose in life. *Might as well whistle and scream for eternity, if it's the only thing you can ever do.* She watched in horror as the machine "cleared more room", a dump of garbage, unwanted things. Forgotten, and destroyed, dilapidated. The boxes toppled as she tried to crawl back, away from the horrible nightmare. *Just make it stop!* Her head stung with the imprint of echoes of screams of pain. She crawled forward, reaching desperately for something, literally anything, reaching the wall once again. She could feel its painful heat on her skin. She tried to stand up, the pain disappearing slightly, but smashed her head on the top of a shelf and burnt a patch of her hair out. She fought with her might, but the screams pulled her back like a puppet, and she fell backwards, her head just inches over the cliff of the pit. She began to sob, letting her tears flow off her face into the massive landfill of death, everything in pain as she began to fall and join them.

"M.L?" Sasha asked out-loud. They were walking now, in the open void, dodging shelfs and random walls and holes. She looked at Sean for answers, and he nodded. "Yep." To this, she made a face of disgust and confusion, with a hint of offense. "What do you mean, **yep**?" Sean shrugged, hopping over a crack in the ground, where a forklift had fallen, still slightly sticking out of the void.. "I mean: **yep**," he repeated, nodding profusely. "Okayyy?" She asked, having absorbed no info. Sean seighed. "It's two letters that have caused a ton of chaos." He brushed his hair out his face aggressively, ducking under a shelf. "That's all I know." She waved him off. *At this point, I don't even care.* "Okay well.. all we have to do is find the elevator," she directed, withdrawing the map and pencil from a pocket that was too small to fit them. "And our friends," he added. She nodded. "Right, obviously." They were silent for a moment, as they kept walking forward. "Okay, so elevator, elevator, how hard can it.. beeee?" She stopped, her eyes widening as she searched the map intently. Sean walked back to her, and shrugged, taking the map from her hand. She didn't intervene. "Right, so we've got **elevator: two, elevator: blue, elevator: new, elevator: B.L.U, elevator glue**, which is apparently a section of the warehouse, I didn't know they made glue for elevators, weird." Sasha looked at him with fiery eyes, ready to punch him. "Uh yeah, well uh right, next is elevator **zoo,** and elevator 359566789. My bets on that one." Sasha seighed, and gridded her teeth. "We could split up and look?" Sean offered. "NO!" She yelled, smacking her face hard. Just then the room went silent. She dropped the angry attitude, and stared with warning eyes at Sean. He nodded, and she turned the flashlight off, leaving them in the faint blue light of the katana. Sean jerked his head the left, and she nodded quickly. He took a quiet deep breath, and began to move to a shelf where they could hide. As soon as he took one step, a whistle echoed out violently, matching his speed perfectly. Sasha gridded her teeth and shook her head. They locked eyes. *3, 2, 1.* All at once, both of them dove into the shelf to the left, and landed on the other side of it in an old nasty pile of laundry. Sean moved the sword around, and the faint blue glow revealed they were in a giant donut shaped box of shelves, with another set of them at the center. It was perfectly silent once again, for what felt like several minutes. Sean began to make his way to the middle of the shelves, stepping carefully. **It** followed him, perfectly in sync with the sounds. The ground cracked with a loud bang, and another whistle echoed, seemingly from all around them this time. On edge, he held the sword fiercely in front of him, ready to defend at any moment. The light of the sword flickered just slightly as he held his breath, walking very carefully backwards. Something collided on his back, and he turned around, thrusting his hip backward, ready to strike. Sasha was frowning, perfectly still where she'd flinched. Sean sighed in relief, and *it* did the same in the distance. They stood back to back, each with a dim, almost broken, worn out light. Sean turned backwards slightly, and they both nodded, locking eyes. "Come out then!" He yelled, holding the sword ready. "*Neht tou emoc.*" Came the voice in the distance, in a quiet, female whisper, though it felt far closer. Sean stared out, and raised the katana higher. "Who's the coward now, huh?!" Sasha yelled, holding the flashlight even higher. "*Huh won drawoc eht sohw* " It echoed back, in a deep faint male voice. They turned to each other briefly. *It's..* their heads stung with pain, as if something was projecting their thoughts back at them- catching them and chucking them back like a rock. *Mirroring us..*

The world began to shake, and the air rippled visually, physically becoming solid. They dropped to the ground, and started coughing violently, as if they had entered a vacuum in space. Sean's knees collapsed, and he slammed his head hard on the ground, sending the katana sliding across the floor. As it moved a figure was illuminated in the soft blue light. *Blue eyes..brown hair.* Sasha thought, as she fell to the ground. They tried with all their might to get up, but the air weighed them back down, no longer simple weightless matter, but a solid block, frozen, in a mini pocket of **absolute zero.** They stared out, and the word began to close in on itself, blackness as their eyes were shutting.

"Father?" A little girl's voice called. Suddenly the tension stopped, one single breath echoed loudly through the world, then the air became air again. Sasha picked up her head, gasping for oxygen, It was all that mattered to her in that moment. Sean rose shortly after, and they stood fast. The world was still spinning, but he could just make out the sword's light in the distance. Sasha reached her hand to stop him as he ran into the darkness and grabbed the katana. For a moment he was gone, then the blue light appeared rapidly, and his face emerged in it. She sighed, and leaned against a shelf, staring far into the distance. *darkness. Nothing but it.* Something caught her eye as she randomly glanced around. Alone, standing next to a tiny light in the distance was a little girl. Her silhouette was unknown, she looked forgotten, and out of place. "Father?" She whispered, and her voice stung their ears with immense volume. "***Father, it was them..***" Something began to stir in the darkness, and the girl emerged further into the light. She was tiny, and wore a greenish blue shirt, and donned soft brunette hair. She was smiling, but she was not happy. She was confused. "Father.." She repeated, lost.. "**I saw them steal me.**" The world grew silent, and the light by the girl flicked off. Sean turned from where she just was, and held his katana again. He looked in the blue light at Sasha. *What.. the hell is happening?* She shook her head, fear deep rooted in her eyes. "Sean," she whispered, very carefully. Her jaw dropped slightly open, her eyes fixed on what was behind him. She gestured her head to the left, and something whisked painfully loudly in the distance. *"Run."*

"Over here!" Sasha whispered sharply, but Sean was not behind her. "Sasha?" Sean called out, but Sasha was directly opposite of him. She nearly tore off her face as she ran forward. *GREAT!* Sean shook his head, and raised the katana high. *Just survive, we'll find her later.* He bit his tongue, panting out of breath. *We'll find **everyone** later.. right?* He stopped, and leaned against the wall. *Rest or die, I'd rather rest to not die.* He took a deep breath, and held the katana to the front of him like a shield. Sasha was doing the same, on the opposite side of the shelf donut, resting to save energy. They didn't get a second to do so. The whistles exploded into a fiery scream of death, no longer a hunter toying with its prey, but a predator starving for its meal. Sasha jumped out in surprise, and *it* ran forward at her. She dove forward, breaking into a run around the corner of the donut. Sean echoed her, except on the "fight" side of fight or flight, swinging outwards as something began running around the corner at him from the right. He wasted no time with the "threat" and darted forward, bolting around the other corner. Sasha cramped up against two boxes, but something caught her eye in the distance. A figure had run around the other corner where she'd just come from. She shook her head. *There's two of them..* Breathing began to echo throughout, and the whistles continued. She stood, totally still, Footsteps *BOOMING* next to her, behind her, all around her. It whistled in a playful tone: *Where are you?* Sasha shut her eyes. *Please, do not see me. Do not smell me. Whatever the hell you are.* She moved slightly from her position, as it crept around the corner. Tactically, she matched it perfectly, one corner ahead of where it was, moving against the wall, as it scooted along. Suddenly, it stopped, but Sasha did not. *Okay.. just get out of the box, and we can run.* The whistles continued, and she kept migrating backwards. She was in the hallway section of the donut now, still holding her breath for dear life. Her back collided with something, and said something yelped. Sasha let out a scream as Sean turned around, ready to strike with the katana, but only found Sasha. They had backed into each other. The whistles became even angrier in the distance, and the shelf began to shake. "It's okay.. it's on the other side," Sean whispered, but Sasha shook her head violently and her eyes began to widen in pure fear. The shelves shook with the force of an earthquake, and light shone down from above, directly on top of a shelf. It whistled once again in the same tone. *Found you.* They both took off into a sprint, but it was too late. It leaped from the shelf's and landed directly in front of them. They both screamed in terror, and the floor began to crack and break. For the first time ever, they could see it now. **It** was a shadow, with the face of man. An inky black, massive looking body, with the head of a human. It didn't whistle this time, it screamed, and they were both knocked to the ground. It **SHRIEKED** loudly with a horrifying sound that echoed through the entire building. As it did, its face split open. Sasha screamed and cried, trying to unsee what was unfolding before her. What should've been a skull were a bunch of wiry bloody tendons, there were no bones in it, except for extremely sharp missing teeth. "WHAT THE F-" She clapped her hand over Sean's mouth as she watched the thing screech. The bloody strings that connected it looked like they were barely attached, and its eyeballs had nearly fallen out. It swung with *one* of its limbs, and sent them flying across the donut hallway, smashing into the metal frame of a shelf. Sean fell to the ground, with Sasha nearby. They were both bleeding now, suffering awful pain. Sean's chest had been ripped open, and his ribs were exposed, and Sasha's leg was mangled, barely still attached. They screamed in agony, and **Something** whistled in the distance, making Sean drop the katana. *Kill me. Kill us. Just end the pain. Just end it.* He waited, and waited, but the thing didn't come. The whistles continued, but they were different. They weren't calls of death, they were calls for a friend. A fellow, the whistle you make when you call for a horse. The katana began to glow very brightly, and suddenly, without even realizing it, Sean was standing up, holding it. His chest began to seal, and ribs began to grow. He was healing. *Power of all things good.* He recalled, and stood up fast. *What the.. I'm... totally fine?*

The pain was gone, and the sword had stopped glowing. He rushed over to Sasha as the whistles continued in the distance. She was coughing, barely breathing, her lips sunken in a puddle of her own blood, rough, and sticky against the solid concrete floor. She was sobbing, begging for the same death he was wishing for, except out loud. Her hair was mangled and torn, and her eye was clouded. Sean held the sword to her, and it began to take effect. She started to breathe as her blood retracted from the floor, and back into her body. The whistles continued, but they were now far off in the distance, no longer an immediate threat. Sasha rose, and her eye filled back in with its usual brown. "What.. I don't." Sean smiled, and helped her up. "You okay?" Sasha looked down at her hands. "How.." He held up the katana. She nodded, still too full of adrenaline to even question the *literal magic* she'd just witnessed. "I do-.. We don't have time," she snapped, running into the darkness. Sean followed behind, but stopped shortly where Sasha was. She was staring at a competition in the distance, standing atop a fallen over shelf. Sean joined her. *What.. the?* In the background was a massive pit of fire and flesh. But that wasn't what they were looking at. A girl was limping through the darkness, whistling loudly, mockingly and yelling insults at *it* Sean's eyes widened. "Avery?"

"Here boy! Here giant monster thing! Whoooo wants a whistle?" Avery yelled, as she ran through the darkness, whistling. *This is a bad idea.* Her mind told her. But she chose to ignore it, and continued mocking *it.* "You can have two! I promise!" She yelled, ducking around a shipping container. She emerged on the other side, and ran through it. *Okay.. left, right, left left, straight.* She ran out of it, and to the left. "Ohhh boy! Look at that!!" She yelled, and ducked to the right. "A nice tasty human!!" *It* lunged out, and she ducked, barely dodging it. She threw herself to the left, then jumped over a massive crack in the ground. "Don't you want a whistle?" She called, and ran strait ahead. *It* lurched out, this time succeeding, sending Avery flying, and landing directly at the edge of the pit. She tried to get up, but new injuries kept her down. *Well.. this is familiar.* *It* was faster, and approached her with booming footsteps, whistling in the opposite way of how she was. *Well.* Avery thought, as she stared death in the face. *At least I tried.* She let her head, and her tears flow. It continued to approach, and raised one of its arms into the air, preparing to strike her. She stared up. Its hand had thousands of tiny needles. *Maybe the physics museum will save me?* She thought, recalling back to when she made Grey lay on a bed of nails. Before she could finish the thought, *it* split its face open, and sreecked, and thrust its arm down, digging into her body. Avery screamed, and the world went dark. ***Expect it didn't.*** It stopped. She opened her eyes. Its wiry, awful hand was just inches from her face. The katana echoed as it slid from its body. Which crumpled and fell like concrete, half of its face split from the tiny tendons, followed by the other half. All of ***it*** fell into the pit. "Avery!" Sean called out again, smiling. Avery smiled back, her face covered in blood, wincing in pain still. "Hey."

"Then get on my back!" Cam yelled, they were halfway up the ladder now, and Nate was struggling to climb without both of his legs. Cam shook his head in defiance. *You're the climber! Why is it my job?* The door echoed below, with loud banging, and Cam exhaled. *It's still there.* As if in response, the door burst open, with the sound of horrific tearing metal. ***It*** thrashed its legs against the wall, and began to climb up the walls like a spider slowly, stalking its prey. "GET ON THEN!" Cam yelled, and Nate did. "Sorry," he whispered, slightly scared. Cam immediately began to struggle against Nate's weight as he pulled his hands up the ladder. *One hand in front of the other.* He forced himself to think. The walls were crumbling now, and *it* continued to climb, destroying the concrete with each massive deadly step. **It** whistled playfully once again. Cam shivered but kept climbing. His hand slipped, and the bars of the ladder grew sharper with each passing moment. They were at the top now, right in the open door of the elevator shaft. But it was too much. Cam held on tightly, but his grip was letting go internally. The world grew darker, still illuminated by the red lights of the elevator shaft. "NATE!" Cam yelled. Nate grabbed the latter with one hand as he slid off cams back. *It* was a mere second away now, climbing the elevator shaft, somehow even more like a spider.. Cam reached up, but he couldn't find the strength to hoist himself out of the door opening. "Cam!" Nate yelled, trying desperately to crawl out, his efforts crumbling as he kept letting go. "I can-" Cam tried to speak, but his world had gone black. "I"… *can't.* He was too exhausted. His body went limp, and his hand let go. But Nate grabbed him. *It* was now directly at Nate's ankle, and he held on desperately to Cam's hand, stretching between falling, and holding on. "AHH!" He screamed, as his shoulders started pulling muscles. *It* was now pulling Cam down, ripping him from Nate's hand. In one final desperate attempt, Nate reached out and his hand caught *someone's*. He pulled up, and a figure dived down next to Cam, grabbing onto the handlebar and thrusting a sword deep into *its* mouth. *It* screamed in pain, but did not give up. *It* reached out wide with one of its arms, and grabbed both Cam and **Sean**, pulling hard. Sean's wrist began to tear, and he could feel his blood vessels popping. He winced in pain, but still held on, looking around, and up. It tore him from the ladder violently, but he grabbed the next bar, and held on tight, stabbing hard, downwards. Unfortunately, *it* dodged. He looked around desperately, and something caught his eye. *The cable.* He was too far away, so he fought hard to bring them to the corner, struggling against the force of the massive inky arm. It pulled him to the middle, and he let it. At the last second, he smiled. "Bye, fucker!" He yelled, and slashed the elevator cable. It was silent for a moment, and *it* stopped pulling them. A horrible scraping noise began echoing down the shaft, getting closer as it went down. *It* looked up, and *its* dark eyes widened. Sean seized the opportunity, and pulled himself out of the way, holding Cam in a hug, just as a massive fleet of sparks and shrieks flew past them, forever crushing **it** into the darkness, its inky crusty body disappearing in the faint red light.

A moment passed, then a massive loud bang echoed up the shaft, and the walls shook with the impact. Sean recoiled slightly with Cam in his hand, he could feel it shaking his entire body. His muscles relaxed as he exhaled with relief, and began to climb back up, Cam still in a hug. He reached the top, and handed Cams hand up to the others like a lifeguard. Exhaling, He stared at the fresh blood on his hands, then back down into the void of the elevator shaft. It looked as if nothing was there at all to begin with. *Safe at last.*

Chapter 8

"So that's it? We're just gonna murder people, with zero costs to us?" The second man leaned in slightly, scratching his chin. "Who ever said removing threats was bad?" His voice was higher pitched, and sounded slightly uncertain of itself, a hint of insanity. The third man's lips formed into a glare of hatred. "Threat..?" He asked, his voice full of concern and caution, echoing deeply through the interrogation room. "Threat," the second man repeated, calmly, and slightly mockingly. The first man clasped his hands together. "If an asset discovers too much, it becomes a threat. To mankind, to the operation, to everything, ever known." - "To your money," the third man countered, coldly, backing into the shadows. The second man stood up, and began to pace around the tiny room. "There is nothing stating what is good, and bad. The world is a void, and it's meant to be.. tested." The third man shook his head defiantly. "I once had a daughter.. many would believe it was wro-" - "DONT!" The third man yelled, sending booming crackling sounds through the tiny room. The second man cleared his throat mockingly. "Killing… someone. Is no different than removing a fly from your home, or disposing of a plant. After it's.. gown too long." The third man stood his ground as the second one approached him. "Everything dies eventually, there is nothing saying what's.. right.. and what's wrong." The third man stepped away, his *faint handlebar mustache* visible in the yellow light above. But he was stopped before he could reach the door.

"Everyone has their own beliefs, but sometimes emotion affects logic, and scientific thinking." - "Don't try to-" The second man stopped him, waving him off. "Just.. Don't do anything.. rash… *Garrison.*"

"Alright, I know this sounds weird. But just hang on," Sean alleged, holding the katana above Cam. He flicked his wrist just slightly, and the blade suddenly de-materialized, bursting into a mess of strange ripples and pixels, leaving nothing but the handle remaining. Cam eyed it excitedly. "Woahh I didn't know that thing was a light s-" A random mouse scuttled across the floor interrupting him.

Sean nodded proudly. "This thing's just full of surprises." He flicked his wrist again, and the blade re-appeared. Sean aimed it carefully at Cam. "It worked for me," Nate said happily, dancing with his "new leg" Avery nodded, though her head faced down to the ground. Cam winced slightly as the blue light fused his flesh back together. "Yep," he coughed out. "that's uh.. yeah so we're just not gonna question the magical ass sword?" Sean chuckled, and nodded his head. Cam shrugged, and stood up immediately. "Wow, yeah you weren't wrong." He nodded, and they all rose up once more, as if nothing had ever happened. *But something very much had.* "So are we all good?" Nate asked out loud, gesturing to the elevator shaft. No-one nodded, except for Sean. "Oh SUREE, no, sure let's just move on!" Sasha began ranting sarcastically. "It's not like any of us just broke our fucking legs and witnessed horrors beyond our comprehension or ANYTHING!" Sean shrugged, noticing Avery, who was covering half her face, looking sorely down at the floor, trying to be unseen. But it was painfully obvious she was indeed: not okay. "Av you-?" She shook her head, showing her face. She was crying, but stopped, forcing herself to bottle it up, and face forward with a straight face. Sean gave a sad, lonesome nod as he watched her do this, knowing full well it wouldn't help anything. *Practice what you preach, coward.* His consciousness called back to him, and like every other time in his life, he ignored it, remaining emotionally numb. "So magic is real," Cam blurted out, now accepting what he'd seen behind the fence just a few hours prior. "So is the boogie man," Nate added.

They all nodded, out of breath and barely listening to him. Avery stood up, frowning, and pulling back her tears. 'Alright, let's go."

*A knock sounded at the door, echoing through the chamber metallically. "This is not the time, I need to focus right now!" An annoyed muffled voice came through the synthetic tile door. Loud sounds of typewriters could be heard from the inside, the man was clearly busy. Regardless, **he** ignored it, and wrenched open the door violently. "LITERALLY ANY OTHER TIME! ANY OTHER TIME AND YOU PICK NO-"... The man stopped, his strange, inky eyelids widening at the object shown before him. "He's leaving, One. He's gone."... Neither of the **brothers** moved, or spoke, as if a sudden force had just banned the concept of breathing. The first began to claw at his desk, his hand becoming a fist, his shadowy face curving with anger to match. The white light above turned a hue of red, matching his body, and after a few intense moments, he spoke. "Let me read it." The second was silent, the mark of the same anger embedded, burned on his face, combined, somehow, with a grin. The first nodded in his seat as his eyes darted near the bottom. "Wh-" his heart skipped a beat, his* *face growing cold, his hair standing up. His eyes began to shrink, his pupils becoming small white dots in two empty voids. He gritted his teeth, and started to shake uncontrollably, the light above turning purely blood red. His mouth dropped slightly open, his head fell to the side,and his nostrils flared aggressively. Moments passed, and a knock came gently, innocently at the door. "I know you said not brother you, but there's an urgent situation!" The first's eyes moved on their own volition the second **brother**, who nodded understandingly, and opened the door. "Oh th-" the worker didn't make it even an inch in before he was pinned against the wall, the face of a man of extreme power now a very prominent threat, eyes locked with his and the first man withdrew a small metal machine in the shape of a spider from his pocket, wrenching the worker's throat open, and shoving it down. The spider's eyes lit up, and it began to crawl fast down the worker's body. Immediately he fell to the ground, and began gasping for air, the sound of his organs being eviscerated from within now loudly playing like a record player through the room, his heart beating extremely audibly. "I..'m .. sor-" his vocal cords were sliced before he could finish the word, and in an instant, the loud echoey heartbeat* *ceased. A tear formed violently in the worker's pants, and the metal spider plopped out, freshly soaked in the worker's insides, a pool of blood immediately forming around it. The second* **brother** *nodded once more, having seen this a thousand times. A thump erupted loudly as the first brother dropped the worker to the ground like a child with a broken toy. "Get the cleanup crew ready.. He's not leaving us that easy." With that, he walked ominously out of the room, leaving the second brother standing before the pile of flesh that was now the worker. He should've been full of sorrow, or disturbed having just seen what happened, and yet he smiled. His lips red, his eyes a pit of psychotic ideas, Fresh genuine delight on his face..*

"No elevator, no 'smelevator," Cam's voice traveled through the strange concrete, metallic halls, ringing annoyingly with reverb. "Well if you have a better idea, we're all ears." Sasha responded, kicking in a door. Nate was ahead of them, climbing a massive mountain of stairs with ease. Their footsteps echoed loudly as they made their way up, a sharp metal clicking on the hard steel floor. Avery stared bluntly at the walls as they passed by, something about their architecture *felt familiar.* She squinted, stopping in place for a moment subconsciously. *Curved metal slits, three branching out, two branching down. So on, so forth.* "Oh!" She said out loud. *"That's at my house!"* She began walking again happily, the others waiting for her a few feet ahead. But she **stopped.** Her feet ceased to move, her eyes angled themselves at the walls forcefully, unwillingly. *That... that is NOT and has never once been **at my house**!* She spat to herself in her head. *Why did I just think that?* A chill formed in her spine, and her knees caved in against the wall. The halls grew blurry, all of them zooming towards her at once. Something was in the distance, it **made up** her friends, a combination of their mangled, twisted body's. The same thing from the basement, it had the head of.. *dad? No.. what? How?* Her head span in a thousand directions, ones incomprehensible to the human mind. *It's not safe. It's not real!* She felt her head smash on the metal wall, gasping for breath, the world itself in danger everywhere, an **error** of horror. *I'm not safe.. they're not real. Nothing is.. no.. GET AWAY! GET AWAY!* She yelled in her head. *I KNOW YOU'RE NOT REAL! I KNOW YOU'RE NO-* "Avery?!" *Ave-* Avery- **Avery.** "Av, It's okay. We're here. He glanced quickly at sasha, who was at the other side of her, nodding. "Hey, I know that might've been too much, and believe me I wish we could sit here but-" "There's no time," Avery finished, hopping up, and acting like nothing had happened once again.

A fan buzzed in the distance as they continued up the stairs. "Avery, I-" She waved him off, too busy in thought. Sean sighed, and gave her space. "Well," Sasha interrupted, checking her map, which appeared to extend throughout the entire facility. "It's not like we're gonna just be able to mar-" she was cut short, tripping, and falling flat across the stairs on her face. Cam reached his hand down, and she took it, begrudgingly. "Uh?" He asked to the world. "Ooh!" Nate echoed him, in the exact opposite tone. In front of them was a hole in the stairs, just big enough for a human to fit through, an ominous red light peering just out of the cracks. Immediately, Nate took off, squeezing through the gap and breaking into a crawl. "What.. the," Sasha squinted in disbelief. "Nate, wait!!" Avery yelled, but it was too late. "God damnit," She muttered, and positioned herself to crawl in after him. "Wait." A voice repeated behind her as Sean grabbed her arm. She yanked it away from him. "We can't lose him, cmon!" She ordered, and he sighed as she disappeared just as Nate had a moment earlier.

They emerged from a damp crawlspace and into a cavernous open room, where alone lay a massive square container. Lined with glass, and glowing with nauseating LED lights. One single thing stood separate in that tiny room. A little girl. She was peacefully asleep, her body flat down on the cold, white clean, but clearly concrete floor. She was smiling, her blond hair sprawled out on the ground, with a hint of purple in it. She wore a friendly silver hat, fallen off from her impact on the ground. By all accounts, she looked like a content little girl, enjoying time sleeping at home. Cam smiled, slightly enthralled by her cute childish nature, but Sean and Avery shook their heads, joined by Sasha. Avery felt a chill down her spine, as she stared at Sean. *It's a prison.* He nodded. *And she's the prisoner.* "But why?" Sasha inquired, seeming to have read their minds. Cam shrugged. "She seems happy." Sasha shook her head defiantly. "No. Look at the way her body is. She's clenching her chest." Avery nodded, and Sasha pointed her finger at the glass accusingly. "I'm willing to bet that smile is just relief from finally being free of whatever sick DISGUST-" She stopped. "The point is, we can't leave her here. Who knows what the hell these freaks will do to her!" Sean nodded, his brown hair bouncing slightly in the sickening purplish light. "Okay, well," Cam offered. "There's gotta be people taking care of her? Maybe this is her home?" Sean shook his head. "No. She's in a random crack in the stairs buried deep in some weird government bunker, I mean do you see ANY food or water?" Cam made a face of concern, nodding. "Okay, then how do we get her out of here?" Avery shrugged, analyzing the glass. *Bullet proof, well good at least she's not gonna get shot, because that's definitely a concern I thought I'd be having today.* Cam's facial expression grew slightly angry. "Okay, can we just stop for a second and address *WHAT* she is?" They all did as he asked, and Sean pointed his hand out like a stage performer, giving him the floor.

"I almost just got eaten by a massive meat spider monster thing. Gods, myths, monsters. They're all VERY clearly real down here.

WHO KNOWS if she's not a vampire or something.." Sean shrugged, and went towards the glass. "That's a risk we have to take." The others affirmed in suit. Cam turned around *"that's a 'wisk we 'hev to 'tek,"* he muttered, mocking him, and making a stupid face. Though he was not quiet in the slightest, and everyone immediately turned around, looking disappointed. Sean nodded, a pensive, slightly annoyed look on his face. "Uh.." They stopped. The room froze. Avery and Sean stood together, a warning look fresh on their faces. She was awake now, standing, and leaning against the glass, her head cocked, glaring at them curiously and twitching slightly. It was clear she was looking for something. "Great, told you so," Cam snapped, whispering. The little girl cocked her head to the right, and her smile faded. She looked troubled. Not scared for her safety, but rather: for theirs. Her eyes rose to her left, and they focused directly on Avery. She shivered. *Hiii.. creepy little girl, you good?* The girl did not blink, nor did she move an inch. She just stood, studying her, idle. Avery stared back at her, but she didn't seem threatening. More confused. *Why are you here?.. I told you not to.* They all sat, not in danger, simply watching the little girl. She cocked her head again, and looked down at her hands. Moments passed.. then the light flickered and she fell back to the ground, sleeping peacefully again, as an innocent little girl. Avery looked at Cam. He nodded. "Okay well.. she seems friendly?.. probably?" They all nodded, their faces purple in the bright LED light. "Oh right!" Cam yelled, *a little too loud*. The others glared at him, confused, as he thrust his hand into his pocket, and retrieved his new favorite object.

"Guess the **CAM-era** is helpful after all, ha!" He jeered at the others. Sean looked at him disappointedly, as Cam snapped a horrendous, badly lit, terribly angled shot of the little girl. He stood proudly, the camera up to his eye, admiring his new prized shot. "Well, hopefully this is good enough for the cops." Avery shook her head. "Yeah, I'm sure the cops will be THRILLED to hear you're taking pictures of little girls in cages." Cam scowled, taken aback, and Avery smirked, looking at Sean. "Hey who knows, with your track record, you might have a future in that!" Sean said, finishing her thought. Cam rolled his eyes. "Yeah, yeah, well it's for EVIDENCE so if you're calling me a detective, thanks." Avery cocked her head. *Welllll.* Sean smirked, and laughed under his breath. They stared at each other for a moment, once again enjoying each-other's sarcastically lovable company. "Uhhh, guys." They paid no mind. "GUYS!" Sasha yelled. Their instincts kicked in, and Sean pushed her aside, grabbing both Avery and Sasha by the wrists and running to the corner, leaving Cam alone in the center.

For just a brief second, it felt like time stopped. Cam looked out, not able to comprehend what lay just in front of him. A laser pointer shaped like a triangle lay static, directly on his forehead, purple, and accompanied, mere milliseconds later with a loud piercing pop. His *own* instincts kicked in as the bullet flew towards him, and he turned his head away, looking directly into the glass box. It should've been impossible, he should've been shot and dead. And yet he was awake, with time still at his fingertips. *What?!* The little girl was gone without a trace….

Where am I? Am I dead? He glanced around, again, something that should've been impossible. His friends weren't moving, nor was the bullet coming towards him at light speed. It wasn't just adrenaline. *Time's frozen?* As if in response, a shadowy figure appeared down the hall, in the faint red light. Cam pushed to run forward, but could not. "Hey!" *no response.* "HEY!.... What the hell.." He looked down at his hands, and tried to grab the floating camera. It wouldn't budge. "Where.. Who?" The world flew by, oxygen necessity not even a concept in his mind. Then, in an instant, the figure grabbed the bullet out of the air, and shifted it back towards the guard. Cam looked back, in pure confusion, and the little girl was standing, once again, in the glass box. Then he looked forward again, but the figure was no longer there. *What.. the fu..*

BANG! The guard holding the gun was now shot, straight to the head, leaving him standing there, eyes blank, breathing heavily, finally accepting what he'd been denying the whole time. *The signal jammer.. It's real.* He looked down. A stream of blood ran to his feet across the hallway, but he was unable to move. *It's.. all. Connected... She was ri-* "LETS GO!" Sean yelled, grabbing the inside of his armpit, and hoisting him into a run. His hearing returned. A loud alarm had apparently erupted into action, accompanied by ominous green lights, somehow even more alarming than the typical "red-alarm".

"What do we do?" Nate asked, panicking as they sprinted down the hall. "Just run, for now!" Sasha yelled back through layers of confusion and stress. Nate stopped abruptly, backing into a corner of the hall, and collapsing into a fetal position. Cam nearly kicked him in the face, in rage and confusion. "Yo, what are you doing?!" - "I… I don't… I don't.." - "Nate, we need to go!" Sasha commanded, but despite his efforts, he couldn't budge. He began hyperventilating, the green lights feeling blinding, the sterile metal walls sickening. "Nate, get up!" Sean heaved, determined, but out of breath, attempting to pull him up into standing position- yet still, he didn't budge. "HAUL ASS!" Cam yelled. Avery shook her head, breathing, and thinking hard. "He can't. He's having a panic attack, or something, his breathing, it won't allow him to stand!" Cam smiled like a circus clown, and crossed his eyes, and the green lights continued to intensify. "It's not the fucking time for a science lesson Avery!" She shook her head, ignoring his ignorance, biting her lips, and glancing around intensely for solutions. *An empty metal hall, GREAT!*

"There! I hear them!"

Their eyes all moved towards the direction of the guards voice for just a brief moment. "Nate we need to go!" He didn't respond. Loud footsteps started to echo down the hall, its circular architecture making the noises all the more more threatening. "Sean, we're sitting ducks!" Sasha snapped. "You think I don't know that?!" He snapped back.

'Foccus!" Avery commanded, eyeing around the hall. The footsteps grew louder. Sean's face swayed, realization forming in his eyes. "He knows we're here!' "What?" "The guard, he knows we're here." Sasha shrugged aggressively, her face reading mostly laser focus, but her eye's reading: *WHAT THE FUCK DO WE DO, YOU IDIOTS?!* Sean bit his teeth, and Avery scampered away, a plan hatched. "NATE GET UP!" Yet again, he didn't, continuing to breathe faster and faster. **The footsteps grew louder..** 'NATE!!" -Nothing. *Screw it.* In a single moment of quick thinking, Sean kicked his stomach in, causing him to have the wind knocked out of him, and go completely unconscious. *Pray this works.* "CAM!"

He yelled, and Cam nodded, his eyes flying wild.

They each grabbed an armpit, hoisting him, with bad posture and high effort off the ground. A loud bang echoed out, and Cam flinched, dropping Nate's unconscious shoulder slightly, but quickly picking it back up. "What the hell are you doing?!" Sean grunted. He shook his head, he could do nothing *but* shake his head. Sasha looked around, guiding them through the panic. She squinted, unsure if what she was seeing was even real. A metal cover of sorts now stood dormant on the floor, adjacent to it, a girl with a strangely confident expression, sitting inside of a now opened vent. "Go!" Avery commanded, and The two boys didn't hesitate, shoving Nate's unconscious body through the vent with a god awful scraping sound.

`"YOU'RE ALL GONNA DIE TODAY!"`

Cam gritted his teeth, and widened his lips at the sound, a somewhat cheesy, unintimidating thing to say. But in the moment it felt terrifying: "You're gonna die today."

"Get in!" Sean yelled, violently kicking Cam through to the other side.

The footsteps stopped.. Bang.

"Cam?" A young Sasha spoke out. Cam did not respond. "What are you doing, idiot?" She chuckled to herself, liking the word. Still no response. "Okayyy then, well more cake for me then." She smirked, somewhat sadistically for a child. "Had the ten candles and everything." "Ten?" A small, shy voice echoed out. "Ten!" She repeated, happily, a giddy grin on her face. "Janice, I'm twelve."

.....Sasha shook her head unwillingly, her throat feeling tight all of the sudden. Parts of her world began to glitch out of reality, their concepts within existence refusing to exist. The brightly lit bedroom around her became an uncanny valley of confusion, and surfaces blurred randomly into grays and blacks. "What?!' "Cam?!' "Who is that?!" "CAM?!" Cam did not respond. The walls grew closer to her, folding in like a living being, the floor

beneath her crumpling into madness and randomness. "CAM!!" She screamed, but her mouth could not move, somehow sealed shut. A single shadow appeared within the chaos, in a way impossible to describe, the symbol, the center, the figurehead of all of it. It reached out, but she resisted. One word formed on the tip of her tongue, which she still couldn't move: **The signal jammer.**

Boom. The projectile flew past Sean's head at a speed even faster than a standard bullet, a silhouette looking heavily armed in the background matching it. For the split second he had, he stared at the guard. The guard held a rifle of some-sort proudly over his shoulder accompanied by a metalic, angled helmet that covered his entire face. Its seam was glowing purple where his eyes were in the helmet. He was dressed in a tactical, leather outfit, black and gray, with various weapons strapped to parts of his body.

`"May your blood be of use to him"`

Sean, for some reason, found himself ignoring every instinct in his body, and simply stood, eyeing the guard up and down. The guard reciprocated this action, almost, for just a brief second, feeling unthreatening entirely. Two animals, curious of each-others presence. Something grabbed his foot, breaking his daydream, and dragging him to the ground. "What the?" He whispered, almost relaxed. "SHUT UP," Cam snapped, dragging him through the vent and into a corner of *presumed* safety. "What the hell were you thinking?!" Sasha demanded. He shrugged, laying inactive on the ground, exhausted, staring up at Nate, who was now conscious again, and scowling at him. "Body's are easier to transport if they're not breathing." He sighed, taking a peek behind him outside the vent. The guard ran forward, studying their movements through the vent, but for whatever reason, he did not try to stop them, nodding, satisfied, and walking back down the hall.

Sean sighed once more. "Learned about it from Avery's brother.. a long time ago." Cam raised an eyebrow. *Grey?* "Well, great, Sean. Great! I'm so glad Avery's family murder tactics helped you out there." Avery made a sour face, caught in the crossfire, still recovering from the adrenaline. They waited, all staring at Sean expectantly. Sasha shook her head like a disapproving mother. "Well?" - "Well, what?" She rolled her eyes. "Apologize!" Sean looked at her like her whole life was a joke, and began laughing gently. "apologize?..For making sure no-one got shot yes I'm so sor-" Avery shot him a look, and he signed once more, letting go of his ego. "Fine, Nate, I'm so sorry I saved your ass too, instead of leaving you to die. My bad there, champ." Sasha's frown grew exponentially, her eye's becoming pits of hell. "Look, I'm sorry, okay? I had to do something or else we'd all be dead. We're not safe just sitting here, we need to keep moving." Avery nodded, eyeing the path ahead.

She knew that they were, in part, in imminent danger, but something still bothered her. *Why would Grey know that?* She scoffed to herself, brushing it off as they continued down the vent. *Why **wouldn't** he know that?*

"Wait!!" Sean called suddenly from ahead, leading the pack. The strange green alarm still blared all around them, with an ear piercing ringing to accompany it. 'We can't!" He barked, turning around, his face full of fear. Cam moved his hands into a shrugging position. "We *can't* what, dipshit?" - "We can't leave her here!" Nate, and Sean responded in sync. "We'll come back!" Sasha yelled in response. Avery shook her head. *Who's to say we even get back in here.. If we get out?* "How can you be sure of that?" She called back to Sasha, staggering over a vent-fan. "Well, we'll have a better chance next time then right now!" Sean exhaled defiantly, turning his head side to side. "We have to go back!" Sasha waved him off, coughing briefly from the amount of dust in the vents. "And get shot?! We'll *COME* BACK!" Avery nodded. "She's right," she concluded, though one heard her. "Fine!" Sean yelled, and they kept crawling. "Okay, but where are we going?" Nate asked, at a completely normal tone. He no longer seemed panicked, now oblivious to the situation. "Why should I know?" Sasha replied, passive aggressively. Cam cackled. "I don't know, it's not like you have a goddamn map or anything!" She shrugged, and gave a soft, admitting nod. *Hm.*

"Kill switch?" A man asked, he was dressed in a simple hat, and camouflage security uniform, staring at a silver static monitor before him. "Nahh," the man adjacent to him replied.. "As much as I'd love to Jimmy, it's the boss's orders." Jimmy shivered, fiddling with random military dog-tag beads. "Which boss?" The other man chuckled slightly. "The **BIG**, Bad one. Yep.. the first." Jimmy covered his face with his right hand,looking uncomfortable, his shoulders raised for protection. "Ay' listen, Jimmy. I get it's your first day, but you'll warm up to i-" - "There they are!!" Jimmy yelled, his hat flying off his head, and by some miracle, back into his face. The other man slammed on a comically large red button, and the guards on the monitor next to the vent cover rose, immediately alert. Jimmy's eyes exploded with excitement, watching the monitor like a TV-show, as the pack of teenagers messily flopped out of the vent.

"Cam, Shh!" Sasha snapped, landing smoothly like an assassin. She peeked around the corner, and her eyes squinted, searching and scanning efficiently. "Okay," she signaled to the others, extending back. "There's two guards… what's our plan?" The two guards rolled their eyes ahead of them, very easily hearing every detail of her "plan". Unlike the leather wearing threatening guards, these one's were ghost white, and looked as if they had zero personality or purpose, *almost Stick-man like.* "What do we do?" Avery asked. Sasha shrugged, remaining in a stealthy position checking her map. *Why aren't they.. Oh.* Above the previous unmarked section was a new section labeled: **fish Imports**. "Yeah, that explains it," She muttered. Sean peered over, his face serious, about to make a decision. *Two guards, presumably both are a bad shot, opportunity to take one hostage.* He nodded, and looked back at the group, then prepared to jump out, un-crouching from the corner. "Wait!" Cam asserted, grabbing his shoulder and bringing him back down. "I got this." With that, he reached into his back pocket, proudly retrieving a tiny model helicopter, complete with a remote. Sean raised an eyebrow, as he watched him turn it on, and the group exchanged looks of confusion. "What the?!" Nate startled as it jumped to life, flying into the air. "Hey?" A guard called, more of a lackluster question than a warning. Cam smirked, his blonde hair flying in his face as the propeller spun annoyingly, creating the sound of a house-fly. Suddenly, it lit up brightly, and the group watched as he jammed the stick forward and flew it down the hallway with nearly perfect precision. "They've got a drone!" One yelled, and Cam nodded, flying it far out of the hallway by some miracle not smashing it into a wall. "We gotta stop that thing!" The guard yelled and they ran out the hallway. Sasha rolled her eyes. "I cannot believe that actually just worked."

Sean bit his lip, disappointed but impressed. "What? It was a great plan!" Cam raised his arms like a toddler. Avery couldn't help but smile. *A toddler with the precision skills of an airforce pilot.* "It *WAS* a good plan," he repeated. Sean sighed. "Alright, yeah, you win. Let's go before you have to repeat that." Cam nodded. *That's what I thought, jerk. Good plan. "The greatest plan,"* he muttered, leaving the controller on the ground and walking down the hallway with the group.

"Well, we didn't die, yippee!" Nate exclaimed. Cam ran his finger around the gate in front of them. "Hey Avery, look at that! It definitely *was* electrically powered." She stopped momentarily, shooting him a glance, completely out of breath and astonished at his stupidity. They were back in the cave now, stepping out through the previously locked metal gate. Avery squinted her eyes, bending at her knees."Back.. here," she managed to cough out. Sean nodded, slipping out of his hood. "Well it hasn't changed for the.. Hours.. We've been gone?" He stopped, and the others all looked at him, understanding his exact thought. Nate frowned. "Yeah, I'm pretty hungry." Suddenly it dawned on them. "What time is it?" Sasha asked out loud, nervously. Cam smirked, his tough guy confidence returning, as he walked into the cave they'd been in just earlier…*earlier..?* For just a single second he narrowed his eyes, confused. "Eh, only one way to find out." Sean opened his mouth in disbelief. "Yep, and just like that his vulnerability is *erased* from the earth." Cam rolled his eyes, now a decent bit ahead of the others, pushing on into the cave. "Yeah, sorry. I almost died in an old creepy elevator shaft, but don't worry about me!" He smiled passive aggressively. Sasha stared daggers at his back with exhausted frustration. "You're the one suppressing it, not us." She mouthed to Avery and Sean. They nodded, shrugging. Nate was in a corner, having found a -*Rather fancy looking rock, yes.. perfect.* He smiled, and began picking at it, paying zero attention to anything else. "You comin'?" Cam yelled, now far ahead into the tunnel. "Yeah.. I guess," Sean responded, not able to yell quite as loud, still out of breath.

The brush blew vigorously in the wind as they emerged from the thick trees back to the campsite. Avery scratched her chin, something about it felt off. *It looks no different?* She rolled her eyes at her own thoughts. *Why would it be any different, we've been gone for..* She stopped. "What time is it?" Each one of them shrugged individually. Cam gestured back at the tent. "I did bring a little clock, but it stopped working, I just checked." Avery nodded, and Sean pinched his fingers together, putting them up to the sun. "If I had to guess, around eleven. But I'm pretty damn hungry, so who knows." Cam gave a thumbs up, and began to turn around to walk to the van. "Alright then, let's get the fuck out of here," he smiled, proudly. "No," Sasha said, firmly. Cam raised an eyebrow. "We can't just leave her here!" - "Ah," Cam muttered, nodding just slightly, trying not to scowl.. "Well how's about this?" He began to propose, gesturing his hands in the air like a stage performer. "We sleep as much as we can and ignore the *Eldridge horrors* we just witnessed, and then head back to.." He searched the air for the word. "Save her." Sasha shook her head again. "No, who knows how long she has before they.." She pursed her lips, and spun around slowly, an emotional defense mechanism. "Look, we can't do it alone, we're gonna need help. This is very clearly a bigger operation than five teenagers can handle." Sean shook his head, but gestured an agreement, begrudgingly. "So we go to the cops?"

Cam nearly burst out laughing, his hair flying in his face from the wind. "The co- HA, the cops.." Sasha glared at him impatiently. "Have you SEEN the cops in our town? Yeah, I don't think they're gonna be any different than us trying to do it ourselves." Avery tilted her head for a second. *He's got a point.* "Plus," Sean jumped in. "Whatever *this* is, it's clearly funded heavily, there's no chance this isn't the government, even the most rich companies couldn't afford a facility like… that." Sasha waved him off. "Yeah, well we don't know till we try." Cam palmed his face. "Counterpoint, we don't know until we *die*." Avery scoffed, and immediately tried to hide it. Sasha raised her jaw, taken aback. "Alright Ms. Funny, what's your take on this? Since you're the one who got us into the mess in the first place." Sean frowned, and raised his hand at her. "Hey," he muttered, surprised at her random change in tone. Avery took a deep breath, and shrugged "Well, we're clearly dealing with some crazy stuff here, I think Cam has a good point. I mean, who's to say that innocent little girl isn't some kind of.. Decoy?" Sasha scratched her face in frustration, but gave a nod of listening nonetheless. Cam gave two confident thumbs up to Avery's opinions. "Yeah, like some kind of like vampire-robot." Sasha stared at him blankly. "Vampire.. robot?.. yeah, really Cam? A vampire robot?" Cam shrugged angrily. "I don't know, but we shouldn't disregard the fact that it might *not* be a normal human being." Sean nodded. "He's got a point, we can't be too careful." Cam rolled his eyes, and began leaning on a tree, recoiling slightly from its cold temperature. "Plus, I'm not wasting gas driving all the way back to town, just to drive back here." Sasha's jaw nearly fell off. "AN PRISONED LITTLE GIRL, AND YOU'RE GONNA CHOOSE GAS MONEY?" Cam shrugged, ignoring the other penetrating stares of shock and disappointment from Nate and Sean. But not Avery. *I've seen a room like that before... that girl is familiar.* Sean and Nate stood by his side, though they both were still glaring at him. Sasha stood on the other side, looking like a time bomb, ready to explode into anger. "So?" They all looked at Avery expectantly "Avery?" *Grave... Pit...ML. Why the hell would they be keeping those things down there?* **"Av-"** "Yep. Yep yep. Couldn't agree more." Sasha smacked her face, and widened her eyes, expecting an agreement between the two. "Uh, let's talk it over dinner?" Avery offered, whispering a bit. Cam smiled aggressively. "Why, that sounds like a great idea Avery! Let's just eat all our magical food we have unlimited access to!" She shook her head, and looked at Sean, who frowned and shrugged. "You didn't.." Sasha started, her eyelids being hidden as they raised beyond a healthy threshold, her eyebrows angling to match. "YOU DIDN"T FUCKING PACK ANY FOOD??!!" Cam shrugged. "No Sasha, I didn't. I'm not your third grade mother that packs your lunch every morning. I figured we'd go get it on our own." She began grinding her teeth at him, genuinely striking fear into the other three. "SO WHAT, WE WERE JUST SUPPOSED TO GO GODDAMN HUNTING?!"

Cam, once again, dragged his shoulders up and down, brushing it off. "Yeah, and?" She gently bobbed her head side to side, glaring with a rage that couldn't quite be described in words alone. Sean sighed, in just as much disbelief as her. "Well, we've got a map. Let's at least take a look at what's around." Sasha gave a passive aggressive thumbs up, refusing to speak, and handed the map to Cam without another word. He looked at her, confused. "No, not that one." Sasha rolled her eyes, and yanked it back, turning around and staring at the ground.

Quickly, Cam ran back over to the van; which had now sunken just slightly more into the mud, and grabbed something, running back as quick as he left. His eyes narrowed in as he focused on 'the right map". "Let's see, Mountain, mountain, mountain. Oh here we go!" He yelled, summoning the group. Nate looked up hopefully. "Yeah, this will work!" He continued, his eyes lighting up. "It's another fucking mountain!" He concluded delightfully, throwing the map to the ground. Sasha rolled her eyes, and picked it up, investigating the bottom half. She didn't look for even a second before immediately staring daggers with immeasurable disappointment. "So uh, you ever look at the back half?" Cam stared at her blankly, and the group watched. "Uhhhhhh… yeah!" He threw out. Sasha seighed, shaking her head. "Well there's nothing here anyway, so it wouldn't even matter." She dropped the map angrily, and stared at Cam. "More fucking mountains?" He asked. "More mount-" She stopped mid sentence, smirking slightly, staring at him, still with anger, but a hint of mischievousness. "More *Fucking* mountains," she confirmed.

"Welp," Sean began, shrugging. "So that we don't all starve to death, we might as well randomly drive down the road and look for a place to eat, right?" Avery yawned. "I don't see a better way." - "Orrrr, we could take the ol' bow and arrow for a spin," Cam countered, drawing an invisible bow. "Pew," he muttered, letting go. Sasha frowned, and shook her head. They sat like this, staring at each other awkwardly for a minute. "Alright, hop in my van kids." Cam said, breaking the silence. Avery Couldn't help but laugh, and ran up to the van, followed by Sean. "Is there candy?" Sasha asked quietly, for some reason warming back up to him after her outburst. He chuckled, he liked her sense of humor, sharing it. "There's food, hopefully." She smiled, kicking the van door open. It screeched like a dying pig as Cam jammed the keys into the ignition. "Phew," He exclaimed as the engine roared to a start. "Okay…" He took a deep breath. "Let's go," he said with a smirk, *YANKING* the stick into reverse, and flooring it back, then zooming forward and out of the campsite. Everyone laughed as they were thrown around in the back, tension from almost being killed several times releasing. Then they rounded the corner and began back down the old overgrown road of uncertainty.

Chapter 9

*O*ctober 26th.

To: Jeramy,

What the hell is happening? I just saw someone devour their wife's arm like a wild animal. The enforcers were supposed to regulate this, like they were even a government to begin with. But I haven't seen any activity in the radio tower in over a week. We need to start thinking about defending ourselves. Whatever this thing is, it isn't normal. More artifacts are showing up each day, and no-one is batting an eye. "2056" What even are those numbers, a date? These things aren't FOR us., brother. They can't be. Yesterday they shut down the roads, horses killed, blood spilled all over the dirt. I don't understand, none of us do. Everything on that road yesterday died..

*Every. Single. Thing. There's something in the air. I can feel it. My teeth feel sharper than normal, and my impulse feels high. There's massive buildings forming here, and I don't understand why. It's like something outside of us is bleeding into us. They've gone insane. They've formed some sort of cult. Worshiping something they just call "the creator." I was ambushed yesterday, at **The Disposal**. They tried to brand my skin, they tried to make me join them. I refused. But I barely made it out alive. No matter what, we **have** to stand our ground. I don't think it's a question anymore. I hear those loud pops everyday now. Those "gun" things... they're clearly some sort of weapon. There's no denying it. They've overthrown our leaders. We're on our own. I'll see you up ahead. Be careful.. please.*

-Garrison.

It was dark and rainy now, as they drove down the road. "Ooh," Nate exclaimed, like a kid in a candy store. Cam braked to a stop, not bothering to check his mirror, knowing not a soul was behind him. "Ronnie's silly dilly dally diner," Sasha read aloud. Sean let out a chuckle, and Avery echoed him. "Well, sounds like food to me." Cam announced happily, pulling extremely fast into the lot, and parking directly in the heavy rain. They all stepped out. The moonlight reflected rigidly in the puddles, illuminating the tiny roadside diner ahead of them, dark and freezing cold. "Ladies first," Cam said, gesturing for Sean and Nate to go through the door. "Yep, sure," Sean muttered, too exhausted to argue. Nate followed behind, raising an eyebrow at Cam as he passed though. Sahsa and Avery waited for a moment, and Cam stayed, smirking with devious intent. "Gonna slam the door on us?" Sasha asked. He nearly flinched, taken aback. *How could they..* "Alright buddy, like you said." Sasha exclaimed, pushing him through the door. "Ladies first." She smiled slightly, enjoying the feeling of superiority. The air was thick with the smell of not so pleasantly cooked meat as they approached the counter. It was loud, and cavernous, the sound of the heavy rain pummeling the roof echoing throughout the building, feeling somehow amplified by a thousand. A man stood behind the counter, faint in the yellow light that illuminated him, barely effective against the darkness of the storm. Avery glanced at Sean and he nodded. The man looked like he hadn't gotten any sleep in years. He donned a curly, messy unshaven mustache and beard, with the same hair to match. They waited, and he simply stood there, completely frozen, staring at them. "Uh," Avery asked gently. "Hel-" - "WELCOME TO RONNIE'S SILLY DILLY DALLY DINER!" He shouted, his eyes bloodshot. Avery blinked, standing back awkwardly. *So I take it you're Ronnie?* Ronnie stared at them for a moment, eyeing them up and down. "So you wanna like.. you know… order something?" Avery glanced at Sasha expectantly. "Um, yeah I'll just have a burger." Ronnie leaned into the counter slightly, coughing., his long neck cracking disturbingly. "Okay, what kind?" Sasha glanced at the others for guidance, but was only returned with a reassuring smile. "Uh, yeah, you know. Just the um.." He blinked a few times, impatiently. "Just a cheeseburger is fine," Sasha finished, shrugging at the others. "M'kay, and the rest of you?" He asked. They all exchanged glances. "Um. Uh." They stared at the menu, glancing over its options, though there were scarcely any, the glass cover shattered, illuminated only barely by a dim orange light. Ronnie began shaking, his eyes growing impatient. "Okay," he spat, rather loudly. "You're all getting cheese burgers then." Cam shrugged. "Alright, I'm not complaining." Avery nodded, and the others followed suit. Though by the evidence around the building, it was probably the only food they had. "Good," Ronnie scolded, quieter this time. Then once again, he stood perfectly still, staring them down. "Uh, so what time did you say we had to be out of here?" Sasha asked, growing uncomfortable. Everything about the man sent red flags. Sean stared back at him, matching his coldness. *I ain't afraid of whatever you are planning, old man.* Avery stared out the window, trying to avoid Ronnies extremely direct eye contact, but the rain blocked everything there possibly was to see. "Uh yeah, like ten for-" Suddenly, Ronnie RAN forward, his arms frozen at his side like a puppet, and eyes wide, sprinting up to them at an alarming pace. Cam startled backwards, and Avery began to back away slowly. Sean gave him a warning glance, puffing up his chest, and Nate stood next to him, with his firsts clenched. "Right this way," he spoke, through his scruffy beard. They relaxed, and exchanged glances, then followed behind him.

The tables were old, worn thin of paint, with the walls matching, too dark to see the dilapidated yellow that made them up. "Wait here, I'll be back in a minute," Ronnie said, disappearing before anyone could acknowledge him. "Alright then?" Sean asked aloud to no-one, as they sat down at the old, cramped table. It had a cloth thrown hastily over it, barely covering the rust on the shell of the red cold metal, which was still visible in the threadbare tears. Cam smirked, laying back and instantly taking up all the leg room. "So, what's our odds this food is any good?" They all shrugged, yawning in a chain. Sasha rolled her eyes. "It's food, Cam. You don't want it, go drink some rain." The table cloth ripped to his side, as he pulled himself to an interrogation pose. "You know what? Maybe I will!" He waited, his face blue in the wet depression that lay outside. "Seriously though, I need to get the van in a parking space that's not gonna flood it. That things Ollld." Sean nodded. "I'll go with him." The others followed his guidance, collectively wanting to get out of the creepy old diner. "Avery?"

Her eyes were in a different world, focusing on the yellow slashed paint, and old dirty napkins and drinks scattered across the floor. Almost as if dreaming about it, not sure what space she'd found herself in. "Aveeryyy?" Sasha called out, waving her hand in front of her. Her brunet hair curled down messily in her face, obstructing her cheeks and forehead. Sasha seighed. "Prince charming, you wanna try?" Sean scowled sarcastically at her, but gladly approached Avery, still in her own world, struggling.. fighting to get back. "Hey, Av." Her neck began twitching gently, and Sean recoiled, staring back at Sasha. *Somethings not right.* "Av?" *Grave.. building.. woman… room.. basement… it's all there. But ho-* "Avery?" Her eyes darted back to normal, back to the world, her physical form. "Yeah?" Sean looked at her, concern in his eyes. "You okay, Av?" She nodded, smiling with her classically overused "very, definitely totally safe and comfortable smile" - "Yep!" She answered brightly, though her tone didn't fit the environment. "Cams gotta go park the car-" - "Van," Cam muttered behind him, showing off to absolutely no-one. "Oh," she breathed, staring blankly at him. "So, you want to come?" She shook her head, ridding her daydream. "Uh…" She stopped, twirling her hair anxiously. A defense mechanism that is very indicative of a "not so okay" person. "Here, why don't you come with?" Sean asked, smiling gently, sensing her distress. She took his hand, and the table cloth slipped a bit, then she got up to face him, matching his smile.

The rusty old table swayed slightly as the group brushed past it to the main entrance. Avery stared out into the rain blankly as she let her legs carry her, her mind just a passenger. "HEY!" Came the voice of Ronnie, booming through the restaurant. He emerged shortly after, and began speaking in a calmer, more reasonable tone. "One.. of y'all has to.. *stay* here." Avery recoiled slightly. *Yeah.. that's not a red flag at all.. and the.. voice.* She shivered. They looked around at each other, shrugging. Cam rolled his eyes. "Well then us four will go move the van, while *Schizophrenia* over here sits and ponders her imaginary friends." Sean shot him a warning glance, and Sasha echoed him. "Av-" - "No, he's right. I'll stay," she volunteered. Sean's eyes narrowed, growing with concern. "You sure? I.. don't know Avery? Maybe I should?" She shook her head, her hair flying in the dark blue light, taking out her switchblade for a moment, and gesturing at it. "No, it's.. it's alright. I need some time to think, you guys understand, right?" She looked out hopefully, letting a tiny bit of her venerability slip out. Sean bit his lip, his gut feeling wrenched the wrong way. *No. This is not safe, this is not right!* The others began to walk out, and he joined them, his head still turned at her. He nodded, and smiled, his look more-so of trust and an agreement rather than assurance. *Stay safe.* The door slammed shut, as the four of them disappeared into the rain. She laid back in the chair a bit. *Finally, some time to think.* After a few breaths, closing her eyes. *Everything is okay.* She smiled, but thoughts began to creep into her head. *Girl. Figure. Dad. The cage. No, no how can you sit back like this doing nothing when there's a little girl out there suffering. I don't understand.. What even was that? Why even was that?* She sighed. *Okay.. okay we'll figure it out. At least it's nice to be alone for now.*

"Why do you think we see darkness when we die?" A voice came from directly behind her, subtle, and whispery. "What?" Avery replied, her *own* voice trembling slightly. Behind her, against the window sat a dark, hooded man facing away from her, hidden in the void of the rain. "What do you think of when you think of nothing?" His voice was deep, and ominous, *a hint of insanity buried within it.* Avery curled her lips, disgusted by his sudden appearance. "I don-" She stopped. *What **do** I think nothing is?* "I don't know." She tried to look around his hood, but saw no face, it was too covered and dark. "When a baby is born, it's untouched.." She recoiled at the word *untouched.. What the hell is this guy talking about?* "It hasn't yet learned what anything in the world is. Color, senses, mom.. **dad**... it's moldable cement.." - "Wha-" The man interrupted her. "What exactly do you think that infant would do, childish, and innocent, incapable of living on its own.. If it was never shown any of the world, no sights, no sounds, simply *darkness..*" She began grabbing the table cloth for a sliver of support, severely uncomfortable, yet for some reason, curious. "What kind of being would you then be creating, deliberately, contriving..?" *Contriving.. creating? God tell me you're not a parent!* "Have you ever heard of the Mandela effect?" The man cocked his head slightly, the hood following his movement. "I.. no?" Avery half asked, admittedly intrigued by the stranger's cryptic nature. "You know, you could be living in a world that started just last Thursday, your memory's only there to create a life you never had, to deceive, ***to betray***…" The man finished with a hint of anger. She opened her mouth, but once again, he interrupted her, as if sensing her trying to talk, though he had no sight of her. "You know.. these are the words of a very great man. He died a long time ago.. and yet it feels like he's here every day." The man stayed perfectly still. "Something tells me.." He shook his head. "Something tells me you know that man.." Avery moved her hand to the salt container, lifting it up and down in thought, half in pursuit of a weapon, forgetting she even had one in her pocket. "How would you know that?" The man stayed still, and did not respond. The air was silent for what felt like an eternity, then he spoke again. "Answer my question." Avery dropped her hands in confusion. "What? The man?" he shook his head. "Last Thursday… What if everything began last Thursday?" She sat still, thinking. *What are you doing? Get away! This guy's probably a serial killer!* Yet somehow, in some way he felt familiar. Comforting, but threatening, and blurry. The very nature of a random hooded stranger. "Why would that matter if it's the life everyone lives?" She found herself asking, still very much afraid of the man. "Hm, to each their own.. I suppose." She nodded, not sure what else to do. "But.." The man began. "Why wouldn't it?" He responded, ominously. "What if you're the *only* one living it.. when everyone else can see the world, you're blind." He began to turn around, but immediately stopped, retracting back. "And yet. It feels.. like you choose to continue being blind.. rather than.. opening your eyes.." He swung his head down, as if fighting against a need for self violence. "Is *someone* blinding you.. or are ***you blinding yourself***?" Avery cringed at his last words, a tingling feeling flowing through her body. "Ignorance is bliss.. Right.. **Avery**."

"Wha-" A chill shot down her spine, and the world began to spin, blood running to her stomach, as the air became thicker and harder to breathe. "What?" *No.. no.. I don't.. who?* WHO ARE YOU!? HOW DO YOU KNOW MY NAME!?" She yelled out, but her voice was quiet, and horse, her world slowly fading as she passed out. She fought to grab the man by the throat, a wild animal registering a threat. Yet the man remained still, and confident. *No..*

no you're wrong! You're not real, you're not real.. GET OUT OF MY HEA-

"What are you yapin' about back here?" Ronnie stood, directly in front of her, his scraggly beard hanging near her face. Avery breathed heavily, grasping the table cloth desperately, as if barely holding onto her sanity. "There.. there was a man, he knew my name! He knew m-" The man was gone. In his place was an empty wooden chair, perfectly centered under the counter, as if he'd never been there. "Little girl, what in god's name are you talkin' about?" Her vision blurred, as she looked around desperately. The man remained absent. "Look, be a crazy stoner all you want, but I'm trying to hear the rain. It's peaceful, so stop bothering me!"

The sound of the rain was echoing, entrancing, and above all else loud, but it was far from peaceful. It stung in her mind like the static of an old television, loud and rapid, neverending. The checkered floor grew infinite like a mirror reflecting on itself as her head collapsed to her knees, impacting with a sharp loud crack. The world was no longer clear. Not just in her vision, but in everything else, sanity, clarity, reason. It was all a blur now, with her vision being an epitome of everything. *He knew. I know him. He knows me.* The door creaked loudly in the distance. "Y- ye wel- let see- ou d a- bett job!" The voices echoed, unclear in her mind. "Avery? You okay?" Sean's voice pierced into her perception. "Avery?" Sasha asked, her voice ramping up in panic. *How did he know my name, how did he know my name? Pain..pain...all i fell is pai-*

Sanity returned in an instant, and she felt calm. She shook her head, no longer seeing visions, no longer in her own world. As if someone had pressed a button to pull her back to the real one. "There was a man here… I don't-" Her voice cut off, shrill and full of fear. "Okayyy crazy?" Cam asked, once again taking the leg room, putting his hands behind his head to relax. "Cam!" Sasha snapped, and Nate shook his head at him, genuinely concerned like a puppy for Avery. "Hey, I believe you. It's okay, you're safe with us." Avery shook her head, her face buried in her hands and knees, curled into the fetal position. *We just got chased by some crazy mythical creature that VERY clearly almost killed me!! Almost killed ALL OF US!* She sobbed into her hands, and Sean looked at the others. They unanimously shrugged, though they made no physical movements. *HOW IS THAT SAFE?!* Avery yelled in her head. Her back grew warm as she felt Sean's hand rest upon it. "I know it's been a crazy day. But we're safe right now. It's okay, we're here. Your friends are all here." Cam shrugged, a tiny, just a tiny bit of empathy fresh on his face. "I saw him.." Sean began alternating his hand, comforting her slowly. "I know that man." Sasha stared at the back of Avery's faced down head, a chill running down her spine. Sean nodded at her. "It's okay, take all the time you need." Avery stopped, sitting up for a moment as if finally fighting back. "He asked me a question I've heard before." Sean raised an eyebrow. "Where did you-" - "My house. My dads basement." She stopped suddenly, a tear running down her check. "I remember.." They all waited, as she finally sat up completely, her eye's angling, mouth opening, replacing her sadness with complete determination. "His name was J-" *SHUT UP! SHUT UP AND GO TO BED. HE DOES NOT CARE ANYMORE! BOTH OF US CAN ROT DOWN HERE. HOW CAN I FIND FOOD FOR YOU IF I CAN'T GET ANY SLEEP!! Now is not the time Avery. Be a good a girl. Be quiet. Be quiet. Do not think about things that could harm you. Stay here where it's safe. When we get out of here.. I will have made things better.*

Her head **Exploded** into pain as her heart accelerated, and her mind began to hurt. A thousand screaming thoughts at once, ones she didn't want to hear. *Stay. There are no answers. You don't need to remember. "I will hurt you for your own good."* It was as if the mental part of herself was trying to give answers, but failsafe's were screaming at her, blocking out her ability to hear the sound. She clutched her head, and fell back to her knees, writhing in pain. "Avery??!" Sean yelled, but even the physical world wasn't loud enough.

"Alright y'all, here's ya burgers!" Ronnie stood before them, his scraggly beard dripping down like the rain that surrounded him, into their faces. It smelled of wet dog, and they tried to lean backwards to get away from the stench. He waited for a moment, watching for someone to make a move. His eyes glowing like an angler fish, waiting for its prey. Cam took the first bite, and gave a "crisp thumbs up." - "That's uh.." he bit his tongue. "Great, Ronnie. Thanks." **The man** dropped his jaw, absolutely appalled at Cam's *ignorance*. "Excuse Me?!" Cam squined, cocking his head as the others tended to Avery. *Uh, what?* "YOU THINK THAT.. THAT JUST BECAUSE I WORK HERE MAKES ME RONNIE?!" He began to inch closer to the table, only amplifying the wet dog stench. "MY GRANDFATHER BUILT THIS BLASTED COUNTRY, AND YOU…**YOU!**.. THINK THAT JUST BECAUSE I WORK HERE I GET THE PRIVILEGE.." Cam began yawning. "NAY, THE **HONOR** OF THE TITLE OF **RONNIE**?! SHAME ON YOU, BOY. I.. AM.. APPALLED. YOU HEAR ME?? **APPALLED**!! Cam delivered a "Cam-shrug" and took another bite of his burger, glancing at Avery, who seemed awake and doing fine. "YOU, YOU IGNORANT CHILD MAY CALL ME: **MISTER. WAITER**." Cam sighed, glancing at the others who wore the universal teenage *"Fuck if I know"* face. "Alright, well, *Mr. Waiter*, how much will this cost?" **The waiter** shrugged, staring up at the old moldy ceiling. "Hmmmmm… TEN RUBIES!" He concluded. Cam leaned his head forward, and stared outwards. *Holy good god, what the hell does that even mean?* "I don't have rubies, Ronnie. NONE of us HAVE any rubies."

Surprisingly, The waiter nodded calmly. "Well then maybe you should get a little more.. Mmmmmm," he hummed creepily, using his clearly massive index of thinking skills. "Richer," he finished, after a solid thirty seconds straight. Cam palmed his face. *There's no way way on this fucking planet that you're a human being.* He glanced at Sasha briefly, who gestured back for him *alone* to handle it. *Great.* "Well, Ronnie, best I can do is twenty bucks."

The waiter shrugged leaning in, and licking his lips, spit dripping out of them disgustingly. "Well, I 'spose sense ya *finally* called me my real name, instead of that damn nickname Goodman gave me.." He stood for a moment, as if literally lagging in his own body. "I 'spose you can have it for free." The others turned around at the sound of the word, and each nodded in gratitude. Cam smiled genuinely, for once showing his teeth instead of smirking. "Well, that's really kind, Ronnie. Thanks." The waiter sniffled his nose directly in Cam's face, and then widened his eyes. "What did ya just call me?!" Cam gave up, and wheezed with laughter, leaving The waiter to grit his lengthy total of nine teeth, nodding. "Well, I see we have customers. What can I get y'all?" Cam glanced at the others, still laughing hard. *There's no way this guy is real.* "Welp, anytime you wanna order, just holler.. Oh and by the way, you can call me Mr. Waiter." With that, he ran back at full speed to the kitchen, muttering something about "doing onto other competitors"

"Avery?" Sean asked. She was awake, but shook her head violently. The pain inside of her mind had won. Cam turned around, re-joining the group. "Thanks for the help, gang." - Sasha responded with an apologetic nod. "Yeahh, about that.. We've decided to seek help from the police." Cam raised an eyebrow. "We.. *We..* Did?" Sasha raised her hand to counter but he waved her off. "See, I'm not seeing much *WE* here, guys. I see four idiots and one chauffeur that's *APPARENTLY* been outcast." Sasha exhaled sarcastically. "Look, you were busy handling Mister. walking-corpse there, so we took the valuable time we had to vote." Cam scoffed. "Oh, a vote! Great, sasha! I'm so glad *YOU* took a vote." Sasha rolled her eyes, and Cam echoed her, doing it even more aggressively, as if trying to found a new form of staring contests. "Alright, well, this vote.. What are the options?" Sean jumped in, breaking apart their bickering. "Optio*N*, singular. And it's to get help from the police." Cam stared him down, and he shook his head, faking confidence as "the alpha." - "there, Cam. You voted. Now let's get out of here before Ronnie decides he wants twenty gems or whatever the hell, instead of just ten." Cam blew up his cheeks like a balloon, and slowly sighed out in acceptance. "Fine, but next time include me, alright? That shouldn't be too much to ask, especially since I'm the one driving you-" He stopped, biting his lip and circling his head. "I'm the one driving *us* assholes around." Sean nodded genuinely, and the others echoed. "Alright, sorry man." Then without another word they walked out the door with the burgers, and got back in the van. "Police?" Sean asked. "Police," Cam repeated.

A man sat at his desk, rubbing his eyes. Exhausted from his shift, having been on an early, old computer all day. His eyes were slightly cloudy, blurred and damaged from the piercing orangish light in the dark. His face was dropped, his body slouched. On the computer lay a file, barren of any life or personality, info hastily scribbled down from the recent digital case transfer. The walls were white, with brown baseboards at the bottom, completely sterile. No decorations, or any form of personality existing, except for a poster taped long ago that read "Firearms prohibited in this room." The cubicle surrounding The man was wooden, and painted with a Matt black finish, an extremely boring color he had every right to change. One window held strong at the north most wall, bringing in the warm winter light of..*night*.. Night time. The man fought to keep himself awake, his noticeably fit body falling in the old office chair. "Man arrested for trying to eat gas station pump." He rolled his eyes, and slammed his fists down on the table, gripping his face in contemplation. "thirteen years of this shit, and I'm still doing.." He stopped, eyeing the person on the monitor for a moment, a flare of suspicion in his eyes. "This.." A noise echoed from outside the window, and a group of teenagers passed through, interrupting his **precious** tiny dot of light. *Great,* he thought, as he watched them through the window, pressing his face against the wall due to how limited the view was. "twenty bucks they're going.." He muttered, tracing their path with his finger on the dirty glass. "Yep," he confirmed sarcastically, as the group entered the compliant window portion of the building.

"Yeah, we'll turn you in while we're at it," Cam snarked at Sasha. "And what exactly is your reasonable suspicion, or immediate probable cause?" His face went blank, his golden hair blowing in his eyes as he walked. "Uh.. I don't know, being short?" Sasha ignored him, and walked ahead of his "manly" walking pace with ease. "Okay, well what evidence do we have?" Sean asked, in a much more serious tone. "Not like they're just gonna launch a full fledged investigation in the middle of nowhere." Avery nodded, considering their options. "Well we go-" Cam stepped in front of her proudly holding up the **Cam-era** "Yep, that," She affirmed, disappointingly. Sean nodded, looking at Nate for input. He was walking above and next to them, on the edge of the median of gravel next to the path they were following. "Uh, Ow!" Sean stopped, and extended his hand to him, who had once again fallen on the ground, wet asphalt claiming its place on his face. "Well, we know where the entrance is," He spoke through the ground, making his voice muffled.

The door buzzed loudly as they entered the building, a friendly, bright and happy face awaited them through the stained, church-like glass window ahead at the desk. "Hi there, how can I help you?" The woman asked, her fingers crossed over each other on the reception desk, her black hair long and flowing, perfectly symmetrical, just barely touching her hands. They all stopped. "Uhh," Avery spoke aloud. Sean patted her on the back, and stepped in front of her. "We'd like to report a person who seems to have been kidnapped." Avery gave a cheap thumbs-up, echoing the others' nods. *Yep, and a secret government coverup murder facility.* The woman's face did not change, still keeping the happy robotic like appearance. "Okay, do you have any idea where this person might be being held?" She asked calmly. Sean glanced back at the others, taking a deep breath hesitantly. "Yes," He stated, and the woman nodded back. she was silent for a few seconds, continuing to stare at the group, expectantly. "Butterfly sanctuary," Sean answered, his body position cautious. The woman's eyes jumped slightly, her face turning red, chills clearly running down her spine. Just then, a door burst open to the back of the right, and a tall, buff looking man walked out in panic. "Oh, John I can hand-" The man shook his head, and walked her out of his way, his eyes wide, now right in front of them. "Monarch?" He asked, his voice deep, and full of apparent anger, staring forward, angling his eyes up at them.

"Monarch," Cam affirmed in the corner, tossing him the camera.

The man nodded, and stared into it diligently. His jaw began to

clench as he saw the images before him.

Quickly, he locked eyes with the woman, and she shook her head

warningly. "There's other ways," She muttered, biting her lip in

concentration. "A little girl goes missing in the facility, and we've

got probable cause." She frowned, her pulse visibly beating fast in

her neck. "There's gotta be another w-" - "There will *BE.. NO*

other way," he replied sternly. The woman eyed the group, her face

not at all convinced. The group eyed each-other as the two officers

turned around, talking privately. "No judge is going to approve

this, much less your own team." - "Like I said, we've got all the

probable cause we need right here," he assured, holding up the

camera. "And as for the team.." He glanced over his shoulder

briefly. "I've got the help I need a few meters from where we're

standing. We hit them while they're not expecting it, we play it

smart, and we're golden." The woman turned back around, and

stared at the others for a moment, an extremely concerned look on her face. Then she walked back behind the reception desk and out of sight.

"Alright, listen," The Man began, unlocking a drawer, and pulling out a small revolver. Sean and Avery looked at eachother confused. *Well, that went from zero to a-hundred in about two seconds.* "We're gonna drive there, and you're gonna stay outside," The Man continued, shoving a number of mechanical parts into his pocket. The woman suddenly reappeared from the corner, stepping in his way, her face looking offended. "What about the others?" The Man grabbed her arm, and brought it down gently. "I've waited long enough," he replied, his voice sad, almost desperate, in a whisper. "Let me have this." … The woman shrugged, her body language indicating panic. "Fine, but you are NOT bringing *them* in with you." She scowled, her receptionist act long gone. The man nodded, and turned around. "You guys have a vehicle I assume?" Cam nodded, confused, intrigued, and eager.

It was nearly midnight now, as they trudged down the old dirt road, passing by signs and protest banners strung long ago across the trees occasionally. They led, and the officer tailed them, his look menacing in the distance just behind them. "Think he's gonna call us metaling kids?" Cam joked. Sean snorted "Well we're in a van, and he's got the look for sure." Nate stared blankly out the back window, like a kid in a candy shop fascinated by the police car. *A child who never grew up or saw the world.* "Cam, how are we on gas?" Sasha asked. Cam shrugged, back in the driver's seat once again. "It don't matter." Sean and Avery exchanged glances. *Uh, I'm pretty sure it do matter.* Hours passed as they went back up the windy road. Avery cracked the window just barely, a chill running down her spine. The road looked even more ominous than last time, the barbed wire fence looking more like a promise of death than a threat. The trees sprawled over them like an ink splotch, growing over the road like fingers. Cam shivered as he drove by the lookout spot, the memory from the previous days flashing back. *There's something behind you.* He shook his head, still opting to not tell the others, and made a rather violent hard left. The officer palmed his face behind them, moving forward and **gently** turning behind him. At last they reached the camp sight, still completely void of any life. The long grass blew in the wind, and the tire swung in sync with it. The bright blue tent still stood in the ominous fog and rain, as if they never even left. "Well," Cam exclaimed. "Home sweet home," Sasha said sarcastically, as the van pulled to a stop. The Officer parked behind them, his headlights illuminating the foggy air, spilling around the van. He stepped out of the car carefully, scanning the area quickly. "This it?" He asked, though by his facial expression he already knew. Cam squinted *No it's actually another three hour- yes of fucking course this is it.* "Yep," he said politely, holding back his actual thoughts. "So, no more road?" The officer asked. "No more road," Sean affirmed, gesturing at the path to the left, their remaining footprints only slightly visible from the rain.

The trail felt no different, unchanged, still unnerving, as if time itself hadn't ticked a second. The sky around was night-black, and the mountains towered over, barely visible in the dark haze in the distance, like giants looming over the clouds. The Officer led the way with a much brighter flashlight in hand. "So uh.. what's your.. ya know?" Cam began, trying to make small talk. "What's your deal with this place?" The Officer did not reply, and simply stared at him for a brief second, then refocused on the trail. Cam nodded fearfully. *Yeah okay, sure just don't acknowledge me then.* "This place used to be an amusement park," he began, his voice deep and authoritative. "I remember playing here as a kid." He sulked for a moment, his green jacket reflecting in the rain, then immediately focused back, suppressing all emotion. Cam slowed down a bit, tailing behind them. Hair stood up on his whole body as he remembered what he saw across the fence days prior. *Amusement park.. what.. Right, then what happened to it?...* Sasha whistled quietly, looking behind her, and beckoning for him to speed up. "Hehe," he laughed sheepishly under his breath as he joined back up with the group. She looked at him, a genuine concern that was not her normal stick of shaming him. *You good?* He nodded. "Well as far as we know," Sean chimed in, interrupting the awkward silence. "something, or someone.. uh- either- dug a tunnel into the facility. So that's our entrance point. Assuming it's still there. We found these weird papers that had…" The cop shot him a glance, half suspicious, and half curious. "But I mean, uh-" Sean trailed off, and Avery patted him on the back. *Alright why don't we stop talking now?* She smiled passive aggressively, but he knew she didn't mean any harm. Sasha opened her mouth to speak. "Well if I remember right, we've only got a few more miles and we'll be-… there." She stuttered, staring out at the muddy hill before them. It was completely compact, no entrances or holes in sight. Avery began to panic, looking at the mountain of crap where the entrance stood just hours prior. "No, I swear, it was right here! This was it! I swear, we're no-" - "I know," The Officer affirmed, scratching his chin.

Just then a stick snapped behind them. "Hey! The Officer yelled, showing a bit of fear. They waited, and he kept his hand at his hip, ready to draw his revolver at any moment. They sat, waiting, each of them afraid. Every tree in the wind looked like the shadow of a killer in that moment. The air was tense, threatening to jump out at any moment. But nothing came, and at last he lowered his stance, Exhaling in relief. "John," he said. "The names John." They all nodded. "So, you got a plan B?" Cam shrugged and consulted Sasha. "She's got a map." John nodded, and Sasha handed it over, her face looking a bit more timid than usual. "Fake rock, hahaha no one will ever realize," John read aloud, pointing at the map. Sean scoffed, and Avery held her mouth, trying not to burst out laughing. "You're telling me.. for the world's most powerful government.." John rolled his eyes. "Is.. stupid?" Cam shrugged. "Maybe." John didn't move, and still stood staring at the map in pure disbelief. "Well it won't hurt to check," he concluded, handing the map back to Sasha. "It also doesn't hurt if they're not versed in combat," Sean added. John tilted his head, acknowledging his statement, though based on his body language he did not like Sean one bit. "Alright," John confirmed, gesturing for them to follow him.

Their footprints landed softly as they made their way back through the rain. Sasha curled her lips, disgusted, and Avery looked at her, nodding. The ground was far more slippery than it was hours prior, and the hill of black inky mold now poured down and across the trail like a river. They nodded at each other. *The black mud.* Avery shivered slightly. Something about witnessing it outside of the enclosed tunnel felt wrong, and disturbing, the very essence of a place she shouldn't be. The flashlight peered into the gaps between the tree's making the rain shine ominously. John looked down at his watch. "Well, how about that?" He muttered, holding up his wrist watch. Cam shivered. "It's frozen.." John nodded cautiously. 'That it is. Avery furrowed her brow. *So ours stops, and yours does too? ... What is with this place?* "Alright then," John shrugged it off. "West."

Avery felt a tap on her shoulder, and turned around as the others kept walking forward. "Could we talk?" Sean asked, standing behind her sheepishly. She nodded. "He looks like he's been here for like.. way longer than a day. He's basically trespassing, granted we did that, sure, but no one's watching him.. there's no way the P.D approved this?" Avery shrugged. "I don't know.. nothing here actually.. feels right. But he's helping find the girl-" Sean nodded begrudgingly. "I know but if this.. Government.." - "M.L?" Avery asked, with no problem uttering the letters. "Yeah.. if they're supposed to be trafficking alien artifacts or whatever, who's to say they're not watching right now." Avery frowned. "I don't know." Sean nodded, finding nothing he was looking for. "Just.. look at the way he's walking, constantly checking around." Avery shrugged. "Looks like a typical police officer to me." Sean rolled his eyes.

"And what if he's trying to kill us?" He waited for a response, but Avery had nothing to say. "You two coming?" Nate yelled, and Cam stood next to him, with his arms crossed sarcastically. "Yep," Sean muttered.

"Well then," John exclaimed, pointing out at the rock ahead of them, illuminated by the faint beam of the flashlight, just down a steep grassy hill. "Fake rock," he stated aloud. "Fake rock," Cam repeated, and John nodded at him with a tiny hint of a smile. "Stay put," he commanded, making his way down the steep hill, and over to the rock. He pressed and pulled on it cautiously, but absolutely nothing came of it. "Cool," he muttered angrily. Avery raised an eyebrow, and joined him, pressing on the rock, and feeling around for any sort of lever. "Yep," she nodded. John stood up, annoyed. "Seems pretty real to me." Sean shrugged, puzzle solving not being his specialty. And Sasha stared ahead, her eye's laser focused on: *something.. Something about the trees.. They're growing brighter, it's the middle of the night, there's no-way that's the damn sun.* "Let me see the map again," John commanded. Snapping her out of her gaze. She handed it to him swiftly, but eyed him with uncertainty, whipping back around and focusing on the trees again. *Even brighter… Okay, what the hell?* "Hmmm," John nodded, having studied the map, reaching for the rock, and knocking on it a few times. It didn't budge. To this, he licked his lips, seeming to understand something. "Uh guys?" Sasha's voice echoed. *The trees grew brighter.* John's eyes widened as his silhouette became bright and a shadow cast forward in front of him. Sean balled his fists threateningly, keeping a defensive stance against the ominous bright light that now stood before them. The others hid. John stepped in front of him, gently pushing him aside, and drawing his gun, preparing to aim. Sean gave a nod of understanding, and ran back to hide with the others.

"POLICE! Come out with your hands up!" John yelled, a command from muscle memory. "Seems inappropriate, considering you're the one.. **trespassing**," a voice echoed from the bright light. It sounded disturbed, as if running through a faulty radio signal. "Who are you?!" John demanded, aiming his gun out. The group all watched from the undergrowth a few meters back. The voice laughed slightly. "Not important, good friend."

John gridded his teeth. He recognized the tone. "I have to go. But

believe me, I'll let Travis know you'd said hi." - "What…?" John

suddenly dropped to his knees, lowering the revolver in defeat. The

group watched, but none of them made a move. Then suddenly, in

an instant: John RAN into the light, yelling and swearing.

"WHERE ARE YOU, YOU SICK PIECE OF SHIT?!" The light

remained, and John joined it, becoming a black shadow inside of it.

"WHERE IS HE?!" He screamed, fighting nothing. "WHERE'S

MY FUCKING BROTHER?!" He demanded. Nothing came of it.

Suddenly, the light dimmed down into a single strange, dusty

beam, and John was left punching thin air. "Ahem," A man cleared

his throat, appearing from a tree. "John?" John turned around, and

immediately lowered his gun. "I thought I told you to stay away

from this place," The Man scolded, his voice intimidating, clearly

his superior. John shook his head. "I don-" The man waved him

off, looking disappointed. "Look, I get it. But it's as simple as this:

you're not authorized to be here." He shook his head

disapprovingly and started walking forward, stepping down the hill

with ease. His figure became more visible. He wore a simple, official uniform with a bullet proof vest. Avery squinted. The vest looked old, as if from a very long time ago. The man sighed, and waited a moment, studying John. He reached down, and behind his back, grabbing something, but stopped. Something caught his eyes as he stared behind him. Avery hid her face immediately, but he'd clearly seen her. He nodded curiously, and let go of his grip. "This is your last chance. Come here again, and I'll turn you over to *them*." Avery shivered, the word once again not sitting right. *Them.* "Look, I have reason to believe there's a little girl being trafficked in here," John spoke quickly, and loudly, not willing to be interrupted this time. The Man shook his head. "*This place* is none of your business." His eyes fell downwards, taken aback at the man's statement. "You KNEW, didn't you?!" He demanded. The Man remained where he was, no fear in his eyes. "Joh-" "YOU FUCKING KNEW?!" He yelled, getting up in his face. The man, once again, showed no signs of emotion. "THIS WHOLE T-" The man reached out, and grabbed him with strength that shouldn't have been possible, and threw him to the ground, grabbing his gun and crushing it in his hand, the firing pin falling off like a broken bone. "Go home," he commanded, a simple, yet threatening command, kicking John towards the others, who he knew well were all there. "Don't return," he warned, turning the now dim flashlight off, and disappearing into the darkness. None of them said anything, and John got up slowly, turning on his flashlight disparagingly, and taking the lead, heading back through the rain that awaited them. They followed him without question, fearful of what he'd do if they didn't.

"Go home," John relayed to the group, stepping into his car, mimicking his boss's stern, robotic attitude. The only thing stuck in his head. The only words he could utter. *"Go home."* Cam raised his hand to argue, and John shot him a death glance. He gulped, and slowly let it down. John sighed. "You need help getting back?" They looked around at each other for a moment collectively. The same thing in their eyes: *"We are home."* - "We're good," Cam answered, pretending to stretch in preparation to drive. He gestured to the van, and the group followed him. "Then don't let me see you again," John grumbled, stepping into his car, and flooring it into the woods with no headlights on.

The group made their way into the van, each taking their respective seats. They were silent for a couple minutes, the pitter-patter of the rain filling the void of sound. "Okay then," Sasha asked aloud. No one responded. They resumed their silence, and Cam nearly fell asleep. "It's late. Let's sleep, we'll talk in the morning," Sean mumbled. Avery nodded in agreement, and pulled open the van door, heading off to the slightly damaged tent without the others. Sean followed her close, and unzipped the tent to talk to her, but she was already sound asleep. He sighed, and laid down on the other side of the interior, drifting away fast. The others followed suit. Cam scoffed. *What a damn day.*

Chapter 10:

The walls were gray, and the ceiling was dry. A young Avery shivered, hiding *in the corner of her room. Words echoed through her head, The only words she understood. "My* room." *"My room." She smiled, staring up at the dots on the ceiling. Mold. "Stars!" She exclaimed, mesmerized. She looked around the room as she had countless times. It was circular, with two large glass doors at the front, pipes and wires scattered everywhere. The hallway outside was dark, and barely visible. The room itself was sterile, as if meant to keep something alive. "Avery!" A woman called, her voice muffled through the thick glass. Her figure appeared in the dark hallway beyond, and she knocked on the glass as if addressing some sort of animal. "Avery!" She called again. Avery did not budge, not wanting to address her existence. The woman smiled, her teeth glinting in the faint dark yellow light. "Avery, I brought you friends!" She called, holding up another figure's arm: a small, shivering little boy.*

Her eyes jilted open, and she rose up. It was freezing cold, and the tent shook violently in the wind. *Or from the snoring boys.* Avery smirked to herself. It was the perfect peaceful camping night. Freezing cold- *but like in that good way.* She stared at the others as they slept, considering how they'd react if she left her sleeping bag. She smiled. She had a lot to think about, and finally the time to do it. The moon peered behind the clouds far off in the distance, the pitter-patter of rain freshly impacting the flimsy ceiling. Owls *Who'd* in the far distance cheerfully. It was peaceful, nice to be awake. *Finally, some time to just relax.* She sighed, gathering all the unspeakable horrors of the day in her mind. *Ok.. so, terrifying whistle monsters exist, apparently Grey's fictional shadow government is real, and we've found a human trafficking victim. Could this trip get any cr-* **BOOM!** A flash of bright light exploded through the night sky, with the sound of a gunshot combined with an electrical cable. Avery startled back, her pupils freshly awake from the blast. She looked around cautiously, but the others were still sound asleep, and hadn't seen or heard a thing. *It had to have been lightning?* She tried to recall back, but the adrenaline made it difficult. *Bright flash of light, a deer in the distance.. Holding a stick? I...* She was at a loss for thoughts, the desire to sleep creeping in. She shook her head. *It's just lightning. I need sleep.* But the sound did not repeat itself, and the rain was suddenly not coming down at all. As if someone had flipped a switch on the weather. She fought to try to sleep, but to no avail. The owls in the distance grew louder, as if warning of something, communicating to each other. The world began to feel much colder than normal. *Something is definitely not right.* Suddenly her vision changed, her sleepy eyes darting open, the world growing only colder. *The face. Those weren't antlers… that was a mask. And the stick… that's a rifle.* A chill shot down her spine as the realization crept in. She thought back to the poster she'd found earlier.

"They're watching." She shivered, her senses now cranked to max. Something about the environment was different than before. Not the temperature, or the lack of rain, no. But there was something else. *Is that.. water?* The sound of water dripping and flowing could be heard just outside, and not just dripping. *Footsteps.* Avery realized, her eyes wide with terror. She began to reach under her sleeping bag, drawing her switchblade, which felt like grabbing dry ice. Then, suddenly, the sounds came to a dead stop outside, as if the world had been put on mute. *The water..? I could go check?* And then came the sound. A sound previously barren of meaning, but now filled to the brim with terror. One single whistle. The whistle of a chickadee, calling out for its friends. *I don't dare,* She thought, as the footsteps continued echoing all around the tent. She closed her eyes, begging to forget. But all that stared back in what was meant to be peace and darkness, was the man's face in the woods. *A mask, and a rifle. So… it's a human?* The whistles continued once more. But something was different about them. They were interrupted, and dry. Avery opened her eyes. *It is a human.* The footsteps grew louder as the person circled the tent. One single sound echoed out, and the footsteps stopped at the head of the door. It was silent for what felt like hours, Avery sat, begging in the darkness. Begging it wouldn't come in. *Human or not, we're fucked.* Time passed, she didn't know how long. After a long while, she exhaled slightly, and the footsteps exploded outside, coming nearer to the tent with each passing moment. She drew the knife, and bit down on the sleeping bag. Then it was silent again, the only thing audible being Cams snores, that could be heard from miles. A little too much… without warning, something echoed like a gunshot outside. A sharp, deep male voice. **"Huh?"** The door BURST open loudly with a BOOM, and Avery held the knife high, praying it was too dark for the man to see. Despite the sound, the others still slept sound asleep. The man simply stood there, staring. He was wearing what looked to be night vision goggles, and a jet black leather uniform. *Please go the fuck awayyy!* Avery begged, in a panicked musical number in her head, clenching her face. The man didn't move one inch. It was as if a statue had been standing inside the tent the entire time, just a few inches from her bed, from her safety. His greenish eyes glowed in the faint moonlight, blending his black clothed body. To the unsuspecting eye, he'd look like not a man at all, just a green pair of dotted eyes. Standing, alone forever in the darkness. Hours passed, and the man did not move. Nor did Avery. They just co-existed, staring at each other intently. She fought to stay awake, but the sleep deprivation didn't let her. *No.. don- it's.. not.. sa-* it was too late. Her eyes collapsed unwillingly. with the man blurring into darkness. *He began moving...*

A rooster croaked in the distance, loud *like a gunshot*. Cam rose first. "Do you wanna AR-A-AR-A-AROOO somewhere else, maybe?" Sasha chuckled, and reached across her sleeping bag, throwing on her jacket. Sean stretched, followed by Nate. "Wellll, how'd we sleep?" Cam asked, in his annoying VERY caring voice. Sean yawned. "Like a rock." Nate nodded. Still not speaking. "Well," Cam began. "I'm thirsty," he said, like a child complaining to a parent, unzipping the door and hopping into his sneakers. Sean looked over at Avery, who was still sound asleep. Sasha eyed him. "Rough night for her?" She asked. Sean shrugged. "I hope not."

She nodded. "Ohhhhhh… goooood," came a voice from outside. Sean raised an eyebrow, and sat up, cracking his back to go outside. "Ohh.. good," He echoed Cam, staring at the mess on the ground. Sasha snorted, and joined them. "Oh….." She frowned. "fuck." The ground below the table was completely flooded, and the gallon of water that was previously there was now completely empty. Sean seighed angrily, and turned around, kicking a pinecone. "Well what are we supposed to do now?!" Cam spat angrily. Sean shrugged, palming his face with regret. "We could go back?" Cam offered, but both Sean and Sasha shook their heads. "We have to rescue her." Sasha nodded. "Or at least try."

Cam sighed, but gave a thumbs up. "Well then we'd better hurry up before we die in the cold dry woods," he smiled passive aggressively. "One of you go wake sleeping beauty, I'm gonna salvage this," he ordered, determined, pointing at the muck on the ground below the empty container. Sean shook his head and blinked a few times, scraping his shoe off, then left entering the tent. "Okay," Cam exclaimed, Sasha rolled her eyes, but stopped mid way, something caught them. "Okay, we get the little girl, somehow fend against the shadow government," Cam muttered, swearing, pacing back and forth. "Cam!" Sasha called. "I'm sure that won't backfire, we'll just grab the toddler and somehow man-" - "Cam!" Sasha called again, snapping her fingers. "Then what, we just say yeah child hop in my handy dandy van! Hell, I probably have candy in he-" - "CAM!" Sasha yelled, smacking him across the face.. Cam snapped out of it, and his eyes focused on what she was pointing at. One perfectly round hole sat in the side of the water gallon, with burnt shreds around it, as if the plastic had been melted, yet everything around it was perfectly fine. *Wet wooden pine trees, relatively dry ground.* "What the…" Sasha shrugged, and felt around the hole. They exchanged glances. "That's…" Cam nodded. "Yep," he confirmed, confidently, drawing an invisible revolver. Sean's face emerged from the light blue tent, followed closely by Avery. She shook her head, and frowned angrily the moment she saw the commotion. "I saw someone last night," she said aloud. *Green synthetic eyes, gas mask all around.* Cam raised his hand politely like a child in a school. Avery squinted, confused, and shrugged. "Yeah?" He rose from his squat. "So uh.. all knowing Mrs. Avery, WHY didn't you FUCKING stop them?"

Avery simply looked at him, disappointed. "Well genius, clearly he had a gun." Cam scoffed. "Then why didn't we hear it?" Avery returned with an even more violent scoff.. "I did." - "Then why didn't you wake us up?!" She frowned. "It's.. complicated, okay?" *Gee I don't know, the weird demon asshat in my brain doesn't like me moving when it's having ptsd.* "Wha-" Cam began, about to go on a **Cam Rant.** Sean intervened. "Okay, okay stop. Look, it sucks, yeah. What's our next step?" Cam sighed again, and pointed at the infamous dark trail in the bushes, grabbing his backpack from the ground where he'd dropped it. "We hurry the hell up."

The sun rose in the dark clouds as they made their way to the infamous fake rock. But it was far from beautiful. What should've been a gorgeous mountain vacation sunrise was a dim, ominous *red dot* amongst the dark depressing clouds. As if its light wasn't able to shine through, a place unable to be inhabited. "So, how exactly do we open it?" Avery asked. She received no response. "Avery?" Nate asked. "Yeah?" She replied, gently, confused. *Well, you, my friend havent talked for several hours.* She narrowed her eyes. *Or yesterday..* "If they shot the water to stop us.." He began, struggling to form his words. "Wouldn't that be a warning to stay out?" Cam nodded, in agreement with him. "They didn't kill us before, they clearly saw us with John.." Avery shook her head, but Cam interrupted her. "Who's to say third times not the.. charm?" He asked. Sean and Avery shrugged simultaneously, and Sasha curled her lip, offended.. "For the sake of another human it's worth it," Avery replied, after much thought. Cam bit his lip. "I hope you're right." - "Okay," she sighed. "So last time we tried knocking on it." The group nodded. "We tried feeling for a handle." They all nodded again. "Welp, I'm shit out of ideas." She shrugged, and Cam chuckled just slightly, sharing her humor. They emerged over the hill, the mountains towering ominously, with the dark dripping trees below, like ink drops, stragglers **left in time**. "Well," Avery gestured, echoing John from the previous night. The group nodded again. It looked as though it hadn't changed one bit. *Which honestly made perfect sense.* She reached down, and around again, looking for any sort of handle. Nothing came. Sean joined her, kicking at it hard. It didn't budge. It was a rock. Cam shrugged. "Beats me." Sasha stood there, thinking. "Maybe it is a fake rock… just not a door?" She offered. Sean squinted at her, taken aback. But then his face changed. "I mean.. you could be r-"

Something metal clanked in the distance loudly, and a crow jumped into motion, flying away frantically. Avery cocked her head, and Sean rushed to her side in protection. But she brushed him away, drawing her switchblade. The others waited, each standing their ground. "What the hell was th-" The horrific metal scraping continued echoing. Sean raised his fists, and backed one foot up. The trees ahead did not move, quite the opposite. But ones behind them did, all around them, as if a sudden hurricane had just turned on. Avery and Sasha's hair blew in their faces, and they struggled to keep sight. Suddenly the environment grew dark, as if the sun had just been blocked out, not just the distance, but the small mile wide circle they stood in. The trees grew black like ink splotches, the weeds and ground turning a sickly greenish black. Avery's eyes widened as she quickly looked around, a mix between confusion and horror in her eyes. "SOLAR ECLIPSE!" Nate shouted with delight, and Cam clapped his hand around his mouth, grinding his teeth. Avery shook her head. *God I wish.*

The metal scraping continued, an awful sound like a dying animal. They peered ahead curiously, half wondering what it was, half terrified of knowing *what* exactly it was. Sean eyed Avery, and she shrugged. Simply staring forward cautiously, her hair blowing softly in the wind. *Why does every single thing in this place have to defy physics?* As if in response, the ground beneath them shook violently, and the dark fog drew closer, surrounding them. Cam began coughing. "WHAT THE HE-" his breath stopped short.

Something emerged in the distance, rusty brown metal, erupting like lava out of the ground. Avery braced herself, and took a deep bre- *why can't I breathe?* She looked around briefly. Everyone else seemed to be experiencing the exact same thing, each grabbing their throats desperately. She began to feel light-headed as the air grew colder. *WHY CAN'T I FUCKING BREATH?!* The oxygen was literally depleting around them. They all looked at eachother now, panic in their eyes. Sasha clenched her chest, and fell to the ground. Avery fought to hold her breath, the only thing she could do. Sean joined her, his expression fierce but determined. The distant thing continued to rise, and the fog grew darker. The only thing now visible: the rusty sharp metal in the distance, its egregious sound the only thing that could be heard, next to the frantic heart beats of the group. three more sides joined the rusty beam, a box, like an elevator, rising quickly. Cam knelt down to check on Sasha, trying to remain calm. But he did not get back up. Collapsing with her. Avery's knees buckled, and Sean forced himself to keep standing, pain in his bloodstream.

The scraping stopped, and the metal fully emerged, the world growing blurry as they desperately tried to stay awake. It was then that a familiarly dark, inky figure stepped out of the metal box. Avery shivered, the only mechanism her body had left. The air was freezing, and she could feel her skin literally flaking into ice. The figure looked curiously at the group, and coked its head. *A puppy, whose only purpose was to pillage and kill.* Sean angled his gaze in one last angry gesture, relinquishing control, and collapsing with the others. Yet, somehow, Nate stood, tall and proud, as if not even affected by the lack of extremely vital oxygen. Avery could barely see, down on her knees, her body giving out. But she fought with all she had to stay awake. The figure walked forward calmly from the metal box, gently, sadistically, as if its prey didn't even possess the ability to run. *And it didn't.* Its body was barely distinguishable, partly due to Avery's vision, and partly due to how well it blended in with the murky dark trees. Despite her determination, her vision blanked, and she felt herself fall on her stomach. *You want to die? Don't give up!!* She yelled at herself internally, and her vision restored just barely, now on all fours. The ringing in her ear wouldn't stop, replacing her entire world. The figure was directly in front of her, withdrawing something of a knife from its inky black body. It rose for the kill, but stopped. Staring into her eyes. Though its own eyes weren't visible in the slightest. Once again it cocked its head, looking surprised, shocked, and nodded smoothly, more human than animal. **They** stayed like that for a long moment staring at each other. She: barely awake, and him: studying her like a long lost science experiment. Though it had no face, it was clear it was no longer a threat. *He knows me.* She thought, and her final sliver of persistence left, sending her down, collapsing violently on her head with the others.

The figure snapped its fingers, and the world resumed to normal, no longer a dark oxygen deprived nightmare. It nodded once more, curiously staring at her unconscious body, something of shock in its now **emerald green** eyes. Then it leaped backwards in a flip, and took off running like a cheetah into the woods, tearing through the trees and the bushes.

"V-r-y!"… "Ev-er-v…."

The world blurred into view, sharp, and contrasted. *Friends. Awake… Safe,* she concluded, resting her shoulders. "Avery?" Sean's voice bled into existence. She nodded. "I'm good." Sean sighed, relieved. "Well, about time." A voice echoed strangely- her head had not fully recovered. She sat up. "Ready?" Cam asked, impatiently waiting, tapping his foot next to the others, who were all awake. "Yeah.. sure," She affirmed, slowly getting up. The metal box structure still stood in the distance, it hadn't moved. "I think…" Cam began. "That's our ticket down." Avery shrugged in protest, but the rest of the group nodded, having apparently already discussed her concerns while she was asleep.

They let him take the lead temporarily, cautiously. Avery squinted her eyes as they walked closer. *Is it getting… bigger?* She brushed it off, but in the back of her mind she knew fully that the metal had grown. "Huh," Sasha exclaimed, feeling around the old metal rust. "It's made out of copper." She reflected, curiously. Cam made a face, mocking her. "Erm, it's actually made of copper." Sasha rolled her eyes. "Y'all see a button anywhere?" Sean asked, feeling around the structure. "Since when are you a Texan?" Cam demanded. Sean rolled his eyes, and continued to feel around the metal. Avery looked around at her people. She nodded, Sasha was slightly trembling, Nate was biting his lip anxiously, Sean was breathing heavily, and Cam was standing uselessly, smirking. *Yep, everything is right in the world.*

"Anything?" Sasha asked. They all shook their heads collectively. "Well, I see a chain, we could cut that." Cam suggested. Sasha shot him a glance, and he shrugged dramatically. "What, it would go down?" She rolled her eyes. "Ohh," Nate exclaimed, finding a small, rusty old valve. They group fell silent. Avery stood still. *Alright, so we-*

"So what the fuck was that thing?" Cam demanded. There was a collective sigh, not vocal but they could feel it, relived they could actually talk about it. "I have absolutely no idea," Sasha replied, simply. "I guess.. just another crazy…thing.. this place houses," Sean responded, echoing her tone. Cam smiled passive-aggressively. "So we can just have a weird ink monster say fuck oxygen and knock us unconscious but that's totally fine right, that's *PERFECTLY* normal, right?!" Sean furrowed his brow. "Let's focus on the girl, then we can ruminate on whatever we want." Cam nodded begrudgingly, "Alright fine, but if you ask me we've seen enough evidence to NOT go down there again." They were all silent again for a minute, then Sean shook his head, and joined Nate to look at the valve. Avery smiled awkwardly, moving her hands as if giving a speech. "We're only going because it's another human, once we find her we'll leave and never come back." She nodded to herself confidently, though admittedly that was not the only reason she wanted to go back down. *You're a lier. You want answers.* She frowned at the thought. *I know. But we can't leave her down there.* Something in her mind shook her, making her head twitch ever so slightly. *Don't pretend like you care...* She felt a tear drop from her eye, but forced it away, shaking her head and getting back to the mission at hand. "Okay, so it's a manual," Sean announced, his voice bouncing off the metal pillars that formed the elevator, and into the distant woods. Sasha coughed out something of a laugh. "What does that even mean for an elevator?" Sean shrugged. "Well, it's attached to a chain, so I guess we're *manually* going down." Sasha sighed, but nodded. "And who's to say there's a way out?"… Sean looked down for a second as they all looked at him, thinking. "Well, the shadow, uh, man managed to get it back up." Avery made a face of concern. "You mean the mysterious, shadowy, all powerful demon that just knocked us unconscious?" Sean gave a confident thumbs up, accompanied by a *not* so confident nod. "Okay then," Avery replied, the only thing she could think of. *Very reassuring.* She opened her mouth to talk again, but Cam interrupted her. "Where the hell does one even get a chain that's like a mile long?!" Sean shrugged, and couldn't help but laugh. "Maybe it's an alien artifact too." Cam scoffed, and Sasha pushed him aside. "Think on the bright side, if we ever need a mile long fucking chain, we've got one." Avery sighed, but nodded out of habit anyway. Cam bit his lip, and hopped in the elevator. "Well, I'd rather not die of dehydration, so let's make this quick." - "Alright," Sean responded, and gave a thumbs up to Nate, who began cranking the valve. It didn't budge. "Well?" Cam demanded. "You wanna try?" Sean barked, impatiently, attempting to crank it backwards again. This time it allowed movement, but just barely.

As time passed, they took turns, each watching as they all went down, the light of the surface leaving, and mossy molded concrete following them, growing more and more, spider webs and tree roots in between. At last they made it to what seemed like a half-way point, and Sean gave a firm tug on the valve, to test their hope of reversing what they'd just done. "Ah!" Sasha yelled, the chain had snapped, resuming their descent a couple hundred feet downwards. They screamed for several seconds, but it came to a screeching, *some would call safe*, halt at the very bottom.

"Well, what now?" Cam demanded, disapprovingly, embracing the impact. Avery shrugged, the falling elevator having not even fazed her in comparison to everything else. "Let's just hope the fake rock isn't fake on the other side." They nodded, and Sasha withdrew the map. "I know where we are." With that, she took off running without another word. Sean reached out in caution, but she was already far away from them. Cam leaped off the elevator, following her into the darkness, and Nate followed quickly after. "So much for smart," Sean sighed, turning towards Avery for guidance. She couldn't help but laugh. "Hey, they're alive. And so are we."

The lights burned brightly once again- artificial stinging LED's, harmful, almost as if designed to deter emotion. The group emerged frantically from the hallway they'd been in just a day earlier. Sean knelt down, glancing back briefly. "Alright, let's make this quick," Sasha whispered sharply. Sean nodded, wearing a determined, yet pensive look. "They could be back at a moment's notice, we gotta work fast." Avery edged around a pillar, peering into the ominous glass box ahead of them. The girl was right where she was before, sound asleep. She nodded, waiting to the side, not entirely sure of how to help. The room was still cold, with visible condensation in the air pouring into the walls, and through the loud open vents above. The group made their way cautiously around the glass box, observing its ins and outs. "How do we get her out?" Avery whispered. "Dunno," Sean called back, studying the height of the wall. "Nate." Nate turned around in response, breaking out of his "super-stealth-crouch". - "Think you could scale that wall?" He studied it quickly, then shook his head sadly, straddling the corner where a metal support pillar stuck out. Cam echoed his tone. "And then what, throw her over?" He shook his head, planting his feet on the other side and peering around. "No, there's no way they got her in there without it opening, there's gotta be a way to open the glass." Nate nodded confidently, staking his "cool" stance. "The question is… how?" Cam stared at him blankly. "Yep." *Yes, cheesy horror movie character, it is.* "Alright, well.." Sasha whispered, in imminent distress, backing up against the wall to take a wider look. Avery and Sean exchanged glances through the glass window, each on the opposite side. He smiled for a brief moment, and she smiled back. The world felt paused to her briefly once again. Everything a void of light and happiness. Sean felt his cheeks flush. *This. This is what i mi-*

"Get down!" Cam snapped, pushing Avery into a protection pose with his arm behind a pillar.

"I don't know.. kids breaking in again?"...... "Why's that our job, make cleanup crew do it."... "yeah well they ain't dead yet.".... "let them mind wipe, you really wanna kill another kid?"..... .... "What if I said I do?"... "Hehe."

"Stay low," Sean commanded, whispering sharply back to the others. Avery shivered at the guards words *"**again**." - how many innocent children have they murdered in cold blood?* She shook her head, and craned her neck forward, focusing, a sudden need for revenge awake inside her. Sasha planted her feet, and broke into a sprint. "Sasha do-" Sean reached for her, but it was too late once again. *Fucking great.* A disturbing clown-like laughter broke out through the chamber. Sean zoned in intently on the guard, who was now at the door, stepping ever closer. Avery ducked her chest down desperately, trying to squeeze herself under the glass box.

She stared up, not daring to take a breath. The ground cracked

slightly, and the sound of the guard's leather uniform spinning

towards her direction echoed through the room. She bit her lips.

That laughter, that pride... She shook her head confidently. *That's

no fish market guard. This guy's out to kill.* She forced her eyes

shut keeping her legs out for mobility, hoping to god once again

that the guard would miss her position. The bottom frame of the

glass container stung, cutting sharply into her back. She gritted her

teeth, desperate to survive. *He WILL kill us if we get caught,* she

reminded herself. *There's living proof of that.*

"Avery..." Her eyes rocketed open. **"Oh Sean.."** She tried to slow

her now loud echoing heartbeat, and forced her face closed, her

head up against the glass, holding her breath. *He knows our

names..* **"come out... come out, and..."** the guard paused,

priming his rifle. **"And I'll make it quick."** His footsteps echoed

louder and louder. Avery let out a slight tiny breath of desperation

through her nose, and the man spun around instantly. **"Fine then.."**

She began to scooch along the floor, her jean buttons creaking loudly as the guard's footsteps got closer. **"Oh? Hiding, are we?"** He laughed, a deep disturbing voice that sounded excited. A hunter, hyped about its kill, its prey. Avery bit down hard. *Now or never.* She took a microscopic deep breath, and started to maneuver around the glass box behind the other pillar. *Stay low, just stay low, and stay slow.* She lowered herself to the ground, scrunching her face. She could feel her own sticky blood merging with her cotton flannel, the threads tearing at her new opened wound. Her body began to physically shake, staring at what now lay before her. A single green line had appeared in the distance, and was actively making its way to her. *That's exactly what I didn't need.* She fought hard to keep her breath held, staring into the distance at the laser, which was now slightly closer to her. **"Fine,"** the guard's voice echoed out, rather annoyed. The green laser began to approach faster, each passing moment one single *frame* of safety. *Okay just to the right a bit. Just a bi-...* She peered out, her face mortified. In the distance, directly to her right was now another tiny purple laser. *That's EXACTLY what I did not need, for the second goddamn time.* **"You know I'm just waiting.."** Avery gritted her teeth. **"Makes it more fun."** She shook her head, curling her nose at the guard's voice. *Fun to give me time to escape? Perfect!* She bit her tongue hard, rotating around the pillar, the laser following her directly. Shivering, she cracked her neck silently, and peered out the glass to the other side. To her surprise, a face stared back. It was distant, and hard to see, but there was no mistaking it. *Sean?* He nodded, his face in a battle pose. Avery looked away, back at the guard, but he did not. She glared back to find him still staring, his green eyes glowing from the purple laser. *Why isn't it affecting him?* "Do you trust me," He mouthed. She nodded, her face matching his. Sean raised his arms in a cacophony. "Make some noise!" He mouthed. Avery bit her lip, but nodded back. "So what's your thing," She asked, her signature smirk illuminated by the two approaching lasers. "I mean you clearly love keeping little girls in basements so…" She chilled her teeth, laughing genuinely. The guard rounded the corner, now pursuing her at a very fast pace, the laser following him. *Cmon Sean..* "Hey I mean, I don't judge. Well, Actually yes I do. Who's your boss anyway? Some kind of pedophile kingpin?" - **"I'll SHOW YOU!"** The guard yelled, but he remained at the same pace, the green laser now bouncing around the glass box as he walked. Avery ducked her face uselessly, as The guard's silhouette rounded the corner, giving her a tiny window of opportunity to get a good look at him. He held his rifle high as he trudged towards her. He wore a black gas mask with the same black uniform to match, tiny green dots glowing where eyes should've been from the reflection of the laser in the glass. His face *itself* was not visible, crammed into the mask *as if his body matter had been modified.*

He let out another disturbing laugh, and aimed the laser directly into her eyes. It stung, and she let out a cry of pain,The world clouding into a blur in her eyes. His mouth was invisible, but it was clear that he was smiling. **"Or maybe I won't."** Avery forced her eyes shut as The guard primed his rifle, he immediately pulled the trigger, and Avery ducked as a last attempt.

But his gun had not fired. "Argh!" " Sean yelled, as he struggled to choke the man out, the rifle now a strangling device in his hands. The guard doubled over, and grabbed Sean's jaw, ripping downwards. Sean tried to counter it, but The guard shoved his arm in between the rifle and his neck, grabbing it and smashing in Seans shoulder with the butt.

 "Nice.. try, kid!" The guard yelled, as he broke free from Sean's grip. He recovered quickly, and primed the rifle immediately at Avery. **"Alright, say hi the cre-"** The pipes above exploded with water as someone landed directly on The guard's head, full force, a 190 pound teenage boy, directly to the skull. *Nate* smiled, and The guard collapsed, a fresh splatter of blood now on the floor.

"Clear," he announced, and Cam emerged from a wall panel, the same panel the purple laser was emitting from. "Who are you, spiderman?" Nate rolled his eyes. "Oh, I'm sorry, it's only like we were about to die. I saved us!" Cam shrugged. "Yeah, pretty sure Spider-Man does that a lot." Nate smirked, and high-fived him. "Damn right he does."

Cam sighed in relief. "Everyone okay?" Avery nodded, her heart still racing. Nate gave a thumbs up. "Sean?" Cam asked, looking over at him. "Yep," He said, struggling in pain. He revealed his shoulder. It had a decent chunk of flesh taken out of it, bleeding alarmingly. Avery let out an exhale of fear, and rushed to him. "I'll be okay Av, don't-" Sean's face went from angry, to worried, to confused, to happy in an instant, as he felt her arms wrap around him. They sat there for a moment, Nate and Cam both rolling their eyes. *Lovebirds.* Avery smiled, resting her chin on his good shoulder. Then she reached to his back, and withdrew the katana, which he'd handily mounted on his back. He nodded as she held it in front of him, and its blue healing glow immediately took effect. This time, it was more powerful, almost feeding off her energy. They both smiled, both in pain, but both happy to share it. She rested her head on his other shoulder as the sword healed it, Her brunette hair getting in the way of his face. He laughed, enjoying every bit of it. Cam cleared his throat. "Alright you two, I'm glad your fairytale ass sword gave you love powers, but we need to get our priorities straight." Avery glared at him, but nodded in agreement. "Where's Sa-" - "Hello again," Came a voice from the hall, snarky, smart, braggy, and female. "Oh, well, yeah that makes sense, sure," Cam muttered, but he was clearly happy to see her nonetheless. "Where'd you go?" Sean demanded. "I'm sorry, how about a thank you? Did you really think Cam possessed anything resembling a brain enough to turn on that laser?" Cam shrugged, jeering at her. *Yeah, well I'm great at turning.. Other.. Things.. O-* he sighed, accepting defeat. "Security," Sasha replied, finally. "I sent an alert that we're at the complete other end of the facility, which by the way is literally HUNDREDS of miles away from here." She brushed her hair away, smiling with pride. "Anyway, for whatever reason, that laser turned on when I activated it. Turns out they got some crazy tech. Like, light speed train kind of tech." No one reacted, as none of them understood: *What the hell does that mean?* Cam shook his head. "Okay well that's all great, but back to the task at hand. How do we get her the fuck out?" Sasha raised her hand like a giddy school girl. "Well the interface wasn't hard to use, just hard to sneak over to." Cam dropped his hands to his knees, slapping them in confusion. "So what, we just James Bond our way in? Activate a switch in the vents?" Sasha rolled her eyes. "Yes, as a matter of fact. That's exactly my plan.. and it's gonna work, thank you very much," She finished, pushing Cam's face away. "Alright, one of you is gonna have to stay here while I do a sequential order of button presses." She paused, tapping the control panel at the wall. "Just whatever you do don't-" The glass SHATTERED behind them, and the entire chamber collapsed loudly. "Touch.. it." She put a palm to her face.

 The culprit emerged standing proudly, his arms looking bigger due to the shattered glass. "Well, if it ain't broke." Cam slapped his face, "I don't know man, that looks pretty "broken" to me." Nate rolled his eyes, walking out of the newly shattered frame. "Reminds me of your bank account," His voice came into hearing distance. "Sh, guys not the time." Avery snapped, and Sean nodded. A new member stared at them, eyeing them side to side, her hair falling in her face. "Hey, it's okay," Avery smiled at the little girl, who was cowering behind her bed, if you could even call it that. "We're gonna to get you out of here," Sean assured, keeling to her height. "The.. outside?" The little girl asked gently, her voice was shy and timid. Cams face curled, genuinely disturbed a bit. "Uh.. yeah, the outside. We want to take you there." Sean smiled, shrugging a bit as Sasha eyed him, nodding.

*"What are we just supposed to just trust them?" The third **brother** asked, resting his hand on an old wooden house. "I see no other way," the second brother responded. "Where would we even have room?" The second brother shrugged, staring out into the sharp pine trees that surrounded them. "**They'll** provide the room." The third brother took his hand off the house, and brushed his **long brown** hair out of his face. "Make a deal with the devil, he says, and we're just supposed to trust it?" the first brother interjected, waving his hand to the side. "You wanna end the war or not? I don't care what it is, if it means an end, I'm in." The third brother shook his head, angling it to the corner, still skeptical. "You could use some time, **Garrison.** We'll meet you up ahead." Garrison nodded, and the two left **the third** to ruminate.*

Chapter 11

Shadows loomed ominously through the halls as they guided the little girl. "Hey so uh, what's your name?" Avery asked her, grinning as genuinely as she could. "It's…" The girl thought for a moment, looking up at the ceiling as she walked next to them. "It's Pearl!" She concluded, proudly, though still keeping her head down shyly. "That's a really nice name, Pearl," Avery replied, while looking at Sasha, her face of confusion and chaos. *How the fuck do we get out of here?* Sasha shrugged with her eyes, and glanced around at the hall, trying to gain her bearings. "Okay, west, north and back out the stairs." Sasha nodded, taking the lead. Cam shrugged, looking around the dark ominous hall.

Time passed as they made their way through the facility, checking carefully at every corner, following Sasha with every footstep. "So, uh.. Peal," Cam began, smiling awkwardly with half his mouth. "Could you maybe, uh, tell us what this place is or… why you're here?" Avery shot him a warning glance. *We don't know if that's a good idea.* Pearl furrowed her miniature brow, seeming to gather her thoughts. "Uh, well, a scary man told me I would hurt my parents if I stayed where I was." Sean and Avery exchanged concerned glances. "Mommy and daddy didn't want me to go, but they didn't let *them* keep me," she added, her face sulking a bit. Cam nodded, his eyes fiery in the orange light above. *Typical secret government assholes.* Just then, Sasha stopped dead in her tracks, backing against the wall quickly.

```
"Yeah, well they're moving around back here
and that girls missing. We either kill them
or they make it out."
```

The group joined Sasha against the wall cautiously, hearing the woman's voice echoing down the hallway threateningly. Sean looked at Nate, hatching a plan. Avery shook her head, and gently hugged Pearl, shielding her from the two boys' plans. Though admittedly she loved the idea they came up with. Sean nodded, and they moved Sasha out of their way gently, who looked at them, offended. Sean peered back, and Nate gave a thumbs up.

"Yewwwhooo," he whistled, exiting the hall and running quickly

into the next one. The woman gasped, grabbing her pistol, and

breaking into a run. Sean waved his arms around crazily and the

woman ran towards him, her pistol primed and ready. "GET OV-"

Nate appeared, grabbing her neck from behind with one arm, and

yanking the pistol out of her hand with the other, dropping it to the

ground. Sean smirked in her face, and waved "bye-bye" as she fell

to the ground, unconscious. Cam nodded, though his face looked a

little disturbed. "Is she.." - "Nah, just out cold," Sean responded,

reading his mind and fist-bumping Nate.

Avery let go of Pearl, and they continued moving down as if

nothing had happened. "Okay, this should be.. it." Sasha's

enthusiasm drained as she stared at the sealed shut wall that was

supposed to be their way out. She dropped her hands to her knees.

"I don't, what?" Avery sighed, checking their safety, looking down

the halls in both directions. "We can find another way, it's okay."

She rested a hand on her shoulder. Sasha nodded, standing up tall,

immediately getting *back on the horse.* "Okay, well, any ideas?"

Sean shrugged. "There's downstairs, and there's here. That's all we know." Cam nodded disappointedly. "We could always go back downstair-" Sasha fired beams of threats into his eyes, and he immediately backed down.

Avery paced back and forth next to Pearl, who looked confused and scared. "Let's just keep going along here, there's bound to be more exits." The group nodded collectively, and continued down the hall. "I heard a weird man say there's another door," Pearl interjected. Sasha's face brightened. "That's good, Pearl, do you remember where he said it was?" She shrugged, her shadow moving rigid in the white light above. "*The dungeon* is too big to know," She replied, sadly. Avery nodded. "Yeah. Yeah it is."

"So, uh.. where did you used to live?" Avery asked, as they walked down the long thin corridors. "I don't know. I don't remember," Pearl replied. Avery felt a chill down her spine. *"I don't remember."* the words didn't sit right with her. "Do you.." She glanced at Sean, crafting her approach cautiously. "Do you remember much about what's.. out there to begin with?" Pearl shrugged. "'No," she replied, simply. Their faces grew sour, listening to how she'd been treated. "I've been out before, but they stopped me. They always stop me." - "It hurt, it hurt badly," She added. Sean's face curved downwards, anger setting in. He looked at Avery. *Okay now I really want to take them down.* She nodded, sharing his sentiment. "Oh good," Sasha smiled genuinely, lighting up with joy. "West exit 99-3, that's the fake rock." Cam echoed her attitude. "What was the specification on that exit again?" He asked, holding back a very obvious chuckle. Sasha sighed, knowing instantly what he wanted.

"Fake rock, hahaha, no-one will ever suspect this." Cam, as expected, burst into laughter. The others followed more gently, and Pearl joined in, not fully understanding the humor but happy to laugh with her new friends either way.

"Hmm," Sasha scratched her chin, glancing around the map, amused. "Front yard, Back yard, Side yard, hahaha we're so rich moth-" She scoffed, staring at Pearl. "Uh, the page cuts off," She concluded, not wanting her to learn some new vocabulary. Nate looked around the hallways, something in his face unhappy. "You good?" Avery mouthed. He nodded, but was clearly anxious about something. Avery stepped to the side for a moment to talk to him. He released the bite on his upper lip, and stared directly at her, as if activating a different, more intelligent version of himself. "They're supposed to have an army, yet only one person has come. Something isn't right." She nodded. "Yeah, I don't know. But let's get her to safety first." Sasha smiled. "Well, fake rock it is!" She announced, and she and Cam took the lead.

They emerged now, in a large square room, with a ramp taking up half the space, and a second story just a few feet above where the ramp led, a door just off to the right. "Fake rock." Cam stated, pointing proudly at the large metal vault-like door in front of them. Sasha nodded. "Should be." Avery shot a quick glance at Sean, concerned. *I'm not the only one who hears that right?* He angled his eyebrow, acknowledging her. The sound of tapping echoed all around them, as if something was rapidly hitting the ground. Sean looked around for the source, and at last his face relaxed, seeing a large metal fan on the ceiling, spinning quickly. Avery gave a thumbs up, but the sound direction didn't add up.

"Alright, there ya go," Nate smiled, trying to wrench open the door. It didn't budge even slightly. "Uhh, we're gonna need more than that," Sasha lectured him gently, running up the ramp to a massive control panel. "Okay," She inhaled, muttering to herself as she searched through functions, typing on an old keyboard. "Wall, battery, trains?… huh. Ah, door." Avery showed an "okay" with her hand at the sound of the good news, but still kept her eye on the fan cautiously. Pearl looked around at them gratefully, as steam blew out of the giant door, activating inner hydraulics. "I don't… I don't know how long it's been," She coughed up, tearing up at the view of the trees outside. They all smiled, except for Avery and Sean. She gestured at the wall to the side. *I'm gonna check it out.* He nodded, and kept watching the room. She walked decently far out through several twisting hallways. *Well, the weather outside improved.* A chill shot down her spine, and her eyes widened. *Wait.. weather…trees?! We're a mile underground. How in god's name..* Pearl began stepping forward with a smile on her face, and Avery looked up frantically. She twisted her head, disgusted. What looked to be gas emitters were directly above them. She glanced at

Sasha and Cam. *What? They're not this stupid. Sasha never actually smiles?!* The tapping noises shifted their source, coming from the upper part of the ramp now, appearing to be getting louder. "Well, you want to do the honors?" Sasha asked kindly. She stopped suddenly, completely. Her eyes went gray, and her skin grew cold, pale blue. "Pear-" She jumped back to life. The excited little girl she just was. Yet somehow it didn't seem right, as if the body she was in didn't belong to her. Pearl turned back and smiled at them, her freedom just inches ahead. Avery Sprinted back, yelling, but the soundproof walls of the hallway concealed her desperate cries. She was fast. *But not fast enough.*

Pearl looked back at them with grateful eyes. "Thank you," she choked up, and a tear shed from her eye. Cam nodded, and Sasha smiled at her, joined by Nate, who looked peculiarly queasy. Pearl smiled back, feeling a million different emotions at once. They all watched as she took a deep breath, and stepped forward. "UY– DOn- IT-" Random cries from a *random* person echoed through the halls. Sean looked up. *The fan blades were no longer spinning...* "SEAN!" Avery yelled, emerging back into the room, the other glancing back at her confused. As they saw the horror on her face, they began to echo her as the stupid flaw of realization washed across all of their faces. "WAIT!" Sasha screamed, and Cam joined Avery and Sean, sprinting to Pearl as fast as humanly possible. But she wasn't listening. She'd reached the door, and slowly took a step into the sun. The group charged forward with all their might, fighting with everything they had to catch her.

She felt her bear foot touch fresh soil, and she looked up with hope. The sun was beautiful, illuminating her new freedom. Her world was aligning with new purpose. She smiled taking in the beauty of it all. *I'm free.* She took a breath, and smiled even more, she'd accomplished her life mission. She was free.

Avery lunged forward without warning to grab her shoulder, but it was too late. The sun shone bright on Pearl's face as she let out a sigh. She smiled, then a loud crack sounded behind her, and then there was nothing.

She stopped in her tracks, time froze for a moment, *but only for a moment*. She collapsed, her body falling limp to the ground in defeat. Her eyes were no longer bright with hope, yet her smile was set in stone on her face. She hit the ground with a metallic bang, but it was followed with a thunk of soft dirt. half her body in the building, and half on "the outside" She rested still, the last bit of life gone, as if never alive to begin with. Just then the sun shut off, the mountains in the distance through the door turned into pixels on a screen, and the beautiful world outside went completely blank, a static sound following it. Her blood pooled around her in seconds, pouring out of her mouth and head, and flowing down to the floor. Yet she still smiled. She was free.

Avery's ears rang in pain, her vision blurred, as she looked in horror. She had no words, no thoughts. Nothing. Sean's mouth was open, frozen in time, pure terror burned on his face. They all stared bewildered at her body, her blood slowly reaching their feet. Avery heard a man's voice boom out, but could barely make it out through the adrenaline and ringing ears. *"S- E..- Ve..- Other.. Curas."* They all stood silent, frozen for what felt like an eternity.

An eternity of having a little girl's bloody dead body burned into your head. At last, Sean moved his head, and it searched the room, finding someone in the corner. Avery finally came to her senses, and followed his gaze. Her vision cleared. A man was leaning against the wall holding a rifle between his legs. He wore jet black a collared soldier uniform, weapons strapped to various places around him. His lips curved in a sick smile as he watched the group stare with desperation, all the more infuriating with his scrawny, sharp face, and a crooked nose.

Sean snapped out of his shock, suddenly accepting their tragic reality. He reached for the katana, and in an instant he was rushing towards the man, blade in hand, shouting at the top of his lungs. The man wasn't scared, and picked up his rifle, aiming it straight at Sean's head. "Wouldn't do that if I were you," He lectured, a tone of satisfaction in his voice. Sean slowed to a stop, and glared at the man with pure fiery hatred fresh in his eyes. "Pass it to me", The man demanded, more firmly this time. Sean stood where he was, his jaw clenched staring into the man's eyes. *Show no fear. I'm not backing down. I'll slit his throat and bite off his face. I'll tear into his lungs so he dies of suffocation. No, dying is too good for him. I'll cut out his tongue so he can't talk, and slowly shove needles into him for years. I won't let him die.* Sean snapped out of his trance. *What the hell are you thinking? Where is this coming from?* He shook his head violently, shocked he was even capable of those thoughts. "Last chance, little sneaker." *Sneaker? What's that supposed to mean?* The man began to pickup his rifle, a cruel smile appearing on his face. Avery darted her eyes between the man and Sean, as The man placed his finger on the trigger. Sean raised the katana. *He's not backing down..* Avery's instincts kicked in "SEAN!!!" She screamed, and his eyes widened, dropping the katana to the floor, landing with the same metallic clank as Pearl. "Ah, a Dike." The man dropped his smile, looking more so disappointed than scared. "Kick it over," he commanded, annoyed. Sean glared at him, his teeth gritted so hard they might've broken. "Fuck you," he spat, as he kicked the handle forward. The blade spun, by some delightful miracle: hitting The man's shoe, stabbing into his foot and up his leg. To Sean's surprise, it turned a violent dark black, and The man yelped, falling to the ground, still clenching his rifle by the barrel. The trigger was too far away, and the sword took its effect, for some reason: doing the opposite of its

norm, weakening the man severely. Life drained from his eyes, but

he reached with all his effort into his pocket and pulled out a

syringe. After struggling with it, he shoved it into the vein of his

bicep, and squeezed the trigger, breathing with limited breaths.

His fingers let go, dangling limp, and the syringe dropped to the

ground, his chest stopped moving. Sean took the opportunity, and

ran for the rifle, step by step, his new purpose. Avery watched him,

dumbfounded and frozen. Cam remained frozen in shock,

something *deeper* in his eyes, and Sasha knelt by Pearl's body, still

crying. Nate had passed out at the sight of blood, and lay softly

against the metal wall. "You're a dead man," Sean exhaled coldly,

as he marched his way to The man, and reached for the rifle.

Suddenly the man jilted upward. His bones snapped back into

place, and his veins pulsed with a deathly unnatural black. He

grabbed the rifle, and stood up at an unpredictable pace, kicking

Sean back into the wall. "Well, I suppose that's my fault I

should've seen that coming." Sean cocked his head, confused at his

apologetic manner. "Third time today," The man muttered, under his breath. "Anyway," he began, as if nothing had happened. Then, casually, he picked up his rifle and aimed it at Nate. "He's already asleep, best not to wake him." They all watched in horror as the man took his aim, and placed his finger on the trigger. Avery let her tears flow, accepting her defeat. But she shook her head at the thought just as fast as it was conjured. *No, I won't let another one die. I.. I can't.* She jumped in front of him, and stood tall and proud, fake confidence she didn't even know she had. "Well, all the more fun. A brave one, okay then," the man responded sadistically. Avery Stared into the barrel of the rifle. *Yeah, uh, yeah, yep, that's death.* Unexpectedly, she started to show her trademark smirk, the thought of dying right there and then somehow feeling all the less scary, and all the more motivating. *I am not afraid.* She eyed the man up and down. *Leather coat that looks like it's from party city, a scrawny figure..* Her smirk grew. The man was beginning to feel a lot less intimidating.

"ANY LAS-" Suddenly, a phone rang from The man's pocket. He sighed and took a long pause, deciding what to do. At last, though, he made a face that indicated a decision, and took his finger off the trigger, lowering the rifle. Avery relaxed her shoulders, and Sasha backed down a bit. Sean coughed, staggering himself into a standing position. The man frowned and set the gun between his legs as he'd done before, stabilizing it with his foot. He reached into his pocket and retrieved what could only be described as an old kids toy-like telephone. "Mhm," He mumbled, holding the phone up to his ear, though he'd pressed no buttons. "Yep." His body began to sink, dropping his shoulders. "Yeah, they're here," he reported with reluctance. Avery felt a thousand emotions at once, confused at every corner. Sean echoed her at the other end of the room, still injured and unsure of whether to intervene. After several silent, awkward moments, The man sighed, and his face slowly became more disappointed, as his lips dropped into a frown, and his eyes sank down. "Yeah," he continued in a normal tone. He bit his lip, and stared at them, frowning, disappointed. Like a teenager who was just denied from going to a party. "Yep," he sighed, finally. He put the toy phone back into his pocket, with force and anger, still pressing no buttons. Cam finally moved, staring at all three of the others with a mix of confusion, and genuine sadness in his eyes, a rare emotion to see within him. After a few quick breaths, he ran to Nate to check his pulse. "He's alive," he reported, and the others each expressed relief. "Unfortunate," The man muttered to himself. He rolled his eyes, and reached down, but his hand didn't meet the rifle. "Okay," he began, clearly annoyed. "My boss wants to see you, so you get to live, I guess," he finished under his breath. Immediately, he picked up his rifle, and held in front of him, walking forward. Sean, who was now fully standing: exchanged a glance with Avery. *Who is this murdering weirdo?* The man spun on his heels, noticing no-one was following him. "Well?" he snarked and glared at them annoyed. Sean sighed, glaring at the man with pure hatred. The four of them nodded at each-other, all understanding the same thing. *There is no choice here.* Cam bit his lip, and struggled to pick-up Nate, who was snoring vigorously.

Sasha stood up from Pearl's body, tears streaming down her face, and turned around to follow the others. Cam and Sean wore a pensive look on their face, and followed but Avery stayed behind. She stared at the body, the stream of blood covering her foot. *This was my fault.* She took one last glance, tears blurring her vision.

She opened her jittering mouth to speak. 'I'm so sorry." But the words didn't come, and she turned around and followed behind the others.

The man assured them through the halls. They were long and marble, each section housing a split-off corridor like a maze, signs loomed above in all directions: **filing, Returner management, Equipment.** They walked for a long time, and the place grew through each hall, seemingly becoming more infinite at each turn. Finally, they reached a large metallic door. They all looked at eachother curiously, Cam still struggling under Nate's weight. The console was labeled with a thousand different departments, ones Avery couldn't even understand. **Weaponry, being containment, reality masks, returning substance.**

The man pressed a button on the panel to the side, and the door slid open smoothly. They stepped inside cautiously, observing the new ominous room. It appeared to be a massive industrial elevator. Avery furrowed her brow. It didn't even look like an elevator, but rather a wind tunnel. There was a hole in the center, with glass and metal railings and caution signs surrounding it. At the bottom was a fan, similar to the one on the ceiling from earlier. "Stupid design," Cam criticized, still holding Nate, eyeing the strange construction that made up the room. Sasha tipped her head in agreement. The man grimaced passive aggressively and glared at them like an offended preteen girl. "Hm," he replied, pressing another few buttons. The fan below spun to life, startling Avery, who had her arms slumped over the railing, her face buried within them. She felt a hand on her shoulder, and allowed it to rest. Sean sighed, patting her gently. He felt the same thing she was feeling. She yearned to be closer to him. *To be safe with him.* As if in response, Sean pulled her into a hug, and held her close. "How adorable," The man groaned sarcastically. Sasha hid in the corner, and didn't dare speak. Cam stared at the fan at the bottom. He was furious in many ways, and desperately wanted revenge, but was still intrigued at the mechanics of the machine nonetheless. He furrowed his brow, curious as to what its purpose was. "Positive wind pressure," the man informed, as if reading his mind. Avery eyes burst open, beginning to tremble violently. Her body went limp, and she fell out of Seans hug instantly. He reached out as she fell, and caught her just before she hit the solid metal floor. "Avery?" he yelled, but she couldn't hear him, shaking disturbingly in his arms. *Positive wind pressure? WHo, WHy ,WHA!* Her eyes locked onto the fan.

*She was a little girl again, searching old shelf's violently and fast, knocking over books and scrolls carelessly. She jammed her hand into a box, breaking through its cardboard surface,and pulling out a stack of papers. She sifted through them rapidly, as the sound running in the distance echoed down the halls. "Avery?" a woman's voice called. But she didn't pay any mind, she'd found what she was looking for, deep in the box, brushing off dead spiders, was an old parchment, with blueprints of a circular room, with a fan at the center. She swallowed, vowing to commit the contents before her to memory. The heading was labeled: **project deceit- grave elevator.** "Come here," The woman reached her, and grabbed her shoulder. "No!" She screamed. "No you can't make me, you won't make me! No never!!!"*

'NO! NO, YOU WON'T! YOU CAN'T! I WON'T LET Y-" Sean looked at the others, concerned. "Avery?" he asked gently, barely audible over her screaming. She gasped awake, nearly leaping out his arms. "Hey, Av' it's us. It's okay. We're-" he eyed Sasha for a second. 'We're safe for now," he assured. Avery exhaled in relief, and let herself lay back in his arms. "Little too much fun?" The man asked, rudely. Sean ignored him. Avery had regained her senses, collecting herself, as she faced Sean, tears fresh in her eyes, bending and blurring her vision. Sean eyed her cautiously "We-" She pulled him into a much stronger hug, and he blushed, not caring everyone was watching, he hugged her back. She smiled. *Yeah, now we're safe.*

The man wrinkled his nose and his face grew impatient. "Enough!" He yelled, in a much different tone, and a deeper, more serious voice. Not the snarky comedic one he had been using. "Get a move on," he commanded, trying to recover from the breaking of his "character". Cam glanced at the two *Lovebird idiots,* then redirected his glance at Sasha. She was already staring at him, her head cocked, but spun her head away the second his eyes met.

"Cmon!" The man yelled, and Cam hoisted Nate into the air again.

"Why don't you take him?" He demanded, handing Nate's left arm to Sean, who was still by Avery's side, post-hug. Sean shrugged, and nodded, taking his hand and carrying him with minimal effort.

After what felt like hours, they finally reached a large stone entrance, upon it: an old relic door-knocker of a lion. The man knocked with it four times, and after a few moments, the door opened with a long echoing groan.

Bright lights spilled through, as they walked into the room. It was a simple, eight-by eight chamber. Nothing more than a box. Avery's vision adjusted and she realized where the light was coming from. Screens. Plasma Tv screens, all along the walls. Except these were.. *different.* They were massive panels, section by section, connected to each other. Together, conjoined, they built the image of a forest, woods similar to the ones she lived in. Sean stepped aside for a second and leaned Nate against a panel, the green light of the trees making him look like some kind of forest goblin. Avery checked downwards, and the others followed her gaze curiously. They appeared to be standing on the same screens as the ones on the walls, except these panels were depicting a brilliant blue sky, rather than trees. Naturally, they all looked up unanimously, quickly exchanging glances. *Yep, same on the ceiling.* Avery squinted. *Is that..* She made a face of confusion, observing what lay above them: A crystal clear image of fresh brown soil. She felt herself swallow involuntarily. The reversed direction was simple, yet incredibly eerie. The emerald green trees, the appealing fresh soil, and the cavernous sky. Despite all of it, the simple fact of the scene being completely upside down sent chills through the air, beckoning unnaturality, demanding attention and power.

A boring normal man sat at a boring normal desk, centered perfectly in the middle of the room. He was, in a way, hidden. His dark, mysterious demeanor didn't fit the room, somehow concealing him in plain sight. Much like the panels, his presence felt *wrong*. Avery shivered upon noticing him. By all accounts, he should have been the very first thing they did notice. And yet he wasn't. Hidden, obscure. That thought alone made his appearance all-the-more intimidating. He wore a dark black business suit, with a sharp looking fedora to match, sitting, studying them.

His fingers were crossed over each other, with his arms resting on the desk. No eyes peeked out, no features of his face other than one ominous, repulsive sharp silver **smile**.

Despite her best efforts: squinting, subtly adjusting her angle, moving her head further back, Avery could not possibly make out a single other detail. Cam gestured to the bright sky on the floor bravely. "Big fan of dentists offices?" He squeaked out. Sasha let out a small scoff, but corrected her posture immediately, straightening her face, partly due to remembering what they'd just witnessed happen to *the innocent little girl.*

 "Thank you for joining me," The Man leaned into the light, his voice normal, almost monotone, yet harsh, a hint of anger in it. "Ernie, you may go." The guard nodded, obediently, still facing towards the man, behind the group in the doorway. Then turned around, and made a jeering face at them, frowning and shaking his head, as if trying to forget about them. "Earnie?" The Man's voice boomed out again. Earnie reached behind him and gave a thumbs up, then walked out of the room, and the door slammed shut.

"Welcome to **Monarch Laboratories.** It is.. interesting to see you here. I'm sorry to see P-e671 go. **It** was a nice subject, had an iron will." Avery shivered at his claim. *Iron will for what exactly?* Sean opened his mouth, and his lips curled into a pure rage. He gritted his teeth "Wh-" Sasha lunged forward interrupting him. "HER NAME WAS PEARL, SHE'S A LITTLE GIRL! A LITTLE GIRL WHO GOT FUCKING SHOT IN THE HEAD!" The Man gave no reaction, and simply lifted and re-clasped his hands, his thumbs sticking up in the natural *"everything is okay position"* - "It's unfortunate that you feel that way." Avery raised an eyebrow, contemplating what he had just said. Something within her erupted, and she couldn't contain herself.

"FEEL? FEEL THAT WAY?! YOU MURDERED AN INNOCENT LITTLE GIRL, AND THAT'S YOUR RESPONSE?! PRETENDING SHE WASN'T.. she wasn't.." Her voice trailed off, her anger draining, replaced by sorrow.

The Man cracked his knuckles together, and raised his hand into the air, making Cam flinch back a bit. "I simply eliminated a valued asset. One that my higher ups would've liked to have.. contained," he muttered, closing his hand as if crushing a bug. Sean had his mouth open, still swallowed in rage, but said nothing. He breathed heavily, his breaths echoing into metallic synthesized scraping, through the room. "I- I just- wha- "why?" He asked harshly, finally. The Man leaned further into the light, but his facial features were still a void, except for the sharp ominous smile moving up and down as he talked, his teeth like knives in the darkness. "The subject you almost… escaped.. with, was a harmful one." Avery stepped back just barely. "How?" She demanded coldly. The Man sat perfectly still for several moments, then, somehow: was suddenly two feet to the right, scratching his chin in deep thought. "Well," he began. "She wasn't alive." Sean's frown grew. "Bullshit." The man didn't move an atom, and simply waited for their collective reactions to wrap up.

"We've kept her here as a simple standard procedure, as well as to protect the world, *us* from *her.* " He relayed the words with disgust, only saying them to avoid being interrupted. Avery squinted at him, again, trying to see him. But to no avail. "Then what the hell were those.. things down there?" Nate demanded, suddenly appearing awake behind them, making Sasha startle. His normal childish expression was replaced with the look of a young man about to punch someone in the face. The Man took a deep breath, shakily, stuttering as he inhaled. "Well, my old…Partners.. departed, like the fools they were." Nate shook his head, his question completely dodged. "But I didn't need their body's to continue our work… only their minds. I reproduced their DNA with a few fellow people in the past." Avery curled her lips, reimagining how the "thing" looked. "The couple.." - "Well, thousand," The Man muttered- "We're not a success. But they may prove to be useful. Think of them as *prototypes.* We keep them down there for.. Well, safety," he finished, crushing his palm once again.

Cam finally spoke, the same rage, but more fear than rage in him. "Why are you telling us this?! Why haven't you killed us yet?! This is clearly stuff we're not supposed to see, why are we still here, why didn't that.. weird man, guard." - "Earnie," The Man interrupted. He spun his wrist in the air, balling his hand into a fist. He opened it again, and a small spider-like figure appeared in his hand. "And to answer your question, I don't like removing assets that have… potential. You my friends.." He eye-balled them, grinning with his smile just slightly. "Have potential." Sasha went to speak but was interrupted. "None of you will leave here with any recollection of what happened, nor any memory of this place ever existing at all. Don't worry, It will do no harm. You'll forget about the subject, and this whole place. I'm simply giving you, you right now. The clarity you so desire. It won't matter in a few moments. To you, it will have never happened. And what is life but not just your own vision?" Avery's eyes grew from anger to panic. *I won't forget Pearl. No. I will not, not for her. I cannot let her-* The Man stood up from his seat abruptly, and performed something like squinting at her, his eye sockets pure glowing white, the eye's themselves just slightly now visible. He stared her up-and-down. Seeming to blink heavily. "Wha-at is you-r name?" He asked, his voice suddenly sounding broken, as if something had caused it to glitch out, not fully forming words properly. his confidence seemed to have dropped just a bit. Avery scowled at him as Sean rushed to her side. "Why the hell do you think I'd tell you that?" The Man's eyes widened, becoming slightly more visible. "Come- ome-ome-here, he commanded. "No," Avery replied, definitely. The air suddenly grew cold, and the man's hat began to morph in physical space, glitching in black and white, like pixels on an old Tv screen. His smile curved downwards into a sick, twisted, angry frown. Avery shivered. *Well that pissed him off.* He began approaching her, the air glitching with him randomly as he moved along, morphing into strange pixels. "Wro-n-ng answer," he spat, his voice sounding amplified like a megaphone. He raised his fist. Suddenly, Avery was lifted off the ground, Thousands of tiny spider-like creatures appearing around her, dragging her to The Man's desk. She tried to struggle, but the spiders bit into her skin, and her arms went limp. She fought with all her might, but could do nothing. Sean leaped onto her, putting her into an "almost" headlock to have the most grip possible. Sasha screamed, grabbing Avery's hand desperately, joined by Cam and Nate, but the spiders bit into all of them, and they were forced to let go, staggering back in pain.

Avery was now at his desk, and the world was fading to black, as the spiders covered her face. Coming from seemingly thin air. The Man clasped his fist, aiming it at her bicep, and the spiders pulled her arm forward to him. Sean rushed to her, but was launched back, as the man made a simple waving motion. The rest of the group stopped dead in her tracks, realizing the situation was helpless.

Avery's neck twitched as she fought back for control of her body. The Man raised both his arms in the air, and moved them away from each other, as if pulling something apart. In response the spiders crawled off Avery's head, and her face emerged from the inky darkness. She clenched her muscles, using all her effort. The Man's eyes widened further, and his mouth dropped slightly open. *He knows me..* Avery stared at him in his 'almost" eyes, matching the same hatred and confusion on his own face. As if she was his reflection. "No, it's… I don't understand. How could he have…" Panic grew instantly in his face, his sharp smile quickly turning to pure unbridled rage. He dropped his arm, and the spiders melted into nothingness, Avery fell to the ground, coughing and gasping for breath, and the others tried to run to her but were held back by a strange, horrifically loud sound, piercing into every fiber of their body's. Sasha screamed, in her genius, over the sound. "AVERY, INCASE THIS HELPS, THOSE SPIDERS ARE ZINC!" The Man yanked a drawer in the desk open, and shoved his hand far into it, retrieving a top. He spun it hastily, and began to speak again. "1,9,8,8… I need everyone down here immediately. This is not a drill. Prepare the River, get me in contact with C1 immediately." Avery screamed in desperation, and the floor opened up beneath her like a classic cartoon. "AVERY!" Sean shouted.

No response. He looked around furiously, but the man was gone. "Shit," Cam muttered, biting his lip. Sasha covered her face and let a tear slip. *Please don't do the same thing you did to Pearl.* Sean smacked his knee in anger. "We have to-" - "Going somewhere?"

A familiar voice asked from behind them. Sean turned around, a wish for bloodlust on his face, he already knew who was behind them. "Let's go kids," Earnie said happily, grabbing Sasha's shoulder like a dog.

*More white halls, **distribution, storage, compost, governance.** They took her… why, who are they? Why did I let this happen?!* Sean closed his eyes, hiding the panic, putting on a tough face as they walked through more massive silver halls, a department door in each section. "Here we are," Earnie smiled, and opened the door. They stepped out. "Wha-" Sasha stepped back, nearly falling over. They stood now, on a flimsy old catrail in a MASSIVE open cave, the light above not quite reaching the bottom.

"Welcome to monarch laboratories," Earnie's voice echoed out into the massive cave, each rock bouncing the sound waves off the other. Cam rolled his eyes. "Yeah, we already knew the name." Earnie stared at him for a moment, both of them looking offended, sly. "Well good for you," He muttered, and continued down the catwalk. "Let's go!" He yelled from ahead, gesturing forward with the same rifle from before. Sean eyed Sasha, but she refused to look at him. Something; however, did accept his glance as he walked by, staring at the massive rock, cave walls, lights illuminating them, casting shadows across the world. *Don't try to be a hero, join **THE ZERO***!

He raised an eyebrow, and chill ran down his spine. Alone on the poster was a man with a clock for a head, with an old fashioned hat, a massive red crack in what looked to be the sky behind him. *Clock-faced man.. You were right, Av.* He felt a tear from as he thought of the name, unsure of her safety or whereabouts, he missed her more than ever.

"I ain't got all day, child!" Earnie's sharp voice boomed down the cave, Though by his leisurely walk, he definitely did. They walked along the cave wall for what must've been twenty minutes, then Earnie opened another old, rusty door. "Alright kids, wait here." He sighed, and walked away temporarily.

They were immediately back in the marble white hallway. "We need to go," Sean snapped. Cam shook his head. "And never get

Avery back? That elevators gone, we don't even know if there's another entrance." - "We spit up?" Sasha asked, Sean gave a thumbs down cautiously. "He'll kill us all!" he spat quietly,. but Cam held his ground. "Look at how cowardly Mr. tall, dark, and creepy. That didn't seem like I'm gonna kill you energy." Sean bit his lip, and stared out at the halls, planning to make a run for it. "Okayyy," Earnie's voice came down the hall. Sean shook his head, relaxing. *Damnit.*

Earnie looked curiously at Nate as he walked back down. The others followed. He was staring out into a display labeled "the museum of weaponry." Cam raised an eyebrow, and scratched his head. "A lemon that will set your home ablaze?" He made a face of confusion, and laughed a bit. Earnie nodded, rather seriously and touched the glass, marveling at the thing. "Ah, Cavournos C. Johnathon. Such a fine man." He slouched for a moment, his face rather sorrowful. Then he stood up, and gestured his head at the hallway. "Let's go."

"So what, you'll wipe our minds!?" Nate demanded. Earnie smiled cruelly, his lips curving blood red. "Yes. Yes you have that perfectly correct. "Now." He said, fiddling with his pocket. He retrieved an old key card, and jammed it into the slot. A computer voice rang out through the halls. **"Agent verified. Welcome, Earnie."** It said his name in disgust, as if it had known him, and had been programmed to do so. Earnie reached for the handle. **"Not. So. Fast,"** The voice said in the same tone as before. Anger grew in Earnie's face. "What now you blasted-" The voice interrupted him. **"To ensure this really is you, please identify the following."** Earnie waited, his impatience growing exponentially. **"Please click the following squares that are: traffic lights."** Earnie slammed his fist on the wall. "We INVENTED the Internet, god damnit! Why are WE the ones doing this!?" The group exchanged glances. *What is this guy talking about?* **"Ha. Ha. Ha."** The voice rang out coldly. **"WRONG!!"** Earnie balled his fist, and held it to the panel as if threatening it. **"Activating robot extermination protocol,"** The voice continued, almost as if mocking Earnie. **"Die, you no good robot!"** It stated, in what one could determine to be a yell. Suddenly, Earnie lurched forward, and tackled the group out of the way. The panel above the floor opened up, and a massive spikey crusher rammed downwards, smashing into the floor. A large quantity of water spilled out just a slight bit, soaking the marble ground below. *Sasha raised an eyebrow.*

"Okay," Earnie began, grinding his teeth, and taking a deep breath. "Then we'll take THE BACK ENTRANCE THEN."

They walked around the panels, passing several strange statues, and more massive entrances to hallways, each labeled as something more obscure than the last. Sean glanced around, trying to hatch an escape plan, but zero opportunities presented themselves. He glanced at the others and they all seemed to share the same thought. Eventually they reached another door. It was old, and dilapidated, with a signing hazard sign that read: ***Brain wipin' room.***

Cam smirked a bit. "Wow, you'd think a super secret shadow organization would've taken 1st grade English." Sasha and Sean shot him an angry glance. *You're gonna get us killed!* As if reading their minds Cam rolled his eyes and began blathering. "What, we're gonna die anyway." Sean gridded his teeth, and Cam nodded at him, a smirk on his face. *He likes hearing us confirm his desires.* "Trust me," he mouthed. Sean scowled, but tilted his head, yes.

 The walls were purely concrete, lit up by floor lights beneath, a metal structural pillar sectioning off every few meters. Ancient markings bled through upon the wall itself, making its aura feel ten times more frightening and confusing. Sean peered at the far end of the room. They had indeed gone in through "the back way" and parts of the giant door looked to be damaged. Sasha's eyes lit up at the sight, noticing more water dribbling from above where "the crusher" had smashed in the other side of the wall. *Now that right there... is VERY interesting.* She smirked deviously, a hunch forming in her mind.

They each took their time looking around as Earnie ushered them further into the room. Several strange barbershop-like seats were scattered about the room, each with a peculiar mechanical helmet mounted above. Wires and random electrical parts hung out the helmets ominous, their purpose of existence unknown, but surely not born of good intent. A certain fog lingered in the air as they marched their way through the massive room, making the bright lights seem dim, and pathetic.

Sean glanced around at the structure before them, entering the jaws of a strangely trapezoid-shaped concrete room, plastered everywhere on the floor with black and yellow stripes, warning of a threat he genuinely wished to remain ignorant to.

Earnie clapped his hands together with joy like a soccer-mom photographing her son's team. "Now, you little children stay here, while I go boot up THE MACHINE." Cam rolled his eyes, laughing in mockery. "Where's the ™?" Earnie frowned at him, and Nate and Sasha chuckled. Sean didn't, however. He was laser focused on the architecture around the room, noticing the pockets and bits of tubing that lined the walls.

Earnie began to lean against the entrance, wagging his finger dramatically. 'Well, don't even try to take one TINY step outside, lest you want to be cut in half by 400,000 pounds of pressure." He gestured to a massive industrial blade-like-door above, casting a shadow over the hazard textured floor. "Fitting," Nate commented, glancing about the group. In an instant, Earnie had disappeared back through the fog.

"We have to find our way out of here, now," Sean commanded, sternly. Cam shrugged in anxious aggression. "And get killed, he said it himself, the moment we step out there, we're dead." Sasha cocked her head towards Cam in agreement. "We're better off trying to make a run when we're out of the room, plus i don't think he knows what he's doing." - "No, you're no-" - "Look at him, he's navigated the place like it's first day on the jo-" - "Shut up!" Sean snapped, his eye's of urgency, no time to apologize. Sasha glared back in offense, but understood. "See these?" Sean snapped, pointing at a strange speaker-like mesh hole in the wall. The group checked about the room, noticing more on each part of the walls. Sasha's eye's began to widen in genuine terror. "Yeah," Sean assured, matching her appearance. Cam bit his thumb, and turned towards Sean. "Are those-" - "Gas emitters," he replied, finishing his sentence. "Like holly world dictator that's gonna fucking kill us- gas emitters?" Sean gave a quick nod, and continued searching around, laser focused on any possible way of escape. Nate nodded, only half understanding the situation.

"OH THIS IS BULLSHIT!" Earnie's voice echoed out, muffled. Sean raised an eyebrow. "PROFESSIONALISM, SHROFESSIONALISM!" He continued yelling. Sean peered at Sasha hopefully. "Well," His voice continued, a slight bit calmer. "BY WHO'S ORDERS?!" He shouted. It was silent again as the group waited eagerly, then, without warning, an ear piercing industrial alarm sounded, and the door in front of them slammed shut.

Almost immediately, clouds began emerging from the walls, dark in the faint beams of light. "SEAN?!" Cam cried out desperately. His vision blurred, and Nate collapsed behind him. "Ca-" Sasha began to hyperventilate, letting out a small scream. "HOLD YOUR BREATH!" Sean yelled. "NO, DON'T!" Sasha yelled, taking a whiff of the air. "It's not lethal, it's nitrous!" Cam began cackling passive aggressively. "HAHA, THAT"S GREAT, WHAT DOES

THAT- heheh, mean?" Sean relaxed his muscles, taking a deep breath. "Nitrous-Oxide," he confirmed, coughing out a chuckle, then falling back against the wall. Cam continued laughing uncontrollably, trying to speak, but unable to. "INHALE!" Sasha commanded, laughing with him. "WHAT?!" She smiled at him in the midst of the *fog of death*, both cackling involuntarily, now completely delirious to their consciousness. "Inhale, idiot," she spoke softly, some part of her still awake. She stared at him for a single fleeting moment, then leaned forward, bringing her lips to his, and kissing him gently.

Cam grinned genuinely as he stared into her eyes, both of them unaware of their world. Then they collapsed on-top of each-other with a hard metal thunk.

Chapter 12

The shadowy guards struggled under her rebellious spirit as they

forced her down the hallway, her limbs sprawling desperately in all

directions. "Where are you taking me?! What are you doing?!"

They showed no interest, and continued to walk forward

robotically, with the man in the suit leading in front. His body

language mirrored his face, curved and turned away from Avery,

facing in front, pure hatred fresh in his smile, the only feature

visible of his face. It glowed in LED lights above, like a wolf in the

woods lit by the moon. "Thirty four!" He barked ahead of them,

his voice much harsher than how he'd just been talking to them.

"You want me to take out your legs? Get a move on!" He yelled

ahead, rounding a sharp corner, and veering left through a circular

door.

Avery fought to stand up, but the guards knocked her down,

tearing at her hair, and cocking their heads like a curious puppy, hungry for some sort of meal. One of them reached to her chest, and began to crawl up her torso. She fought against its grip to get away, kicking and spitting, but her arms would not budge. Their faces were not visible, but it was clear they'd been programmed to chase lust. "Cease!" The man yelled ahead, as Avery fought against one of the guards, who now had its hand over her mouth, she bit at its fingers, and it jumped back, yelping and whimpering like a puppy. "Not. This. One," The man commanded, his voice echoing back through the door ominously.

She stared into the blank masked guards eyes, violence now her immediate desire. *And that will get us killed.*
Begrudgingly, She settled down, finally relinquishing her battle, giving in temporarily. *Save the energy. We can't get out right now.*
A small, wooden door covered in hieroglyphics and hazard symbols laid just ahead of her. "Now," The Man began ahead of them, retracting his arms from behind his back, and retrieving something from his pocket. "If I took you in here…" He began to look behind, but yanked his head back as soon as he stared, discarding an idea immediately. He shook his head. "Your brain

would melt," He continued, a slight hint of disappointment in his voice. "So.." He exclaimed, bringing the item behind his back. "Your mind needs to be somewhere else."

She narrowed her focus. *Somewhere else? The hell does that mean?* Her eye's shot open as the man withdrew an object from his pocket: a cold, black, giant syringe. She struggled in the guard's arms as he began to turn around to approach her, but he did not prime it, nor did he even look at her. He snapped loudly, and the guard raised its hand, while the other one held her down. The Man clasped his hands behind his back again, as the guard raised the syringe into the air high. "NO!!" She screamed, but it was too late. The sharp knife-like pain came stabbing down before she could even finish her plea. "Dot d- it." Her words began to slur, and though the guard had no visible features, she could tell it was smiling with pleasure as it got in her face, shrouded more and more in darkness. *NO DON- No. no.* The world was gone, only an empty void of rest left within her consciousness. Her body lay limp as the man pulled a lever, and they descended further into the darkness of the endless facility.

She looked around as her eyes opened, and felt a drop of water hit her face. It was raining, and the green world around her was laced with fog. A river flowed to the west into the miles of mountain cliffs surrounding her.

She squinted hard, her vision dimmed through the weather around her. *Trees, rain.* The cliffs were massive, making her feel trapped.. She took a deep breath of the fresh cold rain. *Smells amazing.* She nodded, noticing its chill running down her chest. *This is real.* "Well then," She began aloud, staring into the distance. "Where to go now?"

The ground slushed as she started forward. Finally, she could see. *Oh..* her eyes grew with curiosity as they focused on her apparent target. Alone, miles in the distance was a massive radio tower, with an old brick building, hundreds of meters wide, separated by the bridge where the water flowed from. "Yep. I'm either a lab rat, or a dead woman," she muttered to herself, as she grabbed a pine tree, hoisting herself up a rock.

The cliffs grew steeper as the hours of climbing passed. She'd taken off her button down, and tied it around her arm. *Survival style.* She smiled, miles of rocks still fresh ahead of her. "Just stay positive," she told herself, dipping her hand into the water before her. *Well, at least we have water. Don't even have that in the real, my, uh- world.* She knew well that this was not her world, though the concept didn't bother her. She'd accepted that anything could be possible two nights ago.

She shook her head, letting her eyes rest on a small waterfall ahead. *Focus Avery, radio tower.* She nodded, standing up again. "Radio-Tower," She repeated, affirming her own existence. She trudged on, hobbling her feet over cold wet rock, shedding small bits of blood along the way. *Okay.. how many.. feet. No. Miles. Miles upon goddamn miles.* She spat at the ground, and flem and mucus came out, merging with the river. Partly disgusted by her own body, she curled her nose, and turned the other way. "Alright," She began aloud, her voice echoed slightly in the canyon rock she resided in. "One foot in front of-" "don't let him get away!" A man yelled in the distance. Avery crouched quickly, trudging cautiously into the canyon formation of a rock to the right, a miniature cave. She grinned to herself. *Perfect hiding spot.*

As time passed, the trees swayed heavily, and several faces emerged in the brush. The first one looking nervous, like he'd been caught red handed. "James, you sure this is-" James waved the man off, gesturing an old style rifle at the ground. "Non believers pose a threat. What do we do when we see a threat Kyle? We fucking eliminate that threat." They went silent for a few moments, the situation clearly heated. "Does it have to be so.. brutal?" Kyle asked, covering up his face slightly in an old leather hood.

"You wanna end up like them?" James demanded, withdrawing a revolver from his belt, and gesturing at a corpse freshly thrown to the ground, their blood dripping audibly off the cliffs just to the side of them. Kyle shook his head shyly.

Avery held her breath, scoping out the situation before her. *Trustworthy, definitely not. "Nonbelievers" that's uh definitely a dead body.. What is this, some kind of cult?* She shook her head, and frowned tightly, shimmying her way around the very little space she had available. A stick cracked beneath her feet and she gritted her teeth.

"Hey, you hear that?" The group all nodded, holding their rifles high. Avery raised an eyebrow as she stared out with one eye into the brush. *Muskets?*

"Circle the perimeter!" James barked, and the others did so sweeping every bush in an apparent mile radius. She looked around desperately, but no answer came. *We're surrounded.* At a loss for options, she squeezed her face tight, and stood her ground, ready for a fight. "There she is!!" One of them yelled, priming his musket at her. "I say we kill her now and save her body for later!" Another one yelled from the other side of the canyon formation. Avery shivered. *What the hell doesn't that mean?* "Get your ass up!" James shouted, yanking her arm into the air behind her. Avery bit down hard, and fought to get away. "Pft," He spat in her face, and tugged at her hair, ripping a few stands out. She screamed, and bit down her teeth, showing them like a sabertooth. "You are one stupid. little girl," he began, drawing his revolver from his belt. "Wait!" Kyle yelled, as James put the revolver to her head. "Are you a believer?..."

Avery stayed quiet and still, a look of bloodlust fresh on her face. "Answer the fucking question deadbeat," James commanded in her face. Avery smirked, *not going down without a fight.* She began to draw quietly from her back pocket, smiling sadistically baring her teeth at the question. "I'm specifically a non-believer.

AND I MEAN SPECIFICALLY." James shook his head.

"Figures," he said in her ear, drawing the revolver closer to her head. "Anything you wanna say before you meet the creator?"

A chill went down her spine, something familiar triggered from the word. "What do you mean by that?" She asked him, staring death straight in the face. James did not respond, only shrugging and holding the revolver to her head. "Wait!" Avery pleaded. James frowned, nodding. "I do have one last thing to say." James nodded. "Get it over with then. You're on a **timer**," he barked, his head twitching slightly, gesturing at the three other men. Avery smiled, completely unsure if her idea was about to work. "WOAH LOOK AT THAT!" All four of the men turned around eagerly like dogs, acting as if killing was their only true purpose. "Haha," Avery laughed behind them, withdrawing her knife. "Made-ya look." She cackled out, and she jabbed into James's throat, holding him before her as a shield. "Who's next?" She asked, nodding at Kyle intimidatingly. "You're gonna fucking PAY FOR THAT!" The man on the left yelled, and dove at her. He was successful, ripping the knife out her hands, and throwing her to the ground. *Welp, I tried.* Avery shrugged, trying to get up, surprised at her lack of fear. But the man wouldn't let her, slamming her back down on the ground. "Say night night little bitch. Hopefully your blood will be more useful than your mouth." The man held his own revolver high, taking aim. Avery closed her eyes, and took a breath. *We'll get out of this, just wait.* She told herself, just as the man came slamming down with his elbow. She blocked it with her hands, and tried with all her might to push him away. But he was too big. His elbow bent into her, crushing a rib. She screamed in pain, and tried desperately to reach her knife. But to no avail. "Burn in hell!" The man yelled, placing his finger on the trigger. Avery tried to fight back, but she couldn't. Her breath was gone, her bones broken. In an instant, the man pulled the trigger...

But not before a figure in a gas mask jumped him, kicking him to the ground, and taking the other man's revolver, shooting them both in the head at the same time, one in each hand. He ran over to Avery. *Red flannel.. brown sneakers, long brownish hair.* his eyes looked frantic despite his face being covered. "Get up," he commanded at Avery, reaching for her hand. "And put this on," he added, withdrawing an old war-time gas mask. Avery stared out, her mind confused in twenty different ways. *Wait.. I just killed a guy... I just KILLED A PERSON! WHY ARE WE OKAY WITH THIS?!*

"Cmon, we gotta move. Put the damn thing on," he snapped, drawing a hand canon and aiming it at a new ruckus of people in the distance.

She threw the gas mask on frantically, digging at the ground to get up. "Sorry who ar-" The Man shook his head, and knelt down, grabbing ammo from the bodies that now littered the cliffside. "Catch up later, we ain't got time." - "There they are!" Another man yelled in the distance. "Fuck em up!" He yelled, igniting his musket, which ricocheted off the rock with a loud **BANG**.

Six more men followed behind him, all dressed like old hunters in leather coats, and thick jeans. They ran forward, emptying gunpowder in their direction.

"Don't let them die too fast!" One yelled, who seemed to be the leader. Avery curled her lips, popping her head above the rock just slightly, for some reason full of confidence. "Get down," The Man snapped, grabbing her and forcing her back to safety. She shrugged aggressively, heaving heavy breaths. *Who the hell are these people?* Something about their nature was different. Violent gangs, but the way they acted was not quite human. Almost like a wild animal, violent, guided to kill. The Man reached into his pocket, and pulled out a grenade. Avery narrowed her eye's again. *Muskets… muskets with VERY modern grenades.. how?.. Why..?*

The man ducked undercover for a moment, popping out the revolver's cylinder, and quickly jamming new rounds into the receptacles via literally biting the bullets, and placing them in the gun, the grenade still in his other hand. "Alright, stay on my back."

She nodded seriously, and primed herself to move, her chest

sinking with the broken rib. "Fire in the hole," The Man muttered,

pulling the pin and throwing at the approaching gang with nearly

perfect precision. Avery plugged her ears and kelt tightly behind

the rock. "Oh shit!" The leader tried to leap out of the way, but the

detonation stopped him dead in his tracks, sending smoke and

debris flying. Her ears stung slightly, but she was fine, and she was

surprised at that simple fact. *I am… fine. Huh, Not as bad as*

movies make it out to be. Also, why am I not in pain?... What the

hell is this place?

"They're armed!" A surviving *straggler* yelled, diving quickly

into the apparent remains of a broken window. For a single

fleeting moment, the strange man looked at her and smiled with his

eyes, something about the two similar. They seemed to share the

same energy, smirking through the masks for a second with quirky

confidence. Avery narrowed her eyebrows, unable to tell what was

so off about him. "Hey boys!" The straggler whistled loudly, and ten more men came barreling out of the woods. Then ten more.

"Shit," The Man muttered sharply, pulling Avery up gently.

"There's too many, we gotta move." She nodded cautiously, and

The Man began counting with his right hand, fishing something

out of his pocket with the left.

1. "You're outnumbered deadbeat!" *2.* Avery nodded. "Give

up now and we'll make it fast!" The Man was now holding

another grenade, this one; however, more old fashion. *3.* The two

bolted from their spot of cover as the man chucked the grenade,

smiling at the gangs with a big sadistic toothy grin.

Yelling sounded off in the distance, accompanied by another loud

explosion, and the two of them booked it. Trees, buildings and

grass rushed by as they ran through the brush. "Cmon! Cmon! We

ain't out yet!" The Man called to her, she was behind him by a few

feet struggling physically with her newly broken bone. Though for

some reason it didn't hurt. "Through here!" He called again,

winding to the right, and under a barbed wire fence, boarded with wood. They ran for what felt like hours, both of them dying for a breath, but not stopping.

"Can.. we.." Avery coughed out, running low on oxygen. "Once we're safe," the man replied, breaking into a crawl underneath a random fallen evergreen. "Okay.. Where.., uh.. are we going?" The Man waved her off militantly, aiming his hand up at the sun as they walked. "Once we're safe," he relayed, checking his measurement again. "And we've got about six more hours till we're not." She shook her head, and started to slow down intentionally. The Man let out a long, annoyed inhale ahead, beckoning for her to speed up. After a few moments, she sighed, and ran to catch up with him.

At last they reached an *apparent stopping point*, and the man pulled open a barbed wire fence. "Cmon!" He whispered to her, breathing thickly. Avery pursed her lips, surprised at his ability to reach into: *Spikey blades of government gatekeeping.* Clearly he'd done it too many times to count. Reluctantly, she followed him through and into an area that resembled an abandoned construction sight. They ran through several brick buildings, the rain bouncing off each one, the sound of the river far away in the distance.

The gang's voices drowned out as they sprinted through the murky trees, and the man slowed to a stop, kneeling down under a wooden pallet, resting from the hook of a long since destroyed crane. "I think we lost em'," he breathed through the gas mask, sighing. "Okay so wh-" He waved her off again. "Follow me. We're safe, but safer is ideal." Avery scoffed, confused, and nodded, a raindrop landing right in her eye. She shook her hair like a wet dog to rid of it, then followed The Man further into: *Only god knows where*

They stood before a massive barricade made of random items, which were stacked and thrown together messily. "In a hurry?" She asked. The man frowned, seeming to recall something. 'Aye." She gave a nod, now understanding why the construction sight looked so abandoned.

The man grunted as he wrenched open the door of an old fallen backhoe. Avery looked around confused, the rain still pummeling down on them. "Welp,' The Man grunted, crouching into the door, and disappeared into the vehicle. She shrugged, and followed behind.

She was led through a tunnel, which looked to have been dug out years ago. "Duck!" The Man called from ahead, and she followed his instructions, quickly dipping down, and continuing upwards After what she assumed to be about half a mile, they emerged out of the other side of the huge barricade. She swung her head side to side, observing curiously. The place was mostly empty, with a few crop fields outside, and random metal chunks strewn about. One thing, however, did catch her eye: a blood-red porta potty stood on a slight slope to the left, behind a wooden fence. The Man nodded, eyeing it. She raised an eyebrow, but followed him anyway. She turned around to look back, still unsure of her safety for a time, and when she returned her gaze back around, he'd disappeared.

"Um?" She looked around Her lips perched, confused. "You.. need a little privacy?"… She waited. "Cmon!" The Man yelled from ahead, his voice muffled in the wood of the structure. "Okay then!" Avery called back, strutting inside cautiously. She searched around, but there was no sight of him. "Down here!" He called. She approached the bowl nervously, staring down it, disgusted. She sighed, *of course.* Reluctantly, she nodded, and held her nose shut, though there was no smell at all. "See, you're not gonna die." The Man scolded, as she landed with the thud onto fresh gravel. The man nodded, somewhat proud, and she stared back awkwardly. "Alright then," he affirmed, and casually walked down the long tunnel before them. Avery rolled her eyes at "god" *Great, more of this.*

She sat quietly, across from the man, their gas masks still on. The room was solid and cavernous, wood and metal gratings strewn together at every wall to keep the foundation up. The light was fairly natural, coming from an orange LED above, giving the place a weird, sort-of awkward feel. An old fashioned record-player sat to the left on a table, and a robot-like body leaned in the corner.

Avery examined the thing wonderfully. Its label had only four visible numbers, etched in precisely on the shoulder. *A date.* She coked her head as she read them. *2-0-4-8.* A chill went down her spine. *Where in god's holly fucking name am I?* "Um.. so.." - "**It's Garrison**," The Man interrupted, smirking with his eyes. She shivered for a second, the name seeming all-too familiar. "Avery," she replied, unsure whether to shake hands.

Garrison stopped, an exact reflection of what she'd just felt. "Huh," he muttered. Then nodded. Avery spoke again shyly. "Uh.. so.. the gas masks?" He nodded, his face still covered. "Yeah, you ain't are you?" She shrugged, her eyes wide, and full of confusion. *I aint what, cowboy?* "You ain't from here," Garrison bit his lip, and leaned forward. "Well, Avery, if you haven't noticed, we're in a war." Avery nodded. "And you're also probably pretty damn confused about everything you're seeing. Like it doesn't fit together?" She concurred again. "Well, pop a squat. It's a story, that's for damn sure."

She gave a nod, and leaned forward a little more. "Our life's here used to be peaceful. They used to be normal. Hunt animals, put food on the table, so on. Then, one day out of nowhere, things started appearing in our world. We don't know where they're from, or really… when." Avery gestured at the robot, and he nodded. "It's been a chaotic storm most of my life. I barely even remember what it was like back then, but it was surely better than now." He stopped, and reached behind into his pocket, drawing out an old, strange pen. "Anyway, this weird.. time-storm didn't just come alone, it brought a disease." Avery leaned forward. "We don't know what it is, but we DO- know where it is." He nodded to himself. "It's goddamn everywhere." He knelt down for a moment, as if mourning. "It drives you insane. It makes you.." He stopped, his eyes growing angry behind the mask. "It makes you a predator. Wild, hungry for blood. For no reason at all. It's like drugs times a thousand. Whole damn British army turned to wild psychos in the course of just 2 days."

Avery's face grew sadder, gesturing for him to continue with her eye's.. "But you know humans." His expression relaxed behind the mask.. "We seek purpose."

Neither of them said anything for a moment, the silent sound of the cave unnerving. "The believers?" Avery asked gently, breaking the silence. "The believers," He affirmed. "It gives them a reason to be alive, some think it even.. helps them." Avery motioned her agreement. "But it doesn't. It just kills. Kills, and kills…" He paused, biting his lip under the mask. -"and kills." He gazed at the robotic body, then back at her. "Artifacts arrive here every day, just: boom, out of thin air." He brought his hand to the mask, thinking. "I collect them, and protect them. Me.. Me and my brothers."

Avery inclined her head, listening intently. "They're out right now, probably be back in a few days." Garrison paused, looking at the exit where they came in. "But because of that." he stopped, handing her a fresh *"2087 lunar-cola."* - "It's my duty to protect you."

Avery felt a chill go down her spine. "What.. What year is it?" She asked, the blue in her eyes wide. Garrison angled his posture down darkly. **"CHRONOLEFT."**

Chapter 13

Avery raised an eyebrow at his weirdly ominous statement.

"Okay.. so.. Uh.." - "We don't know," Garrison replied, already knowing what she had to say. "That's what we call it. I can't remember why, it just is." Her pupils dilated, realizing, truly just how dire the world she'd found herself in was. "So you don't even know what year it is?" Garrison shook his head. "We stopped keeping track after a man named Columbus found this place." her eye's sky rocketed. 'Columbus is the-" - "I know," she interrupted. Garrison gave a nod. "Right." Avery sat up straighter, more comfortable talking to him than moments before. "So.. why.. Like, why did you stop keeping track of the years?" Garrison frowned in response. "The answer to that question is in the palm of your hand as we speak." She squinted, confused, and glanced down. *Lunar soda from 2087.. Oh... right.* Garrison heaved a heavy sigh, stretching his right arm. "Everything that's ever been is falling here randomly everyday." He switched to stretching his left arm. "Time itself doesn't matter, because it doesn't exist here, Avery. At last, in the big picture." She watched him sit back straight, clasping his hands together. "There *is* no time, cause there's nothing to define it."

Avery sat, silently, feeling bad for this random man she'd just met. *So, so far we literally killed a guy, Why don't I-* Her jaw opened just barely. *The time storm... The CHRONOLEFT... I feel no guilt because I inhaled that air.* She sat up a bit more, something within her now active. "Well, uh, I'm from two th-" Garrison shook his head rapidly. "It's best if I don't know." She nodded sadly, and sat back, finally feeling safe with him. Something about him felt familiar, his aura comforting, his accent familiar. Garrison reached over, and withdrew something, bringing his hand back around proudly. She glared at the object deeply. He was holding, now: a familiarly strange katana in his hand, that began to glow blue as it

beard to her. She squinted, but did not object, allowing the blade to

hover over her broken rib. "I know it sounds weird bu-" She waved

him off. "We have this where I'm from too. At least… We do as of

yesterday." Garrison frowned, and gestured his understanding.

Avery sighed slowly, so many questions fresh in her mind, now

amplified without pain in her ribs. "So, uh, you guys have modern

swear words in this.. Uh.. CHRONOLEFT?" Garrison raised an

eyebrow, nodding as if there was absolutely nothing unusual about

that fact.

Avery shrugged, moving her eye to the wall. "So you don't say

thou and thy and all that?" Garrison snorted, amused. "Never heard

that word once in my life." - *"What the fuuuu,"* she mouthed to

herself, her confusion growing exponentially, neighboring her

curiosity. "Shakespeare, old plays, Odysseus, uh, Hamlet, or..

whatever?" Garrison only stared back, just as confused as her.

"Shake-who?" He breathed through the gas mask. Avery palmed

her face, and shook her head. "So history was a lie then?" Garrison shrugged. "How should I know, I'm living it." He glanced to the side. "At least, I think."

Avery made a face, motioning her understanding. "Well, uh… Can.. I get back to my.. time?" Her face was slightly shy, though she wasn't afraid. "I mean I feel bad about this.. war, and all but-" Garrison shook his head. "If there is a way, the desperate souls that appeared in this hell-hole would've already found it."

Her heart sank. "It doesn't really matter though. If you have all of man's inventions from day zero to one hundred, what's even the point of time?" Avery shook her head in disagreement. "People?.. family?" Garrison's eye gleaned just slightly, a spark of hope. "You know what's funny?" He asked, trying to brighten the mood. "What?" Avery replied, feeling somehow very comfortable. "I love that name.. Avery. I thought if I ever had a daughter one day, if all this ever gets fixed, I would name her that, and if it was a boy well.." - "Conner?" Avery threw out the name, not entirely sure why. Garrison nodded, extreme suspicion in his eyes, which he attempted to hide quickly. "Wishful thinking, I suppose." Avery shrugged. "Hope?" She suggested. Garrison looked taken aback, but motioned in agreement still. "Hope."

He smiled with his eyes, and she smiled back, leaning in her small wooden seat, and crossing her legs on the table in front of them. "So.." She began, her spirits lifting as she popped open the can of soda. "How does one go about drinking with a gas mask on?" Garrison laughed genuinely, and got up, leaving the room for a brief moment, then returned with a kids silly straw. Avery burst out laughing. "What?" He squinted. "Um?" She asked, recovering from the explosive laughter. "What?" Garrison repeated, peering into the hole of the straw, confused. "We call this a **sustenance consumption enabler device**. Avery nearly burst out laughing again. "Mhm, yeah. That's uh…" Garrison's eyes were angled in confusion, but it was clear he was laughing with her. "Well where I'm from we call this a silly straw." Garrison fell to his knees, and began laughing uncontrollably. "That sounds so.." - "stupid?" Avery asked. "Yeah," He affirmed, laughing, and they laughed it out together.

"Who taught you to play **quatro**?" Avery asked through the gas mask, across from Garrison at a small, salvaged wooden table. Garrison shrugged. "I don't know.. the future?" The two laughed. It was night now, and the rain was pouring down outside. She'd stopped thinking about the outside world, genuinely enjoying her time with the man.. The stranger, whom she had just met.

 "Hey, you can't stack on a plus four wild!" Garrison rolled his eyes, barely visible through the foggy gas mask. "I don't see no rules." Avery stared him down. "Who's the one from the future here?" Garrison scoffed gently, and raised his hands in mock surrender. "Fine, fine, I forfeit." Avery smiled, throwing down a blue reverse, and a seven to cap it off. "Damn right you do."

Their laughs trailed off, both growing quiet. Avery sighed, and reached for her mask without thinking, beginning to take it off. Her hand was swatted away before she could even lay a finger down. "Don't," Garrison commanded sternly, standing above her. She nodded. "My bad."

It was silent again for a few minutes, both of them staring at a wall. *This isn't.. awful.* Avery smiled to herself. "Well.." She broke the silence. "Have you ever thought about.. where, this.." She chose her words carefully. "Disease.. is coming from?" He stayed silent, leaning against a wall, clearly thinking. He turned around, and opened his mouth to speak, but turned back at the last second. He nodded, facing the wall, and turned to look at her a third time, staring deep into her eyes, a look of confusion on his face, as if seeing someone he knew. An old friend. He shook the thought off quickly. "Let me show you something." Avery raised an eyebrow, and got up, following him out of the room. Slowly, they walked down the left corridor. Several doors and halls passed by as they made their way into a room. Avery's eyes began to widen. They stood now, before an old decrepit basement like room, three shelves to the left, a wall *where a windowsill might've been* to the right. The foundation was of rock, wood and chainmail layered on top to keep its structure. A freshly dug crawl space sat where stairs would've been.

Avery shivered, her pupils dilating at a sudden, quick, violent realization. "This is my basement," She spoke, giving Garrison a look that could kill. "What?" He asked, his eyes squinted. "This is the basement of my house," She repeated slowly, feeling around the shelf's, the three aligned perfectly, no different than her own world. "Well then, that's.. I.." He stopped himself. "A big coincidence." He nodded, clearly hiding something else. "In any case.." Garrison continued. But Avery wasn't listening. *Time doesn't exist here, a world cast out from mine, the one I belong in... Why am I so okay with this? This is NOT WHERE I SHOULD BE! ..*

"So we think they end up here in some sort of vacuum of time." Garrison stopped. "Avery? You alright?" … "Av-" - "Uh, yeah! Mhm. The uh.. the time vacuum." Garrison nodded. "Yes." He stopped again, studying her face, as if searching for something he lost long ago. "There's more," He added, grimly, beckoning her down the hallway. She willed herself not to follow, but did so nonetheless.

They took a left, and passed by an *old gargoyle statue.*

Avery studied the artifacts and posters around as they walked down the halls, the cave seeming more and more like a home. She stopped in her tracks for a second, her eye catching on a framed painting on the wall. It was a simple black and white portrait, showing a basic, leatherbound book, on its cover which read **CHRONOLEFT** A chill went down her spine. *..What..?*

"Here!" Garrison called from afar. The floor cracked as she met him in the other room, leaning against the door frame. "Avery.." Garrison began, his eyes squinted, still searching for something. "Yeah?" Avery asked, the trust from earlier completely gone. He stumbled backwards a bit. "I don't know why.." He began, placing his hand against the makeshift wall. "But I feel I should show you this.".. He ruffled with the open cabinet on the wall, and withdrew a large, thin object. "We found this just a few hours from here, broken to pieces on the floor." He paused, considering whether to continue. "Everyone seems to understand that it is someone doing it, and whoever is doing this, it's for a reason." He reflected, as he bit his lip. "They're some sort of god. That's why we call them the creator.." He extended his hand out to her. "Whatever this.. creator-is, it seems to look like this." In her hand was now a paper folder, sharp and old. She twitched a bit, every instinct telling her to *run*, but her curiosity argued otherwise.

Bismurchfully, she opened it, sifting through the papers inside. Her eyes widened. Alone on every single page were iterations of a drawing of a man with a clock for a face, dressed in anything from a melting wooden dress to a formal business suit with fedora on each paper. She looked up, but its contents were not fully emptied. In a split second, a strange, familiar object landed in her hand, falling out of the folder. Her eye's leaped open like rockets, and she fell back against the wall, holding the thing in her clutches up to her heart, feeling it pound like a rapid-fire-rifle, struggling to breathe through the gasmask.

Lonely in her hands sat a small, weirdly shaped mechanical clock, ticking vibrantly with each passing second. "I.." She couldn't bring herself to speak, staring at it with a look of every emotion both possible and impossible. *Strange ticking, a dog tag-like necklace attached..* Her mind threw a memory at her like a dart, stabbing into her consciousness. *"Figured he'd want you to have this…"* *The figure… that man.. Black hair, emerald green eyes, ..* "HE'D- *want you to have this…* Her jaw fell open. *"HE…"*

"Are you-" She waved him off, nodding, something clicking in her mind. "Why?" She asked through tears, her demeanor changing. "Why show ME this?" She took up a stance of caution, standing with her feet straddled. "I've only known you for a day." She shook her head. "It seems to me that this is your biggest secret.. so.. why trust me?"

Garrison slouched his head, grabbing the wood on the cave wall. "I don't know," He admitted, sadly. "My brothers don't trust me, especially the oldest." Avery shook her head confused, fiddling with the clock necklace. *You're a grown badass man who's acting like a child.* "I don't know why I trust you, it just feels right."

… "Av," He chuckled to himself. She took a huge step back. "What?" Garrison nodded. "fifty-five, and I don't know how much time I have left." He shook his head remorsefully, resting his neck on the wall. "I've always dreamed of having a family. It's stupid, I know." He smiled to himself through the mask, closing his eyes. "Just to have a best friend, someone to nickname, a child." He stopped, and opened his eyes, cold and dry. "But there ain't much left to live for in this world." Avery gripped the necklace tight, and rose into a defensive position.

"Our instinct is to survive, yet no one ever asks why." She was now almost outside the room, her face full of suspicion. *This is fake. He set this up as some sort of fake stupid world to trick me, there is no way this man is **my father**.*

"I guess.. *that's* why I told you." He nodded slowly. "At this point I'll do anything just to have a life, to have a family." Avery held her gaze, not at all convinced. "The sooner I solve *that*." He gestured to the folders she still held in her hand. "The sooner I can die peacefully," he finished, standing back up. *Columbus, British army, literally impossible. It cannot be him.* Garrison cocked his head. "Tell me, Av." She took a step back again, the name feeling wrong." - "It alright if I call you that?" He asked, genuine kindness in his eyes." *No! No it's not! You are no-* her eyes fixated on his deep blue eyes, a mischievous angled nose. She thought back to the name *"Av"* she nodded, something feeling right. A chill shot down her spine, as she stared deep into the man's eyes. *This man **is** my father.*

She nodded. "Sure thing." Garrison reached for his back, withdrawing an old metal pistol. "2056," he spoke, nodding proudly.

"1911," Avery corrected, matching his smirk in the eyes. "Oh… Well, have you ever learned how to shoot?" He asked. "No," She replied. "*My dad* never taught me." Garrison grinned, and gestured to the exit of the cave. "Well… wanna?" Avery smirked behind the gasmask. "Sure."

"Alright, first rule of **shootin'** safety" Avery held a laugh under her breath. *Firearm safety? Right. You guys don't know what anything is called.* She stood now, on a makeshift, rather hairy wooden platform, posed before a home-made target range of trees and various metal parts. Garrison re-holstered his 1911. "Always point the **boom** part away from you." She laughed again, this time out loud. "Something funny?" Garrison asked, mostly joking in his tone. "Uh, just different terms from where I'm from, that's all." He nodded respectfully, and reached into his back pocket, drawing a simple, rugged M9 handgun. "So you always hold the handy handle-" Avery burst out laughing, leaving Garrison staring, confused. Minutes passed, and she regrouped. "You ready now?" Garrison asked, half disappointed, half laughing with her. She concurred gently. "Alright, you always hold your dominant hand as high up near the hammer as possible, without it touching the actual hammer." Avery nodded. *Okay, hammer. That's normal. So something normal passed on. Or.. back?* She nodded, reaching out to grab the pistol, but Garrison pulled it back. "Not yet," He scolded, squinting at her mischievously. She nodded, echoing his eyes. *Father and daughter.* She smiled to herself, she enjoyed this.

"Alright, now you **always** keep your finger on the trigger in case something surprises you." Avery raised an eyebrow. *Do you* *thoughhh?* She nodded, hesitantly. "Always keep it loaded incase you need it in a flash." She nodded again, but common sense told her that was in-fact: not the right thing to do. "Okay," she confirmed, and waited for more instructions. "Alright, now the slide is what loads a game." Avery raised an eyebrow. "Mhm," she affirmed. Garrison gave a thumbs up, proudly. "That's what you call an outlet." Avery snorted. "A bullet?" Garrison shook his head. "An outlet." Avery shrugged, but didn't let it go. "Bullet." - "Outlet!" - "Bullet!"

This went on for minutes, both of them arguing like toddlers. "Fine, how's about big- boom?" Garrison threw out. Avery scoffed, and gave a hasty sign of agreement.. "Okay well, the BIG BOOM.." He began with annoying emphasis, "goes in the bottom." Avery nodded. "Can I just see-" She reached for the M9. "Alright fine," Garrison sighed, cautiously handing it off. Avery grabbed it eagerly, but carefully, placing her domintent hand as he'd shown her, wrapping her other one around it. Garrison stepped back slightly, surprised at her knowledge. "Alright, finger on the trigger," he commanded. Avery's face grew concerned, and she pretended to place it on the trigger, resting in just over the trigger guard. "Alright…?" She waited. No response.

"Shoot," Garrison ordered.. "What about ear protection?" She asked. "Huh?" He responded. "And if those… believers hear?" Garrison rolled his eyes. "Why do you think I just handed you a gun?" She laughed nervously, and shrugged nonchalantly, firing a shot at a random tree stump. *Ow.. yep. There goes my entire ear drum.* The world rang in pain, but she recovered shortly. Garrison stood, not affected in the slightest. *Well, I guess I'm sacrificing my ears then.* She smiled, and fired another shot. Then rested it down safely, placing it in safety with the switch on the side. "What are you?" Garrison began. "Safety," Avery responded eagerly.

Garrison's head nearly exploded, this new switch a completely foreign concept to him. "You guys haven't evolved much with guns, have you?" She asked. "We…." He struggled to find the words. "Well, you seem ready to me." He nodded, with a big dumb grin. Avery shrugged, and spun around swiftly, stepping down off the makeshift wooden platform they'd been practicing on. She extended the M9 back to Garrison, but he shook his head. "It's yours," he smiled, pushing it back to her. She pursed her lips, surprised. "Alright, now let's head back. My brothers should be home." Avery yawned in agreement, and the two headed back in the direction of the cave.

A man smiled, holding an axe proudly, headed home from a long day, dragging an entire elk behind him. "You think he's holding up okay?" The second brother asked. "I could care less," replied the first. "He's family, you know," the second one offered. The first one rolled his eyes. "Family that has know clue what they're doing," He spat. "He's…" The second one thought for a moment, choosing the right words. "He's found a way to be interested in more than just survival." The first one shook his head pathetically. "You really buy into that pig shit?" *A word that was shifted in the transition into the past.* The second one nodded, throwing his musket behind his back. "Yeah, a little bit." The first one shook his head, and spat on the ground.

"There's evidence," the second brother offered. "There's myths," the first one corrected. "Still, the one the many. Someone saw them." The first man rolled his eyes. "Yeah well if *they* are, when-".. "If- I find them," He corrected, gripping his axe tightly.. "There will be a river of blood flowing, and I'll drown every last one of the believers in it," he finished, his teeth gritted. The second one shook his head. "If," he repeated, looking up at the sky.

The LED lights shook gently as they strolled back into the hideout. Avery smiled, having a new found bond with the man. *Dad.* "Well, I think dinner's on its way." She nodded, opening a door gently. "I uh, Avery I gotta be honest." He stopped, his deep southern accent prominent. "I don't know how well my brothers wi-"

A man burst out from behind the door, grabbing Avery, and pointing a pistol at her. "Try anything at all, she's dead."

Garrison nodded, his eyes wide with fear, lowering his 1911.

"Now," The man began, holding Avery together. Her heart skipped a beat. He shook his head, whatever he was saying gone, mentally over-ran. "You know, yeah, you think I'm fucking crazy?" He showed his teeth, buttery yellow with a hint of fresh red, like a shark. "Don't you?!" He spat, shoving the gun into her face further. "You people have it SOOO fucking easy just standing around, doing nothing." His eye blinked rapidly, and his finger moved to the trigger. Avery scowled. *Well, at least he's got good firearm safety.* She closed her eyes desperately, her humorous instincts protecting her from screaming in terror.

"I'm a.. I'm a fucking.. he sent me here, and the goddamn shovel won't-" The beliver trailed off, his head beginning to twitch in sync with his eyes. "The clock, it's the damn Issac, fucking always eating out of the pot BUT I TRIED TO TELL HIM NO, the rat, they don't liKe FoOd TheY like.. blood!!" He broke into mumbles, and his limbs began twitching, smiling, a pure psychopath. Avery looked desperately at Garrison. *We need to do something.. RIGHT NOW.* She breathed, and began to slip her way from the gun, gently. The man didn't seem to notice, his rambling turning into utter nonsense. **"HEY!"** He yelled, biting down on his tongue. It crunched audibly and blood began to pour out of his mouth. **"I FUCkInG tOlD yOu to sto- eati- m rati- THEYRE FUCKIN MINE!"** Avery screamed, and Garrison lunged forward. **The believer pulled the trigger.**

It was morning now, and the sun was still covered by large ominous clouds, as if wanting to shine through, but being blocked out by other forces.

Sean shook his head furiously, accompanied by Nate, who seemed oblivious to their situation as they sprinted down the path to the van, having just woken up randomly with the others. "She's still in there, we can't just leave her!" Cam shook his head in response, his "asshole ego" on pause. "We don't know *where* she is, it's four against who knows how many, clearly some government dickwads way above the actual police." Sasha nodded, ducking under a low tree branch. Sean nearly growled like a lion. "So what? We just

GO back to the police, you saw what that weird business dude did! What makes you think ANYTHING will be different?!" Cam consulted Sasha as they ran by, slowing down slightly, rain bouncing off both their hair. "That's a risk we have to take," Cam responded. "A risk we'll have to take if we want to save our friend." Sasha nodded strongly, standing with him. Sean slowed to a stop, and stood next to the small overgrown tree, rooted like a spider across the ground. "And what do you know about risk, huh?" Cam squinted angrily, and approached him closer. "Me? ME SEAN? I've busted my ass all week for you and your girlfriend to uncover your oh so precious mystery." Sean moved his head, now staring him down threatening with one eye. "One which may I remind you almost and maybe WILL get us all killed!" Sean stepped forward, getting in his face. "The only risks you've taken are shitty jokes and being a terrible friend. And yeah, we almost got killed, and we discovered something teenagers would never once get to see." Cam pointed his finger, extending his arm like a catapult. "YOU?! YOU- wanna talk about almost getting killed let's talk about how responsible you and Avery were with the little girl huh? That innocent little thing.. MAYBE! MAYBE SHE'D

STILL BE ALIVE IF YOUR EARS WOR-" Sean leaped forward and slammed him into the tree, tackling both of them down on top of eachother. Sasha reached out, but it was no use.

"THE ONE YOU IGNORED FOR GAS MONEY?!" Cam shook his head, writhing and struggling in Sean's arms who now held him down. "If we've really gotten into such awful trouble and discoveries.." He coughed out. "Then maybe, maybe it's BETTER IF SHE STAYS IN THERE." - "I'LL FUCKING SHOW YOU STAY!" Sean yelled, barreling his fist at Cam, it collided effectively, breaking his nose. Nate tried to break up the fight, but it was no use. Cam bit his teeth, whimpering slightly in pain. Sounds that drowned out the cries and pulls of Sasha, ambience in the rain. *Unimportant.*

"Go FUCK YOURSELF!" He cried out, his voice nearly gone, deep and dilapidated. "Such a fancy insult genius, but he can't come up with anything better when faced with the truth," Sean jeered, wiping blood off his mouth with his sleeve. "Touch me again Sean, go ahead see what happens **Mr anger issues**. I put up with

this shit for years!" Sean smiled cruelly, something *in the air*, turning them into animals. "You want to suffer?" He asked, his neck twitching a bit. Cam bit his teeth psychotically. "I will plant a seed here with the screams of your agony." Sean smiled in response, drawing a blade behind him, the rain washing off the gashes and tears in his hair. Sasha and Nate screamed and cried, pulling at them but it was no use, insanity had begun consuming them. Cam grinned again, his teeth covered with the blood of his newly broken nose. "I will turn your lungs into a red fountain." The rain itself seemed to grow more intense, somehow appearing blood red. *A common theme in the conversation.* The ground grew seputone, the trees glitching with color in chromatic chaos. *Boys! Boys!* "***BOYS!!***" Sasha yelled, and they turned to look at her.

She too was losing her grip on the world, bent down as if in pain. Yet she held onto sanity desperately. "Look," Nate ordered, sharing their symptoms.

Alone, far off in the distance was a man dressed in an old fashioned suit, only one thing indifferent from his perfectly symmetrical figure. His head was of an old western clock, wearing a sharp brown fedora.

rocks and dirt followed slightly around him, like a planet in a black hole, a leaf in a tornado. He raised his hand and performed a salute, an old western gesture, his pocket watch reflecting his head. Then.. *snap*. The world was back to normal, colors and rain, perfectly surrounding them it was meant to be.

Chapter 14

The believer pulled the trigger...

But there was no pop, only a click. The chamber had no round in it, the recoil of the spring however was still there, and it dug the metal gun into her gas-mask, cracking just slightly. *Screw it.* "HEY LOOK, THE CREATOR!" She yelled, pointing at the corner of the room. The man's eyes widened wider than any normal human could achieve, his pupils completely bloodshot, his eyes nearly red, foaming at the mouth with blood. Whatever sliver of sanity left seemed to have taken its last course, as he dropped the gun, and ran to the corner, falling on the floor. Garrison immediately elbowed Avery out of the way, behind his back. "Cover your ears." He commanded, and she did so as he shot the man in the head. He turned around, horror on his face. "You okay?" She nodded, fresh terror matching his in her eyes. "He had to die, right?..." Garrison nodded meaningfully. "Yes. Avery, he tried to kill you." She nodded, at a loss for words, and breath. He studied the crack in her gas-mask cautiously. "You sure you're okay?".. She gave a small yes, but it didn't seem convincing in the slightest. "Good, cause we gotta move…Right now. Where there's one, there's many."

"Did they get her?!" A woman called in the distance, her voice rapidly approaching. "Cmon," Garrison snapped, grabbing her by the shirt and pulling her into a run. The rain had not stopped outside as they bolted through the old construction equipment. The tree's leaves were dark and gray, almost blue, with the rain pummeling down onto the rusted old metal. "This way," Garrison directed quietly, jumping up to a fence. There was barbed wire, and Avery cringed as she cut her arm half way down, the old rusty spikes digging into her tendons. She bit her lip, half her face covered in bruises from the sharp bits of the mask pressing against her head. The rain washed it off, turning red. *Ow. Ow. Ow. Fuck. Move. Survive.* She told herself. It stung like hell, but she didn't stop moving.

They traversed through the woods once again, narrowly avoiding trees, and diving into bushes on their way. "Avery!" Garrison called, he looked around, making sure the area was clear. "Get that pistol ready," He warned. She nodded insecurely. "Self defense," Garrison assured, surveying the area again. "Self defense," She repeated shakily. "My brothers were headed back," Garrison muttered. "They ain't dumb enough to not notice an incoming attack, we have an emergency path," He nodded. "This is it." He moved the brush slightly and stared out. "We should encounter them if all goes right."

... "I know you're out here!" Someone's voice yelled from afar.

"We WILL find you!" they added, accompanied with the sound of the bolt of a rifle reloading. "Alright, we gotta move," Garrison whispered, cleaning off the glass of his gas mask. Avery echoed him, and they crawled slowly out of the bush, making their way behind a concrete barrier, in a slight crater, hastily thrown from the sky. Hours passed as they made their way across the forest, avoiding enemies as the day faded. "Last resort," Garrison began, "It's an emergency landing spot, our meet-up." Avery motioned her understanding, heaving, exhausted from running for hours. "We're gonna have to find somewhere else," Garrison informed her, rounding a corner of a tree.

"That is, if we find a way to ambush them." he took out a small water-bottle and drained half of it, handing it to Avery. She inhaled the rest gladly. "So, plan is we ambush them." He hesitated. "But we can't do that without-" - "Finding your brothers." Avery rolled her eyes. "Got it." And they continued down the trail.

Cam and Sean both sat sprawled on the ground, covered in traumatic injuries. They looked at eachother, their faces surprised and disgusted, in awe they were capable of ever truly hurting each other. Guilty, in pain, *human*. Sean reached behind his back, and his eyes shot open, surprised he still had what he was looking for. He drew the katana cautiously, watching it expand into its full-form.

Cam nodded, and he held the sword close to him. It immediately took effect, picking up the pieces of bone and blood on the ground, and healing his nose, reversing the events of violence moments prior. It glowed its ocean blue, the opposite of the fresh drawn blood on both of their faces. Sean extended his hand, and Cam nodded, grabbing it and pulling himself up. He gestured to Sean's head wounds, patches of his brown hair still ripped out. Sean shook his head, and bit his lip, shrinking the katana back into his pocket. Cam looked at him confused, joined by Nate and Sasha. He simply shook his head again, and picked himself up, moving forward to the spot the clock man had just been. The others followed, but made sure they kept their distance. Sean frowned ahead, rolling up his sleeves, his shirt now covered in mud and dirt from the rain and the fight. He clawed at his head, feeling the gashes roughly. *My fault, my aggression, my lesson.*

They BOLTED past the tire swing, not looking back for a second, and ignoring the tent and supplies entirely, which were soaked in rain and fallen in mud. Lightning now blared above loudly, illuminating the foggy woods only occasionally, nearly flooded with the fresh downpour.

The van shook as they floured it down the gravel path, which was now partly flooded, a tiny river, each intersection and turn feeling more like a pond than a road. Sean stared out the windshield profusely, driving faster than Cam had been. The others fidgeted their body's, holding the same tenacity. "We get in, we ask, they say no, we're going ourselves," Sean established. Sasha bit her lip, but nodded still, genuinely agreeing with him. Cam gave a quick 'okay" reluctantly which Nate echoed, as per usual, not fully in tune with the world. "And if they do say yes?" Sasha asked, cringing at a sharp corner, looking down. "We storm the place, guns blazin'," Cam responded from the corner, smirking with vengeance. Sasha rolled her eyes "who said you'd get a gun?" Cam shrugged, pulling out the somehow still intact **"CAM-era"** - "God," He responded, still smirking. Sasha turned around, ignoring him, but laughing to herself a little. *Idiot.* They laughed, neither of them remembering the event that had happened between them the previous day.

The usual three hour drive was cut down to one. Sean paid no mind to the speed limit, racing down the dirt roads of the mountains, still flooded like make-shift rivers.

John held a tight grip on his keys, as he turned to lock his office. He shook his head remorsefully. "He's dead," he muttered… "Let it go." He stood idle for a few moments, studying the empty space on his door. Boring old wood, a sterile silver handle, and a perfectly framed glass window, plaid in its interior. A frown formed fresh on his face as he stared at each point. He was the very definition of sad, a normal, boring, un-exciting man. Yet in this one moment, as he stared into his domicile, he longed to *not* be himself. *Just let me let go. Let me move on… He's dead.* "But you won't," he muttered out loud, peering into his small reflection in the glass window. *But you won't.*

At long last he turned around, and walked towards the exit, the sound of the rain becoming more audible as he drew closer. "Well," he began to himself, his voice grumbly and cold. "At least I prevented it from happening aga-" A frown erupted onto his face at lightspeed, and his eyes shot open with pure unbridled rage. "WHY?!" he pounded on the glass, and shoulder-slammed the door open, as two strange old yellow lights made their way closer.

The old minivan came FLYING into the parking lot, running a stop-sign and skidding to a stop into about three parking spots, directly in front of John. He shook his head furiously, covering his eyes from the blinding brights, which were still on in the van.

"Let me guess," he growled as he yanked the unlocked van-door open. "What did I tell you huh?! WHAT DID I TELL YOU?!" He yelled, with a face angry enough to destroy the entire van itself.

Sean hopped out of the driver's seat, narrowly missing John. "Who let *HIM* drive?" He demanded, staring at Cam. "Wasn't my idea," Cam muttered, shrugging with his eyebrows. "Avery's gone," Sean informed, his face still furious. "Oh well shit I wonder why, good thing no one tr-" Sean **slammed** the van door closed, startling Nate, who was still sitting inside.

"We're going there either way. Are you coming or not?" Sean asked, leaning back on the wet metal of the minivan. John scowled, glaring directly at him. "I can't and you know that," he responded, his face cold. "And you shouldn't either," he continued, grabbing Sean by the arm. Sean shoved him away with surprising strength, almost knocking him over. "Yes or no?!" He demanded, standing in a fighting pose, the rain bouncing off his head injuries. John's face shifted for just a second, a small part of him seeming concerned. "Kid, what the hell hap-" he stopped himself, dropping every possible instance of caring. "Need I remind you, I am an off-" Sean grabbed his shirt, and pulled him close to the van. "Yes or no?" He asked coldly. John stared him down, and pushed him away with ease. "Watch yourself boy," He grumbled, his tone a genuine threat. "You've got guts coming all the way out here to the *actual* police, just expecting I'll gladly pickup and help." Sean started approaching again, and John gave him a warning stare. "I told you not to. I warned you. This is your fault, and your burden to bear, NOT mine." Sean shook his head, and approached him again with zero fear in his eye. "You act all big and tough," he began, walking back to the man. "You're just as troubled and childish as us." John gritted his teeth, matching his fearlessness. Sean smiled slightly, he knew he was cutting deep. "If this was your brother, would re-" John **shoved** him hard, making him fall backwards on his back into the flooded street. "You don't KNOW ME!" He yelled, stepping towards Sean. "YOU DON'T KNOW WHAT I'VE BEEN THROUGH!" Sean threw his legs out, sitting up. "YOU DON'T **GET**. TO GO THERE!" John yelled, stepping on his shoe, and knocking him back down. Sean coughed, the wind knocked out of him from the impact. Cam reached out and grabbed the now "untamed wild bear", pulling him back. "Okay! Okay, chill!" He intercepted loudly. John nodded, shaking Cam off his shoulder, not taking it further. "I'm closing the station. If you're gonna get another person killed, do it yourself." Sean turned his head back towards the others, his lip now slightly fatter, glaring at them with hatred. "Told you so."

Cam shook his head, resting his hands on his lap as he sat back down. "Well that went about as well as I expected." Sean waved him off, his face determined and serious, still heading the group at the driver's seat. They'd been taking turns driving, each flying down the now "river" once again paying no mind to speed. Sasha bit her tongue, studying everything at her disposal rigorously. *There has to be another way.* Her eyes darted from point to point only slightly illuminated in the faint yellow light of the headlights. *Okay.. So we know the fake door exists, but we can't get through. And we definitely can't now.* She squinted hard, using every last bit of her brain-power. *The halls were all bright white.. No. They had a computer automated system.. Also no. The rain... THE RAIN!* Her head nearly popped off as she jumped out of her seat. "The geography!" she cried, happily. Cam shrugged. "What about it?" Nate echoed him, looking at her blankly..

"Those tunnels that… thing dug.. that wasn't just mud." Sean raised his eyebrow, which was now close-by to a black-eye, but nodded, following her. "Monarch laboratories," Sasha sighed. "The cave we went through the first time…" She looked around at the three boys, and they motioned their attentivity. "Guys that wasn't a hallway, that was a vent." Sasha nodded aggressively, now smiling happily, a puzzle complete in her head. "A vent made for water… That's why the wall was blown open! AND it's the whole reason the place was fully visible, and not blocked off.…"

Cam gestured to his wrist, ironically pointing at a clock that wasn't there.. *get to the point?* "This isn't a mountain, it's a lake." Sean's eyes widened, the whole situation suddenly making more sense. Sasha raised her arms in the air conclusively. "Whatever this.. "monarch" is, it's underwater, not under dirt."

Cam perched his face on his hands, thinking hard. *But the waters under the dirt?* Sasha waved him off, reading his mind, and he regrouped, letting go of his jokes for a moment. "Alright… okay,, then we just swim into the lake, and we're there?" He asked, though he knew well what the answer would be. Sasha moved her jaw awkwardly. "Yeah…no. It's a few hundred meters down." She shivered. "Or at least… the part we were in was, I think." Cam shrugged, accepting what she'd said, but still a bit scared. Sean sighed. "Wanna switch?" he called out, pulling over. Cam gave a hasty thumbs up, and pushed him aside playfully, hopping back into his: *Thrown.*

"So assuming there's an entrance at the bottom, we descend a few hundred meters and break in." Cam eyed her suspiciously. "Okay… sure.. But where the hell, at midnight, are we gonna find the gear we need?" Nate smirked, hearing one word. In one foul swoop, he wrenched out his bag from under the seat, still struggling immensely just as he had been days prior. They watched curiously as he drew a massive leather strap out of it, and unraveled it. Revealing a scuba mask and an oxygen tank, along with a strange lengthy piece of paper that read: *16, 12, 25, 20, 3, 15, 14, 22, 5, 14, 9, 5, 14. 3, 5*

He smiled, and Sasha returned it with a grin. Sean furrowed his bloody, bruised, beat up brow, watching them through the rear-view mirror. "What's the note about?" Nate shrugged blanky. "Eh, not important." Sean rolled his eyes. *How convenient.*

"Okay that makes one of us." Sean nodded, hope rising in his eyes, reflecting the heavy rain and flooded road outside the window. Cam smirked from the driver's seat as he had many times before. "Sasha?" He beckoned, not bothering to pull over, there wasn't a car in sight. "You wanna drive?" Sasha shrugged. "Sure.. if you trust me with your beloved wife after last time." Cam rolled his eyes, and gave a proud nod. "She'd be honored." He let go of the wheel, and sat up, leaving the van still completely in motion. "Cam?!" Shasha cried, rushing to the driver's seat and buckling promptly. "You couldn't have stopped it?!" Cam laughed in the back. "It's not funny! You could've got us all killed!" He smiled guiltlessly, and raised his shoulder up and down. "Well, we're going into a secret government death building anyway." Sasha took a deep breath, ignoring him and quickly steadying the van to a much more reasonable speed. "Okay," Cam exhaled, cracking his knuckles. The three boys sat around as if they were at a meeting. Nate laughed to himself. *Quarterly reports have been very good this year.. I.. uh...* His brain faded off.

"One at a time," Cam pitched, gesturing at his plan. Sean squinted, not fully trusting him. "Look, we send one down through a chain, we pull the gear up, rinse and repeat. Sean frowned. "And the last one?" The van shook a bit as Cam bit his lip in response. "Well, they cut the rope and hope we find another way out." Sasha shook her head in the driver's seat, staring through the mirror back at them. "And what if one of us doesn't make it in?"

Cam frowned, frozen ominously, his peach fuzz illuminated for a mere moment in the lightning outside. "It's a risk we have to take." Sean covered his face and ran his fingers through his hair. "Even if this DID work, where on god's green earth would we find a chain that long?" He frowned warningly, noticing Cam's smirk reappearing. "Don't, don't you-" - "GEE, I DON'T KNOW," Cam shouted proudly, the phrase that was Seans bane of existence since they'd very first met. "If only there were some kind of fallen abandoned elevator with a chain just as long as we need." Sean's eyes grew with hope, and for once, he too smirked. "Not bad," he nodded proudly.

Sasha let out a small breath of nervousness. "I don't like it.. I don't think anyone here does." *Anyone sane anyway.* Cam shrugged. "We-" Sean elbowed him, interrupting. "If it's what it takes, then it's what it takes."

They were silent for a few moments, then Nate raised his fist in the air slightly. "We in then?" He asked, even if he hadn't fully been paying attention. Cam nodded, eyeing Sasha. She exhaled, and thought hard, but motioned in agreement nonetheless. Sean joined in, with the look of determination still fresh on his face. *Screw it.* He bit his teeth, and withdrew the katana, taking a moment to heal his lengthy wounds. There was a collective sigh, and Cam gave him a genuine, strong, proud nod. *Good on you, Mr. Anger.*

Sasha wiped her forehead. "Okay, so we need to go scuba diving, hope to god we can breathe, and then repeat." She grinned. "Easy eno-" **BAM!**

A fork of lightning **EXPLODED** just a few meters ahead, and the road, by some strange phenomenon, grew nearly impossible to speed through.

As if in kahoots, the radio kicked on in the van involuntarily, and an alarm boomed out, followed by a voice. **"The following districts of the midwestern United States have been placed under severe flood watch. Colorado, Wyoming, Utah. This is not a drill. Please seek shelter indoors or at a high elevation immediately."**

Sean shook his head, rolling his eyes. "They know we're coming." Sasha nodded, her expression grim. "Then what's to say they don't know exactly what we're planning?" Cam and Sean both shrugged in different ways. "Like I said, it's a risk we have to take." Sean nodded, agreeing with him. "Alright then," Sasha replied from ahead, accepting their fate. "Let's go save our friend," Nate spat, attempting to make his voice sound "cool." Cam rolled his eyes. *Yep, Mr action movie, let's do that.*

"Avery!" Garrison yelled, grabbing and pulling her behind a rock. They were close to the radio-tower now, braving a fork in the river, rushing wildly, lightning pounding above like gunshots.

Garrison shook his head, they'd been looking for his brothers for hours but to no avail. "Still got that sword?" Avery breathed out heavily, coughing violently. *Where are we?* She was injured badly, her knee and arms bleeding, her jeans torn all down the legs, their loose threads freshly coated in red.

"Avery, I need you to look at me," Garrison began, pulling her face towards his. "We need to run, we need to get to that radio station, and we need to get as far hidden as possible." Avery nodded, her face serious and determined, but partly laced with suspicion. *Why the tower specifically?* "If something happens to me, you keep going, okay?" She nodded again, her vision swaying, she was losing blood. "Okay." *Leave. Leave this place. Or die.* She smiled out of instinct. *Goal either way.* Garrison pulled her into a small hug. "We let NOTHING stop us."

Rain hit her eye slightly as they peered out from a rock, now out of the fork in the river, and scanning the area. "Alright, on my signal we're gonna run as fast as we can out of here." Avery affirmed silently once again.

They waited for a few minutes, tensions high, then Garrison waved his hand down, and they both leaped from the rock, sprinting towards the tower. The river was somehow now right next to them, flooding fast and rushing violently, taking chunks of rocks with it.

"This way," Garrison called softly. The ground opened up as they ran, the water flooding and taking more and more of the land they had left to stand on. Garrison shook his head. **"We- go- ro-"** His voice was drowned out by the thunderous rain and the rushing of the river. He gritted his teeth concerningly, and pointed to the rocks ahead, drifting, very dangerously in the rushing water. Avery gestured her understanding, and they followed through. Garrison leaped with ease across to the first rock, grabbing a tree branch slightly as he did. A chill went down her spine. *Just like Grey.*

The river washed over their feet violently, threatening to knock them off at a moment's notice, as they both leaped to the first rock. Garrison gestured to the next one, and Avery breathed heavily in fear, it was further away than she would've liked. She sighed, looking at Garrison and began to get ready, priming herself for a long jump. "You.. sur-" She wasn't able to finish her sentence, coughing loudly, desperately wiping away the fog in the gas mask, which made it difficult to see. "Circle the river!" A voice barked in the distance. "Avery, we have to go." Garrison yelled, his voice barely audible, growing in panic. She nodded and took a deep breath, Garrison jumped in front of her, and she followed behind, leaping into the air. Her fingers collided with the rock, but the rest of her body did not. "Shit!" She screamed, as her bottom half was pulled, the river a monster, eager to devour her. "Avery!" Garrison yelled, and threw his hand out. She grabbed it, and he pulled desperately. She would not budge. Her foot was stuck on a rock.

She closed her eyes, and pulled hard with her leg. The rock gave a snap, and her toe became floppy. She screamed loudly, biting down her tongue, only increasing the pain. Her foot was free, but her toe was broken.

Garrison pulled hard, and this time she budged loose, rolling onto the rock like a dead fish. She gritted her teeth, grabbing her foot. "I know, Avery I know, but we DO NOT have time!" Garrison pleaded, dragging her up on her feet. "Can you walk?" She nodded through tears, and forced herself to take a step. Garrison patted her, already a step ahead of her. "We need to go." Avery gave a thumbs up, her hand shaking violently, not willing to speak. Garrison looked around scanning as the river rushed onto the rock, threateningly every second, the world a time bomb of nature.

Garrison pointed to another rock, even further than the last. He exhaled, and ran forward without question, barely making to the other side, his boot slipping on the moss. He breathed heavily, and extended his hand out to her, waiting for her to jump. "I think I found them!" Another voice yelled in the distance. Garrison gestured even more aggressively for her, panic erupting in his eyes behind the glass of the gas mask. She didn't think this time, and ran forward, ignoring the pain, jumping into the rock.

Her head collided against the side of it harshly, and Garrison grabbed her arms, and pulled her in. The world went blurry, and she let tears flow, mixing with blood, her face no longer looking human, like a pulverised shrimp. Garrison's face turned stone cold, somehow even more so than the soulless gas-mask. "*Ave-*" his voice blurred out in her ears. He touched her mask, and came back with shards of plastic and glass. His eyes widened, his face horrified. It had been broken, and severely split in half.

"They went in the river!" A woman yelled from the distance, though the distance was not far at all.

"We have to go!" Garrison snapped, shaking his head for the thousandth time. They were on land now, across the last rock.

"THERE!" A man yelled, and Garrison threw his feet up, hoisting Avery up. It was silent for a mere moment as he looked around desperately. Then the air EXPLODED into gunfire.

He was already running as the first bullet ricocheted off a tree. Avery at his side, barely awake. *I could give her my mask but if I do we're both dead.* "GET 'EM!" A man yelled in the background.

The rocks thrashed past violently as they ran around trees, heading for the radio tower, survival their only goal. Gunshots filled every corner as they bolted behind massive wooden planks and trees, dropping through a tunnel in the muck. Garrison let go of Avery as they fell, and she army-crawled forward with all her mite. Her wounds filled with nasty wet mud as she fought for her life, her face beaten, her gas-mask gone. The rain pounded loudly above, combined with the sounds of yelling and running. Garrison grabbed her hand as she made it the other side, and hoisted her forward and up, helping her out the tunnel. "Where'd they go?!"

The voices called in variations. Garrison gestured at the outside of the tunnel, the river rushing like a hurricane with the wind around the flooded land, which was now almost everything around them. The water thrashed against rocks violently, as if a new ocean had been created. Avery looked desperately around at the literal island they now stood on, sitting in the middle of the deadly flood.

"FOUND 'EM!" One yelled, and footsteps began echoing again.

"Avery…" She nodded, the only thing she could do at this point. "You ready?" She repeated herself, priming her nearly non-functional body. *Alright Mr Jenkins 6th grade track practice, don't fail me now.* Garrison shook his head, drawing his pistol. The roar of an old boat sounded in the distance, and more believers swarmed them from every direction. Garrison pointed, his hand shaking at the radio station, its first floor and half the building now victim to the flood. They exchanged glances as the guns began to fire, not much mattering now. They nodded, understanding each other perfectly. Only one thing left to do for the final time… ***run.***

*The woman dropped the flashlight, running into the brush, leaving Avery behind. **Garrison** stood, defending his daughter, a magnum revolver strapped in a holster, a certain switchblade in his back* *pocket. Avery put her tiny hands out in front her eyes, the blinding lights ahead of them stinging like a burning sun. "Step away from her," a man commanded.*

He was dressed in a suit, with eye's just barely visible, a sick glowing smile embedded on his shadowy face. Garrison shook his head, gritting his teeth. "I'm immortal you son of a bitch you REALLY want to do this?!" The man smiled, only his mouth visible in the faint beams of the trees, and the ominous shadow of the flashlights. "I'm not here for you," He said, stepping forward. Garrison drew closer to Avery, guarding her with his life. "Do anyth-" - "step away brother," his opposition interrupted. Garrison scowled with genuine hatred at the man. "I told you before you're not my fucking brother anymore."

The man let out a small laugh, patting one of the guards on the shoulder, its rifle still aimed prominently at the two. They waited. "Garrison, step away from the child." His face grew angrier, and his blood vessels were visibly bulging, eyes bloodshot as he defended his daughter. "Well then, I hope you remember what being shot in the he-" Garrison SPRINTED to his brother,

dodging the bullets of the guards as he went, combating them with

the speed of a bullet himself. A guard fired their rifle, and he

grabbed the gun faster than any of them could react, pointing it

back at his brother.

The man let out another laugh, and stepped fearlessly directly into

the path of the gun barrel. "You said it yourself, we're immortal.

You want to waste valuable ammo? Garrison glanced over at

Avery, who was being watched by no one. All the attention on him.

"Why would it matter?" He snorted in his face. "You're just gonna

*enslave more imports from **NITROPLANE** anyway. His brother*

frowned slightly, stepping closer to the barrel of the rifle. "Come

now, you don't think I'm that bad." Garrison rolled his eyes. "I

don't think, I know." His brother nodded. "Then how about all

*those times you needed **returner**, huh? How about that?" Garrison*

snorted, sending thick snot into his brother's face. "I'm not

*Jeremy,... **one**," he said coldly. "You really think you ca-"*

Garrison spat again, and landed in his brother's eye disgustingly.

His brother curved his lips with rage, and Garrison smirked, the *polar opposite. "I don't need your permission anymore. You're not my brother, and no matter how hard you try, murdering my daughter ain't gonna do a damn thing to bring **her** bac-" The man slammed the butt of the rifle back into Garrison, interrupting him, and throwing him to the ground, and stomping on his nose. Blood began to pour out, but Garrison paid no mind. He laughed as loud as he could. "Ha, that all you go-" The man slammed his face in with the front of the rifle, then shot him. Garrison smiled, and his brother grabbed his knife and sliced away at his leg, cutting off the chunk of skin the revolver was strapped to. Garrison gritted his teeth in pain, blood pooling in the floor, but he did not care. "You know?" He coughed out, jeering. "It's pretty damn ironic that I'm the one smiling right now, ha." His brother gritted his teeth, kicking him over, and waving a command to someone. Then the scream of a little girl sounded in the distance as his brother prepared the blood covered revolver. The air popped loudly, and something hit the floor.*

Her mind blanked for the first two seconds, not present in the waking current world. Then her vision focused. Her legs flew in front of her as if she was riding a bike, carrying her through the mud and rocks faster than she knew she could even run. The air rang with pain, and bullets ricochet around her violently. As she ran her senses returned, the smell of blood and gunfire enclosing around her, with sounds of pops and cracks to match. Her brain was on autopilot, and she could barely think. *Water.. flood.. father ahead.* She focused on the word, as bullets rained past her. *Father.. dad.* Her consciousness returned, and she dodged just as a *massive purple shockwave* exploded behind her. Some sort of weapon not from her time. "AVERY!" Garrison yelled ahead. This time she yelled back "YEAH?" Garrison came skidding to a stop in front of her, sending mud flying into the distance, which was now a flooded ocean. She stopped with him, and crowds began to surround them, yelling in every direction. They stood, preparing for a fight, before the last remaining willow tree, which somehow still had a wasp's nest attached to it, clinging on for dear life in the now "hurricane" they stood in.

"It's not too late ya know!" A man laughed out, only half speaking, his voice high pitched, loud and psychotic. "You could joi-"... He coughed up blood, and his eyes turned even more red, vessels audibly popping. "You know what's right.. you could...believe.. with us." He aimed a rusty massive metal axe at them, which had a shotgun on the handle. Another off, *obscure* weapon. Garrison stood his ground, and aimed his revolver out at the crowd. "Listen, you let us go-" The believer fired his shotgun, and it violently bashed the axe outwards, bending it down. Avery squinted, confused, her ears slightly ringing. *Not very smart for an army.* Garrison shook his head, adjusting his body position into a run. He jerked for a second, then went back cautiously. Avery frowned.. *Too outnumbered.*

The believers drew closer, each with a rusted metal weapon, gun or not, it didn't matter, they were all deadly. Garrison side eyed Avery cautiously, and a chill went down her spine, she held her pistol out in front of her, matching him. He began to blink, and she nodded quickly, reading his mind. The group grew closer and the air grew tenser by the second.

Garrison took a deep breath, not moving the gun. *3,* he blinked once. *2,* a second time. *1* He pulled the trigger, and the believers immediately echoed him, a hundred different bullets flying out at once, all, by some miracle missing by inches. The fire ceased. Garrison's shot had landed perfectly. Yet it landed nowhere near the opposing gang.

It landed on the wasp nest above, creating a fresh cacophony of screams and running. Avery smirked, and he echoed her through the mask. Then they ran as fast as they could back in the direction of the radio-tower.

 They quickly found that there was absolutely nowhere to run that didn't lead to the promise of a watery death. Garrison looked around, and his eyes lit up. "Saving damn grace," he muttered, pointing at an old rusty canoe, the only single thing not flooded in the distance, and miraculously still on land. Garrison eye'd her carefully for just a single second, fighting a mental debate. *If I give her my mask, I go insane, and she probably dies. If she stays without a mask,..* He shook his head definitively. *If my mask goes, she dies. There might just be a chance of her living if I'm the one to keep my sanity.* "Cmon!" He yelled, grabbing her arm and breaking into a run towards the boat.

Avery shook her head., quickly studying the: *Shittyness,* of its structure. "You can't be serious?!" Garrison threw his arms up, slapping them on his knees in defeat. "You got a better idea?" She shook her head, biting off a loose thread of her jacket.

A moment later, the voices of believers started to make a comeback, echoing throughout with horrifying screams of war declaration. Mud turned to river as they trudged to the boat, leaving footprints behind, only to be washed out by the rain in seconds. "Okay, help me push in." He yelled, waiting for Avery. She got down on her knees at the front and began to push forcefully, groaning in pain, but biting it away, Garrison pulling at the opposite side from the back. The metal was freezing cold and sharp, rusty and dilapidated. "Okay!" Garrison confirmed at last, as the canoe slid into the water, nearly being washed away immediately.

Avery bit her finger, stopping more bleeding, her vision still blurring in and out. "I don-" Garrison nodded, pain in his eyes watching her *pain. Give her the damn mask,* his consciousness screamed. He echoed her, bottling up the pain. *If I do, we're both dead.* "I know, I know it's okay, you're gonna be okay, just grab my hand" She struggled badly, and Garrison resulted to leaning, nearly tipping the boat, and helping her on-board, simultaneously pushing off with her weight.

"Don't lose 'em!" A woman's voice shouted in the distance.

"Stay low," Garrison commanded, and Avery followed, ducking in the passenger compartment. The river, as if a living monster, pondered zero hesitation, and immediately accepted them into the flood, the canoe speeding up instantly. Garrison reached into his pocket's quickly, setting the paddle down, and retrieving a leather pouch. "You know any first aid?" Avery shrugged, her hearing not fully recovered, only made worse by the now very loud sound of the rushing floods. She took the leather pouch anyway as he handed it back. *"Pat- your - woun-"* She ripped it open with her teeth, and found an old soaked bandage, grabbing it and wrapping it around her forearm, biting it off. It didn't work, and she was left with it falling off embarrassingly. Though now, she didn't seem to need it. The pain was subsiding, and her hearing was improving. *Confidence...* The word rang through her head.

They hit a ridge and the canoe leaped into the air slightly, sending the first aid pouch flying. "Damnit!" She cursed under her breath. A part of her was taken aback, surprised at how easy it had just been to breathe. "Fucking go!" She yelled at him, her eyes becoming bloodshot, the disease in the air taking effect. Garrison shook his head. "Avery.." He warned, battling the flood. "WHAT?!" She demanded, her face muscles twitching, her hearing back surprisingly strong. "I need you to stay sane for a little bit longer okay?" She frowned, and her pupils grew, humanity fighting back inside her. "I'm trying!" She cried desperately, angrily. The canoe nearly tipped all the way as the flood grew stronger in front of them, almost at the main part of the rushing river now. The trees stuck out like fingers, blocking their path. Garrison steered around them, as the water sped faster and faster.

"KILL THE NON BELIEVERS!" The same woman from earlier yelled, and an army of screams of terror echoed ahead of them. "Shit," Garrison spat, looking around quickly. "Avery?" He called back. *Death?* Her mind focused on the thought. "Can you shoot?" He asked ahead of her. "Fuck yeah!" Avery responded, devilishly, bloodlust fresh in her system, not fully human. "Okay, then get ready!'

She nodded eagerly, and withdrew her pistol, her lips curving into a smile, her teeth now slightly sharper, peeking over them, glinting in the dim sun. "FIRE!" The woman yelled, and all kinds of gunshots fired in their direction. "Avery!" Garrison ordered, as the canoe merged with the river, speeding up like a car on a highway. "On it!" She reported, smiling, aiming in seconds as the canoe rocked back and forth, tipping violently. She shot, and a believer screamed in pain, the blood from their leg flying into the river. She shot again, and an opposing shot went by, veering into the river. "Miss!" Avery called out jeeringly, shooting one off to the left in the head. More gun shots flew by, by a miracle not hitting the boat. "Hey bitch-lievers!" Avery yelled. "DEATH TO THEM!" They

replied, in variation. One raised a grenade into the air, getting ready to throw it. Avery shot quickly, landing it perfectly on the grenade, blowing them up. "Fuck you!! HAHA!" She yelled, adopting the psychotic chaos of the air. Happily she smirked, firing another shot at a random head. "Keep that up Avery!" Garrison called back, only using the paddle for drag now, having given up the hope of actually steering minutes ago.

The water rushed by, splashing them in the eyes. Avery coughed, but did not let up. She shot, and several opposing bullets shot back, this time, one of them landing on the side of the canoe. "Uh, **dad!**" Avery yelled. Garrison shrugged her referral off. *We don't have time.* "Shit." They began both frantically scooping out water, just as three more shots landed on the canoe. "SINK THEM!" The believers yelled, firing a barrage. Avery dodged left and right, still keeping the gun trained on the group all around them. The radio tower was coming into view now, lightning striking behind it. "DON'T LET THEM LEAVE!" A man yelled, and one leaped into the river from the cliff side above. He tried to swim like an alligator, being swept away by the current and slamming head first into the canoe. He grabbed it without hesitation, and forced his way aboard, taking hold of Avery before she could shoot, and holding her in a chokehold. "Gar-" She cried out, but her breath was cut off. Garrison thrust the paddle behind him, and it split in half, now a spear. He stabbed it into the intruder's eye as a bullet went by his head, barely dodging it.

The man fell into the river, shrinking behind them as the water rushed chaotically. Avery coughed, and her eyes grew more bloodshot. "OKAY NOW I'm PISSED!" She yelled, firing at two of them, disabling them both. "JACKSON!" One pleaded to the left, sounding sad. "YOU'RE GONNA FUCKIN DIE FOR

THAT!" He screamed, throwing a grenade into the canoe. It

landed surprisingly perfectly, and Avery frantically picked it up,

throwing it back at them, matching the precision. "HAH!" She

barked, growing more violent as four of them were blown to

pieces. "We're almost there!" Garrison yelled, using the

"half-paddle" to steer across the sharp curve. Avery slammed her

chin on the rusty metal as he made the turn. She gritted her teeth,

anger taking over. "Sorry!" He blurted, and she let go of tension

for a moment, still scooping water out of the boat, her teeth

sharper, her eyes more keen, more red, like a hyena.

Suddenly the commotion died down. Avery furrowed her now

sharper brow, genuinely confused. She ran her hand through the

water in a moment of curiosity, and her eyes shot open. It was

blood red. She looked up, finding Garrison already doing so.

Something in the sky was changing dramatically.

They all stared ahead, stopping the violence in a strange moment of peace. The water seemed to slow, flowing gently, almost safely. The sun too had turned blood red, with a dark circle around it. Faintly within it was an old western clock. The world was now a horrifying orangish-red, and everything in sight was now covered in-part by a massive shadow of looming clock hands. Red lightning struck ahead, and the thunder clouds turned a sickly black. It was silent for a moment, and the water fully calmed down as if the universe had paused.

Then the clock ticked one second, and everything resumed. "What the hell is that?" Avery demanded, her voice shaking, literally in the air as the canoe zoomed by. "I have.. no idea!" Garrison called back. They both nodded, their mission clear. *Get to that tower, or die trying.*

"HE WILL SAVE US!" The believers screamed proudly nearby, marveling at the sky as they ran. Avery shivered, her humanity returning to her for a second. "The creator," She said aloud, looking at the clock in the sky. Garrison nodded. "It's real."

She shook her head, violence returning. "FOR THE CREATOR!"

A woman yelled, leaping as far as she could, landing right next to the canoe. She immediately began drowning in the blood colored water, grabbing the rusty metal, and slicing her finger. Her blood was sent into the river, impossible to tell which liquid was the real one.

She drew a pistol and shot at Avery, barely missing her by a single centimeter. Avery shot back, and nailed her in her arm. She smiled cruelly and Avery pressed the trigger again. "Fuck!" She yelled, the gun clicked, she was out of ammo. The woman shot but not at her, shooting the canoe until her mag had only one round left, Avery grabbed the gun from her, and she roared like a lion, screeching psychotically. Avery recoiled back in disgust, and shot her in the head, collapsing her body into the water.

"PROBLEM!" Garrison yelled. "Yeah!" She responded, and he exhaled. The canoe was beginning to sink into the **blood river**, with more shots landing every few seconds. The radio tower was close now, only a few hundred meters away. She felt herself rise with the water, which was growing to be even more violent, sweeping believers into it, and threatening to tear the boat apart at any moment. The roar of an engine echoed in the distance, and rusty green metal appeared in the tiny stripe of ground left above them. "PROBLEM, THE FUCKING SEQUEL!" Garrison began, knowing exactly what it was.

An impossibly loud crack sounded, and the canoe gained another giant hole. The thing roared into the trees mercilessly, speeding up and crushing its fellow brethren beneath it. The sound of a hydraulic mount boomed into the world, then immediately, the fiery whirl of a Gatling gun.

"THEY HAVE TANKS?!" Avery cried, frantically scooping water from the canoe. "That thing's a motorized quad wheel transporter!" Garrison yelled ahead, doing everything in his power to go faster. "SO *A FUCKING* TANK!" Avery confirmed, staring, horrified into the barrel of the mounted Gatling gun. "SAY NIGHT NIGHT!"

The operator yelled in the distance, and the gun jumped to life, firing a hundred shots at the poor little injured boat below. Garrison closed his eyes, no point in having them open, somehow dodging the bullets. "Shitty aim!" Avery bragged, having also survived. She could hear the operator yell in rage at his failure.

Garrison shoved the broken paddle in hard, beaching them on a tree root. "We have to swim!" He yelled as the truck roared in the distance. "WHAT?!" Avery demanded. "AVERY IT'S THE ONLY WAY!" He pleaded, sinking with the boat. "Okay!" She replied, and he grabbed her, jumping back into the rushing river. They spiraled out of control, not daring to let go of each other as the bullets rained above. Avery opened her eyes, a sudden pain in her pelvis. She looked down, she was spirting blood from a bullet wound, but it wasn't visible in the already bloody water. Garrison reached up, and ripped off his gas mask, thrusting it against her face, and buckling it on. She felt her teeth go square, and her eyes return to normal, her humanity resuming. They sank, smashing into sharp rocks and trees, the flooded world below. Both their visions blurry and uncanny. Something gleamed above, and both their jaws dropped, staring at the only visible thing in the universe: A man dressed in a ripped black suit with a clock for a face reaching down. Avery screamed, humanly, as the man grabbed hold of Garrison away from her. He yelled in the water desperately, and Avery tried to hold on, but it was no use. He slipped out of her grasp and the clock man pulled him out of sight, into the endless "god knew what" of hell.

They sat staring at each other for a moment, frozen in time. Avery's mind focused on one word. *The creator.* The clock man nodded, and the ground split apart below her, sending the water and everything else in the world tumbling into an infinite void. Her eyes closed involuntarily, and she felt herself falling, then for one final time, the world went black.

Chapter 15

Cam's knife shined brightly, proudly stabbed into a point on a

map. "Here?" He asked, briefly showing it to Sasha. "Yes, Pirate,"

she added. Cam nodded, and rolled his eyes playfully, before

looking at Nate, who was fashioning the scuba diving suit rather

hastily. "So that won't drown us, right?" Nate "sort of" nodded.

"Not all of us." Cam and Sasha stared at him blankly. "Uhhuuuh."

Cam replied, clearly *not concerned in the slightest*. Sasha moved to

the front quickly as the tire swing came into view, once a symbol

of a fun camping getaway, now a remark of danger and mystery.

"Give me the map," Sean ordered gruffly, his mind exhausted.

Sasha patted him on the back gently, handling the situation

carefully. "You alright?" Sean nodded, taking the map from Cam's

hand. "I *Will* be," he sighed. Sasha nodded, and moved to the back.

"All set?" She asked Nate. "All set," he affirmed, putting on the

scuba diving helmet, and giving a crisp thumbs up. "Alright, so

here's the plan.." Sasha clapped her hands, and began to stand tall, even as the van sped fast down the flooded path, not bothering to park where they normally would. "Writing on the wall says the black-mud is metal, so we'll have to break through the ground once we're at the bottom of the lake." She nodded, confirming her own statement. "I'll jailbreak the panels once I get in, that will likely trigger an al-" Cam's eyes crossed, spacing out. *Bla bla bla alarms are super dangerous and stuff! Bla bla bla, one at a time, water pressure bla...* -"Right Cam?" - "Uhhhhhhhh…. yeah!" He concluded, having *definitely* heard what she just said. "Are you lying?" She asked casually, throwing her finger up in accusation. "Uh, noooo?"

Sasha smacked her face, and lay back in the seat. "Great, then you can be the one to lead the way.." - *"Into hell cause that's where we're going,"* She added, under her breath.

The van skidded to a stop in front of the trail, covering the windshield in mud. "Well that's the last time you're driving," Cam scolded, rolling his eyes at Sean. "You would've done the same!"

He countered. Cam smiled. "Yeah I would've." Nate nodded. "Yeah you would've." Sasha didn't join in.

"Alright, so should we just…" Cam waited for a response, staring hopefully at Sasha, his guide on how: *not to be him.* Sean had unlinked the elevator chain, and was in the middle of pulling it, alongside Nate, the lake residing ominously in the background, a few feet higher, due to the rain.

After another hour of arguing and hard labor, Nate was finally hooking the chain onto the scuba-suit. They'd managed to yank the spool out of the ground, and had mounted it, and the chain into the ground, secured down by heavy-ish rocks.

Sasha scouted the water, squinting through the rain. "Okay, if we're really careful about where we place i-" Nate grabbed the chain and threw it into the lake like a shot put. Cam nodded, proudly, and Sasha rolled her eyes, retrieving the crumpled map from her back pocket. "Right, so right here there's a hatch. It's in this lake, that much I know. The three boys nodded.

"Everything's pressurized, so unlocking that hatch causes..

holes?..In the vents, I guess? She asked the world. It did not

respond. "So it makes sense why that mud was there, the vents

flooded, and it washed away the foundations of the mountain."

Cam once again raised his hand sarcastically. Sasha sighed, and

immediately smacked it down hard. "Your passive-aggressive,

dumbass little school-girl technique- isn't gonna work forever."

Sean stifled a laugh, and Cam shrugged, accepting defeat. "Right,

well, Sasha, I get why the mud exists, what I don't get is why it

made us trip absolute balls for a period of time we're still not even

sure of." She stared at him blankly, and moved her eye's,

consulting Sean. He bit his tongue gently. "Look, yeah, what's

happened to us lately is…" He shook his head, unable to even find

a word. "...Our friend is in danger. AFTER we rescue her, we can

have a little book club, *all about* the messed up crap we've seen.

But till then, we need to move. We're burning daylight, and we're

sitting ducks."

"Alright well then who's going first?" Sasha asked, after a moment of silence. The group looked at eachother, and at last Sean raised his hand.

After several minutes, he'd finally made his way into the suit and the helmet, his cheekbones jammed into an involuntary "cutesy" smile, which Cam, as expected, laughed at jeeringly like a jerk.

"You said it's a hatch right?" Sasha nodded. "What kind?" She shrugged sadly. "Like I said, the map is VERY vague. But it's deep down there. I know that.." Sean straightened his face in acceptance, unable to nod through the weight of the helmet.. "Okay, how deep exactly is *deep*?" He asked, staring at the old rusty chain. "Well, aside from death-by-pressure, I think a better question is how much oxygen does that tank have?

"It'll only last a little bit," Nate replied ominously. "And how long is that?" Sean asked, his voice in a weird echo in the helmet. Nate shrugged. "However long it lasts." Sean shivered slightly, exhaling. "Well then… Is the chain secured?" Nate gave a very hasty thumbs up, and Sean gestured his understanding. *Extremely reassuring thanks buddy.* "Straight down?" Sean asked Sasha. She nodded. "Straight down." "Okay." Sean sighed, and stepped further down into the lake, wading cautiously in. *For her,* He reminded himself as the cold water began moving up his body. He gave a small, effortful salute one last time to the others, then his face submerged fully, and his feet fell off a cliff, the rusty old chain following behind him ominously.

"Okay.." Sasha exclaimed, nervous. "twenty meters."

Deep, cold, freezing water. Plants?

Cam joined her, staring at the tiny tracker screen, which she'd rigged to follow a device on the suit. "seventy meters.".. He ran back to Nate.

Darkness. Light above. Just faint blurred light, it doesn't look… real.

"One' twenty… He's getting there, I hope." She added cautiously, taking her eyes off the tracking screen for a moment, as she watched the chain wind and pull down, manned by the two other boys.

How deep can "deep'" be? His vision began to dwindle, as the pressure grew more intense.

"Okay… four-hundred meters!" Sasha called out, glancing into the water briefly.

No light left in the world. Sean smiled to himself. The pure solitude of being alone in inky darkness felt somehow… relaxing.

"Five hundred fifty!!" Nate yelled, watching the tracker from afar, excited. Sasha dodged out of his way briefly, as he moved around with the chain.

Why is the chain moving? He laughed to himself. Can't.. see. His senses blurred into oblivion, but something below was visible. "Oh right." His voice echoed out into suppressed nothingness, and he reached over his shoulder, turning on a flashlight. "Thank you, highschool scuba-class.

"Okay, any day now he's gonna-"

"Ow!" His feet hit the ground violently, and he fell over on his back, grunting, barely able to breathe at the extreme depth. He could feel the suit crinkling, cracking at a concerning rate. The ground shook slightly as he dug in one of his hands, to try to get up, but it only landed him on his stomach, still weighed down by the heavy metal suit. He dug into the dirt and grime of the ground again, the pressure killing his sinuses. "Okay.. focus." He said aloud to himself, in the tiny pocket of air that was the helmet. "Hatch." He nodded, and pushed as hard as could with his hand, attempting to get himself back up. "Ow!" He yelled again through the suit as his hand hit pure sharp steel. His eyes widened as the dim beam of the flashlight revealed a metal plating.

"YES!" He began digging, using his hands to clear the grime away.

"He's down there for sure but…" Sasha eyeballed the chain, it was barely moving. "No… no he's okay. He's gotta be." She nodded, confident. Cam's expression looked grim.

*Okay.. okay losing oxygen. Sean thought as tore away at the ground. He dug hard, not caring about pain or exhaustion, searching like his life depended on it. And it did. "Yes!" He cried, holding open a pocket where he'd torn violently through the grimey ground. Along the sharp metal plating was indeed a word and a number. "**Hatch 4b**" he smiled to himself, and pulled open the ground further, finding a handle. "Okay.." he breathed what was left to be called a breath. "Cmon." he pulled the handle with all his strength, still on the ground faced down. "CMON!" He cried desperately, a tear forming in his eye.*

"Sasha!" She waved him off, but Cam did not back-down. "Sasha, it's moving too much!" She shook her head, her face determined.

"He's gonna fucking die down there, come on!" He yelled, grabbing the chain from Nate. "Don't, Nate!" Sasha ordered, her face still completely determined. "Cmon… cmon." She whispered desperately to herself.

"COME ON!!" He yelled, pulling violently, trying to adjust his position. He shook his head in defeat, it didn't budge. "I tried." He said aloud, pulling above him at the chain. It didn't budge. He didn't move. "Guys?" He asked, his voice scared.
He tugged at it again. **No response.** *He shook his head desperately, and rested in the helmet for a moment. He closed his eyes.*

A boy sat alone in the woods, small, snowed in trees, stood pathetically, and he stared below him into the icy pond. Nothing stared back. No brown eyes. No crazy hair. He wore a gray, blue camouflage jacket, with simple thin khakis. No noises could be heard in the distance. Just solitude. No-one else in his battle but him. He thrust his hand into the ice violently, but to no avail. It stayed solid, as if refusing to melt. He picked up a stick and chucked it into the pond.

"Hey.." a shy voice echoed behind him. "Hey," He responded gruffly, his breath steaming out into the world. "Can I…" The boy nodded. "Yeah." They sat together awkwardly for a few minutes, then the girl cleared her throat cautiously. "So.. uh.." The boy didn't respond, not even acknowledging her existence. Staring into the cold frozen pond. "Are you-" - "I'm fine," He interrupted. "Youuu sure about that?" She asked, smiling awkwardly. The boy didn't respond. "Cmon bro, I've seen you hide emotions better than this." She smirked, nudging him with her shoulder. "You gone soft?" The boy rolled his eyes, but smiled just slightly. "I mean if you're gonna say: "Oh I'm Fine," she moved her arms like a gorilla, teasing him. "At least don't make it obvious that you're not."

The boy shook his head, but his smile grew. "I mean.. I've seen twelve year old girls hide their emotions better than this, what am I gonna tell Cam and Sasha? My best friend is a twelve year old girl?" She laughed, and he echoed her, again just slightly. They went silent again. "Seriously though. I'm here for you." She smiled, taking his hand without asking. "You can tell me whatever you need, Sean." Sean shrugged. "I can't see my reflection. The ponds froze over." Avery cocked her head, curiously, but nodded gently. "Well, why do you feel the need to see your reflection?" Sean shrugged, and waited for a bit, grabbing a bit of snow, bare handed. "I don't know.. I just don't feel like I know who I am lately." Avery nodded, and sat for a moment thinking. "Well.." She reached into her back pocket. "Maybe all you need is a little help from someone else." She smiled gently, withdrawing a lighter and picking up a stick, touching the tip to it. It easily lit ablaze brilliantly, illuminating the tiny pocket of trees around them. She held her smile, and put the stick up to the ice. Warmth, burning away the cold uncertainty. It began taking effect immediately, and within a few minutes she'd burnt a hole into the entire thing. Sean stared into it, and his reflection stared back. Avery smiled, wrapping her arm around him, and Sean finally echoed her, fully grinning as they both stared into the murky, dark, yet calm and reassuring water.

His eyes burst open, and he gasped for breath but none was there. He was still lying flat on the ground, his hands still holding open the tear in the grime and algae. He nodded confidently. "For her," he repeated, not giving up until death. He RIPPED open the ground with all the strength he had, and stared at a new panel. A nine digit code pad. "Shit."

"Wait!" Sasha cried, her voice evermore nervous. "He needs a code!" She yelled. "WHAT?!" Cam screamed, frantically, staring down at the water unsure of what to do. "HE NEEDS A CODE!" Sasha screamed. "AND YOU WAITED ILL JUST NOW TO-" "THREE, FIVE, ZERO, FIVE!!" Sasha yelled at them. Nate's eyes were wide with stress, as per usual, oblivious to the reason behind the comotion.

"HOW AM I SUPPOSED TO TELL HIM THAT?!" Cam demanded, panicking. "Nate pull him up it's too la-" Sasha waved him off once again. "No!" She yelled back to Nate. Cam looked back like she'd just killed an entire family. "WHAT ARE WE JUST SUPPOSED TO LET HIM DIE?!" Sasha shook her head.

"The pen!" Cam raised his arms. "WHAT FUCKING PEN?!" Sasha frantically dug into her pocket and threw out an old ink pen. Cam nodded, understanding. "There's no way in hell that's gonna work!!" - "We have to try!" She yelled back. "God, fucki- FINE!" Cam replied, running as fast as possible into the water, biting off the pen cap and frantically pulling out the cartridge. He hovered above the massive pit, and began to dump the ink in numbers. *This is it.*

*This is death. Sean smiled to himself. 4356.. 7685... 2345... 911.. 1911. 1983..."COME ON!!" He yelled desperately, entering in random codes. "No.. no.. it can't..." His vision blurred, and his breath was cut short. He relinquished control and began looking up to the waking world one last time. "Wha-" He shook his head, but remembered his earlier words. "For her." He bit down his teeth and tried with all his might to stay awake, just as he had a few hours ago. His vision restored for just a moment. **"E.S.O.S?"** He thought. "No." He said aloud, but it was real. Black clouded ink in very specific shapes, barely visible in the tiny rays of light. "3505!" He yelled finally, his last breath as the pressure nearly* *caved in his head. He forced out every last bit of adrenaline, and punched in the code as fast as possible, pulling the handle. To his horror, it didn't move. He gave it one more try. "YES!" He yelled, yanking open the hatch. A loud thunderous beep echoed out, and his body was sucked in, the chain following with him. He watched curiously, still panicked. By some way he didn't understand, he could breathe again. strange pipes and lights passed by. He couldn't tell what direction he was in, his head and vision were a blur. It was like this for what felt like several minutes, then his head popped out into a pool, and he could breathe again. He stared out. **White sterile walls, faint dim light, a poster. The words "Monarch labs" scrawled along the wall.** He sighed in relief.*

"Sasha, the chain!" Cam yelled, watching in a combination of terror and relief as it flew out of the spool fast. "Nine-hundred meters.. and he's way off to the right!" She cried with joy. "It stopped moving!" Cam yelled back, panicked. "He made it!" Sasha announced, sighing and falling back on the ground, finally able to think and breathe. Cam nodded, and followed her, lightly sitting down and taking a deep breath. Nate's eyes widened as he felt the chain tug upwards. Cam eyeballed it. "Alright… who's next?"

 Rubble flew by her face, brushing against her bloody nose, and surrounding her as she fell, the darkness swallowing everything. She felt her eyes open forcefully, and the world around her began to form, a tunnel wrapping its stone chunks and metal beams around her world, atoms in the air forming new shapes. Her head hit cold metal, and she looked up. Red lights flew by at an alarming speed, beaming down on the moving surface she found herself on. She moved her head to look down. It was a train, a massive long, VERY fast moving train. She touched her tongue to her teeth, they were square and normal. She nodded, and slowly pulled off the gas mask. *Okay so what the hell was that? What are you gonna say it's all just a dream?!* She rolled her eyes, still able to be herself even when bleeding out. She struggled to sit up, groaning in pain, as her leg twisted. The tunnel was slim, rough and skinny. Everywhere around her was a high pitched electric sound, a sound of technology unheard of, powering a tram going at a speed that, too, was unheard of.

Avery grabbed her knee, and forced it into the roof of the train with her hand. It slipped, and she ended up flat on her back.

"Avery Zeno..." A voice boomed, ominously in the darkness. Avery struggled against the beating metal, and stared up at the figure. She gritted her teeth. *You.* The Man smiled sadistically, watching her struggle in pain. "I must admit, that whole fiasco was… impressive." The Man's face came into the faint red light, his teeth glowing evilly. She coughed out in pain. "Yeah!?" She asked, aggressively. She darted her eyes around, but there was no exit. Simply the train and the seemingly infinite tunnel. "Oh yes," The Man replied, walking towards her. "Just like your father," He added, still smiling. He walked against the force of the train as if it wasn't even there, bypassing the laws of nature. Avery bit her lip, and managed to get one arm to support her. "And just what do you know about my father?" The Man took a step back, his smile slightly fading. "More than you do, believe me," He replied, his face in thought. "Oh yeah? And why's that?" Avery asked, wincing in pain. Blood dripped from her arm, and streamed out behind her, flying behind the speeding train. The Man smiled fully with his teeth, and looked at his hands once again, toying with them like a businessman bored at a meeting. "Quite simple really, He's my brother." Avery made a face of disgust, though she wasn't entirely surprised. "Or.." The Man stopped, looking sideways. "Was, at least.. according to him." She raised an eyebrow, backing up slowly in a crab walk. "Okay well what the hell was that then? Put me in the damn matrix and expect me to believe my father was alive, what? seven-hundred years ago or something?"

The Man laughed, resting his fedora down temporarily. "Oh Avery, believe me that was far from fake." She shivered,but put on a confident scowl, still backing away. "Then why? What was your goal?" She smirked for a second. "Seems kinda dumb to me." The Man did *not* look impressed, putting his hat back on and continuing to approach her, somehow walking with ease against the extremely rapid speed of the train. "Well, since he decided to betray me, I wanted to see if new blood could take his place." He smiled cruelly, putting his hands together in an orderly fashion. "I'm quite satisfied with the results."

He stepped further, and his dark inky body came into view. "Then what did you do to him?" Avery asked, getting another arm to support her. The Man raised his *barely existent* eyebrow, and scratched his chin briefly. "My question is what did he do to you?" Avery stared up at him, he was now almost above her. *Do to me?! DO TO ME!? Who the hell do you think you are? You don't know dad.. You don't know...* Her thought was cut off as the Man appeared directly in front of her, inches away. He made a gesture with his hands, and two guards came from seemingly out of nowhere, onto hovering platforms next to the train. Each paralleling the other. She was up to her knees now, preparing to make a move. "I wanted him back, yes, granted soon. But seeing what you've done here, I don't think I'll even need him." The air rushed against her as it flew by, blowing her hair up out of her face. "What do you want with me then huh!?" She jeered, having an upper hand he didn't know about. The Man scoffed, and returned to his psychotic smile. "Ah, like father, like... daughter." Avery curled her nose. *Just as intelligent as you are cryptic.* The

Man stared off into the distance. "What could've been, what could've been."

Avery planted her feet, and got ready. "We could've conquered the world," he continued, raising his hand as if making a toast. She braced herself, and stared, waiting for the right moment. "I would've never had to see you. You or that.. ***stupid woman***," he scoffed.

The train sped up slightly, and red light began passing even more frequently. The Man walked closer still staring into the tunnel. "But now that I do *have* to see you… I can do what I've always wanted to." She cringed visibly. "And what's that?" The Man smiled, and bent down next to her. "See Avery, I've noticed great talent in you. Me.." He put a hand to his chest, balling it into a fist. "'Me and my higher ups. Employers, if you will." "Bu-" He interrupted her immediately, extending his hand out. "So, Avery, I'd like to offer you a job." His eyes turned slightly more visible, lighting up bright white.

"The names **Ignelious**." Her eyes widened, and a hundred memory's echoed in her head, the name making her angry. "Indeed," he remarked, still with his hand out. "Figured you'd.. remember me." She cringed at his words, and rejected his handshake. He rolled his eyes, which were now fully visible, bright white circles with tiny black pupils. "Well, I tried." Avery dodged back as he made an attempt to stomp on her head. His boot hit the ground violently, echoing through the tunnel. "Well it wasn't much of a choice, **AV.**" He said loudly, the name not fitting for his mouth. "See, you show signs of GREAT." He Smiled with his signature monotone grin, nodding. "Interest."

Avery scowled. "How so, Mr. Big Bad?" Ignelious looked to the side for a moment, then back at her. "Your memory's. Your life form. You're an enigma Avery, a rejected science experiment. Monarch.." He stopped, his lips curving cruelty as he shuffled back into the darkness, only his eyes and ominous smile visible. "I love a good enigma. Especially if it's a chance to.." He stopped, twirling his thumbs again. "Finish what I started." He sighed, and raised his hand to the sky swiftly. A bright red light erupted in his hand, and the shape of a sword began to form, a katana. Her eyes narrowed. *Just like Sean's.* "What a goddamn disappointment," he spat gruffly, swinging it down to her head. He was unsuccessful. Avery leaped forward out of the way of the sword, and fought with her last strength to reach her pocket. Ignelious thrust the sword over his back, swinging down to her, and she dodged again. "You're fast!" He shouted, stabbing down again. Avery smirked, with one hand covering her bloody pelvis, and one with her switchblade now in it. Ignelious ran at her. "But no one possesses the skill to beat m-" She took the moment, knife in hand, diving straight through his legs, cutting into the flesh of thigh, down to his ankle. She rolled out of it, in the move her brother had taught her. *Thanks Grey.*

She now faced behind the man, perched on a small, architectural circle, one hand on her flesh wound, slightly elevated above the surface of the cold metal train. "Oh-ho-ho… really" The man laughed menacingly, his smile increasing, showing no signs of pain. He bled fresh *red* blood from his creepy inky body, and it flew off, decorating the train, just like Avery's. He turned around, picking up the katana, having just dropped it.

 "You!.." He began, still in pain. "Avery you've only seen a fraction of what happens to the souls that even slightly graze me." He spoke calmly, thrusting the katana at her heart with perfect aim. But in an instant, she wasn't there. She was slightly to the left, perched in a ready position, her knife in hand, smiling mischievously. "What's that?" She coughed out mockingly, maintaining her smirk. Ignelious mirrored her, maintaining his sick psychotic grin. "You want to find out?" Avery shivered, but kept up the act. *A distraction.* "Go ahead and show me," she beckoned jeeringly. The man swung at her with the katana repeatedly, but to no avail. "Maybe another day, a day where you're happy at work, doing amazing things for the world." Avery shook her head. *Bs.* "Like killing little girls?" Ignelious did not react in any way, continuing to back her down the train. "Oh Avery." He began, laughing visibly. "She was already dead," he relayed ominously, his voice strangely getting deeper and more distorted. Avery cowered back for a second, surprised. "You are just as incompetent as your father," he spat, his smile growing to a sadistic sharp curve, now full of anger, bearing his silver teeth, his true colors showing. Avery got to her feet, standing in the red light. "You know, your awful, evil, betraying brother.." *My father I guess.* -"was really helpful," she finished, dodging another attack, and laugh-coughing. "Taught me some super helpful tricks on how to avoid idiots with swords." Ignelious shook his head, standing back momentarily. "Well, he didn't teach you how to deal with gods of unlimited power, now did he?" Avery looked down, and raised an eyebrow. The skin of his leg appeared to be sewing itself back together, the wound turning a shade of dark purple, then returning to his normal, pitch black skin tone. In one motion, he threw the katana off the train into oblivion, and it disappeared with a bright flash. He gestured at the guards, still watching.

They began open firing, and Avery ducked fast behind the protruding circle, using it as cover, studying as his skin formed itself back together. *He's immortal,* she thought, hatching a plan. "Who do you think taught him, after all?" Ignelious asked, pointing at himself proudly. Avery nodded. *Can't beat him there I guess.* The guards simultaneously ran out of ammo, and She leaped to the ground, sliding a bit with the speed of the train. They reloaded, but Avery was ready. She stood, just next to him. The first guard opened fire at her, but she ducked, and dodged, letting the bullets hit him. She hid behind him, and used him as a shield. Bullet holes forming all across his body. He reached up, and made a fist, but still showed no signs of pain. The guards immediately stopped.

Avery took off immediately. *No time..* Ignelious walked forward, coughing a bit, his wounds already healing fast. Bullet shells popped out of him, as his body formed back together, his suit melting into an inky blackness, and reforming its structure around his body. He glared out at Avery, who was running across the train. *"Hmmm, hmmm, hm hm hmm,"* he hummed ominously, echoing into awful scraping sounds as the sound grew further in the distance of the tunnel. "Well Avery" He smiled fresh again. "You're good for a child, I'll give it to you." Avery rolled her eyes, ignoring him. "You have confidence to be sure." He nodded, still walking down the train. "But you lack stability," He began, stomping on the train. "You lack self control!" He stepped forward again violently, stretching out his legs to a distance that should've been impossible. "Chasing rumors that get you killed, running from the truth to follow a memory." Avery shook her head, once again trying to ignore him. "Chasing lies!" His voice echoed out in a horrific sound like a broken siren, running after her, speeding across the cold metal roof effortlessly, growing limbs like a twisted makeshift spider out of every point in his body, his true form showing. "Av-re-ey.." He called, his voice shrill and improper, as if it was glitching in and out of existence. Avery shook her head, as she ran through the train. *Screw you, freak.* "Avery, there's more meaning in here than there is out there." She gritted her teeth, trying to ignore him. "False lying memory's.." His body suddenly burst into black and white pixels, and he rematerialized in front of her. Avery's face dropped its confidence, and she ran the opposite direction. "pas-asts built in you-r-r mind jus-just for you."

His legs continued growing, elevating him to the height of a giant, his grin now the symbol of the shadows, perched proudly above in the deep red light. Avery scrambled forward, fear fresh in her eyes, no longer with a goal to beat him but simply: *to get the hell away.* Her vision began blurring, she was losing too much blood. Now his voice BOOMED out in a horrific static sound, the sound one would hear when a microphone is too malfunctioning.

"Par-arents that once lov- loved you, but are now PROGRAMMED TO!" He yelled. Avery covered her ears desperately, his yelling stinging every part of her soul, a painful ringing in her ear. "NOTHI-N-G out there is natural" His voice returned to normal for a moment. "Y-OU-U WANT TO KNOW THE TRUTH SO BA-ADL-Y?" He demanded, his voice like a horrific megaphone, except amplified by a million, glitching like a faulty computer. Avery stopped, her body ceasing to move. The world around her was dark now, and her vision clouded as her pelvis continued to bleed out. Her heart sank as he got closer, desperate, hopeless.

"YOUR FAT-HE-ER" He began, and his voice returned to a normal volume, normal like a human. "Is dead, Avery," he finished. Her knees collapsed, sending her to the ground, resulting in her laying up on her side, her body ceased, but she remained awake. *I don't even know if "My father" is real anymore.*

 "A long time ago," Ignelious interjected, walking down an invisible staircase as his height shrank back to his normal size, somehow not affected by the train. "Garrison left us." Pixels once again erupted around him, and he vanished in a glitch of black and white, and reappeared next to her, still smiling. "He promised he wouldn't share anything. I gave him a chance." He reached down to pick up: *The mess of my niece dying on the cold metal ground.* "But he betrayed me. He and.." The man stopped, suddenly troubled. "And *her-er*" He glanced down briefly with sorrow, his voice glitching for a moment. Then he immediately looked back up, and stared into Avery's eyes. "So I killed the one thing that mattered most to him," he said, grabbing Avery by the hair with inhuman strength. She yelped with all the voice she had left, and slung her arm outwards for a right hook, but it didn't hurt him.

He raised her to his eyes, and began to grow taller, his inky static glitchy body sprouting further and further up. She struggled in his everlasting grip. "I KILLED YOU!" He yelled, damaging her ear drums with the volume that blasted from his mouth, and kicking her thorax in, dropping her several meters to the ground. She landed, and her head hit the metal. She gasped for air, but barely any came. *Please..* "I saw your father grieve, sob," He jeered, bending his figure downwards to her frail destroyed body.

"I watched you die, I saw your burial." He stomped on the ground, and it left a dent of glitching pixels, a *paradox* in the metal. "At least that's what I thou-ought." He said angrily, kicking her chest hard, sending her tumbling to the side. She tried to cough, but her throat was blocked with blood. "And now loo-ook at you." He stepped on her back, as she struggled for air. "Lost. Out of place. You belong here child. If the man your father was didn't want to take part in greatness.." He stopped, picking her up, and forcing her to look at him. She coughed, and blood spewed out, going all over the man's face. He smiled psychotically in response, chomping his teeth mockingly as Avery gasped for breath. Her eyes were bloodshot, and black, both of them knocked inwards. "Then surely the good part of him. The part he passed on.. will." He finished, raising his foot above her head. "However…" He began to grow back to his normal size. "I am a man of fairness, Avery." He began drawing something from the air. She looked hard through her beat-up eyes. A sharp, long blade, with a blue glow. *Sean?* It was all her mind could conjure. An image of Sean standing tall and proud with the blue katana. *The sword of..* her lips twitched slightly as she tried to speak, her skull broken, her body destroyed. *The sword of healing.* Ignelious smiled brightly as usual. "And as much as I'd love to see a *straggler* be taken care of.." He swung the katana down violently, but made sure it didn't hit her. "You are my blood. And letting it all spill would be-e a waste." He reached down, and let the sword take its course.

Immediately she felt her broken bones be pieced back together, and her tendons correct themselves, her blood refilling. Her breathing returned to normal as she regained her strength. She rose to the air, immediately backing away from him and gasping for breath. "So.." She began, breathing heavily. "What are you, too afraid to kill?" She jeered, the only thing she could think of. Ignelious laughed loudly, his voice echoing through the tunnels in a double voice-effect, as if he was simultaneously screaming underwater *and* yelling above the surface. "Most peo-eople believe de-ea-eath is the worst fate." He snorted, walking towards her again as she fully sat up. "They don't stop to think what can happen to them while they're sti-ill ali-live."

Avery crouched down slightly in fear, a chill going down her spine. "Weren't you just trying to kill me?" She asked, her body fully recovered. Ignelious rolled his sharp bright eyes. "Not every sword is meant to kil-il-ill" Avery echoed him, rolling her own eyes. "Yeah okay Mr. plot convenience." Ignelious snarled, and opened his mouth to speak. "You k-" He was interrupted. The tunnel rang out in a deep, sharp, loud beep, echoing across what felt like the entire world. **"Next stop: Monarch H-1, Colorado.**

Avery smirked. *Oh perfect.. probably?* "Alright enough!" Ignelious yelled, his voice sounding more on the human side. Avery raised an eyebrow. "I've had it with you!" He yelled, his voice again sounding normal. Avery nodded, studying him like a scientist, which she knew only made him more angry. *Hmm.* He shook off the *disease* from his skin and erupted into his lanky dark form. `"Congrats,"` he spat. Avery braced herself, eyeing his posture, and took off running down the train, losing balance as she went. `"You're hired."` He jumped upwards, and his spider-like arms sprouted, inky black, grabbing the wall, and speeding away on the ceiling, rotating around the tunnel as he crawled forward at the same speed of the train. "Oh, ok, yeah… FUCK THAT!" Avery yelled, bolting into a sprint as best she could, running for her life.

Chapter 16

"And you don't find that odd…" Cam squinted at the speaker,

who was leaning against a pillar in the shadows. "You don't find it

odd that this technologically super advanced alien force, whatever..

You don't find it even slightly off-putting that there's no alarms

going off, no guards posted?" Sean had repeated his statement, but

it didn't hesitate with Cam any more than before. Sasha strolled in

between the two boys casually, breaking up their: *wasteful toddler

battle.*

They were in a small, black-tile filled old room with that of a

subway tunnel in the background, a slim low curved concrete

ceiling above them, reflecting wet, ominous shadows of the faint

LED lights. Sean waved the two off, and started digging through a

box of old crystals and random mechanical parts."What the hell do

they need this many… artifacts for anyway?" They both shrugged

in response. "Must be one hell of an auction," Cam laughed,

picking up another paper, searching through it with absolutely zero care, then throwing it to the side. "There's some kind of like-" he squinted at the box he was searching. "Pyramid.. On this thing. Got different positions listed. Guards, fielders, and.. **C's**, whatever that means." Sasha raised an eyebrow. "So what, there's some sort of hierarchy for inanimate objects?" Sean shrugged. "Apparently."

"Nothing here!" Sasha called, searching an old briefcase thrown to the floor in the corner. "Okay.. so some random-" Sean's voice cut off, as he stared at the letters on the clipboard in front of him.

 "A.V," he read aloud. Sasha jumped across the room to his position, grabbing it to read herself. "Well, assuming that doesn't stand for **Air vent**, we should probably investigate," Cam confirmed calmly, walking over to them. "Okay.. it's.. in.. a different language?" Sean dug further into another box. "Maybe there's a cypher somewhere?" "I.." Cam began. "I've seen code. This doesn't look like code. It looks like a normal language." - "Maybe this can help?" Sean asked, nervously, pulling an object out of the box. Spiders crawled out of it, and Sasha jumped back slightly. Sean brushed them off cautiously.

Alone in his hands now stood an old, rusty laptop-computer. Cam raised an eyebrow sarcastically. "Looks pretty recent." Sasha nodded. "Haven't seen this thing since I was like two." She reached out, taking it, and Sean dropped it into her hands gently, Dilapidated remains of an image stood wavering, glitching across the old screen. "Wave powered," She read aloud, staring at the bottom. "It might still have an energy transceiver, "She began, hopefully, throwing the lid back on the box, and setting the computer gently onto it. "Okay.. uh… waves.." *third grade science.. uhhh..* She focused on the tile around her. Explosions no, light, barely. *Sound!* Her vision focused again, and Cam's hand was in front of her. "You good?" She laughed. "YEAH!!" She yelled. Sure enough, a tiny spark of life jumped to light on the screen. Cam smirked. "Ah, well in that case, I..SURE HOPE NO BAD GUYS COME GET US!!" He yelled. Sean rolled his eyes, and began yelling nonetheless. "Are you guys…" Nate raised an eyebrow, shyly. "Scream your heart out, bro!" Cam invited, and he joined them. "I'm NATE!" He shouted, his voice cracking. Sasha smiled as she stared into the old pixels of the screen, now lit to functionally. "Bingo." She grabbed it and collapsed to the ground, resting it on her lap.

"Okay.. random documents.. random documents…" Her eyes widened. "A.V!" She relayed aloud, the bright, digital letters reflecting in her watery eyes. Sean rushed to join her, and they looked at each-other. She nodded, an understanding nod, then reached her hands to the keyboard. *//CO0C: OPEN-A.V.* Immediately, the file popped open on the screen in a rather charming animation. "Dammit!" Sean called. Cam grabbed the clipboard that they'd dropped moments prior, and headed back over to them. "It's in the same shitty weird language!" Cam nodded, and consulted the board for a moment, a rarely solemn look on his face. "Call sign…" Sasha covered her mouth as the green text jumped to life in front of her. "This call sign… it's addressed to Avery's house.."

Sean felt a chill down his spine, and he stared at her for a moment. .."Who?" Sasha shrugged, and fumbled with the keyboard again. Cam stood still, his face just as confused, staring into the dim light on the curved tile ceiling. "I- I.. don't know," she responded, her voice shaky. "**MRA** is all it says." She tapped on the top of the computer. "I uh.. I think this thing has a camera!" Sean nodded. "Can you acces the call sign?" She gave a "captains thumbs-up" and entered into the "Cam!" Sasha called. "Yeah?" He replied oddly, standing literally directly next to her. "You have the clipboard right?" Cam nodded, his eyes nearly glowing in the ominous LED lights above. "Yeah!" - "Okay, check next to A.V, there should be a number!" Cam gave a thumbs up. "Nineteen-ninety seven!" He yelled back, his voice bouncing off the tile walls, causing the computer screen to spark a bit. "Nineteen ninety seven," Sasha repeated, muttering as she punched in the code. A message jumped to life on the screen. *CONNECTING.- WELCOME MRA.* "It's working!" Sasha called. Sean nodded hesitantly. *How do we know that's a good thing?* "Yes!" Sasha yelled, as a new image popped onto the screen. Her eyes widened and she fell backwards, the hair on every part of her body standing up. Cam walked over, and sat down next to her. Immediately, his face echoing hers, growing pale and cold. "Is that…" Sean joined them. *Grey?*

"Grey?" A voice called out. Grey's head immediately shifted to **the bear**, a complete deviation from his norm. He stared into its eerie eyes intensely. *What… the…* "testing," The voice echoed out. Grey shot his eyeballs to the alarm clock on his shelf, and his eyes grew wider. Satisfied, he turned around, and gave a thumbs up. Then immediately closed his door, stealthily, violently slamming his windows shut.

"He's there!" Sasha exclaimed, happily, nearly jumping. Cam smiled. "Well fu-" He cleared his throat. "I'll be damned."

"It worked!" The *strange* voice echoed out. Grey raised an eyebrow. "Hello?" He whispered, brushing off his hands on his gray shirt. "We can hear you." A boy's voice came through, statically. Grey nodded. "Grey, it's Sean and Sasha"

Cam rolled his eyes. "And- me" Grey nodded. "I know." He said confidently, for once actually smiling at the old ominous bear. "How did you guys.." - "Listen, Avery's in trouble. We have this *****" Grey squinted, the last part having been a static mess. "We can figure out where she is, but we need your help." "Okay," Grey said simply, his voice still pretty monotone.

Cam grabbed the clipboard hastily. "Okay, ask him if he speaks.. uh... **KROTHAN**." Sasha shrugged at the strange name, but nodded nonetheless. "Grey.."

"KROTHAN, " Their voices came through. "Alright.. yeah I can probably help," He responded. "Okay, uh first.. digit? " Cam began sheepishly, "Is a weird swervy line, it kinda looks like an ocean wave."

"Athenian?" Grey's voice came through. There was silence. "It's A," he concluded, staring deep into the bear's eyes. Sean let out a breath of stress, and nodded. "Oka-a-ayyy..."

Cam prepared, Grey's voice on their end static again. Grey rolled his eyes, and eye'd his alarm clock. "This next one looks like a pine tree, uh it's got some weird squiggles on the base." Grey put his thumb to his chin, thinking hard. "Chrothomian," he muttered to himself. "What?" "That's a v." Grey nodded, confident in his answer. He shook his head briefly, consulting the clock again. "Whe-re a-re you guys?" His voice came through, buffering in audio. Sasha glanced at Sean, and he bit his lip. "Uhhh…" She began speaking into the old computer, the lights flashing above her. "M.L," her voice echoed through the makeshift radio cautiously. Grey did not freeze up, nor did he make a single movement of reaction. "Is she safe?" He asked, simply, his voice monotone as always. "Grey, we-" - "Is she safe?" He repeated, his voice slightly more cold.

Sasha grabbed her face aggressively, a combat tool for her anxiety.

"We don't know, Grey," She responded, half sad, half cautious.

"Uh…." Cam's voice echoed through the chamber. "There's a…

scheduled time here…" Sashas eyes widened. "when?" Sean

asked, closing his eyes. "Uh…. yeah… five thirty, ocean waves,

and something else. Pretty sure we can guess that means AM."

Sasha eye'd the time of the laptop. "Five twenty," she read aloud.

Seans eyes narrowed.

"Okay, Grey we really nee-" -"AVK8p0e3," he spoke

into the bear. Sean felt a shiver down his spine. "How did you

know that?".... *There was no response.* "Grey?" Sasha called out.

Her face lit up green as new words were typed in the terminal. *//c:*

CRITICAL ERROR: MRA does not exist.

 She shook her head, her hair standing up on her arms visibly.

"How.." Cam, asked. Sean stood up ready, "Doesn't matter, we've

got ten minutes, and a code. So… now what?"

Sasha shut the laptop, annoyed, and the two boys sighed

collectively. "Okay, so it could be a prison cell number, or a plane

or, I don't know. For all we know she's on a different fucking pla-"
ALERT: a train is arriving in: sector c, test labs and control facilities in: eight minutes. They watched in horror as half the wall opened up, revealing a sight that stung their eyes.

"Monarch labs…" Sasha relayed, as she stared out into the miles of a MASSIVE open cave, each with a hundred different strange metal buildings, unknowable in a single lifetime. A huge clock at the center loomed in the miles of fog ominously, ticking with the sound of a gunshot in the distance. "Five… twenty..three.," Sean read, his eyes in utter awe.

"What the?!" Sasha's pocket began to feel heavy, and after a few strange tugs, the map of the facility JUMPED out of it, tearing it open and flying into the distance. "I don't.." At the nearest wall it began glowing, and aligned itself to the structure, flattening out, and piercing itself together. Cam's mouth hung open agape in awe. "Oh.. my…holly fuck…"

Upon the wall, thousand other maps formed with theirs, welcoming it back to its long awaited place. Sasha shivered both visibly and audibly. "This place… it's under the entire country…"

Miles-wide, metal, hexagonal spheres towered over them ominously, each with a strange, aleine-like teal light, and architecture like no other in the world, each with a utility tunnel and train running to it, numbered by the thousands. Sean shook his head aggressively, and snapped his fingers. "Okay.. yeah.. That's the most insane thing I've ever seen. But we've got a friend to save." Cam nodded, not even slightly adjusting his gaze. "Where are they going?" … Sasha cocked her head. "The trains?" .. "Yeah." Sean squinted into their newly discovered world, his interest piqued. "It said a train is arriving in eight minutes, what, two minutes ago? Five thirty.. That's gotta be her." Cam shook his head, his face still pressed to the cold glass, fascinated by the "nearly" other planet just a few inches from his face.

"M.L," he began, the word now the most fascinating thing he'd ever witnessed. "This.. M.L, is infinite dude, I mean.. Look." He gestured at what lay before them. "There could be a million other Avery's down here for all we know." Sean nodded, but refused to give up, searching the underground before them for any shred of information that might help.

Suddenly, an impossibly loud crack of pure energy BOOMED through the air, sending them physically falling backwards. It continued, and one of the spheres in the distance shook as a BURST of bright light exploded into sight, filling the entire world with the loudest sound they'd ever heard to match. An intercom rang out, screaming through the underground society: **SECTOR 3503 removed, Subject: A.V arriving at: colorado H-1 in: five.. Minutes.**

"Avery," Sean cried out, half terrified, half relieved. Cam shrugged pessimistically, standing back up from the blast. "I can't think of anyone else with that nickname…"
"Sasha?" … She did not respond. She was standing, her face embedded with a one-hundred-yard stare. "CHRONOLEFT," she relayed aloud. The boys peered at her, confused. "That's how

they're obtaining these items… Time travel." Sean nodded. "Well, yeah, I thou-" - "Not like this," she interrupted, ominously. Cam bit his tongue, confused, but unsurprised. *Every shadow government asshole has to have time travel, obviously.* Sean helped her up carefully. "So you're saying they're traveling to different times to steal the… artifacts?" Sasha shook her head. "No, I'm saying they're *bringing* "different times" right here, right in this place, and destroying them." She shivered. "I read about it.. Evolutionary armageddon, abandonment of time itself, …

***CHRONOLEFT*.**

"redacted… C," Sean spoke, reading a sign in the distance. "That's where we are." Sasha glared at him, offended, but forgave him immediately upon witnessing his discovery. "Colorado, H1.." She relayed aloud, her eyes lighting up in a spark. "I saw that on the laptop!" Sean smiled for once, and ran to it with her.

She stared out at the tracks, fascinated, now back in the main terminal. "Abandoned C, used to control sector C: ZENO-train railways. Her eyes shot open, and Cam read her mind. "They aren't stationary!" he cried in delight, eyeing the subway-like tunnel behind them. Sean nodded with excitement. "Okay.. we've got what, three minutes? Let's start planning. Sasha smirked, cracking her knuckles and reaching for the keyboard. "Already got one."

"You are nothing more than a r-aat in a ma-a–aze!" Ignelious scrambled with a horrifying sound as his nightmarish spider-body bolted down the tunnel. Avery looked back for a brief moment. *What the fuck are you?*

He climbed around the tunnel like a fireman rotating a poll, chasing like a cat at a terrifying speed. **"Why don't you sto-o-0p running and FACE YOUR FEA-r-rs-ears"** She cringed in pain as he screamed, his voice in that same megaphone like pitch. "Quite simple!" She called out to him, limping. "I don't wanna fucking die!" She smiled, and turned around to run. It didn't work.

As she fell she stared out at: *whatever the fuck the man was*, her face a combination of fear and disgust. **"I told you bef-ore-ore you shouldn't be alive!"** He screeched, toppling his weight onto the train. Avery watched in horror as the world around her became completely pixelated, it looked as if nature itself had become an old static TV, and her universe tipped downwards, sending her flying into a now massive teeth filled mouth, maintaining its sadistic smile. New instincts kicked in, and her body dodged, rolling her over to her stomach onto what was left of the side rails. She watched as the train flew into the monster's mouth, its industrial beeping horn echoing into the abyss as it went. *Keep going. Keep fighting.. av. She imagined Sean's face, smiling and comforting.*

His dark fist grew out of the now infinite black void, smashing into the side rails, and sending her falling into the void. She screamed, but in an instant she was back, landing violently on the cold metal roof of the train. "You are scared," he jeered, breathing in anger, his voice fully sounding like a broken record-player. *Wow, no shit,* she thought, trying to roll to her side. But it was no use. Nothing functioned. "Lost, scared. `You-'re just like your fa-father! Unsure, insecure. Un-unstable.`" He turned around, and brought her to her feet again. Her head rang in pain, The electronic sound of the train becoming her new, only frequency. She struggled in her mind, fighting for control, but her body flailed helplessly, as The man lifted her up. **`"Wi-will you choose to live in a world of li-ie-es, deceit, and corruption designed for you?"`** Avery riggled her neck a bit, a motion she fought hard for. "`Or, will you choose to fa-ac-ce the truth-uth, and help me` finish what your father started?" His voice returned to its normal ominous tone, not a hint of any glitching. *Give in, Av. He wants you to. I.. your father wants you to. "NO!"* She yelled in her head, fighting a battle with a demon that had long since been sealed away. But it was out now, and nothing could change that. *"I... know. What's real."* She yelled to the thing in her head, and her facial expressions resumed. She gritted her bloody teeth, ready for anything. "You said.." She struggled, kicking and violently shaking in the man's one hand. "You said he's dead?" The man smiled sadistically. "Avery.." The train made a sudden strange beep, and they were shifted to the side just slightly. Her face ran cold, but she had a hunch of who was behind it. **"All we really are-ree-are is informa-at-tio-tion, and memory's."** He began, squeezing her by the throat tighter. `"Kill those memories and you've effectively killed the person,"` he finished, smiling evilly as she gasped for breath, his voice once again fully destroyed. **"That was a quote from Garrison,"** he spat crudely, in a twisted, deep way.

She fought for control in her mind, the darkness constantly clouding it. Memory's flowing stronger than they ever did before. "Now then, hold still, and I'll make the `decision-ion` **for you,"** he commanded, grabbing a dark syringe again, and smiling psychotically. *Okay.. okay now is the time Avery. Friends, family. Real world. Warm memories.* She stopped in her thoughts, as he drew the syringe closer.

*I... **The grave.*** In a single swift motion, she grabbed his arm, and bit into it hard, tearing out his fine motors. He bled red, and his tendons popped out, exposed, the hand with the syringe left limp. It began to fold itself back together, but it was too late. She was out of his grasp now, she had the upper hand. Another loud industrial beep echoed through the tunnels, and they were both sent flying, the train swerving sideways, and toppling over. **Relocating track at request of: Redacted, C,** a computer voice on the intercom spoke. Igenilous's face grew, for the first time ever: scared. Avery reached up, clinging onto the train desperately as the entire, massive thing was spun and curled around the tunnel. "GOD DAMN-AMNIT!" Ignelious screeched, landing just beneath her, and gripping onto her feet. "YOU ARE NOT LEAVING THIS PLACE ALIVE!" He reassured, screaming at the loudest volume she'd ever heard. Her ears rang in agony, but she held on for dear life, kicking him as the train continued to swerve. Another beep sounded, and the train straightened, bringing them both back into a fighting stance, standing on the now flat, somehow still functioning train.

She stood, barely, everything in her body: damaged and broken. The intercom sounded again, as ignellious dashed for her position. **Please stand clear of the transceivers, as this ZENO-train is arriving..** Followed by a happy-go-lucky jingle countdown.

`"STUPID GIRl, HAVEN'T I TOLD YO-OU-OU TIME DOESN'T WOR-ORK THE SAME HERE?!` He gritted his teeth, and rose to another massive height. `"EITHER-THER YOU JOIN ME NOW-OW, OR-"` **WAM!**

His body went flying behind her as he smashed face -first into a metal support beam above. Avery smirked, as she watched him. "Sure, but spacial awareness does." He appeared completely unharmed, but was flailing about, struggling, unable to part from the beam.

She thought back to what Sasha said. *"The spiders are zinc."*

Ignelious began to writhe in the foggy distance, and his skin stopped repairing itself, his body growing into a static wireframe, black and white pixels comprising his form, changing and glitching his place in the world rapidly. The tiny spider bots were swarming around him now, cringing as if in pain. `"YOU ARE JUST LIKE-IKE HIM!!"` His horrible voice shreeked from afar down the tunnel. Avery smirked with her trademark smirk. "If I'm so much like him.." She yelled back, seeing the light of the stop in the tunnel. "Then I guess I'm leaving too!!"

The train began to slow. "Yeah.. yeah I see why he "betrayed" you." She smiled, she had won, though horrific sounds still screeched in the distance. The train stopped fully, and familiar faces appeared. She couldn't have been more relieved in that moment as she looked at them. "Hey Av!" Sean called, standing proudly next to the others, amongst an abandoned subway tunnel. "Hey," she laughed, leaping down from the metal train. A disturbing cry of death echoed in the distance, and a red alarm bolted into action. "Alright," Cam directed, nodding. "Time to run."

A monotone woman's voice boomed loudly over the intercom: **"Attention all monarch sector C staff: Our operations have been breached by unexpected guests. These guests are… unwelcome. It seems they're under the assumption they rule this place. Let us show them the unmatched power they so-seek. Let that power burn their souls into nothingness. Don't Kill them.. Death is far too good for them. And to the trespassers… struggle. We enjoy watching our prey be hunted.."**

"GET THEM!" A guard yelled, firing an M16 with laser darts at them. Sean jumped and dodged, his arm around Avery in a recovery rescue position, her limping along with them as they ran for their lives. "DON'T LET THEM LEAVE!!" Another guard ordered, running after them with a sword. "Cam we gotta move!" Sean yelled. He nodded, breaking into a full sprint, grabbing

Sasha's hand. Nate passed them with ease, running to scout ahead as best he possibly could.

"YOU'LL DIE FOR THIS!!" A woman yelled, chucking a grenade. Avery pushed Sean away for a moment, catching it midair as it flew towards them. *Done this before bucko.* She smiled, and threw it back as hard as she could "OH FU-" The grenade exploded, leaving their ears ringing violently, smoke now filling the air, a fire behind them, the walls collapsing. They watched as the true structure of the facility revealed itself around them, the massive underground alien world leaking light through the foundations, parts of the sterile white halls collapsing into the endless abyss.

"We're almost there!" Sasha cried, not letting go of Cam's hand. "WHERE IS THERE?" Sean demanded, his voice cracking in desperation. Averys vision dwindled, pure exhaustion catching up to her. "FUCK YOU!" "AHH!" "NO.. NO!!" The guards cried in variation in the background as the ground of the offices collapsed beneath them. "RIGHT!" Sasha cried, Nate threw himself to the right frantically, and the others followed. "HOW ARE WE-" Cam begged.

They stared ahead at the door. Blood covered the floor, and a poor little girl's body lay still on the ground, a symbol of their decisions and actions. "FAKE ROCK!" Nate yelled with glee, stopping at the door. Sasha ran up the ramp by Pearl's body, desperately spamming the button on the panel. "THERE'S NO POWER!" She yelled. Red alarms began balring, sounds of incomprehensible levels booming in the background as the facility fell apart, exposing hundreds of thousands of strange buildings and lights among the caves.

"That there's not.." Came a voice. Sasha curled her lips in disgust as a man walked out around the corner. "*This,*" he pointed at Pearl. "Was this not enough for you?" He asked, waving the power core in his hands mockingly. "FUCK YOU!" Cam spat.

"I warned all of you," Earnie began ominously. "No one gets out here." His cruel evil lips began emerging into the faint red light. "You kids think you own the world, ruining our operations.." He frowned for once, his sick twisted lips curving downwards. "Now who wants to meet the creator first?" He asked, reaching into his pocket for a nasty looking syringe. Sean stood in front of the others, protecting, and Avery echoed him, the others cowering in the corner. "I SAID WHO WANTS IT, GOD DAMNIT!" He yelled, his "sly" persona slipping into his madness. "I WILL make sure each of you live forever," he began, approaching Avery, and getting in her face. "Then I'll cut off your face, and make a hundred different clones of you.. JUST. So that you never run out of pain…He yelled. Avery spat at him, and he grabbed her by the throat, throwing her to the floor, choking her out. Sean leaped on top of him, and stabbed in the back repeatedly, Earnie winced in pain, and Avery cried out desperately as he dug long, scaly fingernails into her back. Sean brought himself up, and stomped on the butt of the knife, stabbing it like a bullet into Ernie's skin. "I WILL MAKE BOTH OF YOU MY FUCKINGS SLAVES!" He cried, psychotically, turning around with ease, and full-on biting Seans neck. He yelled, and Avery crawled away. Nate stepped in front of her, and Cam joined, blocking her off. "YOU ARE JUST ANOTHER LITTLE TOY TO ME!" He screeched, crawling towards Sasha, with sickeningly eager eyes. Sean stomped on his head, and Earnie reached up, firing off his rifle. He hit nothing, and Avery grabbed it from his hands easily, her face in pear rage, her eyes lit fiery red in the alarm above, not scared, not traumatized, just pure and utter bloodlust. "KIll me! YOu can"t bitch! I'M FUCKING IMMORTAL, YOU SL-"

In a single, swooping instant, he was YANKED away into the caves, smashing through the wall, and disappearing into the fog.

"Apologies, my friends. He gets a little too excited sometimes," A voice echoed through the air eerily. "You know, kids.. You've shown a great deal of... talent." Avery scowled, searching for the direction of the man's voice. "Allow me to.. Cut, hm, to the point. You give yourselves up now, and I will grant each and every one of you a life a thousand times better than you could possibly imagine."

Sean glanced at Avery, and she gave a brief, pissed nod.

"It's either that or… you will be turned into biological servants in a position so painful you'll wish you were dead. But we won't grant you that gift… No. You will remain alive and in-pain for the rest of… well, even I don't possess that knowledge."

Cam snarled. 'You can take your job, and-" The wall exploded beside them, and a massive inky tentacle thrashed into the room, lunging at each of them. They dodged one by one, and the tentacle flew back out the wall. "Verywell then," Ignelious said calmly. "...HOW UNFORTU-NATE-ATE!" He screeched in his same horrific pitch, and every wall and ceiling burst open. "GENERATIONS OF WORK, THOUSANDS OF YEARS OF SCIENCE, RUINED.. BY A FEW TEENAGE BRAT-AT'S!" They stared up in horror at the husk of a man before them, making each of them shiver involuntarily. What was once a man in a business suit was now stretched literal miles across the chasm, massive horrific black arms, grabbing and collapsing the cave walls, bright white psychotic eyes beaming with rage, and a sick, sadistic smile, the size of a city alone. `I-I WILL. NOT. HAVE. I-IT!!!"` He screeched, ramming a tentacle into the room, and swiping across the floor, knocking each of them over. `NOW IS YOUR TIME.. TIME AS A CONSTRUCT, IT IS NOW! THE CLOCK HAS COME TO CONSUME YOUR PLACE IN THIS WORLD!"` Avery balled her fists, no longer afraid of the death that towered just before them. "YOU SAY SCIENCE!" She yelled jeeringly, grabbing Seans hand and helping him back up. "AND YET, YOU'RE NOT EVEN THE ONE WHO RESEARCHED IT!"

`STUPID GIRL!"` The monstrosity shouted, his eyes becoming blood red. "SASHA, OPEN THE DOOR!" Sean ordered, and Sasha nodded, running for the terminal. Avery smiled cruelly, and stared the monstrosity dead in his eyes. 'IF YOU CARE SO MUCH ABOUT YOUR "SCIENCE" THEN WHY ARE YOU

TEARING DOWN YOUR PRECIOUS FACILITY.. FOR JUST A FEW TEENAGERS?!" The monstrosity yelled in fury, and screeched with the loudest sound imaginable. "NEVERMIND!" He screamed disturbingly. His eye's erupted into a glowing explosion of blood red, the power of the sun just a short distance away from them. "BEING A SLAVE TO TIME IS TO GOOD FOR YOU.." He shouted, and his eye's became the brightest thing in the entire knowable universe. Two massive laser beams BLASTED out his eyes and flew across the chasms. "GET DOW-" Cam's voice was drowned out by the sheer amount of power headed straight for their souls. One last final shreek echoed out amongst the noise of the laser beams, disturbing, possibly loud, the worst thing to ever be uttered. "Say hi-" The world exploded around her, and time stopped.

"To the creator," Avery finished, peering around, confused. Her friends weren't moving an inch, frozen like everything else in the world. One single figure walked out of the chaos from nowhere, the figurehead of her life, her nightmares, her purpose: A man in a business suit and fedora, with a clock for a face.

His blood red tie seemed to somehow contradict Ignelious's glowing red eyes. "Who-" the man shook his head gently, and snapped his fingers. In an instant, his head began ticking at an incredibly fast pace. Avery looked around, staring, in awe as the events that had just transpired reversed in real-time around her, the lasers returning, the walls re-forming, time rewinding.

She squinted in pure curiosity as The Creator clasped his hands together, studying her, as if reviewing a business investment. They watched each-other for a period of time she couldn't comprehend, given that time didn't exist in that moment. Then at last, he nodded at her, his clock head stopping entirely. He gave one last simple nod, whether of pride or a deal, it was impossible to tell. Then the world's colors inverted, and she was back with the group, who were once again running for the exit. "AVERY?!" Sean yelled, she didn't budge. *This is his facility.. His to rule. And yet.. He prioritized me over every single other thing... Who.. am I?*

"AVERY!" They all yelled, and she turned to face them, not a single sliver worry on her face. "Yeah!" She called back, and ran to the group.

Sasha slammed on a button in the terminal, and the door began to open with a mechanical creak. "THANK GOD it has power," she heaved. Avery felt a chill go down her spine. "Fake rock?" Cam asked, not even willing to process the horror they'd just been through. "Fake rock," The group repeated in unison, even Avery, who barely muttered it, collapsing limp in Sean's arms. Sasha nodded, pressing a button, opening the massive mechanical door, revealing an elevator. The group stepped in, and Sasha waited. Her face grew pale. As she stared into the machine's control module, her eyes lost hope. *It needs an operator.* faint streaks of sunlight bled down from above as they stepped into the elevator, but became shadowed as the door began to close. "Sasha!" Cam yelled, as the jaws of the door came crashing down. *Alright..here we go.* She breathed out heavily, and leaped forward, bolting it for the doors. "Cmon cmon!!" Cam yelled, reaching out his hand in desperation, not caring if it got chopped off as the door closed. *Door.* Was all she could think as she leaped forward into the metal jaws, which did not stop or slow down in any way.

The world seemed to pause for a moment, everything in slow motion as they all processed what was happening. Then Sasha smashed into the wall of the elevator, full force, JUST as the doors slammed shut, violently tearing off the tip of her shoe. Cam exhaled in relief as he helped her up. She smiled at him. "Told you I'm fast." He nodded, and pulled her into a hug. She returned it happily. The machine didn't hesitate, and shot upwards at a pace of urgence. *As if it understood the situation.*

They emerged at the surface, and the infamous rock swung open, finally revealing where they'd stepped so many times before. The world outside was unchained, no resolution, no bright sky. Dark rain with faint orange light, the trees like inky blobs. Avery stretched her arms out, and tapped Sean, gently falling back to the ground. "Okay…" Cam began, his voice shrill and exhausted.

"Let's get water and never do that shit again." The group nodded, Sean sighed, and they walked back to the van for the final time.

"Well, we have the ultimate shadow government on our ass, you almost died and we're probably going to get sick from inhaling lake water." Cam smiled. "Did you find what you were looking for, Avery?" Sean shot him a glance, and went to comfort her. She did not reply. Shasha looked back in the mirror as they flew down the wet muddy road. She shivered.

Avery frowned, staring coldly out the window. *It looks no different than when we got here. Nothing has changed.* She shook her head, staring into the bright sun above with no regard for safety. *This whole thing.. For nothing! NO ANSWERS JUST MORE QUESTIONS!*

"Hey," Sean said gently, snapping her out of her anger. She turned around, and he reached out to her hand. She took it, and squeezed it hard. Sean nodded, and patted her on the back. "At least we're safe," he affirmed, smiling gently. She nodded. *Thanks to things you couldn't possibly imagine and that I probably shouldn't even tell you.*

Frustrated, she closed her eyes. *Brick building. Red valve, open grave, old garage door.* She shook her head, arguing with a thousand demons left burnt in her past. *Stay here. You can't go out. They won't let you. We're running out of food. **I'll find you friends…*** She focused hard, her memory bothering her, not just an agitation, but a genuine itchy pain deep within her mind. *Brick building. Grave stone, old trees… brick building. Brick building.* She opened her eyes.

They widened in disbelief as she stared in front of her, not fully comprehending what lay before the van. "Brick building," she said aloud, staring out the window. Her mind went blank, and she ran to Sasha in the driver's seat. "Avery WHAT THE?!" She yanked her out with strength she didn't know she had, not even aware of her own existence, her only purpose in life simple: *Brick building.* "AVERY?!" Cam yelled, and dove forward to stop her. It was too late. She slammed on the brakes and cranked the wheel hard right, sending them flying into the woods. "WHAT THE HELL ARE YOU-" The van slammed face first into a tree, splitting the front in half, and shattering the entire structure. Glass flew around as they screamed and yelled, blood flying through the air as they tumbled into the trees. Avery felt her head hit the door as she watched the other slam into hard metal, and their worlds went black.

The water flowed gently below, through the beaks and wings, waving in and out, red with the light above. Grey stared out, his expression blank, as if unsure of how to feel, like a photograph, undeveloped. He squinted hard, something about the dead birds feeling wrong. They didn't feel that way before. He never felt that- *"wrong."* His eyes twitched slightly, but he did not move his body. Time passed as he continued to stare, searching for meaning. Yet he found none. *Why?* He asked in his head, to no one. For no reason. And no one responded. He sighed, and withdrew his backpack, jamming his hand inside violently and pulling out a piece of paper. *Okay,* he thought, as the paper shined brightly in the red light, the black ink a contrast in the white. *A house in the woods. Two bears in parallel rooms, a basement mapped below. To the left was a symbol of a drain, mapped next to a barbed wire fence by a river. To the far right was a mountain, labeled with two letters: M.L.* Grey nodded, having read this map a thousand times before, darting his eyes to the bottom where he'd just recently taken notes. *Avery is missing, she's supposed to be back. They found it. They had to have. I need to contact Jane, I need to understand what she knows. Three brothers, but where was the sister? Why is **she** protecting the basement so much?* The writing grew frantic, ink splotches randomly thrown around the paper. *I can't talk here. She's coming. I'm not safe... she's watching.* The handwriting grew nearly impossible to read, scrawled on the page large like a madman. *I feel it coming, but I can't do it yet. Why am I different? Who am I? I don't feel pain when I bleed. I have to kno-* The "W" was not completed, ending his sentence ominously, the ink quite literally flat-lining. He shook his head, setting the paper and backpack aside, and staring down at the birds below. For a moment something changed in him. He felt a shiver down his spine, a body of guilt behind him, showing him something. Then for the first time, he felt.. *sadness. Something is wrong with me.* The walls around began to feel creepy, dark, the unknown laying within them. The environment's entire existence changed. No longer a simple convenient area to perform a task, the walls not mattering, the birds below only a simple element. But they meant something now, and they were not blank. They were… *red?* For the first time ever, he rested his head in his hands, and tried to cry. But no tears came. He looked down below at the birds. *The birds… Birds,* He confirmed to himself, and looked up. But something wasn't right, something was off. He looked down again, and human eyes stared back, their bloodshot veins matching the stains on the wall. He shook his head, not willing to believe it, then got up and leaned against the wall. He looked back, but the walls did not change, nor did the "birds". Something on his arm caught his eye. Red, dripping liquid. *Blood.* He shivered, but not out of fear. He was in pain, his world changed, his existence shattered. Yet still he stood up, and smiled. He now knew his purpose. He now knew his potential. He snapped out of it, not wasting a second, grabbing his bag and running with stunning accuracy up to the pipe ladder. He nodded as he walked, his face filled with a fresh smile, a glint from the red light reflecting in his deep gray eyes. *Thank you… Dad.*

Sean lay on shattered glass, his blood freshly spilled, his leg thoroughly smashed. He struggled to get up, reminding himself how to breathe as his vision returned, blurring into existence. *Trees, broken van, friends asleep..* His mind focused on one thing in the distance. *Girl, holding shovel.* He willed himself to get up, and checked on his friends one by one. He nodded, satisfied. They were all breathing, just unconscious. The girl moved in the distance, and he limped his way out of the shattered glass, blood and light reflecting fresh on the shards. He climbed through the now useless metal structure of the van, using the same break in the glass, the previous person used to break out.

"Avery?" He called, limping over to her. Avery stood in disbelief. In front of her was a large brick building, surrounded in trees, dead and alive. It towered over her, seeming to merge with the forest itself. The wind blew through, cold and nostalgic. She had been here before. To the side of the building was a rusty metal socket, where a valve once was, long ago, long since removed. At the center of the building was a spotted, rusty garage door, sealed shut years ago. It looked as if there were no way in to begin with.

"Av"… Sean asked, as he approached her from behind, the light illuminating his figure in a shadow. Avery looked behind her, guilt surfacing. She shook her head, and willed the memory's to be jetted into her mind. She remained where she was, staring into nothing, the cycle repeating itself. Her eyes widened as they found objects on the wet ground, familiar thoughts rushing through her head. It was a gravestone. *It's… it can't.. how..* Without warning, Avery sprung into action, and Sean didn't bother to stop her. She picked up the shovel, and began to dig. Sean reached out for help, but she pushed him away, violently, her mind not knowing right from wrong.

The dirt flew back into a pile by the garage door as she aggressively scraped and scooped through the soil, ripping away roots from the trees. Something about it felt nostalgic, like she'd been there before, she looked behind her for a moment, her humanity returning. She stared at Sean. He smiled at her gently. The air grew cold and she felt a chill down her spine. *This place* *remembers me… why **does** it remember you?* The air felt thick, and Sean shared the same feeling, as he looked around. *I've seen this place before..* He nodded at her, and she went back to digging.

Sean's eyes were wide, hurting from the dim sun passing through the trees. *Why have I been here?* His thought was broken as dirt flew by him. "Avery, I-" He stopped himself. "I.. don't..know," he admitted, as if some force of the land had blocked the thought out. He thought back to what she'd said days earlier. *A radio signal being jammed.. yeah.* He understood that feeling now. They stood for minutes, and Avery continued to dig deeper and deeper. Voices from the van rose, and at last she'd found something in the dirt. Sean made a face of disgust as he saw what she'd found. *Purple, dilapidated, veiny, dry and destroyed.*

Avery grabbed the object and pulled hard. Five fingers were revealed, and she pulled harder, digging deeper and heaving the person out with all her strength. *Grave… Grave.* It was all she could think, her mind focused on the word. *It will answer everything.*

The other's approached with furious faces, but Sean held them back with his arm. Avery shoved her *own* arm down, and took the person by the hand, brushing over their now revealed eyes. Her heart stopped, She fell back, uncontrollably, still holding the person's hand. Her eyes were wide with fear and confusion, and the person echoed it. There was only one thing left in them now: a reflection. Her skin fell cold, and the world blurred into a thousand memories. *"We need you to be very quiet, Av."* Her friends yelled in the back, but it didn't matter. None of it mattered. *"Be a good girl Avery, one day we'll leave this place"* *gunshots. The elevator. The basement. The room. Who was…. Dad..?* Her body rang in white hot pain, as if the words had been burned, and sliced off her skin. Still there, but not visible. Memory's untold, forgotten, yet evermore present. She stared horrified into the grave, and only one thing stared back.

A child. Blue eyes, beautiful brunette hair. An unmistakable mischievous grin forever embedded on the face. ***It was her…***

To be continued...

Special Thanks:

-Joey (COSMIC)

-An incredibly talented artist, author, creator, and the greatest friend I could have possibly asked for. CHRONOLEFT exists because this one man pushed me to keep making it. Thank you so much, bro.

-Family.

-At my young age, I've made an insane amount of mistakes, and I've ignored way too many assignments and nights of sleep to count. But even after all of that struggle and flaw, my parents never once stopped supporting me through every hurdle of creating this novel. Thanks so much guys, love you.

-Jake, my lizard.

-For putting up with the late nights of being awake, and being my partner in crime.

-The mud by a river on a bike-path.

-The entire reason this universe exists to begin with, haha.

-Beta Readers/ artists/ Inspirations

-Cosmic -reaperz -LURVI -KULANIYT -RENGA -OxxyFC -MOOKsthegreat -SYNTAX3rr -Scott Cawthon -Valve -The mortimer beckett franchise -Steven King -the indie horror game community -The fortnite creative community -stress level zero -MCNF -My awesome YT community

A Note From VEXFC:

I think in many ways, Avery is a direct reflection of me. Mischievous, ambitious, not wanting to follow a system, or listen to authority, the norm. Her memories and hallucinations are partly real ones I've experienced. Life is a really weird mysterious thing, and we have no idea what else is out there we truly cannot comprehend. I honestly wouldn't be surprised if every person that has and will ever exist, ever has experienced this exact story. I have many MANY philosophical, and horrific thoughts, but writing this helped to get them out. it's not just the sassy, lovable teenager. It's the paranoia, the anxiety. The feeling you get when something is right behind you, nestled, deep in the dark woods, next to a black murky pond. This is the feeling I felt for a long, long time. Writing this helped me understand that feeling, and use it to create something I think is pretty damn incredible. "When life gives you lemons, burn its house dow-" Sorry, I mean make lemonade. I hope you think the same. Thank you for reading!

www.ingramcontent.com/pod-product-compliance
Lightning Source LLC
Chambersburg PA
CBHW070300310726
48976CB00005B/1509